MW00364539

"Snowstorm" surrounded the wagon. They had appeared out of the gathering dusk without a sound. One grabbed Lauren's reins and hauled the startled pinto to a stop; another two galloped around the wagon. Then another rider charged up out of the river bank. A long black coat whipped around his legs, and a dark hat shaded his eyes. He carried a rifle in one hand and controlled his plunging horse with the other.

"Ah, my competition has an escort," the dark man said in a voice tinged with a slight French accent. "And who is this fine piece?"

Lauren felt the dark gaze rake her.

"My wife . . . as of tomorrow," Adam said without emotion.

"Mrs. Adam McPhail?" He doffed the floppy hat, revealing an unruly mop of matted, dark hair. "I am honored to make your acquaintance." He shot Adam a knowing look. "A delicate flower cannot be transplanted to the prairie, Inspector. It will wither and die or be trampled down." Urging his horse closer, the man reached out and fingered a strand of Lauren's hair. She struggled to keep her fear at bay, to keep it in some other place. She raised her eyes to the man's and stared at him, challenging him to look away first.

His smudged face crept into an evil smile, and he let his hand drop slowly. "This delicate flower has deep roots, I see." He laughed, a sound more like a grating than laughter. "Perhaps she will live. Perhaps not."

Then, he urged his horse close to Adam, who had made no effort to draw his weapon. The man leaned closer. "You did not hear me, did you? I told you last time that I move on the wind and you cannot see the wind."

His mocking smile faded, and Lauren saw Adam's shoulders stiffen and one hand drop away from his reins.

"Be warned, Mountie. You cannot stop Black Angus. No one can. When the Mounted Police are all dead and buried in their fine red suits, Angus will still be here. He is part of the Territories, part of the land. Leave me alone, Inspector."

Angus looked Lauren's way and smiled again. "And your flower might live long enough to bloom."

Dear Romance Reader,

In July of 1999, we launched the Ballad line with four new series, and each month we present both new and continuing stories set everywhere from medieval England to the American West—the kind of passionate, romantic stories you love best, written by the most gifted authors. At the back of each book, we tell you when you can find subsequent books in the series that have captured your heart.

Getting this month off to a dazzling start is **The Bride Wore Blue**, the debut story in our charmingly romantic series *The Brides of Bath,* from award-winning newcomer Cheryl Bolen. In the most picturesque of cities, the *ton* lives by its own rules—until, that is, love breaks them all! Following her much acclaimed *Bogus Brides* series, beloved author Linda Lea Castle sweeps us back to the spectacular atmosphere of medieval England in her newest keeper, **Promise the Moon.** This is the first story in her compelling series *The Vaudrys,* in which three long-lost siblings rediscover each other against a backdrop of passion and intrigue.

Also this month, Lori Handeland returns with **Nate**, the highly anticipated fifth book in her sexy, compelling *Rock Creek Six* series, in which a pastor's daughter and a gun-for-hire discover how love can overcome even the most difficult obstacles. Another one you won't want to put down! Finally, Kathryn Fox begins *Men of Honor,* a stunning new series on the danger-filled lives of the Royal Canadian Mounties. In this first book, **The Reunion,** she takes us deep into the snowy wilderness—where tenderness and passion are challenged by the hardships of life on the northern frontier. Enjoy this extraordinary selection!

Kate Duffy
Editorial Director

Men of Honor

THE REUNION

Kathryn Fox

ZEBRA BOOKS
Kensington Publishing Corp.
http://www.kensingtonbooks.com

ZEBRA BOOKS are published by

Kensington Publishing Corp.
850 Third Avenue
New York, NY 10022

Copyright © 2002 by Kathryn Fox

All rights reserved. No part of this book may be reproduced
in any form or by any means without the prior written consent
of the Publisher, excepting brief quotes used in reviews.

If you purchased this book without a cover you should be
aware that this book is stolen property. It was reported as
"unsold and destroyed" to the Publisher and neither the
Author nor the Publisher has received any payment for this
"stripped book."

All Kensington titles, imprints and distributed lines are available at special quantity discounts for bulk purchases for sales
promotions, premiums, fund-raising, educational or institu-
tional use.

Special book excerpts or customized printings can also be
created to fit specific needs. For details, write or phone the
office of the Kensington Special Sales Manager: Kensington
Publishing Corp., 850 Third Avenue, New York, NY 10022.
Attn. Special Sales Department. Phone: 1-800-221-2647.

Zebra and the Z logo Reg. U.S. Pat. & TM Off.

First Printing: January 2002
10 9 8 7 6 5 4 3 2 1

Printed in the United States of America

Prologue

Regina, Saskatchewan
Spring 1894

"Oh, Papa." Lauren pushed a curly lock of brown hair off her father's forehead and stared down into the still face. Tanned and muscular, out of place amid the delicate pattern of the quilt that covered him, Inspector Butler looked little like a man barely clinging to life.

"I wish you could be there, Papa." She smoothed his cheek, still damp from soap and razor, but he didn't stir, didn't acknowledge her presence, much as he had not for several weeks. Only thin, blue-veined lids betrayed the frailty claiming the once-robust man. Lauren tugged at the covers, tucking them in neatly and smoothing away a wrinkle. When he awoke—if he awoke—he'd appreciate the tidiness of the room.

She raised her eyes to the scarlet tunic and blue pants hanging on the back of the bedroom door and remembered the care he had taken in preparing his dress uniform to wear the day he gave his daughter away. While he had scrubbed and brushed the material, he had laughed and smiled with gentle eyes and white teeth, treating her first as his little girl, then as the woman she had become, offering bits of advice wrapped up in reminiscences.

From outside, the first hum of voices drifted up to her, signaling the wedding guests were beginning to arrive. Lauren rose and moved over to the dresser. She raised the lid of a wooden box and inhaled the brief scent of cedar. Lying there in a nest of blue velvet was her mother's wedding ring. She lifted it, running her fingers over its smooth surface, remembering her mother's hands lifting her, soothing her, calming and gentling her. How brief that time had been.

"Lauren." Someone knocked softly at the door. "Your guests are here," Mrs. Dawson said gently, almost apologetically.

"I'll be down in a minute," Lauren said, feeling a tear run down her cheek. She replaced the ring and shut the box. "Is Adam here yet?"

"Yes. He arrived a few minutes ago."

Lauren wiped her cheek with her palm. Adam mustn't see her cry. Not today. Today was for rejoicing, not sorrowing. There'd be time for that after Adam left for the Territories immediately after their wedding. Despite her intentions, another tear coursed down her cheek.

Once married, their first assignment together was to have been Fort McLeod. Laughing, she had told her father she was going to be a pioneer woman, and he had teased that Adam had better have plenty of patience. Then, a stroke crumpled Inspector Butler to the floor. The surgeon came, shook his head, and said her father would never awaken again.

"Lauren," another voice urged, "Adam is asking to see you alone before the wedding." Aunt Matilda pushed the door open a crack. "It's bad luck, you know, for the groom to see the bride before the wedding."

"I think we've had all the bad luck we're entitled to, Aunt Matilda," she said, glancing in the mirror and wiping away the last traces of tears. How she wished she could also erase the black circles underneath her eyes.

She turned back to the bed one more time. "I'll be back soon, Father. Aunt Matilda's going to sit with you until I return."

She bit her lip to push down a sob. Then, with a whirl of skirts, she caught the doorknob and opened the door.

"You look lovely, my dear." Aunt Matilda smiled, hunching over her cane. "Blue suits you."

"Father thought so when we ordered this dress."

Aunt Matilda's gaze slid to the bed in the room beyond, and her eyes misted. "I wish I could be of more help to you. He is my brother, after all. You have a whole life in front of you."

"I know you can't, Auntie." Lauren laid a hand on the bent shoulder.

"I can give you this time with your young man,"—a wrinkled hand gripped her arm—"short a time as it is."

Again, the lump grew, and Lauren swallowed. "Let's not talk about what might have been, Auntie. Let's enjoy today."

"Stand back and let me see you." Lauren stepped away and Matilda smiled. "You look like your mother. She wore blue, too. Did you know that?"

"Father told me. I guess that's why he liked this dress." She picked up the skirt and fluffed it out.

"A vision she was, coming down that church aisle." Matilda shook her head. "He's missed her so."

A sob grew in her chest. "I shouldn't be more than an hour. Adam has to leave before dark."

Aunt Matilda's dark eyes calmly fastened on her face. "You've come through your hardship a lovely woman, child, and you'll come through this one. After today, you'll have Adam at your side, and you'll be in his thoughts if not his presence." She glanced back to her father, lying still and quiet, then turned quickly and walked to the head of the stairs.

Adam waited at the foot of the stairs in his scarlet dress uniform. Arms crossed over the newel post, he watched her with a latent hunger that made her blood surge. His blond hair lay in perfect rows that taunted her to run her fingers across the smooth ridges, a fantasy that had haunted her on more than one occasion. His Stetson dangled from one finger.

Lauren kept her eyes on his face until she stopped one step above him. "Auntie said you wanted to see me."

"You're beautiful," he said, his eyes softening into a gentle sadness that made her pulse lurch. He glanced down at his boots, then back up to her face. A sly premonition crept into her thoughts. Perhaps bad luck wasn't finished with her yet. "Let's go in here." He stepped to the side and pushed open the library door. She followed him inside the small room, which smelled of pipe smoke and leather. He shut the door.

"Something's wrong, isn't it?" She turned to face him, steeling herself against the bad news she knew he carried.

"My posting's been changed."

"You're not going to Fort McLeod?"

He slowly shook his head. "No. I'm being sent farther north. North of Edmonton. To Fort Saskatchewan."

Lauren swallowed. "Is there a fort there?"

"Yes, a small one. But I expect to be posted even farther north, into the Yukon Territories. I'll have to put up my own cabin," he ventured further. Not *"We'll* have to put up *our* cabin." Her premonition deepened.

"I think we should postpone the wedding."

Thunderstruck, she stared at him. "But the guests are already here," she said, then wondered at the stupidity of that thought. "Why?"

He twirled his hat, then slowly, deliberately, set it

on her father's desk as if gathering his thoughts. "Life is hard where I'm going, Lauren. Harsh and without any comforts."

She stepped toward him, feeling a void grow beneath her feet, as if the world were about to open up and swallow her whole. "I don't care. As long as I'm with you."

"But you won't be with me, Lauren. Not for a long time. And a lot of things can happen in that time."

The doctor had said her father would only live for days. He'd already lived for weeks, his condition neither improving nor worsening. She could sit by his side for months. Or hours. Her entire future hung on how soon her father would die. The horror of the thought twisted her stomach into a knot.

"It's unsettled country, Lauren. The Cree have only seen a few white men, most of them whiskey traders. The weather is brutal, and there would be no other people for hundreds of miles. This isn't the life I promised you when I proposed."

"I didn't ask you for but one guarantee, Adam. That you love me."

"You know you have that," he said quickly. "But you deserve more. If we marry today . . . you might be a widow before you're . . . truly a wife." They'd planned for Adam to leave immediately after the ceremony without benefit of a wedding night so there'd be no risk of a child.

"You're having last minute jitters, darling," she said, reaching to caress his cheek, hoping the doubts would pass and yet knowing there was a hard truth in his words. She moved forward until her arms encircled his waist and his chest could cradle her cheek. "All I've ever wanted was to be your wife, Adam. I know the lot of a wife of the Force. I know the sacrifices that are expected." She raised her face to look into his brown eyes. But his body wasn't yielding to her touch. In fact, he was rigid, as stiff in his stature as if he were on the parade ground in formation. "There's something else, isn't there?" She raised her head and looked into his face.

"I don't have the right to tie you down." He looked down again at his shiny boots, polished for their wedding. "You may find someone else while I am gone." He looked up then, straight into her eyes. "And it would be unfair of me to expect you to keep vows made to a husband who's a thousand miles away."

"Adam, that's ridiculous. I'd love you even if you were two thousand miles away. Three thousand. I don't want anyone else. I'll never want anyone else."

"I'm not asking you to break the engagement," he told her. "Just postpone the wedding until . . . things are more settled."

"Until Father dies, you mean." She paced to the window and stared out across the vacant parade ground.

"You know I'd never wish that. I love your father, too." He'd come up behind her. She could feel his presence and longed to turn and draw him into her arms. He was slipping away from her, and part of her began to rail at the circumstances that held them apart.

"If we were to . . . conceive a child. There would be no doctors there. No midwives."

She turned then and put her arms around him before he could protest, before he could back away or put up that invisible wall that suddenly existed between them. She only had these few seconds to convince him, only a few moments to salvage her future. "Women have been having babies for centuries without benefit of a doctor. We're healthy. I'm healthy. I'm not afraid, so why are you?" She looked up, but her words had done nothing to change his mind.

"I think it would be better if we waited."

She knew at that moment she would not change his mind. Adam McPhail was the most honorable man she'd ever known, but at this moment she cursed that noble quality and wished he were a rogue who'd taken her innocence in the front seat of a carriage on a warm spring night. At least she'd have that part of him to keep forever.

"I'll make excuses to the guests." He took her into his arms, his touch searing through the thin fabric of her dress. Her wedding dress. "I'll explain our reasons for waiting. You won't have to face anyone."

He was offering her a coward's bargain and she leaped at the chance. She was just too tired and hurt to argue or to dredge up one more ounce of courage. He kissed her again, and she closed her eyes, concentrating on the softness of his lips, the scent of his skin, the solidity of his embrace. All this she stored in her heart.

"You'll write me letters?" She asked as he lifted his lips from hers.

"Every day, and send them to you on passing clouds."

She smiled despite the ache now growing in her chest. "I'll settle for the post now and then."

He pushed a curl off her forehead. "I love you, Lauren. You're the only woman I've ever loved or ever will. We'll be together soon. I promise. I only want what's best for you." He closed his eyes and feathered a kiss on her lips.

"You're what's best for me." A sob caught in her throat with an odd strangling sound. "When do you have to leave?"

He smiled, edging toward the door. "I think it would be best if I left now."

"You'll send for me soon?"

"Yes, soon."

And then he was gone. Lauren sat down on a tattered footstool and sobbed into a handful of the blue cloud that settled around her.

One

Edmonton, Northwest Territories
March 1896

Cold fog swirled and eddied, faceless ghosts circling, taunting, touching with their damp, icy fingers. Inspector Adam McPhail drew his buffalo-hide coat higher and tighter around his neck. In the distance, the lights of Edmonton were swathed and smothered in the thick blanket of mist that rolled up from the Saskatchewan River. A shrill whistle cut through the night. The train was here . . . and so was she.

Fear clutched his throat while waves of uncertainty washed over him. He pulled his horse's rocking canter down to a walk. His stomach churned with the mix of emotions that had been running through him since he'd received her letter. What would Lauren be like after two years? Two years, he thought guiltily, burrowing his chin deeper into the fur of his coat. His heart quickened, whether from desire or anger, he couldn't tell. He'd told her not to come. In fact, he'd forbidden it.

Adam shifted in the saddle as another whistle blasted through the murk. He'd meant his promise to Lauren, but he had also made another promise—a promise to faithfully, diligently, and impartially serve the Northwest Mounted Police. And serve them he had, across the open prairies and high peaks of the Territories. Out here he had learned his own value and come to accept himself as he was. Was he the same man who'd loved Lauren Butler? Was he the same man who'd left her crying in her wedding dress with only a promise to sustain her through the dark days ahead? No, he wasn't the same man at all. And she probably wasn't the same woman, either.

His horse, Jake, stopped, and Adam jerked himself back to the present. They were outside the livery at the far end of Fort Edmonton. When he didn't dismount, Jake swung his head around. "All right. I know you're hungry." Adam winced as his feet touched the ground. He'd been in the saddle since sunup, chasing a pair of whiskey traders for miles over bumpy terrain, and both his backside and Jake's back were aching for it.

He led the horse inside and breathed in the warm horse smells he had come to love. Stimpy slept hunched in a chair that leaned against a center post. A tiny potbellied stove glowed orange from the cracks around its doors.

"Wake up, Stimpy." He kicked at the chair's leg, and the little man leaped to life.

"Inspector McPhail."

"Quarter Jake for tonight, will you? Rub him down and feed him. I'll pick him up in the morning." With a final pat to Jake's sagging head, he turned to go. "Oh yes. I'll need another horse saddled and ready to go about an hour after sunup."

Stimpy nodded and spat a stream of tobacco juice. He caught the reins and clucked to the gelding with the unoccupied side of his mouth. Stimpy's bowed legs and Jake's wide rear shuffled off together into the depths of the warm barn.

Adam grabbed a lantern by the door and stepped

out into the chill. As he strode down the plank walkway toward the ferry crossing, his pace slowed. The first few months apart from Lauren had been difficult, and he had tried to write every day, filling letters with tidbits of the day's events. Then time slowly passed. Soon, he had settled into his job and was excelling. His confidence grew, and he began to move up in rank. With each promotion, he moved from one outpost to another. Sometimes with only his uniform and horse, he relentlessly chased whiskey traders, settled native disputes, dispensed frontier justice. Constable Adam McPhail became Inspector McPhail, and time for writing letters dwindled.

He reached the ferry crossing and paused. The ferry was on the other side of the river, and he would have to wait. Yanking his hands out of beaver gloves, he rubbed them down the coat's rough fur and began to pace, remembering.

After some months, he had spent all his energy on just staying alive. The memory of Lauren became a warm shadow in his mind. Until Lauren's letter found him at Fort Saskatchewan. It said she was coming— coming to claim the promise he'd left her with. Coming to be his wife. She had gilded her words with no explanations or pleadings. Short and straight to the point.

The ferry lines tied to a pillar on shore tightened and creaked. Adam's heart began to thump. What was she like after all this time? Sweat popped out on his upper lip. He loved her, there was no denying that. But she had no place here, where the winter wind could steal a man's breath and his soul at the same time. Here where women aged before their time and buried their infants in the cold ground.

He gazed up into the misty fog, reaching down within himself to find the anger lurking there. Only this anger, fanned into a flame, would give him the strength to send her home. At first, their love had burned like a new flame—exciting, dangerous, all-consuming. Now she smoldered in his soul, an ember burning slowly, steadily, warming him from the inside. Could he contain this smoldering flame, or would it roar to life and consume them both?

Fog, low and dense, snaked around Lauren's ankles as she skidded down the embankment toward the Saskatchewan River. Behind her, the locomotive snorted a final blast of steam. She could see nothing in front of her except wisps of fog illuminated in the faint gas lamps. *He's not coming.* No form approached her through the fog; no one had waited on the rough-plank platform when the train pulled in. Had something kept him?

Cursing her own stubbornness, she clamped a hand atop her Newport hat, and the stem of a fabric rose jabbed her finger. Shifting her weight, she tightened her grip on her valise and stepped into the unlit murkiness in front of her. Somewhere down the steep bank a ferry waited to take her across the river to Edmonton. She'd get a room for the night and a ride into Fort Saskatchewan in the morning. Then she'd settle things with Adam—one way or the other.

Her ankle boots sank in the mud as she blindly navigated the steep path; then two yellow halos of light beamed out of the darkness. She stepped up on the flat ferry, and a hunched figure straightened from bending over the railing. He barely gave her a glance as he shuffled to the front of the ferry and began to untie the mooring ropes. The craft wallowed as the old man hauled on the ropes and sent it out into the current.

Lauren gripped the railing, her face turned into the moist wind that whipped tendrils of hair around her face. What would he be like after all this time? Had he changed? Did he still love her? A thousand ques-

tions tumbled into her mind. Would he be angry that
she had come against his wishes or glad to see her?
Brief pinpoints of light neared until the keel scraped
bottom and the ferry rested on the shore. She reached
into her reticule for a coin, but the old man shook his
head, spat into the water, and secured his line. Lauren
lifted the hem of her skirt and stepped onto land. Peering through the dark, she could make out a shadowy
form coming toward her through the fog. He held a
lit lantern high above his head, haloing his form in
the mist. Then he emerged from the murk.

A thick, furry coat hung from wide shoulders and
gaped open to reveal a hint of the scarlet coat underneath. Dusty blue pants hugged slim legs ending in
muddy black boots. A Stetson shaded a gaunt face,
and a blond mustache drooped over full lips.

"Adam." She stopped short, her heart pounding in
her ears. From what she could see, he barely resem-
bled the man who'd smiled up at her from the bottom
of her steps that last day. Once-smooth cheeks were
now sunken and rough from the weather and covered
with unshaven beard.

"I told you not to come." His voice was raspy, as
if from a man out too long in the cold. His words
were coarser, edged with no hint of compassion, just
an order from a man used to giving them. He moved
a step closer, and she was suddenly angry. Angry at
him. Angry at Fate.

"I'm your fiancée." She tilted her head back and
stared up into his face.

He peered down at her, the lines in his face hard
and etched. Lauren clenched her gloved hands together to keep from caressing his cheek.

His jaw worked beneath the tanned skin, and she
waited with held breath for his words. The Police came
first. She had learned that early as the daughter of a
Mountie.

"You've no place here." He pushed his hat back,

and his dark eyes swept over her. A dangle of hair lay plastered against his forehead, and she imagined her fingers lifting it and smoothing it back into place.

"My place was first at Father's side, now at yours."

He stared at her, his eyes boring into hers, but what lay behind that guarded gaze, she could not guess. Was he glad to see her? Was he angry? No, he didn't look like the Adam she remembered, but the bottom of her stomach dropped out as he took a step forward, capturing and holding her gaze with his. Suddenly, he drew her against his chest, and rough fabric scratched her cheek.

She breathed deeply a mixture of damp wool, wood smoke, and the fresh scent of the outdoors. Gone was the familiar bayberry scent of his cologne and the yeasty smell of freshly starched laundry. Her arms slipped inside his coat and wrapped around his waist. She noticed that even through the clothes his body was hard and muscular—and thinner. Much thinner.

"You're going back on the first train tomorrow." His voice cracked. He paused and cleared his throat.

The words were harsh, but his voice was gentle, vulnerable. The slip in his voice made her heart lurch for the man she remembered, a man who would have swept her up into his arms. "You promised me a wedding and I'm here to collect."

His hand moved slowly up her back to her neck, heating the flesh under his palm. He bent his head slightly, just enough for his cheek to graze hers.

Lauren closed her eyes against an onslaught of long-denied fantasies. She would not think beyond this minute, she vowed again for the thousandth time. Ever since her father's death had released her, she had promised herself she would make this marriage work. Somehow, she would convince Adam they were intended for each other, that they could not set aside what Fate had determined.

"I did miss you," he whispered, the gentle words almost lost in her hair.

"I missed you, too." *How I missed you, wondering if you were dead or alive.*

Adam closed his eyes and rested his cheek on her head. Like water running from beneath the winter's snowcap, his anger drained away. He fought to retain it by summoning all the horror he'd seen. But all he could bring up was Lauren's face, Lauren's body, Lauren's scent. A lump swelled in his throat. How could he have left her so easily? Through the thick wool of her cloak and jacket, he could feel womanly curves, and desire lurched into his veins. Beneath his cheek, her flesh heated his. Nothing should have been able to come between them. But something had. Responsibility. She to her father, he to the Force.

Adam pulled away and stared down at her. Her eyes searched his face, hope making them bright. She wanted what he wasn't sure he could give. She wanted a home, children, security—all the things he'd so generously promised back in Regina where the future was easily mapped. How could he ask her to endure the danger and hardships he had faced when she had already faced so much alone? Especially now that he was on Black Angus's list. The whiskey trader had eluded Adam more times in the last month than he cared to admit. By failing in the capture, Adam had put not only himself in danger but Lauren as well, now that she was here. Angus would see no difference in killing a mounted policeman and killing the policeman's wife.

"Come. We'll talk about this inside, where it's warm." Gently, he set her away. "We had better get inside. It's starting to rain." He picked up her bag, caught her under the elbow, and guided her up the hill to Edmonton's main street.

"Adam. You're limping." Lauren pulled back against his grasp.

Her sudden words startled him. He had been watching her profile from the corner of his eye. She was as beautiful as he remembered, but in a more mature way. Blond hair that had once swirled around her shoulders was now swept up neatly beneath her hat. Her blue eyes regarded him calmly, whereas once before they had sparkled with flirtatious laughter.

"I took a nasty fall from a horse about a year ago."

She slowed and turned toward him, her gaze sweeping him from head to toe. "Were you badly injured?"

Adam shook his head. "It was a simple break. I hobbled around for a few months."

She stopped. "You broke your leg and you didn't wire me?"

"I didn't want to worry you." Adam stopped beside her. "The surgeon said it would heal without problems, and you had enough to worry about."

"That may be true, but I had a right to know."

Guilt gnawed a path through him as he realized he hadn't once thought of sending her a wire. In fact, he hadn't thought of her at all during the painful ordeal. He'd been in too much agony to think of much of anything except a quick end to the pain.

"How are things in Regina?" He changed the subject as their steps resumed.

"The same. Busy since Father died."

His steps slowed. "I'm sorry about your father. Was it a painful death?"

Her sigh was barely audible. "No, not painful. Long. Difficult. He slipped into a coma before he finally passed on."

"I wish I could have been there."

He walked with head down, his hands clasped behind his back, as she had often seen him do. "I wish you could have come, too."

He stopped again. "Lauren—"

"Don't, Adam." Reaching out, she cupped his cheek

with her hand, and her palm tingled from the touch. "I understand; I really do."

The words sounded distant, hollow, as though spoken by a stranger. How could she tell him how much she had wanted him by her side during that time, how much she had wanted to feel his arms around her as she watched the dirt ring hollow against the coffin lid? And yet the inevitability of the pull of the Force again permeated her life as it had in her childhood, when she and her mother waited for her father.

He caught her cupped hand with his. Even through the beaver gloves, she could feel his strength, and a shiver tiptoed up her spine. In the glow of gaslights, his face was half shaded by his hat, but his eyes caught hers, and a little gasp escaped her throat at the intensity of his gaze.

"McPhail!"

Adam jerked his head around. A man sauntered across the street toward them.

"Beggin' your pardon, ma'am." The tall, dark-haired man stopped and nodded to them, his words edged with a soft Scottish burr.

"Lauren, this is Inspector Duncan McLeod."

The man smiled slowly, his teeth white beneath a dark mustache. "Good evening, Miss Butler. Could I have a word with you, Adam?"

"Let me get Lauren settled and I'll be right down to the office."

Duncan smiled and glanced between the two of them. "Tomorrow morning will do just as well." He nodded. "Miss Butler, if I can ever be of service, please let me know." With a curt nod, he strolled away.

"Is he one of your men?" Lauren asked as Adam helped her up onto the walkway in front of the Edmonton Hotel.

Adam laughed. "Duncan McLeod doesn't belong to anyone, but he rides with me, yes. And there's not a better friend to be found in all of Canada." Adam pushed open the door, and a welcome warmth rushed out.

Heated by a cheery metal stove, the hotel lobby smelled of wood and leather. Two brocade-covered couches faced each other, with a small table between. Filmy curtains swathed the window, and a braided rug covered the wooden floor.

"Tom," Adam called out. The curtained doorway stirred, and a man emerged.

"You'll be wanting your key," he stated over spectacles perched on his nose.

"Yes. And I'd like a room for Miss Butler."

Disappointment slammed into Lauren, and a blush crawled up her cheeks. What had she been thinking? That they would spend the night together? That she would lie in his arms as she had dreamed of so many lonely, desolate nights?

Reaching behind him, Tom pulled two keys off a nail and slid them across the counter, turned and shuffled back through the floral curtain.

As they climbed the stairs, Lauren was conscious of Adam's hand on her elbow, of the intimacy of his hip wedged against hers on the narrow stairway. Reaching a door bearing a brass plate engraved with a 2, Adam inserted the key and pushed open the door. The scent of fresh laundry rushed out. He lifted the chimney of a lamp on a small table by the door, struck a match, and lit the wick. Soft light flooded the modest room. A crazy quilt covered a four-poster bed in the center of the room. The walls were paneled halfway up, the rest covered with floral wallpaper. A washstand stood to one side with a bowl and pitcher, and a chamber pot showed beneath the bed ruffle. Two straight-backed chairs faced the fire, and a small pile of firewood lay on the stone hearth.

"It's quite lovely," she said, glancing back at Adam. He watched her with a heated gaze that made her want to yank him into the room and slam the door behind them.

"Mine's next door," he said with a nod. "I guess you'll want to get right to bed."

"No. I want to talk to you first. See you without the hat and coat." And then she did take his arm and pull him into the room.

For a moment, she thought he might bolt. His arm stiffened beneath her fingers, and he glanced to the doorway, then back to her.

"I just want to talk to you, Adam," she said, and took off his Stetson.

He ran a hand through shaggy blond hair. The Adam McPhail she'd known would never have worn his hair so long. "I need a haircut."

"I'll cut it for you."

His eyes widened slightly.

"I used to cut Father's all the time."

"I'll get the post barber to do it."

She tilted her head. "All right. If that's what you want."

Silently, he nodded as her heart constricted, and an edge of hopelessness slid inside. Where was the passionate man who'd asked for her hand on bended knee? The man who polished every button—twice—buffed every smudge from his boots? The wilderness had opened its mouth and swallowed him whole.

Adam glanced down at his boots. "I apologize for the dirt. I've been on patrol for several days."

"It's all right."

He didn't comment further, and the silence grew uncomfortable. "This bed looks wonderful." Lauren set her bag on the quilt, then pressed down on the mattress. Instantly, she regretted her words. She dragged her gaze back to his face and was reminded of the wolves that watched the train from the tree line—cautious, dangerous, mysterious.

"I expect the beds in the train were hard and narrow?" He had edged toward the door, turning the wide-brimmed hat in his hands.

"Yes, they were."

"You go ahead and unpack. I have to go down to the livery and get my things." He put a hand on the doorknob. "I'll see you at breakfast tomorrow morning."

He opened the door and stood there, filling the opening. She didn't remember his being so tall.

"Aren't you going to kiss me good night?" she asked when he made a move to go.

With a quick smile, he moved to her side, reached down, and pecked her quickly. His mustache tickled, but her blood surged.

"Adam," she said as he made another anxious escape to the door. "I still love you."

He paused in his nervous escape and turned his full attention to her face. "I love you, too."

"Why are you afraid of me, Adam?"

He looked down at the hat dangling in his fingers. "A man has a lot of time to think out here. A lot of time alone. Sometimes it does funny things to him. Changes him." The eloquent pattern of speech she'd so admired about him was gone, replaced by short, to-the-point sentences. More efficient out here, she supposed, when a man spoke few words.

"I'll come by for you at seven, then?"

She nodded and opened her mouth to ask another question, but by then the door had closed with a soft click.

Lauren sank down on the bed. Shy? When was Adam McPhail ever shy? But he had almost seemed so. Or was he angry with her for defying the letter he sent forbidding her to come alone? Or was it more? Didn't he want her in his life after all this time? Lauren dispelled the doubts with a shake of her head.

She slid off the bed, pulled out her hat pin, and removed her hat. Then she removed her blue wool coat

and jacket and yanked open her valise. The first thing
she saw was the thin silk nightgown she planned to
wear on her wedding night. White and of delicate gos-
samer silk, the gown gathered in tiny pleats at the
neck and cascaded to the floor. Pink-and-white embroidered rosebuds dotted the shoulders and front.
Scooping it up into her hands, Lauren laid her cheek
against the smooth fabric. She ran her fingers over
the embroidered rosettes and thought of the hours she
had taken over the garment, the nights spent stitching
while sitting at her father's bedside. She imagined herself in the gown, Adam's face when he saw her. . . .

"I won't think about that, either." She stuffed the
garment back into the bag and lifted out, instead, a
sturdy gown of flannel. Thoughts of being alone with
Adam, as man and wife, had filled her mind for days,
making her nervous and edgy. How hard it had been
to wait before the wedding. How difficult to be alone
together and not touch, not explore. But they had both
agreed to wait. *It'll only be a few weeks.* Now those
words held bitter irony.

Lauren rubbed her arms against a sudden chill.
Kneeling by the fireplace, she laid a fire, struck the
match, then watched flames consume first the kin-
dling, then the wood. Outside, rain began to tap
against the window. What would life be like here? Remembered newspaper stories of the Northwest Territories filled her mind. Lawless whiskey traders
preying on the Indians; vast wilderness, so dense only
the bravest men broached it; long, dark winters that
lured men into insanity.

She replaced the poker, straightened, and moved to
the table. The lamplight died with a single puff down
the chimney, and the fireplace filled the room with a
soft glow. Lauren slid between the smooth, cool
sheets, sighed, and turned onto her left side. A dribble
of rain staggered down the windowpane, highlighted
by reflected firelight. Watching raindrops march to

their death wasn't exactly how she'd imagined spending her first night here. In fact, on the trip, she'd convinced herself that Adam would be so anxious to marry her, that he'd meet her at the train with a minister in tow. So much for dreams.

Lauren rolled over and watched the fire, mesmerized by its sensuous dance. All right, so Adam was a reluctant groom. He was still in love with her. She was sure of that. Never once had she doubted that he loved her. Now she only had to get past that wall of silence he'd erected around himself. And perhaps in doing so, she'd discover an Adam she didn't know. As her eyes drooped heavily, a tingle of excitement sang through her. Pursuing Adam McPhail again, far away from familiar eyes and territory, could be an unexpected pleasure.

TWO

The slanting rain stung as the hotel door clicked shut behind Adam. Gratefully, he held his face up and let the cold rain wash away the heat that seared his cheeks. Rigorous activity and constant danger had kept thoughts of Lauren in the back of his mind until he'd received her letter. Then he'd let loose those thoughts he'd kept locked away, allowed himself to start thinking about her—how she smelled, how her skin was soft and smooth.

Leaning one shoulder against the walkway post, he let his weight sag against it, feeling the fatigue of the day. He should go and see what Duncan wanted. Maybe a swift walk in the cold rain would ease the ache in his soul and in his loins. Buttoning up the front of his coat, he stepped into the downpour and splashed toward the low buildings of the Edmonton detachment.

Duncan sat slumped in his desk chair, feet propped on the desk, his head back, snoring softly. A potbellied stove warmed the log room. Behind him, a single prisoner slept on his side in a small barred cell.

Adam smiled and picked up a piece of paper from the cluttered desktop. Quietly, he tore off a corner and traced it across Duncan's tongue. Duncan gasped and coughed.

"McPhail. Are you trying to choke me?" The chair legs thumped to the floor. He picked up a coffee cup, poked a finger in to test the temperature, then turned it up and drank. "What are you doing here, anyway?"

Adam sat down on the corner of the desk. "I thought I'd see what you wanted. Thought it might be important."

Duncan leaned back and laced his fingers across his stomach. "So, you thought it might be more important than the lovely woman waiting for you?"

Adam felt color spread across his face. "I just thought it might need attention before morning."

"It's your brain that needs attention." Duncan leaned forward and tapped the brim of Adam's hat. "Are the waters rough, lad?"

Adam sighed. He couldn't hide the fact long from a man who knew him so well. "We've been apart a long time. We've both changed."

Duncan's laugh faded, and he shook his head sadly. "Distance doesn't always make a heart grow fonder, but the frontier is hard on women."

"How is Pierre's wife? I didn't see him before I left the fort yesterday morning."

"She hasn't spoken since the baby died. Pierre, well, he buries his sorrow in work."

Adam moved to the window and stared out at spears of lightning that shot across the heavens in fiery arcs. "And the surgeon was only a few miles away."

"You can't blame yourself for that, Adam. You did the best you could."

"No, I don't blame myself. Dr. Ferguson said the baby was dead before the birth, but it just brought home to me the dangers of bringing a wife out here, of trying to raise a family here in the Territories."

"Everything's a swap. If you stay here in the Territories, you trade the conveniences of the East for the freedom of the West."

"Lauren shouldn't have to settle for that. She deserves better."

"Maybe she deserves better, but does she want better?"

Adam glanced over his shoulder. "She says she wants me."

Duncan rolled his eyes to the ceiling. "Oh, to be so cursed."

Adam laughed. "Someday some woman's going to catch you, Duncan, no matter how fast you run."

Duncan smiled wryly. "She already did. Remember?"

Adam's smile faded, replaced by embarrassment. "I'm sorry."

Duncan held up a hand and waved away his apology. Then he stretched and eased his chair back on two legs. "Since I didn't see Black Angus in the jail, I assume you didn't catch the scoundrel."

Adam turned from the window. "Nope, but he led me a merry chase. You would think that in country as flat as this it would be hard to hide two men and a wagonful of illegal whiskey."

"Not so difficult for Black Angus. He's given many a man the slip, some more experienced than you, so you're in good company. Are you going to tell her about the threats?" He nodded toward the hotel.

Fear prickled the hair on the back of Adam's neck. "No. No need to worry her while she's here."

"While she's here?"

"I'm sending her back in a few days."

Duncan quirked an eyebrow. "And does the fair lass know this?"

"Yes, but it'll take a little more convincing to make her see I'm right."

Duncan grinned. "I don't know the lovely Miss Butler yet, lad, but I'd say a woman with enough grit to come all the way across Canada for you isn't going back—with or without a wedding ring on her finger."

Adam traced the edge of the desk with his finger. "Griesbach said some of us would be reassigned in a few months. Maybe I'll draw someplace I'll feel safe taking her."

Duncan rubbed his chin. "I heard rumors that some of us might be going north to the Yukon to keep order."

"Then she'd have to wait until I return."

Duncan smiled softly. "You don't know much about women, do you, lad?"

"I guess this is why the Force frowns on marrying."

"I guess so."

"Any place'll be dangerous if Angus decides to make good his threats."

Adam nodded. "What did you need me for earlier?"

"Oh. Turner brought word in from patrol that another operation is starting up north, near Onion Lake."

"Angus's reach is lengthening." Clasping his hands behind his back, Adam walked over to gaze at the prisoner. "Pretty soon he'll be bringing whiskey in from across the border."

"He already is, according to some of the trappers coming up from the Musselshell. The Cree are in a bad way because of it."

Adam turned. "He's gotten a foothold on the reserve?"

"For sure, that's what they say." Duncan nodded.

"Remember how bad it was up there last year when that local whiskey trade was furnishing the reserve?"

"A sad thing it was." Duncan pulled off his hat and scratched his head. "Little children wearing rags, no meat in the whole camp, fathers too drunk to hunt. A sad thing indeed."

"I should get back." Adam moved to the front of the desk. "I'll see you in the morning. I'm at the hotel if you need me."

Duncan grinned and crossed his arms over his chest.

"You've got your work cut out for you sending Inspector Butler's daughter back to Regina against her will. If she's anything like her father."

"He was a strong, stubborn man, all right. But Lauren's reasonable. She'll listen to me."

"God protect the innocent and the ignorant," Duncan mumbled to Adam's back as he stepped out into the stormy night.

Adam's key slid into the lock with a soft click, and the door swung open to a cold, lifeless room. Ignoring the lamp by the table, he went straight to the hearth and laid a fire, content to let the feeble flames illuminate the room—that and the cracking lightning outside.

The room was identical to Lauren's—except that she wasn't in it. She was through the adjoining door, just on the other side of the thin layer of wood. She'd be asleep by now, he mused, squatting in front of the fire. Maybe on her side, one hand curled against her cheek. Her hair would be loose and spread across the pillow like finely spun golden silk. In sleep she'd breathe slowly, her chest rising and falling, the peek of a soft breast visible above the edge of her gown.

He stood, willing away the stirring of his body, the response to his thoughts sudden and urgent. Moving to the window, he sought to leave his thoughts behind, but they followed him like his shadow.

He'd dreamed of lying beside her, her warmth on the sheets between them. He'd rest his hand on the gentle curve of her hip, and the cotton of her gown would slide willingly beneath his palm, higher and higher, baring her long legs. If he peeled the covers back, cold air would caress her skin, and gooseflesh would rise up, spiraling toward her breasts, which he'd bare by unbuttoning the neck of her gown. The soft flesh would spill out, eager for his touch.

He threw a glance toward the door and then followed with his body. The door swung open easily and silently. As he'd imagined, she lay on her side, a hand curled beneath her cheek. But the quilt was tugged up under her chin, and she was completely obscured from his view. Except for her hair. Soft as spun gold, it lay draped across the pillowcase. Adam picked up a tendril and ran the delicate strands through his fingers.

The wait to touch her, to caress her, had seemed interminable. On lazy summer afternoons they'd lain side by side in some secluded place, a picnic lunch abandoned to the ants. Completely clothed, they'd touched through cotton and serge and promised to wait for more until their joining could be with complete abandon and unbound passion. They'd whispered their fantasies to each other, their chests heaving in unison with suppressed passion. Their reward would come, they'd promised each other.

Adam knelt by the side of the bed, his face level with hers and his heart contracted. How could he send her away? To do so would break her heart—and his. And yet how could he bring her into the struggle that was life here, the life of a Mountie's wife? How could he take her from her gentle life of soft fires and fine linens into bitter-cold days and coarse homespun? Did his love for her give him the right to take away her comforts, her safety? She would conceive, and soon if his raging blood was an indication. And then she would waddle, heavy and miserable, around a sparse cabin with no soft rugs or creature comforts.

A hand touched his forehead, pushing his hat off. The stiff Stetson hit the floor with a thump as her eyes opened and looked directly into his. No surprise registered there, almost as if she'd been waiting for him to come to her side.

"You worry too much, darling," she said, smoothing back his hair. "I'm tougher than I will ever convince you I am."

Her intuitive words caught him by surprise, and his studied and rehearsed indifference slipped away. He was sure, by her smile, that his love for her filled his eyes.

Her slim hand slid around to the back of his head and drew him close, closer, until her lips touched his. He sought immediately to draw away, but she deepened the kiss. He slipped his hands underneath the covers, feeling the soft, warm flannel slide against her skin. He wanted to be there under those quilts and sheets with her, cradled in her arms. He wanted her to tell him, to make him believe, that this was all they'd ever need. For a few seconds, he longed to put down the responsibility he carried and be her husband.

Lauren flipped back the covers, and he put a knee on the open space within the curve of her body.

"Lie down with me," she begged, her voice slow and sultry. "Just for a few minutes."

Abandoning all his noble ideals, he shrugged out of his coat, stretched out beside her, and hauled her up against him. The unbound curves of her breasts pressed gently against his chest. She raised up on one elbow, leaned over him, and claimed his lips again. Looking up at her through the veil of golden hair, he thought he would burst if he didn't have her. Right this second. Wedding vows or not.

"Lauren," he whispered, his hands cupping her breasts. One hand smoothed over her ribcage. So slim. His palm slid into the valley of her waist and back up to traverse the curve of her hip, stopping at the hint of fullness he couldn't reach.

"You want me," she said, sliding one bold hand over his torso, across his belt and lower.

He grabbed her wrist. "Don't."

She smiled, her eyes soft, her lips begging for more kisses. "You can't lie to me about this. I'm not the sheltered innocent you left behind, Adam. Death gives one a whole new set of priorities. I know that no matter what your lips say, you want to marry me. You love me. You'll never convince me you don't."

Adam wriggled out of her grasp and out of the bed. He stepped away, struggling for control, ignoring the evidence of his lust for her. After all, it wasn't the first time she'd seen him so aroused nor the first time she'd touched him so. But now, such intimacy weakened his resolve to send her away.

"I won't go away, you know." She sat in the pile of tumbled sheets, her gown hanging off one shoulder, her hair loose. "No matter what you say. I'm my own woman now, and I don't have to do anything I don't want to do."

He turned his back to her and closed his eyes. "I'm only doing what I think is best for you."

"How can you possibly know what's best for me?"

The question came at his elbow. She'd scrambled out of her warm nest and now stood at his side, a wraith in white, in her eyes an unsettling mix of innocence and worldliness.

"You have no idea the misery I watched my father endure or how deep pain can go in one's soul. I've had the misery, Adam, now I want the happiness. You promised me that." She poked his shoulder with one finger. "I'm here to collect a promise from a man who's always stood by his word. Are you going to start welshing now?"

He turned around to face her. "No," he said, and drew in a breath. "I love you, Lauren. I would never break your heart. Will I ever be able to make you see that we should wait until I'm settled someplace?"

"No." She crossed her arms over her chest.

"Then I'll arrange for a minister to marry us day after tomorrow."

His sudden capitulation startled and puzzled her. But not as much as the lack of emotion in his eyes. "You will?"

"Do you need more time?"

"No. No, I brought everything with me."

"Then I'll call for you at seven for breakfast and we'll discuss the details."

Before she could comment or stop him, he pivoted, walked through their adjoining door, and closed it firmly behind him. Cold air swirled around Lauren's feet. She hurried back to the bed, climbed in, and flopped over onto her back. Writhing shadows danced across the ceiling as she reflected on Adam's sudden surrender.

Her mother often said the Northwest Territories were her father's mistress. He was gone at first for more than a year, then months at a time with little or no communication. Had the West stolen away her Adam? Had the vast wilderness taken more than he could give and returned to her a shell of the man she loved?

Lightning illuminated the room, and Lauren noticed her reticule sitting at the foot of the bed. She picked it up, opened it, and pulled out a folded piece of paper. A familiar scrawl wandered across the stationery. Edmund. Her father's doctor. A loyal friend for the past two years. He'd pressed the paper into her hand as she boarded the train with orders that she not read it until she was under way. She'd put it in her bag and delayed opening it, knowing what was inside.

"Dearest Lauren," the letter began in a hasty scrawl barely visible in the dim light of the storm.

> *Please reconsider your decision to pursue your marriage. You deserve better, and I can give you that and more as my wife. If you should ever need me, you have only to telegraph and I will come without hesitation.*
>
> *Yours,*
> *Edmund*

A twist of pain gripped her. She'd long known Edmund would like them to be more than friends, but he'd never said a word nor made an inappropriate motion. She'd just known. Now here it was on paper. Dear Edmund. It was Edmund who had handled all the legal affairs of her father's death and Edmund who had seen to the profitable sale of her father's business. It was also Edmund who had warned her that her trip might not turn out the way she wanted. He had advised that Adam might not be the same man she had known and loved. The men who had risked their lives to tame the Northwest Territories came back changed men, he had pointed out, using her own father as an example.

Lauren let her hands fall to her lap. She should know better than anyone how such a job could change a man, he had scolded. After active duty, her father had returned to Regina and spent the rest of his years in the Force in administrative duties. That was where she'd met Adam. He'd been a young constable under her father's command. She had been attracted to his quick wit and his honesty, but her father had warned her that the West beckoned him. To her father, that was a serious flaw. For good reason, she now realized. He was never the same after the march of 1874 that saw men and horses stretched to their limits. Edmund had reminded her of that.

Picking up the paper, she reread it. Edmund had never pushed or insisted or been more than a perfect gentleman. He had never even tried to kiss her. But he had been there. At the funeral, at the reading of the will, at the train when she left. Carefully, she refolded the note and returned it to her reticule, guiltily hiding it in the lining.

Adam rapped sharply on her door at exactly seven o'clock. With few words other than a short greeting, he led her out of the hotel and down the street to a small café. Muslin curtains hung in paned windows, and delicious smells crept under the door. Warm bread, roasting meat, and baking pies all mingled to make their mouths water. A wave of hunger hit Lauren so strongly she felt weak. Only then did she remember she'd missed supper last night.

They stepped inside, and a waitress sauntered over to their table. "Inspector McPhail! Good to see you again. What'll it be? Your usual?"

As he removed his shaggy coat, Lauren noticed faces turned toward him, nodded and smiled greetings, and she felt a swell of pride.

"I'll take the eggs and steak. And some potatoes, too," Adam said with a quick glance at a handwritten menu. "Sarah, this is my fiancée, Miss Lauren Butler."

The waitress's eyebrows raised. "You're engaged? I'll be . . . What'll you have, Miss Butler?"

"I'll take the same." Lauren handed back her menu and chafed that Adam hadn't mentioned being engaged to someone he apparently saw often. Jealousy pricked at her, ruining what was left of the good humor she'd cultivated since waking.

The woman sashayed off, and Lauren noticed that his glance followed her for an instant before sweeping the establishment, locating and noting every customer.

"Are you always on duty?"

He swung his gaze back to her and frowned. "What?"

"I said, 'Are you always on duty?' "

"Out here it pays to be careful." He glanced around the room again, then back to her. "Did you have any trouble selling your father's business?"

The change of subject was so abrupt that for a moment Lauren could think of no comment.

"No, I sold the store months ago. The responsibility got to be too much with having to be with Father every minute."

His hand crept across the table and enclosed her fingers, sending her hopes spiraling upward. "I am truly sorry I could not come. But with your father in the Force for years, you know how difficult it is to get away."

"I understand, I really do." Lauren's heart quickened as his fingers held hers, entwining with them, caressing them. "I just missed you."

"I didn't get the message for almost a month." Adam leaned back as the waitress set his plate before him and then slid Lauren's before her.

"I know. Really, it's all right, Adam. I didn't expect you to come." Lauren lifted a forkful of the food and savored the simple taste. *But I wish you had.*

Absently, he began to push a potato around the plate, then captured it, sliced it in two and quickly ate it. For the rest of the meal, Lauren noticed that he ate quickly, wasting no time on conversation. Who was this stranger sitting there in Adam McPhail's skin?

"You're so thin," she said, then cringed at the bluntness of her words.

But he looked unperturbed as he quirked up one corner of his mouth. "Not much to eat out there sometimes. The days are long and the work is hard."

"Do you regret staying in?"

His head came up, a look of disbelief on his face. "No, of course not. This is wonderful land, Lauren. Open and wild. Free and untamed. A man has room out here, freedom to do and think as he pleases. Within the law, of course."

"So, you think we'll stay here in the Territories?"

He paused with a forkful of fried potatoes halfway to his mouth. "Yes, I intend to stay here."

Not until now did Lauren realize that she'd harbored the hope Adam would return East one day and take an assignment in Regina. They would spend their lives among friends and family, educate their children in the East.

"I've spoken to the chaplain, and he's agreed to marry us tomorrow afternoon in the chapel at Fort

Saskatchewan. The day after, we leave for the Onion Lake Cree reserve."

There was no hint of excitement in his voice, no trace of expectation or teasing. Just flatly stated facts. She kept her eyes on her plate so he wouldn't see her disappointment.

"That'll be fine with me. Where is Onion Lake?"

"Farther north. There's a movement to deploy men north, in preparation of policing the Gold Rush in the Yukon."

"Will we be going there?"

Adam shook his head. "No, we'll be responsible for one of the trails leading into the Yukon and the Cree territory it crosses."

He put down his fork and met her eyes with an unwavering gaze. One rough hand reached across the table to cover hers. "I've purchased a supply of shields from the physician, and I suggest you purchase another means while we are still here in Edmonton, where such things are available." He squeezed her hand. "I don't want you to become pregnant without qualified medical care available."

The mouthful of potatoes swelled in her throat. Lauren withdrew her hand from his and covered her mouth with her napkin while her head spun. Was she really sitting in a café openly discussing birth control with a man she no longer knew? She glanced around them. No one seemed to have heard.

She swallowed and lowered the napkin. "Adam, this is hardly the place to discuss this," she whispered.

He flushed red and glanced at their neighbors. "I'm so sorry. I didn't think. . . . I wanted you to understand . . ."

She touched his hand. "It's all right. I do understand, and I've already prepared for that."

He looked so relieved that the ridiculous impulse to laugh swelled up in her chest. This was indeed not the Adam McPhail she'd known. This Adam came without the cool confidence of the old, without the pretentious trappings society saddled them all with. But this Adam was delightfully naive and embarrassingly honest.

He lowered his gaze to his plate, traces of his embarrassment still on his cheeks. Lauren took a sip of her coffee and smiled softly into the dark liquid. If she couldn't resurrect the Adam she'd agreed to wed, then she'd learn to love the man he'd become.

Three

Adam's boots clicked on the planks of the sidewalk as he walked toward the livery at the other end of town. Last night's rain had cleansed the air and sky, deepening the blue to azure. Fluffy clouds drifted overhead. The weather was going to be kind to them today for their trip to Fort Saskatchewan, yet in hours the sky could darken and a curtain of frigid air could sweep out of the north, bringing with it stinging ice and snow.

Why was he thinking about the weather, he wondered, remembering his blurted comments in the café over breakfast. Had he been in the wilderness so long, he was completely unable to live among civilized people? His thought had been to make her understand that these were the conditions of their marriage, and yet he hadn't had the courage to issue them to her as an ultimatum despite his sleepless night trying to form those thoughts into words she'd understand. She hadn't been there when Pierre's wife clawed at her blankets and begged for death while he delivered her stillborn child. Lauren had never watched people receive the deepest wound of their life. So, he'd blurted out an almost taboo subject over breakfast. He'd never have entertained the idea of doing such a thing two years ago.

His thoughts turned again to Lauren as he moved farther away from the hotel. Why did he feel trapped every time he was alone with her? Was he such a selfish man that he didn't want the responsibility of a wife? No, he decided, that wasn't it. She had come all this way because she loved him. She wanted a home and children, and he wasn't sure he could give her that. This transient way of life had become part of him—the excitement of new places and new sights, the satisfaction of a job well done.

He raised his head long enough to dodge a woman with a baby carriage just coming out of the general store.

"Good morning, Inspector," she said with a smile.

Adam nodded, sidestepped the carriage, and continued on down the street. Lauren would want babies, and soon, he thought. Again, bloody memories of Pierre's wife clouded his mind and sent an unexpected shiver down his spine.

"Stimpy!" he shouted, entering the darkened livery. "Is my horse ready?"

"Yeah," came the answer from deep within the barn. "Wait a minute. I got a surprise for you."

Hay rustled; then Stimpy stepped out, leading Adam's black gelding and a dainty pinto mare.

"Fellow brought her in last week. She's a beauty, ain't she?" He grinned, pink tongue showing through a gap in his front teeth.

"Why are you showing her to me?" Adam asked as he ran his hand over the mare's neck, noting her small, well-structured head and ears that flicked back and forth as they spoke, a sure sign of intelligence. Her splotched face ended in a nose covered with dainty black whiskers. Adam rubbed her face and around her mouth to see if she'd bite, then walked around her, picking up her feet, testing for ill temper. She obliged each time with a reluctant shift of her weight. When he reached her head again, she raised her nose and nuzzled his ear.

"Last night you told me to git you another horse."

"I did?" Had he said that? Had he somehow known last night that he couldn't argue Lauren out of staying? Or had Stimpy simply had his ear to the gossip mill?

"See there. She likes you already. Thought she might suit your missus."

"Lauren will be delighted. She's always wanted a horse. How much?"

Stimpy rubbed his chin for a moment, then grinned. "Consider her a wedding present."

Adam glared at him. "What is it you aren't telling me?"

"Nothin', I swear." He held up both hands. Then he dropped them and kicked at the hay on the floor. "Well, she didn't cost me nothin'. This here feller from back East brought her in and said he'd got her in Calgary and that she was lame. Bought a nasty bastard I'd had here a while nobody could ride. Well, this little girl had a stone in her shoe. He was just too damned stupid to look. Anyhow, he gave her to me. Said he was gonna shoot her iffen I didn't take her. I doctored her foot and fed her up some. She's a lady's horse."

Adam laughed. "I knew there had to be a story. All right, Stimpy. I accept on Lauren's behalf. Thank you."

He led the horses outside and mounted his gelding. "Whoa, Jake," he said as the black backed his ears at the mare. "She's with us now." He prodded his horse in the sides, and he pranced forward, the pinto shuffling docilely behind.

Lauren raised the window and let the damp morning air pour in. The raucous cry of a whisky jack broke the stillness, and the earthy scent of river water filled her nose. Below, the dock bustled with activity, and beyond the far shore, flat land stretched into infinity.

Elbows propped on the sill, Lauren stared out across endless flat land. Not a tree, save those planted in town, broke the bleak landscape. Down at the river's edge, willows clumped where the steep riverbank gentled and small bars of soil accumulated.

"Hey," someone shouted from below.

She poked her head out. Immaculate in his uniform, Adam sat astride a black horse, a small pinto mare tied behind. Lauren felt a swell of pride at the picture he made, tack cleaned and oiled, his red uniform resplendent against the dullness of the dirt street. He, like her father, was one of the few; one of the men who had captured an entire nation's imagination; one of the men whose motto was *Maintien le Droit* (Maintain the Right). Lauren smiled. How well the words fit him. Always on the side of what was right despite the consequences. It was his strength, yet he saw it as his weakness. Childhood memories of seeing her father ride in review with his detachment rose, and she remembered that then, too, she had felt a sense of pride so strong it brought tears to her eyes.

"I've got a surprise for you," he called up.

"Is she mine?" Lauren pointed at the horse.

"Only if you can ride her."

"You bet I can." Lauren drew in her head and flew down the stairs and out the door.

"Oh, Adam. She's beautiful," Lauren cooed as the mare shoved her nose into her hand.

"She's a wedding present from Constable Stimpy, the liveryman." Adam swung down from the saddle to her side.

Lauren dropped her hand, but the mare continued to probe as a woman passed by and spoke Adam's name. "Does everyone in this town know you?"

"Just about. Here, she's looking for this." He pressed a slice of apple into her hand.

Lauren held it out, and the mare greedily snatched it up with velvety lips. "What's her name?"

"I don't know. He didn't say."

Lauren turned her head thoughtfully. "I'm going to name her Prissy."

"Prissy?" Adam gave the cinch strap another yank and dropped the stirrup. "That's no name for a horse."

"Why not?" Lauren pursed her lips into a pretend pout.

"Well, I don't know. I just never thought of it as a horse's name. Sounds more like a cat or a chicken."

"A chicken." Her eyes danced with laughter. "*I* never heard of a chicken named Prissy. In fact, I've never heard of a chicken with a name. What kind of people have you been associating with out here?"

Adam laughed, and a sensation of relief filled him. How long had it been since he'd laughed with Lauren, watched her eyes sparkle with mischief.

"Just look at her and you'll see what I mean." Lauren pointed at the mare, who daintily picked up a hoof and pawed the ground.

"Okay. Prissy it is. Let's go get your bags." Adam placed a hand on the small of her back.

After packing up her belongings, she and Adam emerged from the hotel and into the street in time to see a detachment of Mounted Police ride by. The patrol punched their horses into a trot and became a cloud of dust on a road that followed the river.

"Who are they? Besides Duncan?" she asked as Adam caught her around the waist and hoisted her into the saddle.

"Some of the men from the fort. They were out with me yesterday."

Lauren caught a note of evasion in his voice, and his eyes flitted away from her. "What were you doing yesterday that you needed that many men?"

The black gelding stood perfectly still once he felt Adam's hand on his neck. When Adam mounted, the horse began to sidestep and fidget, eager to be on his way. "I told you, working."

"Why don't you want me to know?" Lauren turned in the saddle so she could see his face. "Do you think it'll frighten me to know what you do? Well, it won't."

Adam smiled. "I should have guessed that. It was nothing you need to worry about. Just routine stuff. I didn't want to trouble you with the details."

Still unsatisfied, Lauren pulled her horse away from the hitching post and headed toward the dirt road leading away from town.

"I remember when you took great pleasure in doing that," she said softly when he moved up beside her.

"Doing what?"

"Helping me into the saddle." She slanted a glance in his direction, but his eyes were looking straight ahead as they passed the last buildings and rode into the emptiness that stretched before them.

"Still do."

Lauren let the subject drop. She knew from his voice that she'd get nothing more out of him about it. He seemed unusually alert, constantly watching the riverbed, where worn paths climbed up out of the cut. But despite his alertness, his face wore an expression of deep satisfaction. He was content here, but was he happy here alone?

"Look there." Adam pointed across the prairie to a flock of grouse feeding. At the sound of his voice, they took flight, their wings making a throbbing sound, then disappeared over a rolling hill.

Lauren turned her head until her neck hurt, taking in this vast land. She'd never seen so much openness in her life. Everywhere she looked there was flat land or gentle slopes. She felt like a mere spot on the bosom of this mistress that had captivated the man she loved.

What was it about this land that drew people to settle here? she wondered as they rode past a small homestead. Adam touched the brim of his hat to a woman hanging clothes on a line in the yard of a small cabin. Two tiny children clung to her skirts.

"Are you all right?" Adam called over his shoulder after several hours had passed.

"Yes. Fine," Lauren answered, determined not to tell him her legs ached mightily and her bladder was full. Clamping her teeth together, she studied the slow sway of his back for the thousandth time as they moved along a faint path hugging the riverbank. Overhead, the sun broke through thin clouds, spilling feeble light onto the dreary early-spring landscape. The trees clawed at the sky with bare branches, and the grass around them was brown and dry. Green had not quite yet come to the prairie.

"Are we going all the way today?" she called, wincing as her horse stumbled and jostled her. If he didn't stop soon, she'd be in real trouble.

"Yes," he called back. "The weather's too unpredictable, and it's too cold to sleep out tonight. Why?" He turned in the saddle to look back at her. Then a chagrined expression crossed his face, and he yanked his horse to a stop. "I haven't given you much chance to rest this morning, have I? I'm sorry."

He guided them off the dim road they were following and into a group of low willows that leaned over the river. Gingerly, Lauren dismounted and looked around for some place with privacy.

"Go over there behind those willows." He pointed at a place barely concealed. "I promise not to peek."

Lauren looked up into his face, hoping to see a glint of mischief in his eye, but there was none. Painfully, she walked to the spot, and he dutifully turned his back, pulled off his gloves, and began to slap them against his hand.

"You didn't even try and peek," Lauren said, touching his shoulder as she emerged.

He jumped, and a slight flush crossed his face. "No . . . ah, I didn't."

"Two years ago you would have."

He looked away, and Lauren stubbornly pushed away the chill that enveloped her.

"We're only a few hours away from the fort. We should make it a little after dark." Without another word, he untied the horses and handed her Prissy's reins.

"Doesn't all this openness frighten you?" Lauren asked as they moved back out onto the path and a gush of cold wind pushed against their backs.

"No. Out here I can see what's coming."

Lauren moved her horse up beside his as the path widened. From the corner of her eye she watched him sway with the horse's gait. He had always been a good rider, but now he seemed as much at home on horseback as on foot. He sat erect, his hands resting lightly on the snug blue trousers, the leather lines twined gently between his fingers.

"What is it like?" Lauren's legs clamped tight against her saddle as Prissy stumbled, then regained her balance.

"What is what like?"

"Fort Saskatchewan."

"Better than some places I've been. The buildings are sturdy and warm, but sparse."

"How sparse?"

"Very."

"Oh. Well,"—Lauren shifted her position as the increasing chill permeated her clothes—"we really don't need a lot, anyway. I'm sure I can make do with whatever furniture you have."

"That's the point. I don't have any furniture; none to speak of anyway. I've moved so much that I either make or buy what little I need, then leave it when I move on."

"We'll get by fine." From the corner of her eye she saw him glance at her, his face solemn.

On they rode until the cold glow of a winter sunset tinted everything orange.

"Look there." Lauren pointed ahead at a wagon lumbering down the same trail as they. "Are those nuns?" she asked, amazed at what she thought she saw before her.

Adam followed her finger to the wagon driven by two people, their heads draped in black guimpes. "They sure seem to be."

"What would two nuns be doing way out here?"

"There is a mission farther north. They could be going there except"—he frowned—"two nuns came through Fort Saskatchewan two weeks ago headed for Slave Lake. I find it hard to believe *four* nuns would be sent up there."

Urging his horse forward, he soon rode abreast of the conveyance. "Good morning, Sisters," he said, touching his hat brim.

The two women nodded, keeping their eyes straight ahead.

"What are you sisters doing out here on your own in this unsettled weather?" he asked, his voice drifting back to Lauren as she caught up.

Each was swathed in a great bulky buffalo hide coat, knit mufflers pulled over their mouths. "We're going to the mission on the Lesser Slaves Lake," the larger of the two women answered in a squeaky voice.

"Have you been traveling long?"

"Oh, for a few days," the high voice answered again.

"Did you leave Edmonton this morning?"

"Why are you asking us these questions, Inspector?" the soprano asked.

"No reason, Sisters. I didn't see you leave town, and I was concerned that you might not have enough supplies to get you to your destination if you hadn't come through town."

"We are well outfitted, Inspector," the other nun mumbled in a low, rough voice.

"Do you mind if I have a look under your cover there to be sure?" Adam asked.

The two women looked at each other, nodded, and pulled the wagon to a stop.

Adam rode to the back of the wagon and lifted up a corner of the canvas. Numerous wooden crates and boxes were stacked in the wagon bed. "What are all these?"

"Supplies."

"For your mission?"

"Yes."

Adam prodded a box and glass tinkled. "I see. What kind of supplies?"

Again the two women looked at each other. "Medicines."

"Medicines, huh?"

Lauren squirmed under the glowering looks the nuns gave her as Adam poked and prodded through the boxes and crates from his horse's back. And if that wasn't bad enough, he dismounted, climbed onto the wagon, and began lifting boxes and shaking them.

"Yes. Medicines for the poor Indians there."

"Seems a lot of medicine for so few Indians."

The smaller of the sisters frowned. "Do you suspect us of something, Inspector?"

"Suspect, no. Know, yes." He jumped down from the wagon, moved to the team, and caught the side of a bridle.

"Adam, really . . ." Lauren began, already feeling the fires of eternal damnation.

"Step down, please." Adam looked up at the two women.

The sisters looked at each other, laid down the reins, and climbed down off the wagon seat.

"I expected better from you, Whiskey Jack." Adam reached out and snatched off the black guimpe.

Lauren gasped and clapped a hand over her mouth. Had he lost his mind? As the cloth came away, a partially bald head edged with frizzy black hair emerged. A full beard hid beneath the white wimple he tore off next. He pulled off the headpiece of the other nun and long, greasy blond hair tumbled out. "You too, Joe."

"How'd you know?" Jack scowled, his eyes darting to Joe.

"Sweat marks on your horses. Perfect outlines of saddles. I asked myself, Now what would two nuns be doing with lathered-up horses pulling a wagon? Where is it?"

Jack stared at the ground and scuffed at a rock with the toe of his boot. "Under the floorboards beneath the seat."

Nails screeched as Adam pried loose a board and pulled it away. Cradled in a nest of cotton were twelve bottles of trade whiskey. "Getting a little skimpy in your mix, aren't you, Jack? Seems like last time it took at least three cases of real whiskey to make twelve of that rotgut you sell the Cree."

"Times is hard," Jack said with a shrug.

"Is Angus behind this?"

Jack's eyes widened. "No, sir. Now, McPhail, you know we don't run with the likes of him. Joe and me here, why, we ain't never done nothin' bad to nobody 'ceptin' Injuns, and that ain't really bad. They buy the stuff of their own free will. It ain't like we're forcin' 'em to drink it."

"If you knew where Angus was, you'd tell me, wouldn't you?"

"I ain't got no dealin's with Angus, and that's a fact, Inspector. Don't want none, neither. He'd as soon cut his brother's throat as a dog's." Jack shook his head.

"Get on back up there and let's get on to the fort before this storm hits." Adam remounted.

Lauren looked up to see, for the first time, a hint of gathering snow.

Obediently, the men climbed back into the wagon and picked up the reins.

"Why were you so sure those weren't real nuns?" Lauren asked as the wagon lurched forward and Adam rejoined her.

"I recognized Jack when I first spotted him. I just wanted to make him sweat a little."

"Has he done this kind of thing before?"

Adam chuckled. "The last time was in Fort McLeod. That time they were dance hall girls."

"Dance hall girls?" Lauren asked in disbelief.

Adam nodded. "They shaved the hair off their legs, shaved their beards. Ugliest two girls I ever saw, but you know there were some trappers through there so hungry for company, Jack and Joe actually sold a few bottles before somebody got familiar and set off a fight. Frankly, I'm disappointed he wasn't more clever this time." He flashed her a smile. "Makes the game more interesting."

"Is this a game to you?" Lauren's heart beat double time as she realized Adam had not even pulled his gun.

"Sometimes."

"They could have shot you."

"Not Jack. He's too honorable for that."

"Honorable? A whiskey smuggler?"

"He'll be out of jail in a few weeks and back smuggling whiskey over the border. Then he'll expect me to catch him again. Isn't that right, Jack?"

Jack waved his hand over his head without saying a word.

"Why don't they run, since you're back here and they're up there with two horses and a wagon."

"Snowstorm's coming. Even a wagonload of whiskey's not worth being caught out in a blizzard. No, they'll spend the night in a warm jail."

What crazy justice he administered. Prisoners transporting themselves to jail? Playing games with the Northwest Mounted? Lauren shook her head.

But before she had time to finish the thought, riders surrounded them. They had appeared out of the gathering dusk without a sound. One grabbed her reins and hauled the startled pinto to a stop. Another two galloped around the wagon. Jack and Joe cowered together on the seat, fumbling to shed the long black robes. Fear poured through her as Adam calmly, deliberately, watched the melee. Then another rider charged up out of the riverbank. A long black coat whipped around his legs, and a dark hat shaded his eyes. He carried a rifle in one hand and controlled his plunging horse with the other.

"Ah, my competition has an escort," the dark man said in a voice tinged with a slight French accent. Lauren felt the threat in the timber of his voice rather than the words.

She hoped Adam would look back so she could read his face, but he gave her not a glance.

"And who is this fine piece?" Lauren felt the dark gaze rake her.

"My wife . . . as of tomorrow," Adam said without emotion.

"Mrs. Adam McPhail?" He doffed the floppy hat to reveal an unruly mop of matted dark hair. "I am honored to make your acquaintance." He shot Adam a knowing look, but Adam remained impassive.

"A delicate flower cannot be transplanted to the prairie, Inspector. It will wither and die or be trampled down." Urging his horse closer, the man reached out and fingered a strand of Lauren's hair. She could smell his body odor and imagined that some of the scent rubbed off on her hair. But she struggled to keep her fear at bay, to hide it in some other place. She raised her eyes to the man's and stared at him, challenging him to look away first.

His smudged face crept into an evil smile, and he let his hand drop slowly. "This delicate flower has deep roots, I see." He laughed, a sound more a grating than laughter. "Perhaps she will live. Perhaps not."

Then he urged his horse close to Adam, who had made no effort to draw his weapon. The man leaned closer. "You did not hear me, did you? I told you last time that I move on the wind and you cannot see the wind."

His mocking smile faded, and Lauren saw Adam's shoulders stiffen and one hand drop away from his reins.

"Be warned, Mountie. You cannot stop Black Angus. No one can. When the Mounted Police are all dead and buried in their fine red suits, Angus will still be here. He is part of the Territories, part of the land. Leave me alone, Inspector."

Angus looked Lauren's way and smiled again. "And your flower might live long enough to bloom."

Four

Lauren covered her ears and shoved her head beneath the pillow. Despite her efforts, a steady *clop, clop* worked its way into her consciousness. She opened her eyes and poked her head out. The tiny room was even smaller than it had looked last night. And sparser.

She swept aside the covers and planted her feet on bare wooden boards. The fire had dissolved into dim coals, and frost clung to the insides of the window. Dashing across the room, she picked up a piece of wood, tossed it into the stove, then blew on the orange coals until tiny flames licked at the bark. She slammed the stove door and dived back into the bed.

Clop, clop. Curiosity overcame her, and she stood and padded quickly to the window. Through the smeared glass she saw a line of scarlet-clad men working their horses in formation. She dressed, grabbed a piece of the bread off the table, and hurried outside onto the porch.

A brisk, wet wind whipped her skirts to her legs, and she wrapped her short cloak closer around her. Adam and his black horse anchored the center of the line. Anxiously, he glanced from one end of the formation to the other, his horse moving in tiny circles while the others pivoted around him, churning the thin coating of snow into mush.

"They are magnificent, no?" a voice at her elbow said.

Lauren jumped and turned. By her side stood a short, thin, sparrow-like woman. She watched the line of men, the tips of her fingers pressed tightly to her lips, her eyes dancing with enthusiasm.

"My Claude, he is there." She pointed to a little man with a black waxed mustache riding a big sorrel horse on the outside of the circle. As he came around, he glanced over and winked. The woman laughed and waved.

"Is he your husband?" Lauren asked.

"*Oui!* Is he not handsome? Which one is yours?"

Lauren searched the formation again. "He is there, in the center. Adam, my fiancé."

"Inspector McPhail? Ah, *mon dieu*. He never told us you were coming." She pressed both palms to the sides of her head. "We would have made preparations for you."

Lauren watched Adam change places with the man beside him. So he hadn't told anyone she was coming. The formation broke up, and the men clustered together to talk and laugh.

"Here comes my Claude. Claude! *Venez!* This is Madame McPhail."

The little man stopped in front of them and jumped down from the horse's back. He smiled brightly, showing white teeth beneath the carefully waxed mustache. "Ah, Madame McPhail." He spoke with a slight French accent, less pronounced than his wife's. "I am honored." He bowed eloquently as he took her hand and kissed the back of it. "Adam," he called over his shoulder. "You did not tell us that a jewel would soon be in our midst."

Adam rode toward them. Even from a distance, Lauren could see the flush of embarrassment on his face. He swung down and, holding his reins in his hand, stepped up to join them.

"Why did you not tell us so that we could plan a party?" Claude asked.

"We aren't married yet. We will be married tomorrow. By the chaplain."

"Mon dieu. A wedding? And we did not know? We cannot miss an opportunity for a party, *oui?"*

"A party is never any trouble." Claude wagged a finger and laughed. "We must have one tonight." He clapped his hands together, then touched his wife's shoulder. "My Mignon will see to it."

"Oui, tonight at dinner." Mignon nodded.

Adam cleared his throat and looked at Lauren for the first time. "We usually all eat dinner together in the mess hall," he explained.

"I see," Lauren said, tilting an eyebrow at Adam.

Claude looked between the two of them, then glanced at Mignon. "We must be going." He draped an arm around her shoulders. "Mignon has not been well, and I fear for her health if she is out in the damp too long. We will see you tonight."

Mignon started to comment, but Claude gently moved her away.

"Why didn't you tell anyone I was coming?" Lauren sputtered when the couple was out of hearing distance.

Adam glanced down at the reins in his hands. "I intended to talk you out of staying."

Before she could say more, a corporal hurried up to Adam. "The commander wants to see you right away," he said urgently.

Adam nodded. "Tell him I'll be right there."

The man hurried off toward the end of the single men's barracks where a flag floated on the morning breeze.

"I have to go." Adam moved to mount his horse,

but he paused with one foot in the stirrup. "Oh. And good morning."

Lauren watched him swing up into the saddle. Something about his greeting irritated her. Was it the offhandedness of it or the fact that he hadn't awakened her to tell her good morning? He'd installed her in the visitors' quarters in a section of barracks reserved for married officers. He had returned to his home in the single men's barracks. Their parting last night was emotionless and curt, and she was tiring of second guessing his every word.

Wrapping her shawl tighter around her shoulders, she trudged back to her borrowed room. Tomorrow was her wedding day. They had postponed the wedding one more day because the chaplain had been called to a settler's home to preside over a funeral. She scuffed at a clod of dirt and nursed the ill humor rapidly ruining her day. Did she have the patience to break through Adam's resistance? Could she outlast him in this game they were playing with their hearts?

Adam halted his horse by the hitching post in front of the commander's office and swung down. He wrapped his reins around the log suspended between two others and stepped up to the door. A quick rap was answered, and he removed his hat and stepped inside.

"Have a seat, McPhail," Commander Griesbach said without looking up from the sheaf of papers in front of him. A huge wooden desk dominated the room, and the walls were covered with maps of the Territories.

Adam sat in a ragged straight-backed chair and hung his Stetson on one knee.

"You brought your fiancée back from Edmonton, I see." Griesbach signed a paper with an elegant flourish, sprinkled sand over the ink, and carefully laid the document in a pile to his right.

"Yes, sir."

"She's not happy here?"

Word sure traveled fast. "She'll have to adjust, sir."

Griesbach chuckled. "I have found that women in general can be a temperamental lot, Inspector. And our women have more than most to be temperamental about."

"She'll get used to it. Her father was one of the men on the March of seventy-four."

Griesbach's pen paused over the paper. "What was his name?"

"Butler, sir."

The commander slowly laid his pen down, stood up, and strolled to the window. Clasping both hands behind him, he rocked up on his toes, then down again onto his heels. "He was a fine man. But he always regretted leaving his family behind." He turned to Adam. "Had he stayed out here in the West, his opportunities could have been limitless."

"Your point, sir."

"My point, McPhail, is that I'm reassigning you." Griesbach moved back to his desk and shuffled through papers until he pulled out a creased letter and held it up. "And I'm afraid you will be faced with the same decision as your father-in-law—family or the Force."

A sense of impending doom settled over Adam. "Where am I being sent?"

Griesbach looked over the paper in his hand. "To a little settlement north of here where Hudson Bay has a post." He shoved a hand-drawn map of the Northwest Territories at Adam and planted a rough finger on a squiggly black line. "We have knowledge that Black Angus has become well established here, bringing whiskey up the river and selling it to the Cree on the reserve." Griesbach straightened and ran a hand through thick black hair. "The situation with the Cree is becoming critical. If we don't stop this, the whole nation will be wiped out in a few years."

"Is this Eric Ansgar's post?"

"Yes. You are familiar with the area?"

"I've patrolled there many times."

"That's why I'm assigning you there, Inspector. I want Angus put out of business any way you can."

Adam stared out the window. He had expected to be reassigned, and soon, but not to so remote a location. How would he tell Lauren?

Griesbach sat down on one corner of the desk. "I'm aware of the threats against you."

"I don't put much stock in those, Commander. Angus is a coward without his men behind him." Adam swung his gaze to stare Griesbach straight in the eyes.

"This won't be an easy life, Inspector. Not suited to family living."

Adam studied the map. It was beautiful country, wild and untouched, yet very isolated. Lauren would be alone for weeks at a time save for the company of the Ansgars, a Swedish couple running the post. There would be no connection to the outside world and no doctors.

"I urge you to reconsider taking your wife into such an atmosphere." Griesbach leaned back in his chair. "But I won't tell you you can't take her."

"When will I leave?"

"As soon as possible so you can be established before winter sets in. A week at the most."

"I'll see to provisions." Adam started to rise, but Griesbach waved him back down.

"I've taken care of that for you. When do you intend to marry Miss Butler?"

"Tomorrow afternoon, sir."

"You and Miss Butler have been engaged for some time, haven't you?"

"Two years, sir. She remained behind in Regina to tend to her father when I was posted here."

Griesbach slid off the desktop and moved to stand in front of Adam. "Man to man, I want to tell you to make the most of the next few days, but we still have a job to do. Yours today is to ride up to the Cree village. They're holding a prisoner for you. You should be back in time for dinner. Dismissed."

Adam lifted his hat from his lap, clamped it onto his head, and left the office.

Griesbach followed Adam to the door and stood on the porch, watching him trot away on horseback. "How much do you know about Miss Butler?" he asked Duncan as he walked up beside him. Griesbach nodded to where Adam dismounted in front of the married officer's housing.

"She's a plucky lass, to be sure, Commander. A tribute to her father."

Griesbach pulled a cigar from beneath his holster strap and bit off the end. "Do you think she can stand life up at the Ansgars' post?"

Duncan's eyes widened. "Is that where McPhail's being stationed?"

"Not just Adam. I'm sending you, too. Angus has to be stopped. He has the means to put together a whiskey operation bigger than Fort Whoop-up if given the chance."

"And you're sending the two of us to do the job?" Duncan cocked an eyebrow.

"That Scottish irreverence is going to get you in trouble, Duncan," Griesbach said with a slight smile.

"Now, you wouldn't dismiss me, Commander. Who would you send to Edmonton for those cigars?"

"And if I did, when would you get the chance to buy that pipe tobacco you like?"

"Touché"

"And no, I'm not just sending the two of you. I'm sending Mike Finnegan, too."

Duncan smiled. "It'll be a pleasure to serve with a sassy Irishman, sir."

Griesbach slanted him a dark glance. "McPhail's leaving in about a week. I want you and Finnegan to follow him in another two weeks with the bulk of the supplies."

"Are you thinking she won't make it?" Duncan nodded at Lauren, following Adam out onto the porch.

Griesbach struck a match and lit the cigar. "The Northwest Mounted has left a trail of disappointed women."

Adam's teeth chattered as he yanked on the reins of the horse behind him and turned to look over his shoulder. A snow-covered figure sat stoically straight, hands bound behind his back, offering no help with the stubborn beast he rode.

"It is an omen," his prisoner said in a thick French accent. "God does not wish you to lock me up." Snow encrusted his thick black mustache.

Adam brushed the ice off his own face and knew they both looked more like snowmen than human beings. "The only omen here is that if you don't help me with this horse, I'm going to snatch you right out of that saddle and make you walk the rest of the way," Adam threatened through clenched teeth.

"I cannot. I am frozen to the seat," the prisoner calmly replied.

Adam pulled his horse to a stop and massaged his shoulder, aching from pulling on the horse's lead line. A few more miles and they'd be home. He closed his eyes for a moment against the stinging snow. With a gloved hand, he again brushed his mustache and sent tiny icicles crashing into his lap. The light snowfall had turned into a blizzard even before he had reached the village. He could have stayed there for the night, but Lauren was at Fort Saskatchewan alone. Somehow he couldn't bear that.

"Why did you bring me out in this weather," the man asked, "when we had a warm lodge to sleep in?"

Adam ignored his question. Dusk was settling in and with it plunging temperatures. "Come on. Let's go." He pulled on the horse's bridle again and urged his own mount forward. Whiteness swirled around them, nearly obliterating the path they followed. Then, when the snow was thickest, a light appeared ahead.

The main entrance emerged out of the snow, guarded by someone in a buffalo coat bundled head and ears and clinging to a lit lantern.

"We'd about given you up, Inspector," a young corporal called as they rode through.

Adam swung west toward the two-story stable. Moist warmth and the smell of horse manure engulfed them as they rode straight through the wide doors, which Mike Finnegan swung shut behind them.

"Saints above, McPhail. A fine night you've seen fit to go traipsing about in. Why didn't you stay in the Indian village and wait out the blizzard?" Finnegan strolled up to them, blowing warm air into his cupped hands.

"That's what I asked him," the prisoner said as he lifted his leg off the saddle seat and his pants pulled away with a crunching sound.

Adam kicked a foot loose from a stirrup and tried to swing his leg over the horse's back, but his pants were frozen to the saddle seat. He peeled the blue fabric away from the leather and dismounted, but when his feet touched the straw-littered barn floor, his legs gave away, and he crumpled to his knees. Finnegan rushed to his side.

"I'm all right." Adam grasped Finnegan's shoulder and hauled himself to his feet. "My joints are just cold." He hobbled over to the stove. "Bring him over here, too." Adam nodded toward the prisoner.

"Come on." Finnegan pulled the prisoner off his horse's back and shoved the man toward the stove.

Adam bent down and rubbed his knees. He must have been crazy to try to make it home in this weather. It would have been smarter and safer to just stay in the Cree village until tomorrow, then try to make it back to the fort after the storm had blown over. *She* had made him do this; *she* haunted his thoughts and altered his judgment; *she* might one day cost him his life. He shivered with a sudden chill.

"Take him over to the jail, would you? I'm going home." He limped out of the stable, where the wind again cut through even the thick, shaggy buffalo coat. Driving snow stung his eyes and exposed skin as he made his way across the open ground toward the barracks.

Yellow light shone out of Lauren's room, throwing a square pattern on the snow in front of the quarters as Adam stepped up onto the long porch that shaded the front of the barracks. Lace-edged curtains now hung at the window. Smoke puffed out of the chimney pipe that poked through the roof. Home. The word slammed into him with a force that rocked him on his feet. Soon his lonely quarters, wherever they might be, would be a home. All because *she* was here. He felt the familiar confusion surface and cloud his thoughts. He had to tell her they were leaving soon, that she would be leaving behind all she knew and all that was familiar to follow him into the unknown. Did she love him enough? And more importantly, was he worth the sacrifice?

The door swung open just as Lauren reached for it. "Oh, Adam. You startled me. You're soaked through. Come in here and take off those wet clothes."

Snowflakes swept in on a blast of air and made wet spots on the freshly scrubbed floor. Adam slammed the door behind him, took off the buffalo coat, and shook off more frozen pellets. "Looks like it will snow all night."

"You sit down over there by the fire, and I'll go to your quarters and get you some dry clothes."

"No, I'm fine," he said quickly. "I'm going to my quarters to change."

Lauren stared at him and then laughed.

"What is it?" he asked.

She smiled, then giggled. "You look like a snow monster. All except for the print of your hat."

Adam reached up and felt dry hair where the Stetson had covered his head. Along the edges and down to his ears, rapidly melting snow was crusted. He shook his head, and the icicles in his hair tinkled softly.

Laughing, she rushed to him and threw her arms around him. With a quick flick of her tongue, she snatched an icicle out of his beard. The sudden intimacy was jarring, and he stepped backward.

She crunched the ice between her teeth, seemingly oblivious to the fact that he'd spurned her advance.

"Inspector McPhail?" a voice yelled at the door. "Are you coming to supper?"

Adam let her go and strode to the door. A young Mountie stood outside, his coat drawn tight across his chest. His cheeks and nose glowed bright red.

"Begging your pardon, sir, but Commander Griesbach sent me to fetch you. He wants to announce—"

Adam clamped his hand across the boy's mouth. A glance behind him told him Lauren was busy with the stove. He stepped outside, shoving the boy along with him.

"Not a word."

The lad nodded, and Adam let his hand slide away.

"Miss Butler doesn't know about my reassignment yet, and I want to tell her. Tell the commander we'll be there straightaway, that I was late getting in."

The boy nodded, turned, and moved down the long porch that fronted the barracks. Adam opened the door and stepped back inside.

"You've been busy," he said, moving to the stove and sitting down in a chair in front of it.

Lauren glanced toward the window where the lacy bottom ruffle of her best petticoat now hung. "It needed some sprucing up."

"I guess it did need a good cleaning."

Adam rubbed his hands over the stove, letting the snow melt off his beard and drip onto the hot metal with violent hisses. Out of the corner of his eyes, he risked a glance at her. She was carefully coiling her hair on top of her head. Adam closed his eyes, fighting against the remembered feel of that silky hair skimming across his face while she lay atop him, tempting him.

If he stayed true to his plan, she would leave him. He couldn't face the rest of his life knowing he'd left her at the altar. All that remained to resolve this situation was for her to come to her own conclusion that life as the wife of a Mountie was too hard, too demanding. Then she could return to Regina. Friends and family would understand and accept her back with open arms. He would be the cad, the bastard that broke her heart. No matter. His future was forever linked to the Territories. He didn't plan to ever again set foot back in Regina.

Delicious smells struck them as they opened the door to the officers' mess. The aroma of roasted meat, cooked vegetables, and pies and cakes all mingled and swirled together. Lauren's stomach growled, and she realized how hungry she was. Hand-hewn tables sat in straight lines, and accompanying chairs were filled with red-suited men. Only two other women sat at the table.

"We have an addition to our detachment here at Fort Saskatchewan," Griesbach said, standing as Lauren and Adam entered the room. "Miss Lauren Butler, soon to be Mrs. Adam McPhail. Welcome, Miss Butler."

Adam's fingers entwined with hers within the folds of her skirt, offering quiet reassurance. The tenderness of that endearing gesture from a man seemingly bent on driving her away was enough to bring tears to her eyes. Mignon and Claude beckoned to them from the last table. With a hand to her back, Adam pointed her in their direction.

"I didn't know I was so hungry," Lauren said as she sat down and Adam took her cloak.

"The food is *très bien*," Claude said, then winked at his wife. "But not as good as Mignon's."

"Stay away from the blueberry pie," Mignon whispered. "Mrs. Lamoureaux uses too much sugar."

Lauren nodded, turning to glance over her shoulder. Mounties with aprons tied around their waists were serving the ones seated.

"I hear you will be leaving us soon," Claude said as the server ladled a generous serving of stew on his plate.

"Ah . . . yes. I expect to be reassigned soon," Adam said, tucking a napkin into the neck of his tunic. He'd wanted to tell Lauren before they left her quarters, before thirty sets of eyes would witness her disappointment. But somehow he hadn't found the courage to say the words that would send her away from him. Then he realized that if he waited for her to hear the news at supper, she would have all the more reason to be furious with him.

Claude looked confused for a moment; then, with a quick glance at his wife, he picked up his fork and daintily sampled the stew. Lauren frowned and looked between Claude and Mignon.

"I see you brought in the man from the Cree village." Claude jerked his sleeve out of the way just in time to avoid a ladle filled with beans that landed on his plate.

"Yes. We didn't have much trouble. Just the weather and the man's stubbornness." Adam sampled a forkful of the beans, careful to keep his eyes on his plate.

A sense of foreboding crept over Lauren as she smiled at the man serving them.

"You risked your life bringing him back in this storm. Now why would a seasoned policemen risk his life when he could just as well have stayed the night in the village? Hum?"

Claude's black eyes danced with mischief as he looked at Adam over a spoonful of rich beef soup.

Adam's cheeks reddened. "No sense in wasting time staying overnight. We weren't that far away." He chewed a bit of beef for a long time before he swallowed.

"May I have your attention, men?" Commander Griesbach rose to his feet, accompanied by the scraping of his bench against the bare floor. "Several of our number will be leaving us soon. I would like to salute them and wish them well while the weather has us all here together." He raised his glass. "To Inspectors McPhail and McLeod and Constables Finnegan and McDougall, who are all leaving for the Territories. We wish you good luck. And especially to Inspector McPhail, who will, by this time tomorrow, be a married man."

Applause rocked the room, but Lauren barely noticed the noise as she stared at Adam. He barely smiled, his eyes cold, his smile colder.

Wiping his mouth with his napkin, he pushed his bench away and stood. He picked up his water glass and answered the salute. "To the men I leave behind. In both regards. Good luck as well."

Laughter swirled around the room, but Adam didn't look at her even once. She'd expected at least a sly smile, a touch. Some small intimacy between them. He sat back down, brushing against her arm in the motion. She slid toward Mignon, only an inch or two, but enough to draw Adam's attention and a quizzical glance. He wouldn't chase her away, she resolved as she bit into a slice of apple pie. She'd love him despite himself. Damn this man who ran hot and cold at a moment's notice.

Five

"Adam, do you take Lauren as your lawful wedded wife? For better or worse, richer or poorer, in sickness and in health till death do you part?"

He looked down at her, and her heart stopped beating for the breadth of a second.

"I do," he said softly.

"And Lauren, do you take Adam as your husband, for better or worse, richer or poorer, in sickness and in health till death do you part?"

"I do," she whispered, looking up into his gentle brown eyes. But the emotion she'd hoped to see was not there; the Adam she'd hoped would return didn't emerge. He smiled softly, but the wall was still there, a barrier as real as if it had been made of the hardest steel.

"Adam, do you bring a ring for Lauren, a symbol of the eternal nature of your love."

Duncan winked at Adam and handed him a slim golden band, which he slipped onto Lauren's finger. He repeated the words doled out to him by the chaplain, and then he kissed the tips of her fingers and coiled them in the palm of his hand.

"I now pronounce you man and wife," the chaplain said, and applause and happy voices erupted from behind them. They turned and greeted the crowd stuffed into the small chapel. Hands patted Adam's back and reached out to touch Lauren as they walked back up the aisle.

She'd worn the blue dress she'd intended as her wedding gown. No flowers bloomed this early in spring, so Mignon had sewn her a lovely bouquet of collected lace handkerchiefs, all donated by the women of the fort. Outside the church, she tossed the bundle to her assembled new friends, and it was neatly caught by a new bride, a Mrs. Whitman, who promptly returned it to her as a keepsake of her wedding.

They'd enjoyed a reception at lunch today in the officers' mess before the ceremony. Now, as the crowd dispersed and the sun dipped below the horizon, Lauren knew the true mettle of her love for Adam was about to be tested.

They followed a shoveled path back to the officers' barracks, back to the room Lauren had occupied. From the moment the door shut behind them, tension in the room mounted. Adam knelt on the hearth and wordlessly nursed the fire from embers back to flames. Lauren stood in her wedding gown and watched him, unsure what to do next. This was her wedding night, and her heart was hollow. She missed with bitter regret the intimacy of mind and soul they'd once shared. Stolen looks and sly touches had once served to fill them both with pleading passion. Now, standing in her bridal chamber, all she felt was loss.

Adam straightened and turned toward her. He paused for a moment, watching her across the distance between them as if struggling.

"I know this isn't what you wanted," Lauren began, at a loss as to how to approach the invisible barrier that stood between them.

He looked down at the floor, at his impeccably shined boots. "I've always wanted you, Lauren." He looked up to meet her eyes. "I never once didn't want you. I just felt, feel, that you would be safer home in Regina."

She moved within reach of him. "I don't want to be safe, Adam. I want to be with you. I want to live with you as your wife. Good or bad. Right or wrong." She smiled. "Better or worse?"

She thought he would pull her into his arms, but when he didn't, she moved closer still. "You've changed."

A frown briefly crossed his face, as if that were something he'd never considered. "So have you."

"For the better?"

"Different."

"You, too."

"Life out here changes men. And women. Sometimes they find things in themselves they didn't know were there. Sometimes they lose things precious to them. But it's worth the risk, Lauren. It's worth the risk." The emotion she'd hope to see in his eyes for her was instead for acres of wilderness. And for an insane moment, the entire North West Territories seemed to be standing between them. Like a mistress. Or a lover.

Tears gathered in her eyes, making his face grow hazy in her sight. She knew no other words to sway him to her side. She missed the Adam she loved, the man whose laughing voice chattered on and on enthusiastically about whatever was on his mind. But this was not the same man she'd once known. It was almost as if she'd buried two men instead of one.

When no further words would come, she chose action instead. She raised her hands to his brass buttons. "I always wanted to do this," she said as she flipped open the first button. He watched her without comment. When the front of his jacket hung open, she unbuckled the belt that wound around his waist and over his shoulder and dropped it to the floor. Then, she slipped her arms inside his coat and felt the soft cotton shirt he wore underneath.

His fingers flexed spasmodically, paused, then crept to the neck of her dress. He fumbled with the top button, and it gave way. Another and another popped loose. She stepped back. The garment hung loosely on her shoulders. His eyes on hers, he slowly pushed the fabric off her shoulders and down to her waist. Without hesitancy or shame, he allowed his gaze to roam over her breasts, poorly hidden beneath the thin fabric of her chemise.

"You're beautiful," he said on an expelled breath. "So beautiful."

He fanned his hands out on her hips and pushed the dress down. The fabric glided easily to the floor, for she hadn't packed the layers of petticoats she'd planned to wear. She stepped out of the puddle of blue, picked it up, and laid it across a chair. When she turned back, Adam had taken off his coat, yanked out his shirttail and sat down in the remaining chair.

"Come here," he said in a whisper, and she went to him.

He pulled her onto his lap, cradling her in his arms. He pulled out her hairpins and buried his face in the hair that spilled over them both. He held her there a long time, only the crackling of the fire company to his inner struggle. He bent his head and captured the tip of a breast in his mouth, suckling her through the thin cotton batiste. Tingles of joy spread from that spot down to the pit of her stomach where it kindled an urgent fire. Her breath caught, and she tipped back her head in abandon.

"I always wondered how you would taste," he murmured, his face buried against her neck. "How soft you would be." He untied the tiny ribbon that held the neck of her chemise gathered tightly and released her breast to his view. Balancing the weight in his hand, his lips closed around the nipple, his tongue pulling against the sensitive skin. He tangled one hand in her hair and slipped the other between her thighs.

"I promised myself I wasn't going to make love to you tonight. I thought I could come here and sleep by the fireplace and ignore you there in the bed. That I would wait and one day we would be settled and then I could love you like I dreamed and wished. But I can't wait, Lauren. I've already waited so long."

His raw words brought heartbreak with their honesty. He brought her to her feet, turned her away from him and freed the laces of her corset. As the constricting garment fell to the floor, his hands cupped her breasts from behind, caressed down her ribcage, out across her hips and down her legs. He seemed intent on touching her everywhere at once.

She turned around in his embrace and began to undo the buttons of his shirt. When he stood before her with nothing on save his yellow-striped uniform pants and suit of winter underwear, she slipped the tips of her fingers inside his waistband and looked up into his face. "I won't play coy, Adam. I'm not the innocent you left behind. I want you like a wife wants her husband—in my bed."

He pulled the thin fabric of her chemise over her head and guided the batiste pantalets to the floor, skimming the silhouette of her body with his hands as he straightened and boldly, possessively, swept her from head to foot with a searing gaze. Then he gently grasped her shoulders and sat her down on the bed. He removed the last pieces of his clothes and stood before her naked—and glorious. The ridges of his ribs were sharply evident, but the muscles across his chest rippled as he kicked his pants out of the way.

He dropped to his knees between her legs, put his arms around her and laid his head against her shoulder. She stroked his hair, now shorter and lying in the perfect waves she remembered. He was warm against the skin of her sensitive inner thighs.

Lauren pushed away, scrambling back on the bed and dragging the bulk of the quilt with her. For so long she'd dreamed of this moment in time, of lying here with him. Waiting for him to come and lie beside her. He rose and walked to the saddlebags hanging over the back of a chair. Leather rasped against leather, and she heard the rustle of cardboard and paper.

When he approached the bed, she saw a hint of a blue-and-red package hidden in his hand. He sat on the edge of the bed, his back to her, and stared down at the item he held. A French shield. Lauren recognized it from her information shopping in McLean's Pharmacy before she left Regina.

"Just doesn't seem right somehow," he murmured so softly, she wondered if he'd meant for her to hear.

Lauren scooted across the bed to kneel behind him and laid a hand on his shoulder. "It won't matter, darling."

He looked over his shoulder at her. "It matters to me. Doesn't seem right to interfere with the natural way of things. Any other place, any other set of circumstances and we wouldn't have to do this."

Lauren slid her arms around his neck from behind and traced the tips of her fingers through the blond fuzz scattered across his chest. She laid her cheek against his temple and gazed down at the small package in his hand. "There's nothing wrong with choosing when children are conceived. Many couples are careful now that the shields are available."

He dipped his head and glanced at her out of the corner of his eye. "Do I want to know why you know so much about this subject?"

She shrugged and nipped at the lobe of his ear. "Do you think sewing is the only thing discussed in sewing circles?" She leaned down and tasted the depression of his shoulder with a quick lick of her tongue.

He turned and captured her mouth with his, one

hand cupping the back of her head. She backed away, drawing him onto the bed with her until they lay skin to skin. She thought back to those Saturday afternoon sewing circles when Auntie sat with her father, remembering the whispered confessions of young brides and experienced matrons. There were tales of youthful and illicit conquests and of long practiced loving. And in the months between then and this moment, she'd carefully planned her seduction of Adam.

She drew him into her arms with whispered promises and sweet caresses, and he tasted her body in places no one had dared mention. And when he allowed her to sheath him, she drew him inside her with a delicious gasp and the only sense of completeness she'd ever known.

They moved together in their nest of quilts and sheets. Adam loved her with such sweetness and passion that she ignored the pain of her lost innocence. And then he stopped.

"Adam, what's the matter?" Lauren asked, her words breathless with disappointment.

He withdrew from her, rolled to the side, and sat on the edge of the bed. "I can't," he said with a shake of his head.

"It'll be all right," she said, sliding to lean against his back. "The shield is safe. Even Mrs. McDonald said that her daughter—"

He rose abruptly, and Lauren clawed at the mattress to keep from tumbling to the floor. "I don't mean by choice, Lauren. I mean . . . I can't." He kept his back to her and stepped into the shadows. "I mean this is wrong. Our marriage. You here in my bed." He turned and shook his head. "This is all wrong."

Lauren stomped her feet and slapped her forearms. Gray and white wolf dogs squirmed and wiggled in their harnesses at her feet. She stared down into their lean, hungry faces and remembered Adam's warnings that these were work animals and not pets. They were barely tamer than their wild cousins, he had said, and could take her fingers off without provocation.

She raised her eyes and stared across the empty white flatness that stretched beyond the main gate. Nearly as empty as her heart.

A bitter, cold wind spit bits of ice into her face, and she pulled her muffler tighter over her mouth. Adam scowled as he came around the sled and yanked on the latigo straps holding her bag in place.

"You could say good morning," she said, observing that he looked little like a Mountie, now dressed in buckskin pants and a woolen coat. The only things remaining of his uniform were his Stetson hat and his boots.

He glanced at her briefly, then gave the straps a vicious jerk. The dogs stirred and shot him a wary glance. She had no idea where he'd spent the night. Most likely in his office or in the barn. She'd cried herself to sleep, curled in a ball, fighting off the sense of desolate loneliness threatening to swallow her.

He'd said not a word about last night. She'd attempted a few introductory comments, but he'd scowled, as he was doing now, and remained silent, his lips pressed into a straight line. In fact, she'd stood in the center of his room, her bags packed, and given consideration to taking the first train back East. But then she'd remembered his caress and the vulnerability in his eyes. Even if it was only there for a few seconds. Then optimism and love had overcome doubt.

"Are you going to be like this all the way there?" Lauren shifted her feet against the cold that numbed her toes.

He moved to the other side. "It's a mistake to take you, Lauren, a mistake I'm afraid we'll both regret." His words were edged with foreboding, and she felt another chill as the wind whipped around her. "It's a mistake only if we let it be," she said softly.

He met her eyes for a moment, then looked away. Lauren adjusted the men's pants she wore, uncomfortable at how they fit between her legs. But Adam had insisted, saying she would freeze in a dress.

"The rest of your supplies will be up when the weather breaks." Inspector Griesbach stepped to Adam's side out of the small group that had gathered and looked over his head toward the wilderness they were about to enter. "Think you can make do until then?"

"I'm sure we can, sir."

Griesbach stared at her, and Lauren felt her cheeks color beneath the muffler wound around her face and across her mouth. He didn't approve of her going. He'd been very honest and vocal about his objections, but Adam had been undaunting in his support of her. He might not agree with her in private, but in public he had supported her decision quietly and firmly, and she loved him all the more for it.

"Eric Ansgar and his wife will be waiting for you. You should arrive in about three weeks," Griesbach said, rocking up on his toes, his hands clasped behind his back.

"That's what I estimated." Adam yanked at one more strap, then stood back to survey his work. Not another thing could fit on the sled except her.

"Good luck, Inspector." The men shook hands.

Mignon stepped to Lauren's side. "The sky is lowering."

"Yes." Lauren looked up where dark clouds scuttled by. "Adam said snow was coming again."

"I will miss you."

"And I will miss you, too." Lauren covered Mignon's hand with her own glove-clad one.

"Inspector McPhail is a good man. He save my life once." She nodded vigorously as she spoke.

"We have to go to beat this storm." Adam caught the crook of Lauren's arm and gently tugged her toward the sled, leaving her to wonder about this latest evidence of her husband's bravery.

Lauren looked over her shoulder at the little house that had been their first home, if even for a few days. Still hanging in the window was her best petticoat. Maybe leaving it there would brighten some other young wife's day. Tears slipped down her face as she climbed into the sled.

"Are you all right?" Adam leaned over her and asked.

"No." She swiped the tears away with the back of her hand.

"Ha," Adam shouted at the team, and they leapt forward.

"I'll see you in a month," Duncan called as they whisked through the gate.

Adam lifted his hand, and they left the fort behind.

"Are you sure he'll bring Prissy?" Lauren shouted over the wind that snatched away her words.

"He'll bring both horses when he comes. By then, the snow will have melted."

Lauren caught only a few of his words, but enough for reassurance. Settling back against the furs Adam had brought, she watched the endless snow pass, dotted by the occasional brown tree. The constant swish of the sled runners and monotonous passage of flat, snow-covered prairie lulled her until her eyelids drooped.

She was in a room lit only by the yellow glow of many candles. Over her head, a lace canopy stirred with a gentle draft. What am I doing on a bed? she wondered, pushing herself up onto her elbows. A few feet away, a fire burned on a hearth, cheerful and crackling. A man leaned against the mantel, the gentle light turning his skin a tanned bronze. Light touched and caressed the ripples in his bare skin, slid down to his waist and bare hips and back. Desire stirred in her. Lauren rose from the bed, drawn toward him. Soft linen whisked around her feet as she moved. His skin was warm and soft as her hand glided onto his shoulder. Slowly he turned. Adam's brown eyes smoldered, and he enveloped her in his arms. His lips found the soft recesses of her neck. She tilted her head back and closed her eyes, content to let him torment her. He drew away, and she opened her eyes to stare into . . . not Adam's brown eyes but Edmund's blue ones!

"What's the matter?" Adam shook her shoulder.

"What?" Lauren opened her eyes.

"You were dreaming and cried out." Adam was shouting and hanging over the back of the sled as it sped along.

"What did I say?" Lauren said over her shoulder, the dream a crisp memory.

"I don't know." He shook his head. "Couldn't make it out."

The wind was tearing his words away from her, and she was grateful. Shaken by the last vision, Lauren snuggled deeper into the shaggy fur of her coat. Why had Edmund's image been tangled up with Adam's? What did it mean? Guiltily, she thought of her reticule packed in her valise. Why hadn't she thrown Edmund's letter away? She could summon no answer, nor could she part with the note. Were his words her last link to her former life? Was that why she'd saved it? Searching her heart, she could find no love for Edmond, only a deep gratitude and warm friendship. That was why she kept it. Friendship, she told herself.

The storm struck just at dusk, beginning as soft, fat flakes that peppered down like feathers. Adam swerved the sled toward a faint track beneath the snow. They topped a hill, and he dragged a foot to stop the sled, rooster-tailing snow in a plume beside them. The dogs lay down immediately, and Adam rummaged in one of the bags Lauren leaned against.

"What are you looking for?" she asked as he grumbled beneath his breath, then yanked out his scarlet coat. Quickly, he changed and threw the buffalo coat around his shoulders. "What are you doing?"

"Just giving us a little insurance. When we stop, you stay behind me. Understand?"

She nodded to his raised eyebrows. He stepped back onto the sled, and they continued down into a dip that ran parallel to a small creek. Naked willows bent their heads over the frozen water. Through the swirling mist, a light emerged, then two. A whole cabin appeared, snow thick on the groaning roof. So new, the ends of the logs had not yet weathered, the house was a welcome sight. The sled slid to a stop, and the dogs immediately lay down and tucked their noses beneath their tails. Adam helped Lauren out of the sled, but her legs were so stiff, she stumbled.

Raucous voices rumbled, and the sound of breaking glass escaped into the night as Adam yanked the door open. With Lauren close behind, he stepped inside. Rough-hewn tables filled a large room with a short bar in one corner. Chairs, carved from wooden barrels, accommodated three men tossing bent and torn cards into a pile in the center. All eyes raised when Adam swept off his hat and doffed the snow out of his hair.

"Inspector McPhail. Welcome." A man wrapped in a dirty apron stepped out of the dark, drying his hands on an equally dirty towel. "Welcome to Ben's Stopping Place." He stuck out a big paw, and Adam grasped it.

"Thank you. Could you put us up for the night?"

Despite her heavy clothes, Lauren felt the man's gaze rake her up and down. His smile suggested he imagined what lay beneath the layers.

"I'm all full up, but there's a nice warm barn out back. Even got a stove in it. Built it tight for extra

room and to keep the stock warm. You and your missus'd be the first to stay there." He smiled wide and
toothless. "Christen it, so to speak." He chuckled
soundlessly while his stomach jiggled up and down.

Adam's expression never changed, but Lauren saw
a hint of red around his ears at the man's blatant sug-
gestion. "That'll do fine."

"You folks want some food? It's plain, but hot and
plenty of it."

Adam's eyes swept the room, first to the men
watching them, then to the bar. "Are you hungry?"
he said without looking at her.

Warm, beefy smells filled the air, and her stomach
contracted in response. "Yes, I'm starved."

Pulling out a chair, Adam waited for her to sit, constantly watching the darkened corners of the room.
Lauren began to feel uneasy that he was so distracted.
As she glanced at the other men seated a few feet
away, they glanced at each other. More prickles rose
up on the back of her neck.

"Maybe I'm not so hungry, after all," she leaned
across the table and whispered.

Adam smiled. "Nonsense. We're both starved." He
leaned back in the chair and tossed off his buffalo
hide coat. Again, the men looked at each other and
commented beneath their breath.

"The scarlet does have a way of changin' the conversation," Ben said as he set two steaming bowls in
front of them, followed by a plate filled with fried
bread.

"It does at that." Adam selected a piece and took
a bite. "Very good." He nodded, and Ben grinned.

"Always glad to serve one of Her Majesty's finest."
Ben turned and waddled away.

"How can he have no room with only these few
people?" Lauren asked around a mouthful.

"He's only got an attic with a few cots. We get the

better deal out in the barn." Adam tasted the stew.
"This is good. Try some."

Lauren picked up her fork and scraped at dried particles of food clinging to it, fighting against the sudden
revolt of her stomach.

"Coffee, Inspector?" Ben again appeared at their
table, a red-checked cloth wrapped around the handle
of a metal coffeepot.

Adam nodded and shoved forward a cracked stone-
ware cup. Suddenly, a big man in a blue plaid shirt
sitting at the next table shoved back his chair, stood,
and swept the table clean of cards with one beefy
hand.

"Yer lyin'!" he slurred, yanking another man to his
feet by the neck of his shirt.

"I swear I didn't. It was just the luck of the draw."
The man dangled inches above the floor, the fabric of
his shirt stretched tight.

Adam wiped his mouth with his handkerchief, rose,
and strode toward the two men. The man in blue plaid
was tall and thick, an unruly mass of long black hair
falling over his face.

"What's the problem here, lads?" Adam halted at
their side, hands clasped behind his back.

"He was cheatin'," the big fellow boomed, pointing
his free finger at the man hanging from his grasp.

"I swear I weren't, Inspector. Tom's just drunk, and
the cards fell that way. Honest," he squeaked.

"Well, Tom. Maybe if you'd put him down, we
could clear this up like gentlemen."

Lauren felt her throat tighten as Tom stared down
at Adam, a murderous expression in his eyes.

"I'll not put 'im down. 'E's cheated me, and I want
my fair due, and you'd best not interfere."

"I can't do that." Adam looked down and shook his
head. "This is my job. You wouldn't want me to shirk
my duty, now, would you?"

Tom grinned slowly. "Yer job? Now, Mountie, is yer job pesterin' Black Angus?"

Adam's expression didn't flinch. "Ah. I should have recognized the name. You're Black Angus's Tom."

Tom frowned. "I ain't nobody's Tom, Mountie."

"You're your own man, huh?" Adam leaned forward. "Is that why you're doing Angus's dirty work?"

Tom dropped the other man and turned on Adam. Roaring his anger, he raised a heavy fist. Lauren jumped to her feet, fear choking off her air. But before she could blink, Adam's hands shot out and twisted Tom's arm behind his back.

"Ouch. Damn it, let me go!"

"Not until you sleep it off. Then, in the morning, you can apologize."

Tom leaned backward, his feet barely touching the floor as Adam steered him toward the stairs. Together they maneuvered the rickety steps and disappeared above.

Lauren sank into her chair, supper forgotten. After a few minutes, Adam came down, straightening his jacket and brushing spiderwebs from his pants.

"I was right," he said as he sat back down. "There's only an attic and some old, dusty cots up there." He picked up his fork and speared a piece of beef.

"Is that all you have to say about what just happened?"

Fork poised in midair, Adam looked at her, puzzled. "What else do you want me to say?"

"You could have been killed," she whispered.

"I was never in any danger."

Anger replaced her fear. "You're terribly cavalier about all this."

Adam smiled. "I knew exactly what I was doing and what my odds were. I would never do something like that unless I was sure."

As the pounding of her heart calmed, trembling replaced it, and Lauren dropped her fork with a clatter. "What if he'd had a gun?"

"He didn't." Adam neatly finished another piece of bread and leaned back, his coffee in hand.

"How did you know?" Lauren heard her voice crack and felt the sting of tears behind her eyes. Is this how he was always going to be? Testing his mettle everywhere they went?

Adam leaned forward, set down the coffee, and caught her hands in his. "You're cold."

"No, I'm not." She tried to snatch her hands away, but he held them firm. "Did he know Black Angus?"

"Yes."

Tears clouded her vision. "Then that man knew who you were. He could have shot you when we came in."

Adam took her fingers in his hands and smiled gently. "When we came in, I knew he was going to be trouble. He was already partially drunk then, probably on home brew. I listened to their conversation and figured out he wasn't that bright and not very dangerous, despite his bragging. When he took off his coat, I saw that his pants were too tight to conceal a gun and there wasn't one tucked into his waistband. The only place he could have one hidden would have been his boot. The other fellow was harmless, and none of the others were going to risk going up against a Mounted Policeman. Satisfied?"

Lauren looked up into his face. His eyes were unreadable, giving her no hint if his words were bravado or true courage. "No. What if there had been a gun in his shoe?"

Adam shrugged. "He could never have moved fast enough to draw it."

"Aren't you afraid your arrogance is going to get you killed?" Lauren snatched her hands away and shoved them deep into her pockets. "Why didn't you use your gun?"

"I never draw my weapon unless I have no other

choice." His words were dry and hard. "I'm not arrogant, Lauren. I'm careful and methodical. Only a fool rushes into a situation like that. I just saw it coming."

"Oh?" She chafed from her own fear and his mindlessness of it. "And how is that?"

Adam stood and shrugged into his coat. He moved around the table and pulled back her chair. "The other man dealt himself an ace from the bottom of the deck."

Lauren stood. "You saw all that from over here?"

Adam put an arm around her shoulder and yanked on her earlobe. "Caution and logic, my dear. Caution and logic."

Six

Warm animal smells enveloped them as they opened the barn door, scraping a wide path in snow rapidly piling up outside. Reminded of the Christmas story, Lauren gazed around at neatly built stalls filled with fresh hay smelling of summer and sun. The top of the barn was criss-crossed with new pine timbers, and the floor was freshly packed. To the side was a mound of loose hay waiting to be pitched into the stalls. The door swung closed, shutting them in with the livestock.

"Spread out blankets over there." Adam pointed to the pile of hay. "I'm going to check on the dogs." He opened the door, and a shower of snow blew in; then he was gone.

Two horses stood quietly chewing, watching her with big brown eyes. She walked over and scratched one on the forehead and received in turn a soft nicker. In the center, surrounded by a circle of packed earth, was a barrel heater, coals barely alive in its belly. The door squeaked as she opened it and tossed in a piece of wood. She closed the door and wrapped her arms around herself. This is how life is going to be, she told herself. She should have known; she should have remembered. Danger, fear and uncertainty would walk with her every mile, every hour. But so would love.

She closed her eyes, remembering his lips on hers, his arms around her.

You have to make a choice, daughter. Her father's words came back with new clarity, words whispered to her through a haze of pain. Now she realized they were a warning . . . and an urging. *He'll give you love and himself. That's all he will have to give. Those will have to do. Everything else will be cream.*

"A penny for your thoughts." Adam's breath on her neck made Lauren jump.

"You scared me." She put a hand to her chest where her heart pounded.

"Where were you?" Hands on her shoulders, he turned her around. "I made enough noise coming in." His eyes were crinkled with concern, his face shadowed beneath the broad hat. Suddenly, she wanted to step into his arms, to feel them safely fold around her, to lay her cheek against his chest and know that his heart beat just beneath the fabric.

"I was thinking of Father," she said softly.

Adam drew her closer, and bits of snow fell off his hat to tickle her nose. "You must miss him."

"I do. He was very wise." She snuggled against him, contented as he rubbed her back. "He gave me some good advice about marriage to a Mountie."

"Oh." Adam's hands stilled. "What did he say?"

Lauren looked up, her face inches from his. If he would just kiss her, all her fears and doubts would melt like the snow. "He said as long as we have love, everything else will work itself out."

"He *was* a wise man." Adam brushed her lips lightly, then released her, took off his hat and shook off the pellets of water. "The storm's getting worse." He picked up two of their blankets and spread them on top of the hay, carefully straightening each corner. "I'll bet he spent many nights out in a storm like this." Adam threw another piece of wood into the stove, and Lauren noticed he had brought in more.

"He never talked much about the Great March. Only to say it was long and hard and how proud he was of the men." Lauren rubbed her forearms.

Adam squatted down and scraped ashes away from airholes in the bottom of the stove. Cherry flames leapt up from the wood. "I wish I had known him better."

"I wish I had, too." Lauren took off the large man's jacket she wore and felt sinfully light in only the shirt and pants.

"Adam," she asked as she stepped toward the stove, "tell me about your father."

He shot her a quick frown. "What makes you want to know that?"

Lauren shrugged. "I don't know. You never have talked much about him or your family."

Adam stared at the stove as painful memories washed over him with such intensity that he ached.

"Adam?"

"There's not much to tell. You know the story." He tossed his hat onto the foot of the blankets and stood up.

"I know that you left England to come here and then you joined the Northwest Mounted Police. That's all you've ever told me."

He watched her move to the stall and pet the piebald that poked his nose over the boards. The full linen shirt gave little hint of what lay beneath, but the pants that hugged her hips left little doubt. Adam watched her move and felt desire uncoil in him. How long could he last? he wondered. How long could he resist loving her again? How long could he hold out before he got his wife pregnant?

"How far are we from our home?" she asked over her shoulder.

"About three weeks." Adam pulled his buffalo coat tighter around him and stretched his arms over his head. "We need to get an early start in the morning."

Turning, she threw the last of a handful of hay into the stall. "I still want to know why you joined."

"You know why. We've talked about all this before."

She sauntered toward him. "You said we needed to get to know each other again, so let's pretend we just met."

"Lauren, this is silly." He took a step back as she moved closer.

"You didn't think it was silly then." She slid her arms around his neck and stared into his eyes. "In fact, you thought I was beautiful." She laughed, her eyes glinting with mischief.

"Now, how do you know that?" Adam slipped his arms around her waist, then drew her close and inhaled her scent.

"Father told me."

"Well, the two of you had me at a disadvantage. There I was, a fresh recruit, performing difficult maneuvers on a half-wild horse for the OC and all in front of his beautiful daughter." He nuzzled her neck, and she moved her head aside to allow him more access.

"So, why did you join?"

Adam dropped his hands and moved away to a window mostly obscured by snow. "You sight in on something and you just don't let go, do you?"

"How can I get to know you better if you won't tell me anything?" Lauren touched him on the shoulder, and Adam gripped the windowsill.

"You know the story," he lashed out. "Why do you want to make me relive the pain?" He regretted the words the moment they were out of his mouth.

Tears filled her startled eyes. "I'm . . . I'm sorry. I just wanted you to talk to me."

She whirled, walked to the bed, and climbed between the blankets. Pulling one over her, she rolled onto her side and turned her back to him.

Except for an occasional sniffle muffled by the blanket, she was silent. Adam sat down on the pile of wood, uncaring that the snow soaked through the seat of his pants. Staring into the flames winking through holes in the stove's walls, he cursed himself roundly. Why was it so hard for him to talk about his father? To reveal private thoughts? Especially to his wife. In courtship, their brief words to each other had been compliments and light banter, designed to titillate more than inform.

He glanced over at her silent back. Why couldn't he talk to the woman he loved, tell her how afraid he was, how vulnerable he felt with her, how deeply he loved her? Clenching his fists, he put one on either temple and bowed his head. He couldn't leave her behind, not even if he wanted to, and yet he couldn't be a husband to her. Not yet. Fear washed over him like a cold dip in the river, and a woman's face drifted before him . . . white, frightened, eyes wide with horror. He was holding a stillborn baby. Cold. Blue. Lifeless.

"No," he muttered through clenched teeth. "No. That won't happen to Lauren."

"What did you say?" Lauren turned over. Even in the faint firelight he could see that her face was streaked with tears.

"Nothing. Go back to sleep."

Lauren rolled back over and studied the thick post before her face. Why did he withhold himself from her, not just his body but his thoughts and feelings, too? She squeezed her eyes shut against the frustration that welled up. In time, she'd break him down. In time he'd loosen up and let her in. In time.

For three weeks they traveled across a wilderness held in the icy grip of winter. Trappers' cabins, tucked around bends in rivers, hidden in thickets of willows, were their homes at night, when the temperatures dropped and the wind howled across the openness. Faithfully stocked with firewood by each person that had stopped for the night before them, the cabins promised a warm fire without their needing to look for wood in the dark. Adam unfailingly knew where to find each tiny structure, sometimes leaning with weather and age, and when they departed the following morning, he restocked the wood and water and carefully shut the door.

"The breakup's not far off," Adam said when they had stopped at midday for something to eat. "We'll have to be careful from now on when we cross ice." He rummaged in the sled and pulled out an oil-stained canvas bag.

"How much farther do you think?" She bit a cold biscuit, one of a dozen pressed into her hands by a settler's wife when they passed their homestead earlier that morning. Icy wind whipping her skirts around her legs, the woman had waved cheerily from a drooping clothesline filled with garments frozen stiff. She had fed them from a huge iron pot simmering over the hearth without identifying what they ate.

Gentleman that he was, Adam had taken the offered plate, said grace over the whole table, then eaten with relish, complimenting the cook with each forkful. Lauren had tried to smile and appreciate the stew, but it tasted oily and wild. Later, Adam had only smiled when she asked what it was, then said that these settlers had to eat what they could find sometimes during the winter, leaving her to wonder.

"Can't be more than a day to two at the most." Adam left her and moved to the head of the dog team, where he threw each one a fish. The supply of food for the dogs was dwindling. If they didn't reach Onion Lake soon, he would have to hunt for game to feed the team.

Lauren paced back and forth, chewing, grateful for

the chance to stretch her cramped legs. "What do you think our house will be like?"

"I don't know." Adam threw the last piece and washed his hands in the snow. "I'm sure there's something waiting. A cabin or at least a back room, something to call home."

Home. Lauren rolled the word around in her mind, enjoying the warm feeling it elicited. She didn't care if it was just a room; it would be theirs. They'd be home.

"Will there be Indians there?" Lauren pushed back her fur hood, aware that today was warmer than yesterday. Adam had worried that a Chinook might blow up and melt the snow before they got there. Then, they'd be on foot.

Adam laughed. "About all that's at Onion Lake is a Cree reserve."

"You see? There will be women there."

He didn't answer, only cast her a hooded look. Lauren let the subject drop, reluctant to broach the tender subject with him again. He'd never once mentioned what had happened on their wedding night. Nor had he attempted further intimacy with her even when she tempted and taunted him mercilessly in some half-warm cabin.

He glanced over his head at scuttling, fluffy clouds fleeing across an azure sky. "We should camp early tonight. I'll try to find a rabbit or something. I'm tired of pemmican," he said, checking each dog's harness.

"Me, too."

"Better get back in." He nodded at the sled as he pulled on thick beaver gloves.

Lauren stepped into the bed of the sled, and folded back up to fit into the small place she occupied among bags and furs. Adam stepped onto the runners. "Ha," he barked, and the dogs scrambled to their feet and lunged forward.

* * *

By mid afternoon an unseasonably warm wind was blowing. Lauren shed her lap of furs and pulled her fur hood off. The snow beneath the sled runners was soft and wet, spraying her with a fine mist of water as they sped along. They stopped once beside a stream for Adam to check the dogs' feet for ice between their toes. Squatted in the mushy snow, he lifted each paw, spoke a gentle word, then slipped a leather bag over each foot and pulled it tight with a bit of rawhide.

The wind sliding across her face lost its bite. Once, when they crossed a stream, the ice cracked beneath the sled runners. The sled tilted for a moment before a sharp command sent the dogs scrambling up a small incline, yanking the sled out of the water to safety.

"We'll stop there," Adam said as the sun began to drop toward the horizon. Lauren followed his finger to a lopsided cabin leaning precariously to one side, almost hidden in a tangle of underbrush.

"Isn't this wonderful?" Lauren exclaimed as she climbed out of the sled, free of the heavy buffalo coat for the first time in days. She stretched her arms over her head, feeling very light.

"Not so wonderful if you know what's coming," Adam grumbled as he unhitched the dog team from the sled.

"Why? What's coming?" Lauren hoisted her pack up onto the cabin's porch.

"A Chinook. It creeps in just like this, but there's trouble when the weather gets cold again."

"Couldn't this be the thaw?"

Adam grunted and dragged the sled up onto the porch, stumbling over a loose board. "I doubt it."

Ignoring his grumbling, Lauren eased the cabin door open and poked her head inside. Cobwebs laced the room, stretching from corner to corner. Dust turned a rickety table and one chair a soft, fuzzy gray. Tiny scurryings and a disappearing tail disclosed the present inhabitants.

"Do you think this fireplace works?" Lauren called, bending down to stare up the chimney. One night, at the outset of their journey, a chimney had been clogged and smoke had boiled out thick and black. That night they had to sleep with all the windows open.

"Probably, unless the chimney is clogged again," Adam's voice said from outside. She chuckled over his having read her thoughts. Then her smile faded. Three weeks on the trail, alone, together, and still Adam had not touched her. He was kind, considerate, gentle, but not passionate. Talking to him did little good. She wiped at the sooty glass of a window and watched Adam unharness the dogs and carefully remove their boots. Then they scurried underneath the porch.

"I'm going hunting for something for supper." Adam stomped inside and pulled off his beaver gloves, throwing them onto the table in a puff of dust.

"May I come along?" Lauren asked.

He squinted at her, the fatigue of the past days showing in his face. Lauren brushed aside a stray lock of hair, sorry for her words, knowing he worried about her more than himself.

"I suppose so, but you have to be quiet or it's pemmican again," he said with exaggerated admonishment.

"I promise." Lauren put a hand over her heart and feigned seriousness.

He grinned at her, then pulled his Enfield revolver out of his holster and spun the cylinder to check for bullets.

They left the cabin and set out through the woods, black tree shadows penned sharply on the canvas of snow. Tiny tracks in single file, more often in sets of two, threaded their way between the trees and underneath fallen branches.

"Look there," Adam said, squatting where a branch had fallen, retaining its dead brown leaves from the fall. "The birds have been feeding here." He pointed to hundreds of spidery prints around a round area denuded of snow by little feet.

Lauren peeped underneath the branch and smiled. Soon spring would arrive and these little scavengers would be high aloft in the crowns of trees, filling the sky with their songs.

"Spring's on the way. I can feel it." Lauren stood, spread her arms wide, and twirled around as they started out again. Her feet ached and were chafed, but the deep blue of the sky lifted her spirits. Overhead, fluffy clouds drifted idly by, reminding her of summer back East.

Adam laughed a deep, throaty laugh and pushed his hat onto the back of his head. Days ago he had abandoned the thick buffalo fur and now wore only his scarlet tunic. When she asked why he didn't change to the more casual clothes he carried, he had answered that even here the scarlet was respected.

"Don't count winter out so soon. It's still early," he said, slanting a glance at her beneath his hat as she twirled again. "You're wasting valuable energy."

"I don't care. Winter wouldn't dare intrude on a day this beautiful." She held her face up to the sun, grateful for the warmth on her skin.

"Things are not always as they seem here. Remember that. Expect the unexpected and imagine the worst. That way you're always prepared." He shoved his left hand deep into his pocket and again studied the shadows of the surrounding thicket of trees.

"What a pessimist. I can see I'm going to have to change you."

He smiled. "So, you think you can change me?"

"I think I can try."

"And, Mrs. McPhail. What would you change?"

Lauren's heart soared at the lighthearted tone in his voice. "Let's see . . . First I'd take that perpetual scowl off your face. Then, I'd make you less serious."

"Less serious? You mean you want me to laugh and joke all the time?"

Detecting an edge to his words, Lauren hurried to explain. "No, not all the time. I just meant I'd make you think less and enjoy life more."

"Oh, so you'd have me wearing lace cuffs and saying things like 'Oh, I love your gown, my dear. Wherever did you get it?' " He dangled his wrist in a dandy's gesture.

"See?" Lauren shoved a finger in his face. "You can laugh. I remember when you laughed a lot."

His face quickly sobered. "That was another life ago."

Lauren felt the chill and knew that the lighthearted moment had passed. As his eyes again returned to the shadows, she cursed silently the land that had taken the old Adam from her.

"Look there." She pointed to a bend in the stream they were following. Thawed and rushing, the river spilled out way beyond its banks, blocked by a huge pile of logs and branches.

"Don't get too close," Adam warned as she moved toward the pile.

"How on earth did they get all entwined like that?" She stepped nearer and leaned over the tangled pile.

"Lau—"

Suddenly, yellow eyes and teeth lunged at her. Adam grabbed her around the waist and yanked her backward, her feet waving in the air. At the same time, a blast split the air and a cloud of acrid white smoke enveloped them.

He set her down, spun and fired again. On the place where she had stood lay the body of a large wolverine. Her heart pounded, and the flush of panic rushed through her blood.

"I told you not to go close." Adam's chest heaved, and his hands shook as he holstered the gun.

"But how—"

"He found a good place for a den there. Nature provided, and he took advantage. Brush piles like that often have inhabitants."

He stared at her for a moment, then pulled her roughly against him.

"If you had been bitten . . ." He smothered his own words with a fierce kiss.

Confused by his intensity, Lauren encircled him with her arms and tangled her fingers together. When he finally let her go, Lauren stumbled backward. "What was that for?"

"That was to show you that joking and laughing don't make the man." Without another word, he pivoted on his heel and headed back toward the cabin, leaving Lauren to run to catch up.

Sweat popped out on his brow as he strode in front of her, so angry he trembled. If the animal had reached her, she would have been ripped and bitten and probably died before he could get help. He shook his head to dispel the thought. Frozen forever in his memory would be the picture of the wolverine in midair, claws extended, teeth exposed, inches from her face. Only by the grace of God had he snatched her out of the way and his shot been true. A shiver ran down him, and he hoped she wasn't close enough to see. He wasn't prepared for this, not for this responsibility. Why hadn't he insisted she return to Regina, bodily putting her on the train if necessary? The answer came in the burning of his lips, still numb from the kiss. He was hopelessly, helplessly, in love with her. She was as much a part of him as his arms or legs and just as necessary.

Lauren watched from the cabin's porch as Adam disappeared into the dense population of naked trees. Once they were back at the cabin, he'd said he was going hunting; she was staying there, and that was that. Lauren glanced over at the lead sled dog lying on the porch, his head propped on his paws, watching her with blue eyes.

"Traitor," she muttered, remembering Adam's words, "Watch her," to the dog.

She leaned her chair back against the cabin wall, having found a dying patch of sunlight. Soon, she'd drifted off. Something stirred her, something standing close by. She opened her eyes with a start. Adam stood in front of her, staring down, two dead rabbits dangling from his hands.

"I didn't hear any shots," she said.

He raised an eyebrow without answering.

"Stewed or roasted?" Lauren asked as he dropped them onto the steps.

"Roasted. I'll clean them for you." He bent to pick them up, but Lauren reached out and grabbed his forearm.

"I'm sorry I wasn't more careful today. I should have been looking closer. Even I should have suspected we would run into some kind of trouble."

He smiled up at her and started around the cabin to the back.

"Why did you kiss me like that?"

He stopped, his back to her, but he didn't turn around. "It made me realize how quickly I could lose you."

Lauren longed to run to him and throw her arms around him, reassure him she wasn't going anywhere, but some inner voice warned her to keep away, that he had to come to terms with this on his own.

"I believe that I'll wash up some in that little stream over there." She pointed to the other side of the cabin. "I promise I'll be careful."

He turned to follow her gesture. Through the naked forest, a tiny trickle of water made its way through leaves and rocks and patches of ice.

A quick look around assured him he could get to

her in a few seconds if necessary; she hadn't had much privacy lately. "Go ahead."

She rummaged through her pack, tucked garments under her arm, and set out toward the water. Keeping one eye on her, despite the fact that all he could see was her head and shoulders, Adam skinned the two rabbits and speared them to roast in the fireplace. He frowned, watching the smoke rise from the chimney, then hug the ground. Glancing over his head, he noted that the clouds had thickened, blocking out the first stars of dusk. As he suspected, winter was about to make another stand.

"I feel so much better." A wave of lilac scent surrounded Lauren as she brushed past him and stuffed the clothes into her pack on the table. "The water was icy. I think I'll clean up some in here." She picked up a bucket from by the door and set out back toward the stream. Adam closed his eyes against the assault of her perfume. Lilac was his favorite and a scent he identified with her alone.

When he opened his eyes again, she was coming toward him, water sloshing out of the bucket she carried. She flashed him a smile as she pushed past him in the doorway. Setting the bucket on the table, she picked up a rag from her pack, dipped it into the bucket, and began to scrub the table.

Adam squatted before the fireplace and hung the rabbits over the flames. Rocking back on his heels, he stared into the flames, watching the grease drip onto the wood and sizzle. He could hear her humming beneath her breath, in time with the scraping of her cloth across the wood grain. Sudden, intense desire flamed up in him. He glanced at the window and saw the first drops of rain splatter against the pane and drip down. The soft patter of rain on the shingled roof soon drowned out the crackle of the fire.

"There. That's better." Lauren backed away from the table and planted her hands on her hips. The surface was clean and beginning to dry. She set their tin plates on opposite sides along with a fork and a tin cup. Backing away, she tilted her head to the side and surveyed her work as though she'd just set a formal table.

"The rabbit's ready." Adam removed the golden brown meat from over the flames and slid a rabbit into each plate, then threw the spit into the fire.

"You're a very good cook," she said, licking away the grease from her fingers as she sat down.

Adam ate standing, trying to keep his mind off the approaching night. But try as he might, he still felt the urge of desire and dreaded a night so close by her side.

After they ate, Adam added more wood to the fire, then sat down on the floor by the fire, leaning against the wall. Lauren snuggled into the crook of his arm and rested her head against his shoulder. His breathing fell into an even pattern, and she knew he slept. Alone with only the complaining fire for company, Lauren reflected on her marriage. Cradled in his arm, her cheek resting against his chest wasn't enough. She wanted more of this man she loved. No, this wasn't enough. But it would do for now.

Seven

"Do you see anything?" Lauren wrapped her arms around herself and gave in to the shivering that shook her body. Although her teeth rattled, shivering did generate some warmth.

Adam shook his head. Snow skittered off the brim of his hat as he walked in front of the team, now plunging their way through deep, mushy snow. The ice had quickly turned to snow, heavy snow that fell in great clumps and stuck to everything. Saplings bowed under the weight, and limbs snapped and plunged to the ground in the flurry of white. The surface of the snow was an unnatural pink, turned salmon by the setting sun. They should have come to their next cabin an hour ago.

"I know it's in the bend of this river," Adam said, his expression going from mild concern to a serious frown. "Stay here with the sled and let me have a look around."

He slogged away, stepping high in the deepening snowbanks. A biting wind whipped down out of the north and sculpted the snow into formations and angles.

The dogs obediently lay down and curled their tails around their noses. Taking their example, Lauren snuggled deeper into the bed of furs, now wet and cold from unrelenting snow this morning. If they didn't find shelter soon, how would they get their clothes dry? Lauren wondered. She glanced at Adam's tracks, long, gliding furrows in the snow, heading off around a clump of bare willows. The crunching of snow brought her out of her thoughts. Adam was headed back, his head tilted against the driving wind.

"Did you find it?" Lauren asked as he stepped onto the sled's runners without a word.

"I found it."

"Good. How far?" Lauren turned to look at him, and the expression on his face startled her. His lips were drawn and pale, his eyes hard.

"The cabin's gone, Lauren. Burned to the ground. Probably by a careless trapper."

"What makes you so sure?"

Adam spoke to the dogs, and they stood and looked back at him.

"Because I found his body, or what was left of it."

A chill ran over Lauren. "What will we do now?"

"We'll find someplace to sleep. A settler's house, something. Ha!" The team lurched forward.

Twilight deepened into evening and evening into a starless night. Cold, bitter and clinging, crept in on the back of darkness. Lauren shivered and closed her eyes as Adam swerved the sled to miss a rock that suddenly reared up in their path.

"Whoa!" The team stopped quickly. "We can't go on in the dark like this." Adam stepped off the sled runners and moved around in front of her. He pulled off a beaver glove and felt her cheek. "You're freezing."

"I'll be all right. We can go on."

Adam shook his head. "No. We can stay warmer if we curl up somewhere. Maybe in the lee of a rock."

"What about a cave?" Lauren asked, then was confused when he laughed. "What?"

"There are no caves around here and precious few

rocks." Adam pulled the glove back on his hand and looked around them.

"How far do you think we are from the Ansgars?" Lauren asked, stepping from the sled and stomping down a place to stand in the deep snow.

"Less than a day. This cabin was usually the last place I stopped before reaching Eric's, but with this deep snow . . . I don't know. Everything's covered. I could miss a landmark. The snow could get thicker, become a whiteout. We better stop and wait out the worst of it."

"Where will we sleep?" Her wet clothes were increasingly heavy, and her arms and legs refused to cooperate. She stumbled getting out of the sled, and Adam caught her just before she pitched face first into the snow.

"We'll go over there." He pointed at a black spruce, stunted and gnarled with snow-laden branches that swept the ground.

"What if all that snow falls on us?" Lauren asked as Adam grabbed a handful of furs out of the sled and pulled her toward the tree, forcing her to walk.

He grabbed the bottom branches as far up as he could reach and shook them. Snow tumbled to the ground in plops and thuds. Then, he ducked beneath the branches, pulling Lauren along behind him. Soft rustlings said some other creature had sought this shelter before them. In the dark, Lauren could just make out a brown spot against the tree's trunk where no snow lay piled.

"The branches are so thick, the snow only drifted lightly in here." He kicked away the light snow and laid the buffalo robe on the ground. Then, he piled the other furs on top, three thick. "Now, crawl in there while I see to the dogs."

Lauren's teeth chattered together as she shivered uncontrollably. She heard Adam command the dogs to stay, then heard his steps crashing through the snow back toward her.

"Take off those clothes," he said, dropping something at her feet. She was so cold and sleepy, she couldn't make her arms work, couldn't find the strength to unbutton the buffalo coat or her other clothes. Adam frowned at her. "Lauren. Do you hear me?"

His voice was far away, dim, drowned in the soft pelting of snow.

"Lauren!" His hand gripped her shoulders and shook her. Her head snapped back and forward, but she couldn't seem to control it, to find her voice and tell him to stop. She only wanted to lie down and sleep.

Cold cut through her thoughts as she felt her clothes being pulled off. "Stop it, Adam." Her words were slurred, indistinguishable even to her own ears. If she could only lie down.

His hands were all over her, pulling off the outer layers of clothes, then moving to her shirt and pants, stripping her down to her underwear. She caught her breath and roused as he yanked them off, too. His arms were strong, comforting, as he swept her off her feet and shoved her into the furs. With great effort, she cracked open an eye and saw that he was stripping off his own clothes, rolling them into a bundle and pushing them down to the end of their cozy bed. His skin was cold and damp as he slid in beside her and pulled the heavy furs over them both.

"I just want to sleep, Adam." Lauren said as he pulled her into the curve of his body.

"You can't sleep yet, Lauren. Not yet." He kissed the top of her head and smoothed his hand down and across her breast.

"Stop it. I'm so sleepy."

"Well, I'm not going to let you sleep. Not yet. You've got to stay awake or you'll freeze."

Somewhere she remembered reading that freezing to death was not so unpleasant. One simply drifted off to sleep, the article had said, never to awaken again. She tried to rouse herself, to focus her attention on Adam's hand, wandering over her body, knowing he was trying to gain her attention, not seduce her. What an effort it was not to shut her eyes and give into the lethargy taking over her body.

"You should eat," he whispered into her ear. "It will give you strength." His breath caressed her skin, and she clung to that tiny bit of warmth and made her legs feel his pressed against her, made her back feel the hair on his chest, the stubble of his beard against her neck and hair.

"What . . . do . . . we . . . have?" she struggled to ask.

"Pemmican."

Lauren shook her head. Her stomach roiled at the thought of eating the tough, stringy meat even one more time.

He snugged her close, and his warmth became hers, trickling into her body, bringing her back to life. "I'm so tired," she whispered, vaguely aware of his palm sliding across her forehead. As his warmth suffused her, she curled against him and only then did he hold her close and allow her to sleep.

A sharp crack and a spray of snow awoke Adam with a start. He lay still, sleep receding and consciousness taking its place. Lauren was warm—hot, in fact. He laid a palm against her cheek, her forehead. She was burning up with fever. Adam fought rising fear. He shifted her against his body and peeked out from beneath their furs. In the darkness, lit only by starshine, the snow still fell, not in soft flakes but in sheets, driven by a northerly wind. He took a deep breath. He had to think. This snow could last for days, or it could end within the hour. There was no way of knowing.

"So tired," she murmured, and snuggled against him.

A breeze stirred, and tiny shards of ice pelted down, bouncing off the thick fur of their pelts. He hugged her closer, going over what medicines he had with him. He had a little quinine, some sulfur. Outside of that, he had nothing except some willow bark carefully dried and ground for fever. Nothing that would help here. He had to get her to Eric and Gretchen, and soon.

Adam awoke from troubled sleep as dawn lightened the leaden sky. Painfully, he stirred and shifted a still-sleeping Lauren. Prickles stung his arm as the feeling returned. He laid a hand on her head. Was she cooler than before? His hopes climbed. Perhaps he could control the fever with willow bark and snow compresses as they traveled.

"Lauren." Gently he shook her.

"Hmm," she murmured, and shifted her position. Blinking, she opened her eyes and stared straight at him. "Daddy?"

"No, Lauren. It's me. Adam."

"Oh." Recognition returned to her eyes. She tilted her head and looked down at their naked bodies. Puzzlement creased her brow. "Did we make love?"

Adam smiled, relieved to see her eyes clear and bright. "You mean you don't remember? You wound me, Lauren."

She studied his face for a moment, then smiled. "I remember. I was so cold. Has the snow stopped?"

"It has slowed. Stay there and I'll help you get dressed." He rolled away from her out into the cold and quickly dressed. Huddled beneath the still-warm furs, Lauren wondered how he could stand the cutting wind. She sat up, and her head spun.

"Why am I so dizzy?" she asked. "Is this supposed to happen?"

Adam squatted down in front of her, fastening the last of his buttons. "You have a fever."

Lauren searched his eyes for the fear she knew he felt and found it, along with guilt. Smoothing his cheek with her palm, she smiled despite how much the motion hurt. "I'll be all right. You said we were only about a day from the post."

"How do you feel?"

Lauren stretched and drew her clothes from beneath the furs, where their body heat had dried them during the night. "Better than a few minutes ago." She looked up to where Adam watched her closely. "Please don't worry. I'll let you know if I feel worse. I promise."

"Can you stand?" Adam gently moved her hands aside and finished buttoning her shirt. Then he stood and pulled her up with him.

"Of course I can stand." Lauren lurched to her feet and stumbled. "Oh, God. My head." She grasped her temples and sank to her knees. Adam scooped her into his arms.

"I'm so dizzy." She closed her eyes, her head lolling from side to side. "What's wrong with me?"

Adam swallowed. "I don't know."

"Put me down."

"Lauren—"

"I said put me down." She would have done anything to erase that helpless look in his eyes.

Adam set her on her feet. She wobbled for a moment, then took a step forward. "I'll be all right. If I could just have a drink of water." Adam glanced to where a canteen sat beneath the tree, just out of reach and probably frozen.

"Go on. I'll stand still."

Glancing back over his shoulder, Adam retrieved the water and quickly returned. She tipped the canteen, but nothing came out. Then, she reached up and scooped snow off a low branch and popped some of it into her mouth.

"That's much better." Lauren smiled, pushing away the pain of moving her face. She took a step and felt as if her whole body was on fire. Aware that Adam watched, she took another and another, gritting her teeth. What could be wrong?

"Hadn't we better be on our way?" Lauren moved to the tree trunk, picked up one of the buffalo robes, and wrapped it around her, careful not to let him see how good the warmth felt against her fevered skin.

"Are you sure you feel up to moving now?"

"We're not getting any closer standing here," Lauren answered, wondering where on earth she was going to find the strength to carry her pack. Gratefully, Adam picked up both, and she made no comment.

Icy wind pushed against their backs all day. Bundled to her ears, Lauren watched the dogs' bobbing tails as they loped over the smooth terrain. The snowscape passed in a blur of white, and Lauren nodded, grateful to let her eyes droop and sleep.

When awake, she felt Adam's eyes on her and knew he worried and blamed himself for her sickness. As the day wore on, the fever increased. When they stopped midday, she refused the offered pemmican, her stomach roiling at the very thought. Instead, she drank more water and, when Adam wasn't looking, splashed some across her face.

Night fell, and still there was no sign of their post, no house or cabin or other soul alive but them and the dogs. The fever sapped her strength, just as the darkness sapped the light of day, and still Adam pushed on, hoping they would reach Onion Lake. Wondering how he navigated when everything was covered with a thick blanket of snow, Lauren nodded, her nausea growing.

Finally, as night claimed the last sliver of the evening sky, they stopped. Lauren stumbled from the sled, grateful to rub snow across her face, hoping to ease the burning of her skin. She put a handful of snow into her mouth, swallowed the coolness, hoping to wash away the sour taste of bile, and closed her eyes to the dancing world in front of her. Adam's arms surrounded her, lifted her until her cheek rested on his chest. She inhaled his scent, thankful that if she were going to die, at least she would die in his arms. Then, grateful blackness swallowed her.

"Lauren? Lauren." Adam shook the rag doll in his arms, but she didn't respond. He looked around and saw nothing but snow for miles. Panic gripped his throat. Mocking voices inside his head taunted him for his foolishness, for his desire. Why hadn't he sent her back? he asked himself for the thousandth time.

"Adam?"

He bent his head close. "It's all right, darling. I'm here."

She blinked and creased her forehead slightly. "Don't worry about me. You'll take care of us. I know you will." Then, she faded away.

Swoosh, swoosh. The sled runner sliced through the snow, accompanied by the pounding of the dogs' feet, throwing chunks of ice and snow despite the boots they wore.

"Whoa!" Adam called to the team. They stopped and immediately lay down. Adam stepped away from the sled, picking at a blister on his palm from holding onto the sled, despite the thick gloves he wore. He reached his hand into his pocket, pulled out a compass, and flipped it open. The needle swung wildly for a moment, then pointed due north. Adam looked out at the white mantel surrounding him. According to the compass, he was right on course, yet where was the next cabin? They had traveled long enough to reach it. It should be here, near the frozen river they followed. Had he missed some landmark in the snow-storm? Were they hopelessly lost?

Adam snapped the instrument shut and shoved it back into his pocket. No, they weren't lost. Somehow he felt he was right.

"Hup." The dogs stood and looked back at him expectantly. "Ha!" and they were off again. Lauren's head bobbed, and Adam leaned down to look at her face. She had lost consciousness some time ago and before then roused only occasionally to ask for her father or for Adam. Each time, he held her hand and reassured her all would be well.

Fine snow began again, pelting him in the face as he flew along. He looked up at the moon. It's face, bright and shiny minutes before, was now shrouded in thin clouds, thickening fast. "Oh, no," he breathed. "Not now."

As if mocking him, the fall thickened quickly, and darkness closed in; then, finally, a familiar group of rocks appeared. Breathing a sigh of relief, Adam swung with the sled around the bend in the river and saw . . . another scorched cabin.

"Jesus," he whispered to the silent forest, suspicion uncoiling within him. Snow clung to the stark remnants of the house like flesh to a skeleton. The roof was gone, as were two of the sides, leaving the other two to wait for nature to fell them. There was no shelter here. Someone had seen to that.

Adam yanked off his gloves and paced back and forth in the deep snow, his mind whirling. He glanced at Lauren, asleep or unconscious, he couldn't tell which. He had to find shelter or she'd die from exposure if the fever didn't get her first. Then, he remembered the rocks.

Quickly, he moved to the sled and swung the team back the way they'd come. He circled behind the clump of gray rocks and found a small patch of bare ground, a refuge from the swirling snow. Placing a

buffalo robe on the ground, he snugged the battered
fur against the lee side of the rock, then lifted Lauren
into the shelter of the stone. Her head lolled to the
side, and she mumbled. With wind-chapped hands, he
cleared a spot and, kneeling in the snow, nursed a tiny
fire of dry moss he found jammed in a crack. The
flames licked hungrily at the tinder, then slowed their
consumption as he added pieces of wood. Hesitating
at first, the fire caught and blazed small and slow,
casting welcome heat.

He knelt and rubbed her hands and fingers until
she cracked open an eye and blinked. Unsure of what
she saw, Adam soothed her with encouragement.
When she opened her mouth to call his name, he
forced quinine across her lips. Standing over her, staring down at her, he was helpless, powerless to fight
against the thing that controlled her body and mind.
Clenching his fists at his side, he again went over all
the ailments he knew, those he himself had had and
what afflicted other men. None fit the description of
what held Lauren in its grasp. If he could just get her
to the Hudson Bay post, Eric might know what to do.
Maybe he had encountered such a fever before.

The steady breeze and thick snowfall turned into a
wind, then a gale, whipping the snow into a blinding
whirl. Huddled by their sheltered fire, Adam watched
Lauren worsen, her fever rising until she was delirious,
hallucinating and mumbling. He gazed over his head
at a dark sky, lowered by threatening clouds. Again,
he took the compass from his pocket and checked it.
Due north, it registered. Pushing himself to his feet,
he covered Lauren with the last of the three robes,
leaving him with nothing but his scarlet tunic and the
oldest of the robes.

Head down, he set off north, trudging through knee-
deep snow in some places. They were close. He could
feel it. Perhaps the snow had thrown them off a bit,
but they had to be near their destination. In this bliz-

zard, they could be within yards of the post and not see it. He would just walk a short ways. He reached down and scratched his lead dog's ear, commanding them to stay when they rose to their feet with wagging tails.

He didn't know how long he walked. All his concentration was on walking in a straight line, careful not to be thrown off course by fallen trees and rocks. Suddenly, something brushed against him. A wild scream rent the night. Instinctively, he turned and felt something rip into his coat and his back. Throwing an arm across his face, he looked underneath and flailing hooves flashed inches before his face.

Eight

"My God! Inspector!" A thick Swedish accent boomed out of the dark, wet swirl surrounding them.

The big Percheron fidgeted, snorting nervously, nostrils flared in fear. A fur-covered figure slung the lines around the wagon's brake and leaped to the ground. "You are all right?"

Adam's teeth clattered together as the giant in lynx fur grabbed his forearms and shook him. "Eric." Relief made his legs weak, and he sank to his knees in the snow.

Eric caught him by the arm and helped him back to his feet.

"Lauren," Adam managed to say despite the dizziness scrambling his brain.

"Who?" Eric pulled Adam against his ample chest as though he were a small boy.

"Lauren. My wife. She's back there against that pile of rocks."

Eric leapt into the wagon, dragging Adam behind him. "We must hurry."

The horses strained against the wagon tongue and, despite the drifted snow, hauled the wagon forward.

"Here." Adam scrambled off the wagon before it stopped and hurried around the rock. The meager fire still burned, and Lauren lay still, cheeks bright with fever.

Eric knelt. "She is delicate like angel." He placed a hand on her forehead. "Very sick angel." He glanced at Adam.

His head spinning, Adam closed his eyes and hoped the dizziness would disappear.

"You never say you have wife." Eric narrowed his eyes. "How long is she sick?"

"About four days." Adam looked up. "I gave her all the quinine I had, but it's made no difference."

"No." Eric shook his head. "Quinine is no good for this fever." Effortlessly, Eric lifted Lauren and cradled her in his arms.

"You've seen this before?" Adam struggled to follow Eric's long strides.

"Yah. The Chinook bring it." Eric laid Lauren in the back of the wagon. "Many have been sick. Many have died."

The world dropped out from under Adam's feet. "What have you been using to treat it?" Eric was a healer, dispensing medicine to trappers and Cree alike.

Somberly, Eric paused. "There is nothing to give, McPhail. The sick one must fight it off themselves." He smiled and laid a hand on Adam's shoulder. "Come, we are only a short distance from home."

"How did you find us?" Adam shouted over the clatter as the team turned the wagon around. He sat in the back, Lauren's head cradled in his lap, cushioning her from the yaw and pitch of the ride.

"When the Chinook come, I know you would be on foot, so I look." Eric shrugged as if his answer made perfect logic.

"But how did you know where to look?"

Eric grinned and flicked the reins to urge the horses into a faster trot. "McPhail, he always come straight as Cree arrow. Whoosh, across prairie." He split the air in front of his face with the side of his hand.

"Never go around rough country. I come straight, too."

Adam glanced down to where Lauren's head lolled from side to side as the wagon jostled and bumped. They were following no set trail, and the night was dark, starless. Snow fell in sheets before an evil-feeling wind. Adam hunched over Lauren to protect her from the wind despite the buffalo robe Eric had brought.

"See. There is home." Eric pointed through the wall of snow where a faint light beamed out of the darkness.

The dim outline of a roof appeared, a foot of snow softening the usually sharp outlines into a soft hump. One side of the house had straight sides, but the other side seemed to have no specific shape, just lumpy, waving lines tapering into nothing. As they neared, the image did not clear, and not until they pulled to a stop in front of a porch did Adam realize that what he saw were cattle huddled against the south side of the house seeking protection against the wind and snow. Great lumbering beasts with long, sharp horns stared at him from beneath ice-encrusted lashes. Frozen moisture gave them icy whiskers that quivered and grew with each foggy breath.

"Ho!" Eric shouted. The team stopped, and he jumped to the ground.

"Lauren. We're here." Adam touched her shoulder, but her only answer was a muffled moan.

"Here, I will help," Eric offered as Adam scooped her into his arms and staggered to his feet.

"No, I can manage." Adam climbed to the ground and hurried up onto the porch, Lauren cradled against him.

"Open the door, Gretchen," Eric shouted, pounding on the stout barrier before them.

The door opened a crack, and a face poked out, then it swung wide.

"Put her in there." Eric pointed to a room opening off to the right.

Adam noticed little except a welcome rush of heat as he swept inside, past the woman who had opened the door. The dim shadow of a bed sat in the center of the room. Gently, he laid her down, and she settled into the feather tick with a sigh. Adam removed his hat, laid it on the bed, then sat down on the edge. Light slid into the room as someone lit a lamp. He lifted the fur covering her face, and her cheeks glowed in bright red spots against her pale skin.

"Here. Gretchen will see to her." Eric tugged at his arm and set a lamp on a small table by the bed.

"No. I will look after her." Cold water dripped off his hair and ran down his neck. He shivered suddenly, and more droplets fell onto the colorful quilt. He stood, intending to remove the soaked buffalo hide, but he was seized with trembling that threatened to buckle his knees.

A firm grasp clamped onto his upper arm, easing him back down to the bed. "McPhail," a voice admonished in his ear. "You can do her no good if you are sick. Come. Your wife is Gretchen's job; you are mine."

Fuming against his own helplessness, Adam stood and let the big man strip him of the sodden furs. Then, Gretchen Ansgar appeared.

She was facing him, standing between him and Lauren. "You go," she said, a hand on his chest. "I do." Her Swedish accent was so thick, he barely understood the words, but her intent was clear.

Painfully, Adam turned away and followed Eric into the main room, his legs a little stronger. Somewhere in the back of his mind, he recognized the biting scent of cinnamon and fresh bread.

"Winter is not through with us." Eric pulled off his coat of luxurious tawny lynx fur and flung it across a hand-hewn chair. Vigorously, he rubbed his hands together before the fire.

Adam stepped closer, fighting against another wave of shivering that threatened to overcome him. "No, indeed it isn't."

Snapping bright red suspenders against his plaid shirt, Eric turned and studied Adam for a moment, his brows drawn together. Adam sat down in a chair for fear his knees would give way. Water dripped off his thawing mustache and made little circles on his scarlet tunic. He could feel Eric's gaze, knew he had a thousand questions about Lauren. The Ansgars were always gracious hosts whenever his patrols led him this far north, but he had never mentioned Lauren.

"Your trip here was hard?" Eric finally asked.

Adam nodded. "The weather turned sour as soon as we set out." He ran his hand across his forehead and flicked the collected moisture toward the fire.

"Forgive me," Eric boomed. "I talk when you need warming." He strode over to a cabinet, opened a wooden-paneled door, pulled out a bottle, and sloshed some of the contents into a cup. Then he shoved it under Adam's nose.

Home brew. Adam looked up, and Eric grinned. "How is it you say? Do not look at horse's mouth?"

Adam took the cup, winked, and downed the contents. A slow contentment spread throughout his body, and for the first time in days, he was warm.

"Take off your coat." Eric set down his own tin cup with a clank, hauled Adam to his feet, and proceeded to yank off his coat as if he were a boy again. "There. You will be much warmer." Eric ran his hand over the scarlet material and laid it carefully over the back of a chair.

Adam stepped closer to the fire, able now to feel the heat reaching his skin. Gretchen came out of the room, Lauren's clothes clutched to her chest, and closed the door quietly behind her. She moved toward them, head down, then stopped and raised sad eyes. Adam's heart skipped a beat. What had happened?

"She sleep," Gretchen said, then turned and shuffled away.

"I give yarrow tea to your wife. She will sweat; then she will be better."

Adam stared over his head at the plants drying upside down, all shades of gray and green. "I wish I had your confidence in all this."

"God has provided for his children."

Adam glanced at Gretchen rattling pots and pans in the kitchen. "How is Gretchen? Is she better?"

Eric shook his head. "When the little ones died, she rolled up inside. I hoped her heart would heal, but . . ." He shrugged one shoulder.

Fear slithered into Adam's veins, resurrecting demons he thought he had pushed aside. Gretchen and Eric had lost three children. One at birth and two from a fever. He watched Gretchen in the kitchen, stirring and sniffing, drifting alone through her world of grief. Eric watched his wife, a pained expression on his face. Did the same fate await him and Lauren?

"I think I'll check on her." Adam set down his cup and strode to the closed door. Warm firelight spilled onto the polished floor in a wedge as he pushed it open. Snuggled beneath layers of quilts, Lauren slept, golden hair fanned across a pillow edged in bright pink embroidery.

The rope bed frame creaked as he sat down on the edge of the mattress. A single strand of hair fluttered with each of Lauren's breaths. He leaned forward, brushed the hair back, and touched his lips to her cheek. Her fever was higher than before.

"Oh, God," he breathed. Wearily, he slid the suspenders off his shoulders and combed fingers through his hair. Cradling his head in his hands, he stared at the floor, suddenly very tired.

"Surely God will not take a woman so loved."

Adam looked up at Eric's voice and found him silhouetted in the doorway, arms crossed over his massive chest.

"Come." He jerked his head toward the outer room. "Gretchen has coffee and bread. You are hungry?"

Adam shook his head. Then, Eric was beside him, a hand on his shoulder. "You can do nothing here. She needs to sleep."

Adam glanced back at his wife and knew the truth of Eric's words. "Maybe a little. I am awfully tired of pemmican," he said, tugging the quilt higher under Lauren's chin.

"Gretchen will watch her tonight," Eric said as they started for the doorway.

"No." Adam stopped in the center of the floor. "I'll stay with her."

Eric opened his mouth to protest, then closed it and nodded. "You stay."

Slim fingers of dawn light crept in through the paned window and stabbed Adam's eyes. Groaning, he set two of the chair's legs back on the floor and flexed cramped muscles. Sleep faded, and the present intruded. He rose, and padded to the bed in his sock feet, suspenders swinging. Lauren lay on her back, her chest rising and falling in shallow breaths, the only sign she lived. Her skin was pale, almost translucent. Adam ran a hand over a three-day beard and wearily arched his back to relieve an ache. Touching her cheek with the back of his hand, he noted that sponging her skin all night had done little to relieve her fever. Twice he had had to change the bed linens from the perspiration caused by the yarrow tea.

There was a light tap at the door, and it swung open to admit Gretchen, her arms loaded with towels, sheets, and a tray with a bowl. "She is better," she said shortly, dropping her load onto the bed and setting the tray on a small table draped with a lacy cloth. "You go," she demanded, waving him away with her apron.

"Oh. No, I can—"

"Go!" Gretchen placed a hand in the small of his back and propelled him toward the door, then closed it firmly when he was barely outside.

Snagging his shirt off a chair, Adam put it on.

"The fever must run its course." Eric spoke from a large barrel chair in front of the fire. Hunched over, he stared into the flames, rubbing his hands together.

"How long, usually, before the fever breaks?" Adam flopped down in an adjoining chair and inhaled the scent of frying salt pork and baking bread, cinnamon and honey lacing the aromas together.

"I don't know." Eric spread his hands. "A few days with some, hours with others."

"You've seen a lot of this?"

Eric turned to face him. "Much since the thaw. On the reserve, many have died."

Adam walked to the front window. Outside, Onion Lake stretched to the horizon like a crystal sea. "I can't get a surgeon up here until this thaws."

"A surgeon will do no good." Eric shook his head. "By the time he arrives, the fever will have run its course, or . . ."

Adam clenched his fists, hating the helplessness.

"You never say you have wife." Eric's voice lightened as he changed the subject abruptly.

Adam turned from the window. He stared down at his pants and noticed they were streaked with mud and there was a hole in each knee. "No. She'd been waiting for me in Regina for the last two years."

"How long you are married?"

Adam glanced up at Eric. "Three weeks."

Eric drew his lips together. "Ah. She wait long time for you. You have been apart these two years?"

"She stayed behind to nurse her father."

"Ah. Not so sweet a honeymoon." Eric rubbed his hands together and looked into the fire.

The closing of the bedroom door interrupted their thoughts. Gretchen brushed past them, her arms loaded with linens. "It is time to eat," she said, dumping the sheets on the floor in a pile. Without another word, she quickly filled the table with food that seemed to have cooked itself. They ate in silence that hung in the air like a lead weight.

"Thank you, Mrs. Ansgar," Adam said, pushing back his chair. "I think I'll check on my wife."

Adam cracked the door and peeked in. Lauren slept on her side, her face turned away from him. Deciding not to bother her, he started to withdraw his head.

"Daddy?"

Lauren turned over and rolled her head from side to side on the pillow. "Daddy?"

"No, darling. It's me. Adam."

Lauren frowned and cracked open an eye. "Why are you here in my bedroom?"

Adam stepped inside the room and closed the door. "I wanted to see how you felt."

Lauren pursed her lips, frowned, and drew the covers up under her chin. "You're not supposed to be here. You're supposed to be in the Territories."

Adam sat down on the edge of the bed and covered Lauren's hand with his. "I'm right here now. Do you know where you are?"

Her frown deepened. "Of course I do. I'm in bed at home."

A lump swelled Adam's throat as he looked into her bloodshot eyes. "Lauren, you're here with me. In the Territories."

"No," she insisted with a shake of her head. "That can't be true. Edmund's taking me to the theatre tonight."

"Edmund?"

Lauren slumped onto the pillow. "I'm so tired,

Daddy. Just let me sleep a little longer. Edmund will wait. He always does."

"You sleep," Adam said, smoothing away an errant strand of hair. Lauren's eyes closed, and her head sank softly into the pillow. Heaving a sigh, Adam moved to the chair, flopped down, and unbuttoned his tunic. Despite what he told Lauren, the journey had taken its toll on him, too. He closed his eyes and slumped in the chair. As he stretched out his legs, his foot brushed something. Leaning forward, he saw Lauren's reticule on the floor. He picked it up by the ruffled bottom, and the contents scattered across the floor.

"Damn." He picked up items and placed them back into the bag until all that remained was a worn, folded piece of paper. As his fingers brushed it, an odd feeling washed over him, and he hesitated, the letter dangling from his hand. Should he open it? No, a voice said, but another urged him to, offering whispered justifications. Through the smudged paper he could see loops of fancy handwriting. Trembling, he opened the letter one fold at a time. His eyes quickly scanned the script, each word digging deeper than the one before it. When he had finished, he dropped his hands to his lap and stared at Lauren, now deep in sleep. His thoughts immediately flickered back to their wedding night. He closed his eyes, imagining Lauren's face, her hair flung back wildly. Were all her thoughts for him that night? Or did Edmund occupy a tiny corner of her mind? He quickly scanned the note again, looking for something, anything, to ease this tightness in his chest, but the message was clear. Lauren's trip here, her professed commitment to the marriage, her determination to succeed, were all on a trial basis. Carefully, he refolded the letter and slipped it inside her purse. He gazed at her again, so peaceful, so beautiful. When would she give up on him?

* * *

Adam stopped abruptly. Icy pellets pinged annoyingly off the brim of his Stetson. "Is that it?"

"Yah." Eric crossed his arms over his chest. "That is it."

Ahead of them, a small wooden shack sat immersed in a stand of short black spruce. It faced the frozen lake and yawed dangerously to one side. The door hung off leather hinges and grated in the wind with an irritating sound. Half the roof was gone, and the other half was overgrown with now-dead vines.

"It needs a few repairs," Eric offered with a quick glance.

Adam chuckled. "That's putting it mildly. Is this the best the company could do?"

Eric shrugged. "Yes, they say."

"Sorry offering to get a detachment established up here, if you ask me." Adam struck out across the clearing to the little house. Close up, it looked worse. Inside, snow already lay in piles in corners, and in the center was a mound that had fallen through a huge hole in the roof. Mice tracks crisscrossed the floor. Once, beds had lined two of the four walls. Now all that remained were the twisted nails that had once held up the bunks.

Overhead, only the rafters remained of the front half of the house's roof. Farther back, snow filtered in through holes in the shingles of the remaining roof.

"We might as well tear it down and start again."

"There is lumber out back."

Adam walked out the door and around the house, the crunching of his boots echoing against the wall of forest. Stacks of milled boards leaned against the wall. "How did this get here?"

"Two men bring two years ago. They say they build a . . ." He stroked his beard for a moment. "Hunting lodge. That's what they call it."

"Did they never finish it?

"They never come back."

The outside of the building seemed sturdy with two glass-paned windows still intact. The yard led down to the edge of the lake in a gentle slope. Perfect place for a garden, Adam thought. Behind the house, the forest began about twenty yards away. "We could put a few chickens there." He pointed to a cleared area to the left of a vine-choked back wall. "And the corral there. Duncan will be up with the horses in a few weeks, as soon as this thaws." He looked over the structure again. How could he ask Lauren to live here?

After a few more minutes of investigation, they started back around the lake. They walked for a time in silence; then, when they approached the trading post, Eric put a hand on his arm.

"Angus is already here."

Adam stopped at the blunt words. "What? This far north already?"

"I thought you should know." Eric nodded, and little bits of ice fell from his beard.

"Who's he trading with?"

Eric jerked his head toward the west. "Mostly the Cree."

Adam's heart sank. "Has he got a foothold on the reservation?"

Eric nodded.

Adam stared off toward the west, rising anger making his heart thump. Wherever Black Angus went with his rotgut whiskey, pain and suffering followed closely behind. The evil brew he peddled robbed men of their manhood, their minds, their will to live. They became addicted to the contents of the little brown bottles and would sometimes trade their families' last bite of food for another drink.

"I had hoped to get here ahead of him." Adam stared down at his boots. "My job's bigger than I thought."

Eric frowned. "Angus is a dangerous man up here.

He has friends, more than he had in Edmonton. Men from the reserve will protect him."

The shadow of guilt passed over Adam again as he thought of Lauren. "They can't protect him from me."

Lauren opened her eyes to a fairyland. She was in a room flooded with yellow light. Warm, soft quilts covered her, and the delicious smells of home wafted around her. Had she dreamed it all? Was she still in Regina? She tried to raise her head, but pain stabbed her between the eyes.

"Lie still," Adam's voice commanded, then his gentle fingers touched her face.

Painfully, she turned her head. Adam sat in a straight-backed chair at her side, absent of tunic, shirt hanging loose at his waist. Several days' growth of beard shadowed the lean lines of his face. He leaned forward, and a lock of unruly hair fell over his eyes.

"You've been ill," he said with a smile.

"What?" Lauren squinted her eyes against the pain that smashed into the inside of her head as she tried to remember.

His hand covered her forehead and most of her eyes. "Your fever is gone."

She caught his wrist as he pulled away. "How long . . . Oh." Lauren tried to push herself into a sitting position, but as soon as her head left the pillow, the world spun. "How long have I been here?"

"Three days tonight." He rose stiffly, and she noticed the shabbiness of his clothes and the tiredness in his movements. Bits of memory drifted back. Cold. Wind. Darkness. He sat down on the edge of the bed and braced his arms on either side of her, his smile warming the room. "You gave me quite a scare," he rumbled, his breath caressing her face.

"The last thing I remember is being in the sled.

How did we get here?" Her foggy thinking cleared a little, and more memories returned.

"Eric brought us in his wagon."

"He found us? Out there? We must have been closer than you thought."

"We were."

He leaned forward and planted a light kiss on her forehead. "You scared me, you know," he whispered against her skin. Then, he leaned back, and she missed his closeness immediately. She wanted him to scoot under the quilts with her, to feel his arms around her, know he was near.

"Is this our house?" She looked around at the smooth log walls lit by gentle lamplight.

Adam chuckled. "No, I'm afraid not."

"Where are we?"

He smiled, deepening the tiny wrinkles at the corners of his eyes. "We're at Onion Lake, at Eric Ansgar's house. He and his wife run the trading post here."

"What about our house? Where is it? What does it look like?"

Adam shook his head. "Like nothing you've ever seen before."

Lauren frowned, even though the tiny motion made her head throb. "Are you all right? You look so tired." She raised a hand and brushed back his hair, letting her fingers linger on the sensitive part of his ear.

"Yes, I'm fine." Abruptly, he rose and picked up his hat. "The snow's melting. I have to have the corral ready. Duncan will be here in a few weeks with the horses." He stood over her, his fingers worrying the edge of his hat brim. "Gretchen says you might can get up tomorrow if your fever stays down. Then, in a few days, I'll take you over to the house."

As he spoke, he edged toward the door, and she felt the wall go back up. What had happened out there to distance him from her again? "Who's Gretchen?"

"She's Eric's wife. You'll like her," he answered. "I'll be back about midday." He planted the Stetson on his head, tipping it so that his face was hidden. The door opened, and he was gone.

Nine

The sound of the door opening awoke her, and she realized she had slept.

"I am sorry I woke you, Mrs. McPhail," a big man said, one hand on the door latch. "I was afraid the room was getting too cold with the door shut."

"No, I'm fine." She pushed herself up on her elbows, and this time the world stayed righted. "Are you Eric?"

"Yes."

"Adam and I were lucky you found us when you did."

"Yes. The storm was getting worse." His voice went up and down in the melodic Swedish cadence.

"I'm amazed that you even found us as far as you had to search."

Eric laughed, and Lauren frowned at his response. "What's funny?"

"I did not find you. Adam find me. He stumbled out of snowstorm like big bear."

"He was on foot?" Lauren pressed fingers to her temple, trying to remember.

"Yes. He left you in warm nest and come to find me."

Lauren glanced out the window where Adam strode through slushy snow, and even across the distance, she knew his thoughts. She forced herself to look away from the window. "Is he really all right, like he says?"

Eric nodded. "Yes. He was cold and tired, but he is better now. He has spent every night here." He pointed at the simple chair pulled to the bedside. "Your husband is good man."

Quick, hot tears stung her eyes, clouding Eric's form before her.

"You go now," a strange voice commanded, and another bleary form appeared at the foot of the bed.

Lauren blinked and squinted in the direction of the voice. A woman had moved to Eric's side, arms crossed over an ample bosom. She wore a simple blue housedress covered by a muslin apron. Atop her head wound a blond coronet of intricate braids.

"Mrs. McPhail, this is my wife, Gretchen." Eric rested his hands on her shoulders.

Gretchen nodded, leaving Lauren wondering what to say next. "She does not speak the English so good," her husband offered, glancing between the two.

"You go now," Gretchen demanded, giving Eric a shove. Obligingly, he moved away, shutting the door firmly behind him.

Without a word, Gretchen leaned across Lauren, yanked a pillow out of its place, shoved Lauren forward, and planted it firmly behind her shoulders. In addition to being tall and imposing, the woman was also strong, Lauren observed as Gretchen moved her effortlessly. The welcoming scent of chicken soup filled the air. Gretchen spread a cloth over Lauren's chest.

"You eat," she said, sitting down and poking a steaming spoonful at Lauren's mouth. Smooth, warm broth slid down her throat. Another spoonful followed. Obediently, Lauren cooperated while studying the face before her. Gretchen was not a pretty woman. Skin the color of chafed hands covered a broad face. Teeth set determinedly, she drew together thick brows in a frown as she concentrated on each spoonful of broth. Finally, she set the bowl down, wiped Lauren's mouth with a corner of the cloth, and pulled it away.

"Now you sleep." Gretchen rose from the bed, gathered her utensils, and left.

Warmth from the soup spread throughout Lauren, warming and lulling her, but the woman who had fed her haunted her thoughts. Snuggling back under the thick blankets, Lauren turned on her side. What an odd room, she thought, staring up at filmy yellow curtains. Tiny bows of white tied the material into gentle swoops. Near the far wall, a large basket sat on the floor, a matching cover spilling over the edge.

Lauren sat up, steadied herself for a moment, then swung her legs over the edge of the bed. Cold seeped up through the floorboards, chilling the bottoms of her feet as she eased off the bed and padded over to the basket. Inside, a tiny pillow rested near one end, a knitted baby sweater lying across it. "This is a nursery," she said aloud, pivoting to see fluffy cushions in the rocking chair at the bed's side.

She picked up the delicate garment, barely bigger than the palm of her hand, knitted from a soft, fuzzy yarn. Lauren laid the garment to her cheek.

The door scraped open, and Gretchen stood over her.

"I was just . . ." Lauren paused, confused by the expression on Gretchen's face. "I'm sorry. I didn't mean to pry." Was the woman angry? Sad? Lauren couldn't tell, but something in her eyes, something, struck her to her core.

"Mrs. McPhail was only curious, Gretchen." Eric's voice was soothing as he stepped up beside his wife and laid a hand on her shoulder.

Lauren straightened and wobbled for a second before toddling back toward the bed. Why did she feel like a scolded child? Strange sensations flooded over her . . . light-headedness . . . lethargy . . . a feeling of not quite being there. All the while, Gretchen stared.

"I'm sorry," Lauren mumbled, grateful for the pillow that caught her head.

"Lauren?" Adam's voice intruded, bringing the situation back into focus. He had stepped up beside Eric and Gretchen and looked from one to the other. "Is something wrong?"

Eric's fingers gripped Gretchen's shoulder tighter, bunching the blue fabric of her dress. No one spoke. Somebody should explain. "I saw the baby things, and I was admiring them—" she began.

Adam's quick, sharp glance at Eric cut off her words. What was she missing?

"Gretchen, we should leave them alone." Firmly, Eric tugged at Gretchen's arm. With a final sharp look, Gretchen turned and left. Adam stepped in and closed the door.

"What did I do?" Lauren asked, embarrassed to feel tears so near the surface.

He smiled, and icicles on his mustache cracked and fell to the floor. Laying his hat aside, he sat on the bed and loosened his coat. "You couldn't know, but Gretchen has lost three children, the last one a baby." His voice was gentle, caressing, but it didn't lessen the guilt that crashed in on her. "She never changed this room after the last time."

"Oh, dear." Lauren wished she could disappear into the covers.

"She took it hard and has never recovered." Adam pried her fingers away from her face. "It's not your fault, Lauren. You didn't know."

"How awful for her." Lauren glanced over at the basket sitting, waiting for a baby that would never be.

"How are you feeling?" He smiled and brushed her lips with his icy mustache.

"Better. I want to get up. I want to see our house."

Adam frowned, leaned back, and stripped off his coat. "Well, that might take some time."

"What's wrong?"

"There really isn't a house, not a whole house."

"Not a whole house? Adam, what are you talking about?"

He stepped to the window, hands clasped behind his back. The skin over his cheek rippled as he pursed his lips in thought. "Really only half a house; that is, if you don't count the missing roof."

"Adam!"

He turned, boyish chagrin on his face. "It's a shack, a tumble-down shack with no roof and not even four complete walls. We're going to have to build it."

He watched her, expectation filling his face. He was waiting, measuring her reaction to the bad news. "Well, I better get out of this bed soon, hadn't I?" Lauren replied with as level a voice as she could manage. He wasn't going to get a frustrated reaction out of her. No, she'd prove him wrong, prove to him she could do this.

Lauren wiggled her nose and wrinkled up her face. What was that awful odor? She rubbed her nose against the smooth pillowcase, struggling in that space between asleep and awake. There it was again. She brushed her hand over her nose, but the smell persisted. Opening one eye, she gasped and jumped back. Two ragged, dirty men stared down at her, their faces only inches from hers.

"Who are you?" she demanded, clutching the quilt to her chest.

One of the men wore his hair long and loose, black as obsidian, his face pock-marked and scarred from smallpox, she guessed. A dirty length of cloth wound around his head just above his eyebrows.

"You are Mountie's wife?" His voice was velvety and deep and unexpected.

"I am Mrs. Adam McPhail." Lauren cut her glance to the other man, a young form of the first. He, too, wore ragged clothes and a dirty cloth to bind up long, loose hair.

"Humph," the first commented, squinting one eye in concentration. Before she could protest, he yanked aside the quilt, leaving her exposed except for her nightgown.

"I beg your pardon," she said, and pulled the quilt back over her. "What do you want?" Where were Eric and Gretchen? Where was Adam? Lauren looked hopefully at the bedroom door, but no one came to her rescue.

The older man smiled slowly, yellow teeth gleaming, the smile not quite reaching his eyes. "Inspector, he come to my people and bring food, blankets, so I come to bring you this." He whipped one hand out from behind his back, and a dead goose dangled, dripping blood on the quilt.

A scream rose in Lauren's throat, but she swallowed it down and pushed herself higher in the bed, using the time to calm her spinning thoughts. "Thank you very much," she managed to choke out, then reached out her hand and closed her fingers around the goose's limp neck. Whereas before the man's smile had been tentative, now he beamed widely and nodded to his companion. Lauren laid the goose on the foot of the bed, hoping Gretchen wouldn't kill her for the stains. She was, after all, Adam's representative. Hadn't he told her that himself over and over since they'd left Fort Saskatchewan?

"Won't you sit down?" Lauren asked, motioning to the foot of the bed. The men nodded and sat. Now what do I do? Lauren thought. Then she spied a pitcher of water and a glass Gretchen must have brought in while she slept. It seemed polite to offer them something. Was she violating some custom? she wondered. "Would you like some water?" she asked, plunging ahead. "I'm sorry I only have the one glass. You'll have to share."

"Yes," both men answered, exchanging looks again. Lauren leaned over and picked up the clean glass, then poured it full of water. The first man took the glass, drank a small sip, then passed it to his companion, who did the same.

The younger man held it out to Lauren when he finished, expectation in his eyes. Was this the same as passing the peace pipe? She had read incredible stories of the American West about offering a pipe to white men; to refuse was a terrible breach of etiquette. The younger man grunted and poked the cup at her again.

Lauren slid her hand around the tin cup's cool exterior. Her stomach roiled as she brought the cool metal to her lips. Closing her eyes, she took a small sip, begging the water to stay down. She swallowed and opened her eyes. The two men nodded solemnly; then wide smiles split their faces.

"Good wife for McPhail," the elder man said, rising from the bed. He reached into a worn leather pouch at his belt and withdrew a small packet of powder. "You take. Will protect you from fevers. You sick no more." He pressed the pouch into her hand and smiled warmly, his deep brown eyes softening. They left the house as quietly as they'd arrived. Lauren slumped against her pillow and closed her eyes.

"What the hell—"

She jerked awake. Adam stood at the foot of the bed, his hat pushed back off his forehead.

"What the devil is this?" he asked, pointing at the goose, blood soaking into the quilt.

"Oh, no. I forgot." Lauren lifted the fowl and placed it on the floor.

"How did that get here?"

Lauren smiled. "I had visitors."

Adam and Eric exchanged glances. "When?" they asked at once.

"Just a little while ago. I don't know how long I've been asleep."

Adam sat down on the bed, concern crinkling the corners of his eyes. "Are you all right?"

"I'm fine. I just hope I haven't made some breach of behavior."

Adam scratched his head and took off his hat. "You want to start at the beginning?"

Lauren explained about the two men while Adam listened, a small frown playing across his face. Once or twice he glanced at Eric; then, when she was finished, he leaned back and laughed.

"Otter," he said.

"Who?"

"Otter. You've just made a valuable and powerful friend. He's one of the leaders among the Cree."

"Yes. He must have been very curious to come to the house," Eric said.

"Came to look you over," Adam said, "to judge you."

"Oh, and he gave me this." Lauren held out the small package. "He said it would protect me from fever."

Eric took the bundle from her, opened it, and sniffed, then held it out to Adam. "You make good impression, Mrs. McPhail. I cannot find this plant. It is secret among medicine men. It will protect you from sickness in summer, when mosquitoes are bad."

Lauren's heart soared at the admiration in Adam's eyes as he smiled at her. "You handled things well," he said softly. "Just right."

"Do you think Gretchen will be angry about her quilt?" Lauren pointed at the red spot.

"Not if she does not know," Eric said, snatching the quilt off the bed.

* * *

"Adam! Wait!" Lauren hopped on one foot as she slid her legs into the pants and yanked them up to buckle at her waist. Grabbing a coat off the foot of the bed, she charged out of the house and ran to catch up to Adam, now striding along, hands shoved deep into his pockets.

"I thought we talked about this last night," he said as she caught up.

"It's my house, too."

"Yes, but do you want to get sick again?" He stopped, mud sucking around the ankles of his boots.

"I won't get sick. I'm protected. Remember?"

He turned and started off again, head down. "This is hard work, Lauren."

"I've never been afraid of a little hard work." Lauren stumbled over a tuft of grass, caught herself, and hurried along again, matching Adam stride for stride. "Besides, if you let me help, that's two more hands, and we'll finish sooner."

Adam sighed, watching the ground, and Lauren knew she'd won this round.

The shell of a house yawned at them as they approached; at least that's the way Lauren thought of it. There was no front door, and half the roof was still missing, even though Adam and Eric had replaced many of the timbers. Holes dotted the land to the side of the house where Adam was working on a corral. Behind the house, Adam's dogs whined and barked from their enclosure as she approached.

The porch boards screeched as they stepped up on them. "I'm going to put a kitchen in over there." Adam pointed at a bare wall, still bearing holes from the twisted nails he had already yanked out. "I'll order a sink from Edmonton, and we'll go down and get it in early summer along with other supplies we need. The stove will go there and our bedroom over here.

Lauren's cheeks flushed. They'd had no time together since reaching Eric's. Adam worked late and fell into bed when he came home.

His bed.

Not hers.

Using her illness as an excuse, Adam had taken up residence in another of the Ansgars' spare bedrooms. Now that she was better, he'd remained there, using his late hours for his reason. If Eric and Gretchen thought the arrangement odd, they didn't comment.

Lauren sensed a new aloofness in Adam, another barrier to be torn down and conquered. He was attentive and sweet, planting kisses on the top of her head. But something was different. Something had changed. Perhaps it was the scare of her illness. Maybe he'd seen all his fears realized in those few days. Maybe he thought a flesh-and-blood wife too much responsibility for a man married to his job. She touched the slim gold ring on her finger and thought of Eric and Gretchen and the way he looked at her when she didn't know.

"Lauren."

Lauren jerked back to the present, aware that Adam had spoken.

"Where were you?"

"I was thinking about Gretchen."

He caught her hand and pulled her to him. "I'm planning our home and all you can think about is Gretchen?"

Lauren pressed her cheek against him and inhaled the scent now so familiar to her. Maybe she was worrying about nothing. "I'm sorry. Tell me more of your plans."

"I just did. I'd rather hear what you're thinking."

Lauren raised her head and stepped out of his embrace. At the window she rubbed at a sooty spot and looked out at the still-frozen lake. "Something about

Gretchen haunts me. I don't know her that well even though we've been together for more than a week."

Adam joined her at the window. "She's been that way ever since I've known her, but you won't meet a finer person, more kindhearted. I guess she's suffering in silence."

"Being with her and Eric frightens you, doesn't it?" Lauren turned and looked into his face. Surprise flickered in his eyes.

"Not frightens exactly. More like having to look reality in the face every day."

Lauren put a hand on each arm and turned him to face her. "I like looking reality in the face. At least that way we know where we stand."

A sly smile slid across his face as he reached down to kiss her.

"There'll be none of that before house is finished," Eric said, blanking out the light pouring in through the open doorway.

Lauren laughed and ducked as Adam tried to kiss her again.

"Your timing is terrible," Adam protested with feigned gruffness.

"I think my timing was just right. A few minutes later and there'd be no more work today, I'm thinking."

"How can I work with a beautiful distraction like this around?" Adam asked, pulling her close again.

"Go along, Mrs. McPhail, so I can get some good out of him today."

With a final peck on the cheek, Lauren left. They were putting up timbers for roof support today, something she could not help with. Besides, she reasoned, maybe now was a good time to get to know Gretchen better.

Lauren wrapped her coat tightly around herself and stepped inside the low white fence. Three tiny graves, marked with ornately carved wooden crosses, lay in a perfect line. She stopped and stared at Gretchen's broad back as she cleared away a patch of lingering wet snow. Then she righted one of the crosses and brushed the surface of the long-covered ground with her hand. Should she approach? Lauren wondered, crossing her arms against the cold rapidly creeping into her clothes, or would she be intruding? For weeks she'd sidestepped Gretchen's polite gruffness. And yet something drew Lauren to this silent, caring woman, something she couldn't put a name on, yet it existed there between them.

"Excuse me. I . . . uh . . . I saw you here. . . ."

Gretchen's hands stilled. She half turned and stared pointedly at Lauren.

"I'm sorry. I'm intruding. I should go." Lauren turned, her cheeks burning. She should have listened to the small voice that warned her away.

"No. Wait," Gretchen's halting English commanded.

Lauren stopped, her hand on the sagging gate. She heard snow crunch behind her; then the footsteps stopped.

"I am sorry," Gretchen said, her voice low and sorrowful. "Coming here makes me cross."

Lauren pivoted to stare into the ruddy, wind-chafed face. "I shouldn't have stopped. You obviously wanted to be alone."

"No one wants to be alone." Gretchen glanced back over her shoulder at the graves. "I come to remember." She shook her head. "She was little like doll. Tiny hands, like mine but smaller." She held up a rough hand and stared at it, then quickly closed it and smiled. "Sometimes I say too much."

Lauren swallowed back a lump that sprang to her throat. The tragedy was suddenly very real, very vivid, and the emotions Gretchen must have felt washed through Lauren as well. "It must be terrible to lose a child."

"Sometimes I think I lose my mind." Gretchen glanced back at the grave, then took Lauren's arm. "You come." Gretchen pulled her through the gate. "I show you how to make dessert."

Lauren stumbled along behind while Gretchen plowed a path through the snow back to the house, wondering why this sudden change in a woman who had been quiet and sullen ever since they'd met.

The scent of cinnamon poured out as the door swung open. Gretchen took off her coat and hung it on a nail, then stripped Lauren of hers and did the same.

"Secret is yeast," she said, tying on an apron. "It makes the bread sweet, good." She pressed her lips together and closed her eyes.

Before Lauren could comment, Gretchen was off to the pantry; she returned dragging a large sack of flour. Carefully, she ladled out several cups onto a bread-board sitting on the table. She poured a milky mixture into the center of the pile. "Yeast," Gretchen said, then plunged her hands into the mix until white dust floated up around her.

"Turn the bread, like this." She heaved the dough up and flopped it over onto its other side. Lauren watched her, marveling at how different she was from all the other days since they'd arrived. She'd seemed so cold, so distant before, but now she was chattering away as she tortured the heavy dough into a loaf shape.

"You are thinking, why does this woman talk so much?" Gretchen said without raising her eyes from the bread.

"No . . . well, yes, I guess I was."

"I have not been good hostess, and I feel shame."

"That's all right. I guess I wouldn't like it much either if strangers suddenly moved into my house."

Gretchen raised a horrified face. "No." She shook her head vigorously. "No. Everyone is always welcome. Up here in North it must be that way. I am jealous of young bride."

"Jealous? Of me? Whyever on earth?" Lauren stepped back, shocked at the words.

Gretchen turned back to her bread and began to knead it again. "You are like I was many years ago—young, looking forward to future."

"You aren't happy?"

Gretchen's hands slowed, but she kept her eyes lowered. "Life here is hard. People must make happiness, not wait for it to come." Gretchen raised her eyes. "You remember that."

Lauren swallowed down the foreboding that suddenly washed over her. "I never thought about making happiness."

"I make my own sadness. I cannot forgive this north place for taking my babies, and I hate all about it. Sometimes even Eric, because he loves it so."

"So does Adam," Lauren murmured, picking up a piece of loose dough and tossing it onto the table.

"Men, they love excitement, danger." She waved a doughy hand toward the lake. "And women, they love their men."

Lauren snatched back a hand that reached out to grip Gretchen's arm.

Gretchen saw the movement, stopped, and looked up. A slow smile crinkled the corners of her eyes. "It will be nice to have another woman around," she said softly. Then she began to clean the dough from her hands. "Come with me." She dusted her hands with flour and rolled the dough off in little pellets.

Wiping her hands on a towel, she led Lauren to her room and opened the doors to an armoire that sat in the corner. Tiny drawers sat one on top of another. Infant garments, knitted of fuzzy yarn, hung from wooden pegs in the doors.

"No one sees this but me before," she said, tears starting in the corners of her eyes as she fingered the small clothes. "My precious babies."

A sob caught in Lauren's throat. So much time had gone into the tiny clothes, so much love. And now they hung, waiting. Eternally waiting for babies that would never wear them.

"I will have no more babies," she said without looking up. "I have told Eric that I cannot stand pain of losing another." She raised sad eyes to Lauren's face. "And now I miss my husband."

Ten

"Ohhhh." Thick mud swallowed Lauren's boots, and she pitched forward, planting both hands up to her wrists in the goo at her feet.

"I've got you." Adam's hands caught her under her arms and hauled her against him.

Lauren laughed into the wool of his scarlet coat and felt his answering chuckle. "It's muddier than I thought it would be."

He stood her up straight, reached down and pulled her boots free, then placed her feet on a solid tuft of grass. Breathless, Lauren shaded her eyes against the sun's glare and looked out over the frozen surface of Onion Lake. Spring had not yet arrived. Swollen buds were still covered with snow, and the lake lay silent, waiting for the thaw to set it free.

"Oh, Adam. It's so beautiful." His arm slid around her waist and pulled her against his hip.

"Yes, it is, isn't it? Look there." He pointed to a hawk gliding effortlessly in the sky.

Lauren turned her eyes from the bird to her husband's face. Outdoors, he was a different person, a part of the wilderness that surrounded them. Every whiff of wind caught his notice, every creature his attention.

"Come on. Step where I do." He grabbed her hand

and pulled her along behind him. Picking her way, Lauren teetered on the scarce solid ground, the old, ragged buffalo coat dragging in the mud around her feet. They had almost finished the house, but Adam had forbidden her from seeing it for the last week, saying he had a surprise. Immersed in her thoughts, she plowed right into Adam's back.

"Don't look." He covered her eyes with his hand.

"I won't. What are you doing?"

"Blindfolding you."

A piece of cloth went around her head and tied behind her. Adam swept her up into his arms and started forward, his steps uncertain in the deep mud.

"You're going to spill us both!" Lauren shrieked as he lost his footing and stumbled. By the time she heard his boots step up on wooden boards, they were both breathless with laughter. He set her down and moved behind her.

"Now keep your eyes closed until I tell you to look." The blindfold fell away. "Now look."

Bare plank walls were only inches from her nose. She stood on a small porch, staring at a door. The outside wall was a patchwork of new and old lumber. The house was incredibly small.

"Look inside."

The door swung open, and she stepped into a room. In one corner stood an old stove, the door hanging loose, a stovepipe poking out the top and through a small hole in the outside wall.

"Oh, Adam. It's lovely." She hoped her voice sounded as excited as she tried to make it.

"Here's our room." He pushed aside a colorful quilt in another corner to reveal a bed frame laced with rope. "You'll have to cook on the stove for a while. Maybe this summer we can add a kitchen."

"What's that?" In the far corner was a cage structure of metal bars. A door and lock faced the barrel stove.

"That's the jail."

"Here? In our home?" Lauren dropped all pretense of delight and swung toward Adam in amazement.

His face fell, and she felt a twinge of guilt.

"This is my office as well as our home, Lauren. I have to keep prisoners here so we can watch and feed them."

"But, I didn't think they'd be in the house with us." Dismay deepened, and all thoughts of privacy and home comforts melted like last week's snow.

"I don't have a choice. This is my job."

Lauren felt a surge of compassion at Adam's crestfallen expression and mustered a smile. He had spent long hours on the house and was obviously proud of the job he'd done. "I know; I was just a little surprised, that's all. We can put a bench here, and I can make a quilt for the bed."

A flutter of desire fanned heat into her cheeks. Soon, they would be alone, together, in their own home. Then, when she had him all to herself, she'd start chipping away at that wall between them. She glanced at the bare bed frame. And she'd seduce him if she had to. Somehow they were going to consummate this marriage.

"When can we move in?" she asked.

Adam grinned. "How about today?"

"What will we do for furniture?" She glanced around at the empty, echoing room. They had no belongings, save the clothes they wore.

"Eric is holding some things for us from the post. I can make most of the furniture." He stepped forward and enveloped her in his arms, his chin coming down on top of her head. "We'll be happy here, Lauren. I promise," he whispered, and she wondered if his words were a statement or a question.

"We'll make our own happiness," she whispered.

* * *

Crack! Pop! The potbellied monster in the corner groaned. Lauren glanced nervously at the stove from her seat on a wobbly wooden stool. Orange flames licked out from around the edges of the stove door, and she wondered when she had given the contraption a personality. "Adam, are you sure this thing is safe?"

"Sure," he answered from the porch between scrapes and thumps. The door flung open with a bang, and he entered, arms loaded with blankets and pots. "Gretchen sent these." He dropped the load with a clatter. Sweat dotted his forehead, and he loosened the buttons on his coat. "Have you put too much wood in there?"

Lauren glanced back at the stove, now grinning cherry red at her. "I don't know. I've never used one of these before."

Adam stepped forward and was pushed back by a wave of heat. "I think it's too hot." He took the poker and yanked open the door. Flames shot out, and he jumped back in a wave of smoke.

"Be careful." Lauren shielded her face against the accompanying heat. "Maybe if we took some wood out?"

"No, I'll just stir it up some." Clanking against the sides of the stove, he shifted pieces of wood until the stove settled down to a steady blaze.

"Don't put more than two pieces in there from now on." His face was beet red as he turned to set the poker at her side. "Do you think you and it"—he motioned at the stove—"can come to some agreement?"

Lauren peeped around him and swore the stove smiled smugly at her with its warped door. "I guess if I just don't feed it so much."

Adam laughed against her skin as he kissed her cheek. "There's more things on the porch to come in."

"Wait." She caught his arm. "If you go outside damp like you are, you'll catch your death of cold. Here, stay and I'll fix you a cup of water."

Their eyes met. His expression sobered, and slowly he lowered his lips to hers. The kiss was gentle and undemanding. One hand caught the back of her head and pulled her forward, affording their lips more contact. "I'd rather have this than all the water in Canada," he whispered, then straightened and arched his back. "I didn't know two people who have nothing could have so much to move."

Eric and Gretchen had been generous, and Adam had made most of their furniture in a few days. Rough and sometimes uneven, still it was the most beautiful furniture Lauren had ever seen.

"I'm going hunting after I finish bringing in this last load. How about rabbit for supper?" Adam set a pine chest down in their bedroom.

Lauren smiled, her back to him. Rabbit for supper had become a standing joke between them. For weeks they had eaten rabbit in some form twice a day. There just hadn't been time for hunting other game. "Rabbit is fine," was the obligatory answer she gave.

The door closed with a slam. Lauren stepped to the window, a quilt draped across her arm. Outside, signs of spring were increasing. Yesterday she had found a spring beauty in bloom at the edge of the forest, just unfurling its pink flower heads.

Adam kicked open the door and set down another wooden crate. "That's the last of it for a while. The rest is up at Eric's. I'm going hunting," he said. Casting a dubious eye at the stove, he lifted his rifle off the hook over the door and went back outside. Lauren watched him swing off toward the woods, walking with the gentle lope she had come to listen for and love.

Fluffing out the quilt in her arms, she pressed the fabric to her nose and inhaled, reveling in the smell of newness. She flipped it out, and it floated down to settle on the mattress stuffed with dried hay and grass.

She tested the bed with her palm. The ticking crackled enticingly, and she smiled, anticipating tonight.

Lauren moved to the other boxes, pausing before the jail yawning in their living room. Inside, Adam had built a wooden bunk. Over his objections, she had stuffed a mattress for that bed, too. Prisoners or not, they were guests in her house, she had argued, and therefore entitled to at least one comfortable night's sleep.

By the time twilight painted the sky, Lauren had put away all their things and had again tackled the stove. Given to burning either too hot or too cold, it refused to cooperate. Piling on another three pieces of wood, Lauren coaxed orange coals to light the dried grass. The tiny flames paused for a moment, then blazed to life. Smoke rose and disappeared into the pipe at the top. Then, the thing belched a cloud of smoke in her face. She slammed the door and waited for the cracking and straining that always preceded an overabundance of heat.

At first, she thought the faint knock at the door was the stove whining and complaining. Then it came again. Lauren glanced out the window. The last of the sunset was fading from the sky, and night was fast approaching. The knock came again, this time more impatiently. What if it was Eric standing out there? Surely, he would call out. Lauren chewed a finger and wavered as to what to do. Again, knocking on the door. *When Adam's away, I'm in charge,* she told herself, forcing her feet to cross the floor.

She opened the door a crack. "Who is it?"

"Why, itsh me, ma'am," slurred a voice from the dark.

"Who are you?"

"Crazy Wolf."

Lauren slammed the door and leaned against it. Should she let in a man named Crazy Wolf? Maybe he needed help. Already, several people had been by

Eric's. Word had traveled quickly that the Inspector was now the law.

"What do you want?" she shouted through the thick door.

"Well, I want to come in."

"You can't just come in. You must want something." As she spoke, Lauren reached out and grasped a stout piece of firewood.

"No, mum. I jus' wants to come in and lay down. Please, messus." His voice sounded as if his lips were squeezed in the door crack. She listened and heard his breathing against the wood.

"You can lay down out there on the porch."

"But the jail's in there."

"You want to lie down in the jail?"

"Please. I'm tired."

What should she do with him? Let him in? She could just hear Adam railing against her foolishness. But what if the man had something to do with the whiskey trade? He might get away.

"All right. You can come in, but you have to go right into the jail."

"Dat's fine wiz me." His voice was more slurred, slower.

"Do you promise?"

"I swear."

Carefully, Lauren eased the door open, her chunk of firewood held high. "I'm armed," she warned as the ragged man shuffled inside.

He glanced neither at her nor the house. Instead, he moved toward the jail door with staggered, yet determined steps, went inside and shut the door, then flopped down on the mattress. Almost immediately he began to snore. Lauren went over and shook the door to the cell and found it locked.

The door burst open, admitting a blast of cold air. Adam, coat streaked with mud, strode in, a pair of rabbits dangling from his hand.

"Here's supper," he announced, dropping the rabbits to the floor. Then he saw the form asleep in the jail. "Who's our guest?" He frowned and glanced quickly at Lauren.

"He said his name was Crazy Wolf." Lauren let her hand slide off the cold bars.

"And you let him in?" His voice rose.

"He said he wanted to go to the jail."

Adam opened his mouth, anger bringing to mind words he knew better than to say. He clamped his teeth together. "Never, never open that door to anyone unless I'm here."

"I knew you'd be mad." Her face fell, and she replaced the stick of wood. "I didn't know what to do. I thought if I let him go, you might lose some of the information you're looking for."

"Lucky for you it was Crazy Wolf. He drinks like this every week. Eric's been locking him in the root cellar for months when he gets drunk. He's harmless."

Lauren considered his words for a moment, and he waited for her reaction. After a moment, she smiled weakly and bent to retrieve the rabbits. "Why don't you get washed up while I clean these." With that comment, she walked to the door and out onto the porch.

Adam watched her step off the porch and go around to the back of the house. He let out the breath he'd held and shed the heavy, wet wool coat. Lauren had been lucky on this occasion, but what about the next time a stranger dropped by? Next time would it be Black Angus?

He stepped into the still, cold night air and draped the wet coat over the porch railing to keep mud off Lauren's clean floor. The evening chill crept through the fabric of his shirt as he drew a deep, cleansing breath and looked around for Lauren, but she was nowhere to be seen. The moon had risen, casting a silvery glow over the still lake and yard. Adam stopped and listened, then followed a muted sound around the side of the house.

There, by the woodpile, Lauren leaned against the side of the house, her back to the rough boards. Sobs racked her body, her chest heaving. Two headless rabbits lay at her feet. Instinct urged Adam to go to her, envelop her in his arms, and reassure her, but he stopped short of revealing his presence. She had made a brave display inside for his benefit and had hidden to cry out her fears. He propped his elbows on the porch railing and studied the silvery wet ground below. This was something she had to learn to face on her own. His comforting would only delay the lessons she had to learn to live here with him. Chest tight, Adam hung his muddy coat on a nail and went back inside.

He had just finished repairing the fire when the door opened and Lauren entered. She avoided his eyes, although he could see she had been crying. Both rabbits were neatly skinned and dressed.

"I knew you were tired," she offered, laying them on the table under the window. "How about baked this time?"

Love so intense it sent a shiver over him filled Adam as he watched her rinse the meat in a bucket of water and lay each in a pan. She sprinkled precious salt over them, as well as dried herbs. Then, she nestled dried apples and beans in the same pan and covered it with a lid.

"Do you think this will serve our guest, too?" she asked as she brushed by him and sat the heavy iron oven on the stove.

"I don't think he's interested in eating." Adam nodded to where Crazy Wolf snorted on the bunk, arms and legs flung in all directions.

"Well, then, there's more for us." She plopped into his lap and wrapped her arms around his neck.

"How long will it take that to cook?" he asked,

pushing a strand of hair off her cheek. She was so beautiful, and he wanted her so badly. She looked up then, not a trace of deceit on her face. And for a moment he could believe that she loved him and only him.

"About an hour, I think."

"Just enough time for me to clean my gun." He set her on her feet and stood. She glanced back over her shoulder, then walked away from him with a sassy gait. She was well, and they were alone in their own house. Well, almost alone, he corrected with a glance at Crazy Wolf. Tonight they'd share a bed for the first time. He had no more excuses not to sleep with her. Could he resist her? Should he?

He laid his rifle on the table and began the meticulous task of taking it apart. All the while, Lauren hovered nearby, finishing the details of their supper. Time and again, he had to draw his attention back to his weapon and away from the sway of her hips and the way her hair caressed her cheek. The aroma of roasting rabbit filled the room when Lauren lifted the lid of the pan and declared supper ready.

He quickly finished cleaning the gun and put it back on its hooks over the door. Lauren dished out three plates of food. She put two on the table and took the third over to the jail

"Crazy Wolf. Your supper is ready." Amazingly, the man stirred, sat up, and stared at her with bleary eyes.

Lauren unlocked the door and handed him the plate, then returned to her place at the table. Adam stared at her across the steaming food, his appetite for her growing dangerously.

When the meal was finished, she took the plates to a bucket and poured steaming water over them. Then, she walked to the jail and opened the door.

"You're free to go, Crazy Wolf." She held out her hand for his plate.

The man wiped his mouth on his filthy sleeve and looked up at her. "Huh?"

"I said you're free to go." She took the empty plate out of his hands.

Crazy Wolf glanced over at Adam, who shrugged and watched, amused. "But it ain't morning. And you ain't the constable."

"I put you in here, didn't I?"

Confused, he glanced at Adam again. "Yeah, but—"

"Then I'm turning you loose." She shoved a bag of cold biscuits at him. "You won't be sleeping off any more drunks in Eric Ansgar's root cellar. My husband is the law here now, and this is the jail. Since it's in my living room, I figure I make the rules for overnight stays."

Crazy Wolf frowned but didn't speak.

"I won't provide a warm, comfortable place for you to spend the night when you're drunk on illegal whiskey. As far as I'm concerned, you can spend the night out in the cold. Maybe it will teach you a lesson."

Apparently stunned into speechlessness, Crazy Wolf staggered to his feet, clutching the bag of biscuits. He wobbled to the door that Lauren held open for him, pausing in the doorway to throw her another confused glance. Then he disappeared into the night. Lauren closed the door behind him and pulled in the latch string.

"And as for you"—she turned from the door and started across the floor, unbuttoning her shirt—"I want a baby." She dropped the shirt to the floor at his side and unfastened her trousers. "We've been married a month, and you've nursed your doubts long enough." The trousers slid to the floor, and she deftly kicked them to one side. "You're neglecting your husbandly duty, Inspector McPhail."

So stunned was he by Lauren's sudden shift in personality, Adam could only stare at her when she sat on his lap and looped her arms around his neck. "Make love to me, Adam."

Only the thin cotton of her chemise lay between the wonderful softness of her bare skin and his hand. He touched her ribs, a thumb grazing the soft swell of her breast. "I want to."

She stood and slid the straps of her chemise over her shoulders and wriggled the garment to the floor. Firelight brushed her skin with a feathering of gold. "Then come to bed." She held out a hand, reminiscent of some ancient, powerful goddess.

For all the doubts that had once circled his brain, at this moment he couldn't think of a single reason he shouldn't give Lauren what she wanted. What he wanted. Adam stood and shed his belt and lanyard, followed by his tunic and pants. His hands trembled as he worked loose the tiny white buttons on his winter underwear. Lauren had already crawled into the bed, the tick groaning softly, seductively beneath her weight. When he had shed the last of his clothes and stood before her naked and aching, he turned to reach for the shields. Her hand clamped around his wrist. He turned to face her.

"No," she said with a shake of her head. "Not tonight." She rose to her knees and cupped his face in her palms. "I want a child, Adam, your baby. Someone to keep me company when you're gone on patrol. I'm neither foolish nor stupid. I know the risks and the dangers. I've waited two years to love you, two years to begin a family. I don't want to wait any longer."

He sucked in his breath when she touched him.

Boldly. And without mercy.

He eased her backward onto the bed, and she smiled up at him like a lazy cat, her hair splayed out around her head like a soft halo. She deserved more than he was certain he was capable of tonight—to be loved slowly and thoroughly by a man experienced in the ways of love. Which he was not.

They'd never talked of experience or the lack of it. She'd been a virgin until their ill-fated wedding night. She hadn't asked and he'd never revealed that he was as innocent as she. What little he knew, he'd gleaned from conversations with other men. Overheard remarks. And his own imaginings. And now he stood gazing down at the object of those imaginings, the only woman he'd ever love. And she was waiting for him, begging him to love her, to plant his seed deep within her and assure his immortality. Were mortal men meant to be so blessed?

He put one knee on the bed, and she pulled him into her arms. Without the barrier between them, the sensation of her softness closing around him was intimate and shatteringly personal. A sense of belonging washed over him, bringing tears to his eyes even as his traitorous body stopped listening to his mind and sought its pleasure within his wife. He plunged over the brink of desire and knew by her soft moans that she followed closely behind him.

Adam rolled to his side and pulled her into his embrace, their bodies still joined. Basking there in the afterglow, he wondered how he'd survived two years without her at his side and in his bed.

Eleven

The *scruff, scruff* of a brush awoke Lauren. She turned over and pulled the smooth quilt up over her naked skin. On the other side of the hanging quilt, Adam whistled softly under his breath while he brushed his serge coat. Lauren smiled and snuggled down beneath the covers. The same hands that now worked mud and dirt out of fabric only hours before had worked magic on her body. She stretched, feeling sinful and sensuous. They had slept, entwined in each other's arms, then made love again.

His soft melody fell into cadence with the brush strokes. Pleasant childhood memories drifted back, memories of hearing her father brush his uniform every Sunday night. She couldn't lie here all day, she told herself. She had a husband to feed. Reluctantly, she swung her legs over the side of the bed and hastily pulled on her clothes, now strewn on the floor beside the bed.

"Good morning." Adam stepped through the quilt wall, his jacket dangling from one finger. "Did you sleep well?"

Lauren felt heat rush to her cheeks as he blatantly scanned the half-dressed length of her body. "Yes, but I had a little trouble getting to sleep."

Adam stepped into her arms and pulled them

around his waist. "So did I." He grinned, then moved away. Lauren watched him lean over and pick up his cross belt, marveling at how wonderful he could look in clothes that were patched and mended and dirty.

"I did the best I could with this." He slung the splotched jacket around his shoulders. "It'll have to do until Duncan comes."

"When do you expect him?" Although she'd welcome the supplies Duncan was bringing, she wanted to savor their time alone for a bit longer.

"Should be any day now. He left Fort Saskatchewan soon after we did." He did up the buttons and smoothed down the jacket, then picked up his revolver and settled the gun belt on his hips. Lauren's eyes followed his slender hands. He slung the belt across his shoulder and buckled it tight. "Come fasten these, will you?" He tightened his lanyard knot across his shoulder and struggled with the buttons that held his epaulets fastened.

"You'll be careful today, won't you?" she asked, trailing the backs of her fingers along his neck.

He grabbed her fingers and kissed them. "Would you like to come with me?"

"Where are you going?"

"Out to the Cree reserve. Whiskey's running like water there, and they have to be getting it from somewhere." He dropped her hand and picked up his hat. "I need to ask some questions."

"How are you going to get there?" As she spoke, Lauren rustled through her trunk of clothes for something warm.

"We'll walk. It's not far."

Lauren swung a wool short coat around her shoulders and grabbed the buffalo robe from the foot of the bed. "I'm ready."

The air was brisk and cold as Adam led her into the forest behind their cabin. He held aside branches for her to pass, and she ducked underneath the dark spruce and sparse hardwoods. Worn paths crossed the forest floor the deeper into the woods they traveled. Suddenly, they reached a clearing speckled with tumbledown shacks, half-torn tents, and an assortment of other dwellings.

Round-eyed children stared at them from yawing doorways. Skinny dogs wandered between the shacks and tents. Desperation was the word that came to Lauren's mind as she scanned the pitiful collection around her. Wisps of wood smoke rose from small fires outside of plank dwellings, mainly a collection of boards leaned together without benefit of nails to hold them in place. The ground beneath their feet was bare and dusty, littered with a collection of animal refuse.

Adam stopped in front of a house surprisingly well built, when compared to its neighbors, and rapped on the door.

For several moments, no one answered; then the door slowly swung open. A dark and buxom woman stood in the doorway, solemnly assessing Adam.

"Is George here?" Adam asked, removing his Stetson.

"No," she answered, pushing back a strand of black hair, loose from its rawhide strap at the nape of her neck.

"Do you know where he is?"

"No." She stared at him a few more seconds before starting to close the door.

"If you would be so kind." Adam stopped the door with one foot. "Would you tell him Inspector McPhail wishes to see him? It's important."

"I tell 'im."

Adam withdrew his foot, and the door slammed closed. He remained staring at the rough boards, a peculiar expression on his face. Then, he turned, staring downward, and drew on his gloves. "A bloody shame," he muttered between gritted teeth.

"The house?" Lauren asked.

"That and these conditions." He nodded at the rest of the wretched camp. "No one should have to live like this."

"Why do they stay?"

Adam moved around the house, staring at the ground beneath his feet. "Because this is home. Has been for years." He stopped, studying the ground beneath hide-covered openings where windows would be.

"What are you looking for?" Lauren squatted down beside him, feeling eyes on her back.

Adam held a finger to his lips. He traced a faint outline in the dirt at his feet, then rose and dusted off his dark blue pants.

"What did you see?" Lauren asked as he grabbed her elbow and walked away.

"George was here and recently, too," he whispered, guiding her deeper into the village.

"Who is he?"

"He's a trapper. He mingles off the reserve a lot, mixes with traders and the like. Eric thinks if anyone would know where this whiskey is coming from, George would. If he'll tell."

Lauren struck her toe against a bottle and stumbled. On the ground around the houses, bottles were broken and jagged, lying in piles. Then, a house at the very edge of the village caught her attention. Rusted cans and broken bottles rimmed the dwelling, each containing dead plants, almost as if someone had grown them there. They neared, and Lauren saw bunches of dried herbs hanging upside down in the windows.

The house was of the same weathered boards as the rest of the village, but each one was carefully fitted and nailed together, straighter than the others. As they approached, a young woman came to stand in the doorway. At least she appeared young—until Lauren drew closer. Her face was slim and tanned, although furrowed above her forehead and cheeks. A strip of cloth wound around her head and tied in a knot at the back. A colorful striped blanket covered her shoulders and dangled to her feet. With light eyes, she solemnly watched them pass, as silent as the deep forest that snuggled up to the back of her cabin.

A chill ran up Lauren's spine when Adam touched the brim of his hat and the woman responded with a slow nod of her head. Lauren turned to look over her shoulder, but the woman was gone and the door closed.

"Who was that?" she asked, directing her eyes back to the trail they followed out of the village.

"Fox. She's a healer." He chuckled and put an arm around her shoulder. "She calls herself a medicine man. The Cree don't like that much. That's why she's out here, away from the rest of the village."

Lauren glanced over her shoulder at the silent house receding behind branches and trees and knew instinctively someday there'd be a connection between the two of them.

Adam led them home a different way than they had come. The weather was mild, and the sun had warmed the chill morning air. They walked for a time along the northern edge of the lake, but the water and the woods were silent, expectantly so, waiting for the return of spring and of song to the barren branches.

When they reached the cabin, Crazy Wolf waited for them on the porch, straddling a wooden crate, his heels propped up on the railing.

"Crazy Wolf," Adam said with a nod. "Can I help you?"

Crazy Wolf wasted only a second assessing Adam's face, then shifted his gaze to Lauren.

"You a good cook?"

Taken aback by the question, Lauren glanced at Adam and was confused by the smile playing across his lips. "Yes. I think so."

Crazy Wolf regarded her solemnly for another minute and shuffled past them and toward the lake.

"Well, we'll be seeing a lot more of him." Adam opened the door.

"Why? Because he drinks often?"

"No." The keys jangled loudly as Adam hung them up. "Because now he knows you can cook."

Cold seeped in under the door and around the windows. The wind picked up outside and scraped itself against the corners of the house. Lauren hugged a quilt to her and slid the rocker a little closer to the stove. Darkness had closed in hours ago.

Supper warmed on top of the stove, but Adam wasn't home yet. He'd been called back to the reserve by a messenger about midday. Lauren wished she had a watch so she could check the time, but some inner timing told her it was late. She had scrubbed the floor and every stick of furniture, then aired all the bedding. As she began to nod, thoughts of her encounter with the mysterious woman returned to haunt her.

The door blew open with a slam, and cold air whisked in. Lauren jolted awake.

"Did I scare you?" Adam shut the door. Snowflakes dotted his hat and buffalo robe.

Her heart pounding, Lauren took a deep breath. "No. I was waiting for you."

"Another storm's coming in." He slapped his hat against his leg and hung it up by the door. "What's for supper?"

"It's on the stove." She pulled the robe off his shoulders and threw it over a chair to dry.

He lifted the pot's lid and sniffed. "Smells good. I haven't eaten all day."

Lauren filled his plate, then huddled next to the stove and watched him consume his food. He ate as though he were half starved, and she regretted not sending food with him when he left.

"What was the business on the reserve?"

Adam chewed slowly, gazing absently at the plate in his hand. "A murder."

Lauren caught her breath and drew the robe closer around her. "Oh, no. Who? Why?"

Adam swallowed, then took a drink from his tin cup. "A Cree named Asini. He was drinking with some men that had come to the village. They argued. One thing led to another, and Asini was knifed."

Adam glanced up, and Lauren saw concern and weariness in his eyes. She rose from the chair and knelt in front of him, resting her elbows on his knees. "This murder is different, isn't it?"

A smile crinkled his eyes, and he smoothed her hair with his hand. "You read me well, woman." Then, he leaned back in the chair and sighed. "I hadn't expected the whiskey problem to be this bad this quickly. I haven't been up here in more than a year, and from the patrol reports I received, the whiskey trade was just getting into this area. That's not true. It's been here for some time, long enough to ruin the peoples' lives."

By the light of the fire, his face looked gray, old. Lauren blinked, wishing away the trick the light played. He ran his fingers through his hair, and she realized for the first time how very much he cared for these souls in his charge. She thought back to the tattered village and wondered how they had lived before. She had heard stories of great tribes of people living nomadic lives, wandering where they pleased, obeying no man's will. Adam leaned forward and rested his head against hers. A sigh made his shoulders rise and fall. A small streak of blood clashed with the scarlet of his jacket sleeve.

"Take that off and I'll clean it." She tugged the tunic off him and rose, but he caught her arm.

"You take good care of me, you know."

Lauren touched his cheek. "I enjoy taking care of you."

"But can you take care of yourself?"

Lauren frowned down at him. "What an odd thing to say. Whatever do you mean?"

He ran a palm across his eyes and stood. "I don't know; I'm just tired. I'm going on to bed."

"I'll be along shortly," she answered, sprinkling water from her bucket on the sleeve and rubbing it.

When she had finished, she hung the coat carefully across a chair to dry and blew out the lantern. Only the light from the stove lit the room. Once inside their bedroom, she could barely make out Adam's form beneath the quilt. She slipped in quietly beside him. He turned in his sleep and enfolded her in his arms.

She awoke with a start. Something crashed against the wall, then thudded to the floor. Dazed by sleep, Lauren fumbled her way out of the bed, clutching the quilt to her chest. She parted the quilt and peered into the dark outer room. She could hear grunts and thumps near the front door but couldn't make out what was happening.

"Adam?"

Her eyes adjusted a little, and she could see two distinct forms struggling in the center of the floor. The scent of soot and scorching wood was strong. "Adam."

"Stay back," he ordered, his last word cut short with a grunt.

Lauren crept closer. Adam and another man struggled on the floor amid scattered table and chairs and glowing coals from the stove. Adam wore only his suit of underwear, but the other man was dressed for the outdoors and more than outweighed Adam. A pair of handcuffs clinked and tinkled as Adam fought to get them on the man's wrists and was clearly losing the fight.

Lauren bit her fingers, trying to think of what to do.

"Get back in there," Adam growled at her. The big man locked his arms around Adam and rolled him over.

She had to do something. Lauren dropped the quilt, skirted the scuffle, and slid along the wall of the house. She picked up the coal shovel and stood over the thrashing men trying to take aim in the dim light. They tussled and rolled back and forth. Lauren watched, then saw her chance. She whacked at the man's head, but he rolled out of the way.

"Ouch!"

Lauren felt the metal connect, then saw she had hit Adam. Stunned, he allowed the man to roll on top of him again.

"If you want to help, cuff him," Adam slid the jangling set of handcuffs across the floor toward her.

Lauren watched the flailing arms, trying to discern who was who. Then Adam braced his feet against the man coming at him from above and shoved him over his head. He landed with a loud *oof,* and Lauren saw her chance. The cuffs clicked around one wrist. Adam flipped over and quickly pinned the other arm with his knees and snapped the other cuff shut. The fight went out of him, and the big man lay on the floor, gasping for breath.

Adam staggered to his feet, his underwear hanging torn and sooty. His chest heaved, and he held the top of his head.

"Are you all right?" she asked.

"Fine. How about you?"

"I'm not hurt." Quickly, Lauren lit the lamp from the bedroom. Her house was in shambles. Broken furniture lay in pieces everywhere. Coals from the stove were now burning holes in the floor. Her few dishes were scattered and broken.

Adam caught the man by the cuffs and hauled him

to his feet. "Into the jail with you, Rogét." He gave the man a shove that sent him stumbling forward, then clanked the barred door closed. Rogét threw himself at the bars, and the whole assembly trembled.

As the rush of fear passed, tears took its place. Lauren touched the lump on Adam's head, and he winced. "Oh, Adam. I'm so sorry. I couldn't see."

Adam drew her close. "It's all right," he said breathlessly. "I think I'd have lost the fight if not for your help."

"Look at this mess." She lifted the lamp, and the damage appeared worse.

"We have to get these coals up." Adam grabbed a metal shovel and scooped up the coals from the little black hollows they had made in the new floor. He righted the stove and reattached the pipe, then threw the coals inside, along with some wood.

"Let's go back to bed. We'll clean up in the morning." He dropped the shovel by the stove and took a cloth off the sink. "I'm going outside for some snow for this lump."

Lauren swung her gaze toward the prisoner leering at her from between the bars and was suddenly aware she wore nothing but her nightgown. He barely looked human, so covered was he in fur and leathers. A long, dark beard hung down to his chest, the ends twisted into grotesque spirals.

"I have not had a woman for many months," he drawled with a strong French accent, then smiled.

Lauren hurried into the bedroom and sat down on the bed. She buried her face in her hands, willing herself not to cry in front of Adam.

"Behave yourself, Rogét," she heard Adam say as he slammed the front door.

She waited, and he came though the curtain and sat down beside her, holding a cloth filled with snow to his head.

"Where did he come from?" Lauren whispered, taking the cloth from him and pressing it to the lump.

"I don't know. I woke up and heard something in the other room. When I went in, there he was, standing in the kitchen, eating leftovers from supper."

"Do you suppose he was that hungry?"

"No."

Lauren was surprised by Adam's curt answer. "Do you know him?"

Adam paused for a second. "No."

Lauren didn't ask more questions, but something in Adam's answer didn't ring true.

"Do you think you can patch these?" He stood and removed the now-ragged suit of underwear. His naked body was covered with cuts and scratches.

"I doubt it, but I'll try."

He climbed into the bed without bothering to look for his other underwear. His body was warm against hers, but they were both too tired to think of making love. His arm tightened around her, and he slept almost instantly.

"I'm thinking of youuu," came softly from the other side of the quilt as Adam's breath evened. "Mountie's wife. Your man is asleep, but you are awake. Come in here and Rogét will give you what your man cannot."

The words grated on her like fingers on a blackboard. Should she wake Adam? His chest rose and fell against her back, and she decided not to wake him. But she lay awake, the quilt over her head, trying to shut out the obscene words Rogét whispered.

"How could he have gotten away?" Lauren eyed the steel bars, aware of the cold floor beneath her bare feet.

"I don't know." Adam ran a hand through his hair and sat down on part of a broken chair.

Lauren shivered against the chill that ran up her spine. Somehow, Rogét had gotten out of the cell and vanished. When? She remembered the string of obscenities he had mouthed in the dark. How long had he wandered around their cabin before leaving?

"The door's still locked." Adam sprang up and rattled the door. "No bars are missing. I don't understand it." He strode back into the bedroom, and Lauren followed.

"I'm going out to have a look around." He yanked on his other suit of underwear, his pants and coat, then picked up his hat on the way to the door. "Stay inside and I'll help you with this mess when I get back." A few snowflakes skittered across the floor as he opened and closed the door.

Lauren quickly dressed and began to pick up the broken furniture and dishes. She jumped when the door opened and Fox stepped inside.

"Mountie's wife. You keep bad house." Fox scanned the room quickly.

Lauren felt as if her feet were frozen where she stood. The woman looked relaxed, at ease, unaware she had barged into someone's house unannounced. But maybe the Cree didn't obey the same rules of behavior as everyone else, she thought.

"You're Fox, aren't you?"

The woman leveled almost yellow eyes on her, and again, Lauren felt a chill. Fox's skin was brown, but light, her hair the same color. Those eyes. Lauren was drawn into her gaze, and the word *exotic* came to mind.

"I am Fox."

"Can I offer you something to eat, to drink?"

Fox again scanned the room. "No. I do not come for food."

"No . . . I meant . . . We offer food and drink as a courtesy." Had she insulted the woman?

Fox looked at her again. "What is this 'courtesy'?"

Lauren tried to still her trembling hands and will her mind to work. She hadn't intended to get into a conversation with the woman, merely satisfy her until Adam came back. "It means we do this as good manners."

"Oh." Fox nodded. "That is not why I come, either." Again, she glanced down at the broken chairs.

"We had a visitor last night." Lauren offered.

"I know." Fox moved closer and sat down on the one remaining chair.

"You know?"

"Big man. He come to me and ask for potion."

"What kind of potion?"

"Kind to make you want him."

A handful of broken pottery clattered to the floor. "Me?"

"I think to come and warn you; then I say this is not Fox's concern."

"Well, I wish you had. You might have saved us all this trouble." Lauren swept the littered room with a motion of her hand.

"He say more." Fox lifted her head, and Lauren blinked.

Were the pupils of her eyes like a snake's?

"He say he kill your man and take you; then he rich man from whiskey."

"Angus." Lauren breathed the word with a shiver.

"You know this man?" Fox slanted a glance at her.

Lauren sat down on a wobbly broken chair, all the strength drained from her legs. Adam had lied. He knew all along it was Angus and not a man named Rogét. But why had Angus gone along with the charade? Why hadn't he killed them both when he had the chance? "He's the man Adam's been after for months. I can't believe we had him locked up."

Fox glanced over at the jail. "Where is he now?"

"He got away."

Fox smiled slyly. "He has magic, this man."

"No, he doesn't have any magic; he's just very clever."

Fox leaned closer. "Some say he is not man at all but spirit. He move fast, quick." A slender hand sliced the air.

"You can think what you want, but he's no magician; otherwise, he'd never have let Adam capture him."

"Maybe he want to be caught, at least for last night. Only way he can get close to you."

The words rippled across Lauren, leaving goose-flesh in their wake. Fox had said he got a potion from her. She walked over to the water bucket and peered inside, then swiped across the dark bottom with her hand.

"He not waste potion on chance you drink it. He would be sure."

"I think you should leave now. I have a lot of work to do." Lauren didn't turn around, not wanting to see the smirk on Fox's face. How did she get into this? Was she Angus's woman?

Fox spoke not another word, and Lauren knew she was gone when cold air coiled around her ankles as the door swept open, then closed.

Twelve

"I have to go, Lauren." Adam stuffed a shirt into his bedroll and yanked on a rawhide strap. "You know that."

"I know. I just don't like it." She handed him a pair of socks, which he took with a quick pat on her hand. "How long will you be gone?"

"A week, maybe two."

Fear clutched Lauren's throat, and she swallowed against threatened tears.

"I want you to go and stay with Eric and Gretchen." He dropped the roll to the floor and turned toward her. "Stay there until I get back."

"Adam, I can't run to them and hide every time you go out on patrol. I'm a Mountie's wife, and the people here have to respect me as well. Didn't you tell me that?"

Adam laughed and drew her to him. "I hate it when you turn my own words on me."

Lauren snuggled her cheek against his coat. Angus's unexpected visit had shaken Adam. He was afraid, not for himself but for her.

"There's some dried pemmican there and two more rabbits outside. One of the men from the reserve will be by with some meat in a few days."

"Be careful." Lauren caught his arm as he bent down to pick up his bedroll.

"You can be sure of that." He kissed her cheek. "And you'll be careful, too?"

Lauren nodded, fighting back the urge to cry.

"If you get frightened or lonely, you can always go up and stay with Gretchen and Eric. They've extended an open invitation anytime I'm gone."

"This is our home. I'll be fine here." She raised her chin and hoped he didn't see the tears in her eyes.

He started to go, then pivoted and swept her into his arms. His lips crushed hers in a kiss long and hard, as if branding her his. "I hope we made a baby last night," he whispered against her lips.

Before Lauren could comment, he was gone. She stood in the door, tears streaming down her face, and watched him stride away, the split in the back of his jacket flapping gently over slim hips. A man swathed in a striped blanket waited for him at the edge of the trees.

What an admission those last words had been and how hard for him to admit. Last night he had loved her greedily, passionately. Perhaps Adam had finally laid his fears to rest. She pressed her fingers to her lips and waved as he turned his horse and trotted away toward the forest.

"How long have they been here?" Adam whispered to the man at his side.

"Many days. Make whiskey long time." George peered over the edge of the scrubby bushes separating them from a busy liquor operation tucked into the brush.

"Who's in charge?" Adam removed his Stetson and risked a better look. In a clearing where the undergrowth had been stomped and chopped into submission, five or six men tended a still that belched smoke and the intoxicating odor of fermenting mash. Tents dotted the outside perimeter, and clotheslines were strung between poles, heavy with garments.

George shrugged. "Big man with black beard. Mean eyes." George pulled the colorful striped blanket tighter around his shoulders. "Mountie man not cold?"

Adam turned to face the man that had led him here. George huddled beneath two blankets, a fur muffler pulled right up to his chin. Although the day was warm for May, a cold wind had picked up right after sunrise. "My feet are freezing."

"You shoot men today?" George asked, nodding in the direction of the camp.

"No, I'm not going to shoot anybody, I hope. I want Black Angus. He's the man you describe. How long since he's been here?"

George shrugged. "A week or two. He leave in wagon loaded with wooden cases. Head south."

"Headed for the border, probably." Adam shifted his position. Cold mud had oozed up around his knees, and his joints ached. "We'll wait until he's here. This is a pretty big operation. Does anybody else come here for their liquor?"

George didn't answer or turn his head.

"George?"

"Some men come from reserve," he said finally.

Adam sat back on his heels. "I thought you were smarter than that."

"I don't say I come."

"Do you?"

George was silent again. "Sometimes when winter is cold."

"Where do you get the money?"

"Sometimes wife, she have."

Adam shook his head, knowing to pursue the conversation was useless. Illegal whiskey had already done irreparable damage to the Cree, a salve to an unhappy people penned up on a reserve far too small and far too poor.

"Let's go." Adam stood, then froze as the hammer of a revolver clicked back beside his ear.

"Well, what do we have here? One of the scarlet-clad," the voice said with a sneer. "Raise your hands, Mountie."

Slowly, Adam raised his hands over his head.

"I'd ask you to drop that gun, but I know it's tied to your fool neck, so I'll do it for you."

Roughly, someone yanked him around, and he faced a man a head taller than himself, grizzly with beard and mustache. The sour smell of liquor permeated the man's clothes. Rotten teeth grinned at him through lips streaked with tobacco juice. "Pretty little Mountie. Yore lettin' that uniform get mighty ragged, ain't ya?" He yanked on the lanyard, popping off epaulet buttons. "Guess I might have to keep this as a souvenir. Ought ta bring a purty penny down below the border." He swung the revolver by the white rope. "Spyin' on us, wuz ya?"

Adam remained silent, assessing the man before him. He glanced at George, expressionless beside him. He'd be no help.

"Spying? No. I've come to see your boss."

The man grinned. "How do you know I ain't the boss?"

"You better not let Angus hear you say that."

Fear, fleeting and intense, flickered through the man's eyes at the mention of the name. It was all the edge Adam needed. "I thought he might be back from across the border, and I came to bring him a message."

"What kind of message?"

"I'd like to deliver it in person, if you don't mind."

"Well, now, I do mind. You can't just waltz in here and expect Whoop Up Jack to let you see Angus."

"You being Whoop Up Jack?"

He frowned. "Yeah. How come a Mountie's bringing a message to Angus, anyway?"

Adam waited to give his answer, knowing that the longer the pause, the more power he had over the situation. "How do you think Angus gets the liquor down the Saskatchewan past the fort?"

Jack frowned again. "I don't trust you, Mountie. Yore comin' with me."

Jack reached out to grab Adam's arm, and Adam brought a knee up into the man's gut. While he was bent over, Adam twisted his arm behind him. "You tell Angus that Inspector McPhail is looking for him. Now, I'm going to leave you here, all wrapped up like a present, and I'm sure some of your friends will find you later." Adam yanked a short piece of leather tether out of his pocket and wound it around Jack's broad wrists, then secured them behind his back. With pain as his leverage, he yanked the man to his feet. "We'll just put you over here—"

Adam spun around from the impact. Something slammed into his shoulder, and the world tilted. The soft, boggy ground rushed up to meet him. Darkness consumed him as he tasted the grittiness of soil.

Teacher, teacher, teacher, teacher! A bird's insistent call drew Lauren's attention away from the muddy boards of the porch. Stretching her back, she leaned on the broom and followed the lilting notes up into the bare branches of a tree near the lake's edge. An ovenbird hopped nervously from branch to branch, then flew away toward the forest. She followed his flight until he disappeared; then she lingered, her chin on the broom handle.

Two weeks had passed without a word from Adam. Sweat popped out beneath her cotton dress as the sun topped the trees and heated her back. Swallowing against another wave of nausea, she pushed away from

the porch post and finished sweeping away the last of
the mud. As her hand fell on the door latch, she again
looked in the direction he had ridden, hoping for the
thousandth time to see him riding back toward her.
But all she saw was the waving grass, just greening
with spring.

The cool interior of the house made her shiver. She
shut the door and moved to the cracked mirror on the
wall. Lazy strands of hair fell over her eyes. Pushing
them away, she admonished herself for letting her ap-
pearance fall into such disarray. She smiled at the wan
face looking back at her. She was pregnant.

She must have conceived the first time they made
love, she thought with satisfaction. The nausea had
started the day before yesterday. At first she'd thought
she'd eaten bad food. Then, as the day wore on, the
nausea had subsided.

"I need to see some people," she mumbled to herself, untying the apron and hanging it on a nail. "I
have to tell somebody."

Minutes later, she was trudging up the path around
the lake where the trading post and Eric's house sat
alone in a clearing. Her stomach roiled again as the
gentle heat of the morning sun warmed her.

By her side, the lake lapped gently at its bank. Tiny
wrens hopped through the grasses collecting newly
hatched insects. Spring had arrived overnight. Fixing
her eyes on the house ahead, she tried to ignore her
stomach and keep her mind on the woman she was
about to visit.

A broad wolverine hide was tacked to the porch,
and metal traps tinkled in the soft breeze. Lauren
dodged the hanging goods on the common porch
shared by the post and Eric's house. Gretchen answered her knock.

"Hello," Lauren said brightly.

"Hello," Gretchen returned, then stood aside to let
her enter.

"I got lonesome and brought you some bread." She held out the cloth-covered basket on her arm. "In return for your nursing me."

"Yah. Eric will like somebody else's cooking for change." Gretchen bustled toward the kitchen.

"I see you're baking," Lauren said, sniffing the air, now filled with yeast and cinnamon. "You know yours is much better than mine, but thanks, anyway."

Gretchen laughed, and Lauren smiled at the sound. It had taken her weeks to get Gretchen to talk to her, and then it was only about everyday things, nothing personal. Lauren wanted very much to ask her more about the children she had lost.

"Where is the inspector?" Gretchen asked as she moved through the kitchen, taking out cups and saucers, plates and spoons, then depositing them on the table. Lauren watched her bring a kettle of hot water from the stove and slosh it into cups, then plop a pinch of tea into each one.

"He's still out on patrol. He's been gone more than two weeks, now." Lauren's stomach rolled again, and cold sweat broke out on her upper lip. *Oh, dear,* she thought, swallowing. *I'm going to be sick.* The door flew open, and Lauren barely made it to the edge of the porch before losing her breakfast. As she raised her head, she stared into the startled face of two Cree men, covered in fur from head to foot, just about to step up on the edge of the porch.

"I'm sorry," she groaned, grasping the porch post for support.

Eyeing her nervously, they picked their way around her and hurried into the trading post. Cool hands caught her forehead and pressed a damp cloth to her face.

"Come inside," Gretchen said, a supporting arm firmly around her shoulder, guiding her.

Lauren gratefully sank onto the couch and let Gretchen raise her feet.

"When will the baby come?" Gretchen asked with a faint smile.

Lauren studied her face and saw a flicker of envy in Gretchen's blue eyes. "In the winter."

Gretchen smiled. "Ah, a Christmas baby?"

The smile was contagious. "Yes, I think so."

"Does Inspector McPhail know?"

Lauren looked down at her hands. "No, he doesn't."

No comment followed. Lauren raised her eyes and stared into Gretchen's wistful look.

"He wants a child?"

"I think so."

"He does." Gretchen rose from her seat by Lauren's side. "He say many times." She moved to the kitchen and brought back a cup of tea. "You drink and I bring medicine."

Lauren wiggled into a sitting position and sipped the strong tea. Expecting it to aggravate her stomach, she was surprised when the liquid actually quieted the roiling.

"Here." Gretchen pressed a paper packet into her hand. "Put bit of this into your tea every morning and stomach will behave."

"Thank you," Lauren said, surprised.

Then, Gretchen sat down and took her hand. "You take care of baby. No heavy work. No lifting."

"No, I won't."

"And when baby come, you send for me."

Lauren stared into the round face, now softened with concern. What did she know about this woman? Was she really crazy? Should she trust her with her baby?

"You better?"

Lauren took another sip. "Why, yes. What is this?"

"Herb," Gretchen answered shortly, and rose. "You lie down awhile." She shuffled off to the kitchen, leaving Lauren on the couch alone.

For the first time, Lauren noticed how cozy and

beautiful loving efforts had made the rough log dwelling. Intricate needlework covered every chair. The rough board floor was strewn with braided and hooked rugs.

"You have house done?" Gretchen's voice echoed against the ceiling.

"Well, it's livable, but not as pretty as yours."

"Thank you." Gretchen sat down on the end of the couch again, flour dusting the front of her apron. "I show you how. Pretty things make cabin a home."

"I never was very good at handwork." Lauren picked up a doily from the arm of the sofa and ran her finger over the delicate interlacing threads.

"Anybody can do." Gretchen waved a hand. "Only take patience. Like marriage."

Lauren slanted a glance at her.

"You like being Inspector's wife?"

"Yes." Lauren chuckled. "I like being Adam's wife very much. Did he never mention me to you, Gretchen?"

Gretchen looked away. "Once he say there is woman back in Regina."

"But he never said he was to be married?" Lauren spread the doily back across the sofa arm.

"No. Inspector McPhail never talk much about himself."

"But you said he once said he wanted children."

"He say he wanted babies someday but that here is no place to bring woman."

Lauren looked out the window at the lazy sky, their ordeal in the snow fading into memory. Adam had been sore and bruised for days but never said a word about his own discomfort. Only halting steps and soft groans had belied his own pain. For days he had worked on the cabin, sometimes far into the night, to make it comfortable for her. What was her presence here doing to him? Would he put himself at risk unwisely for her sake?

"Well, he's wrong." Lauren picked up her cup and saucer, listening to the gentle scraping of china against china as she turned the cup. "I see now why he is so drawn to this country. It's fresh and new, not trampled and used like the East. This is a wonderful place for women and children."

Gretchen slowly shook her head. "I hope you think so after winter, Mrs. McPhail."

"Please." Lauren leaned over and gripped Gretchen's arm. "Call me Lauren."

"Do not let all that you see here fool you. Much sorrow built this home."

Lauren looked around her again. "Did you do all this after your children died?" *Dear God, what had made her say that?* Embarrassment flooded her. Why had she said such a thing?

Gretchen didn't answer. So long a silence passed that Lauren despaired of the woman ever speaking to her again.

"Gretchen—" Lauren started to sit up.

"Yes." Gretchen cut off her words. "Work helped fill emptiness." Her shoulders sagged, and she stared out the window toward the lake.

"Will you tell me about them?" Lauren set her cup on the floor and swung her legs over the edge of the couch to sit up.

"I never tell anybody, but I will tell you." She turned from the window, then walked across the room and sat down on the other end of the couch. Her fingers picked up the lace edge of her apron and began to worry it. "My little Eric. He was good boy." She smiled, and tears glistened in her eyes. "Only two." She held up two fingers.

"What happened to him?"

Gretchen sighed. "He died of summer fever. We were young. Had just moved here. Eric liked to play in puddles. Bad." She turned toward Lauren, frowned and shook her head. "Never let your baby play in puddles."

"I won't." Lauren felt a niggling of fear. Perhaps she had opened up something she shouldn't have.

"He get sick. All my medicine and all Eric's not help." She shook her head. "He die in my arms, reaching up for me to hold him."

A sob caught in Lauren's throat, and love for her own unborn child flooded through her. How alone Gretchen must have been then.

"My other son die in winter—"

"You don't have to explain," Lauren said quickly.

"No. It is all right. My daughter die being born. I see her." She nodded her head, staring out at something Lauren could not see. "Little girl with red hair like Eric's." She smiled through the tears that ran down her cheeks. "She die before she breathe. But I name her," she said with a nod. "You think baby should die without name?"

"No, I don't think so either." Foreboding crept over Lauren, shadowing the bright day outside.

"If they have no name, how does God know who they are?"

"I don't know." Lauren dabbed at the tears on her own cheeks, anxious now to be away from here.

"Anselma, I name my little girl. That means protected by God." Gretchen nodded her head. "She is now. My baby boy I name Aesir. With the gods, it means. I bury them all out there where you see me that day." Lauren rose and followed her extended finger to the window. A tiny white picket fence, now bent and twisted by winter, coiled in a circle in the yard. Inside, lay the three tiny graves. Trepidation increased. Lauren placed a hand on her abdomen. *It won't happen to you, baby. It won't.*

Then her attention was drawn to the edge of the woods. A wagon rattled out of the forest followed by three men in scarlet jackets.

"Adam," she breathed, and rushed for the door. She flung it open, then realized the party was coming from the wrong direction. They drew closer, and she recognized Mike Finnegan's waxed mustache.

"I must go. My husband's detachment is here from Fort Saskatchewan." Grabbing her basket, she turned to go, then went back and hugged a surprised Gretchen. "Thank you for the tea and the medicine."

Gretchen smiled and nodded. "I am sorry if I frightened you."

"Oh, no," Lauren said, backing away toward the door. "I will come back." Then, she shut the door behind her and flew down the steps.

"Mike!" she cried, running and waving.

Finnegan stood up in the wagon, the reins in his hands, and doffed his hat with a great flourish. Shaking off the lingering feeling of impending doom, Lauren hurried up to them as they pulled to a stop in front of her house.

"And where's the good inspector?" Finnegan asked with a lopsided grin.

"He's away. I expect him back any day."

Mike jumped to the ground, caught Lauren's hands, and smiled until his sky blue eyes squinted shut. "Marriage is agreeing with ye, girlie." She laughed out loud. If there was such as thing as leprechauns, she was looking at one. Soft auburn hair, badly in need of a cut, curled over his ears, and the corners of his eyes crinkled from much laughing, she guessed.

"Thank you. I'm so glad to see a familiar face."

"Are ye tired already of lookin' at that ugly husband of yours?"

Lauren colored as Mike's eyes twinkled. "No, I'm just glad to see somebody else."

"Well, then, you have three bachelors on your hands, all starvin' fer a home cooked meal, I might add."

Lauren stared at the other two men who now made

up Adam's detachment. Constable McDougall was light-haired and short. Constable McLeod was tall and dark, older, and moved with an elegant grace that told of a past spent in more gentlemanly pursuits than taming western provinces.

"Afternoon, ma'am," William said with a curt nod.

"Mrs. McPhail," Duncan said with a nod and soft smile.

"Is McPhail treatin' you right, 'cause if he ain't, Mike Finnegan's here to remedy the situation." Mike screwed his face up into an outrageous wink, and Duncan chuckled. Young William nodded enthusiastically. "A hot meal would be a treat, Mrs. McPhail."

"Please, call me Lauren. All of you. Now, get down and come in. I think I have some rabbit left and—"

"No need to bother." Finnegan moved to the end of the wagon. "I've brought supplies." He whipped back the canvas cover. Underneath lay crates of canned supplies, barrels of dried and salted meat, canned fruits and vegetables, and other necessities to establish a station.

"I figure we should be able to fix a fine supper with what's here," he said with a grin.

"Oh, all this looks wonderful." She raised her eyes to Finnegan's. "You don't know how tired we are of rabbit."

"Finnegan," Duncan said softly.

Mike turned, and Duncan pointed toward the north, where the edge of the lake met thick woods. Finnegan stepped forward and squinted. "Holy Mother," he breathed. "Get down, McDougall, and give me your horse."

Constable McDougall swung down. Finnegan leaped into the saddle and lashed the horse into a gallop, Duncan close on his heels. Shading her eyes, Lauren stood on tiptoe to see. A horse emerged from the forest, paused for a moment in the open, then wandered down to the water and lowered its head for a drink. Lauren caught her breath. Her whole body went cold. Clinging to the horse's back was a flash of scarlet.

"Oh, dear God, no. Adam."

Thirteen

Lauren heard the anguished words pass her lips, but her vision was focused only on the scarlet speck flung against Jake's neck. Finnegan slowed his horse's charging gallop when Adam's horse threw its head up nervously. In a slow, casual walk the pair approached Adam. Time dragged by. Finnegan began to whistle. Jake lowered his head to drink, and Lauren caught her breath as Adam slipped, then grasped for a better hold. Fear gave flight to hope. He was alive.

Jake raised his head and pricked his ears forward as Finnegan stopped, slid to the ground, and walked closer. Sidling away, Jake looked back toward the woods, but Finnegan advanced, his arm extended, his words lost in the slapping of the lake's waves. Then, she saw his hand close on the reins. He moved to Jake's side and raised Adam's head. Seconds stretched into hours before Finnegan leaped up on Jake's back, hauled Adam's limp body against his, and urged Jake into a rolling lope.

Jake came to a nonchalant stop at the edge of the porch. Lauren moved her feet only by sheer will when she saw the blood streaking Adam's blond hair.

"Bring him inside." Her words were amazingly calm even to her own ears. "Over here." She hurried in ahead of Finnegan half carrying, half dragging Adam's body behind him. Yanking aside the quilt, she pulled down the bedcovers. Finnegan heaved Adam onto the bed, and his head settled on the pillow with a groan.

"At least he's alive," Finnegan said under his breath.

"Did you bring any medical supplies?" Lauren asked, gently pulling off the coat, redder with blood than with Mountie scarlet. Blood dribbled through his hair, ran down the side of his neck, and smeared across the shoulders of his shirt. She clamped her teeth against a rising tide of fear churning her stomach. There was so much blood. Where was he injured? Layer by layer she removed clothing until her finger sank into a gaping hole in his shoulder. The world spun and the room darkened as the sticky warmth of flesh closed around her thumb.

"Get me some water," she asked McDougall standing white-faced at the foot of the bed. He raised frightened eyes for a moment before scurrying away.

"I probably scared that young constable to death," she whispered to an unconscious Adam as she ripped his undershirt apart. "I know my face is nearly as pale as yours." She placed a hand against his forehead to smooth back sticky, matted hair and felt the sliminess of another wound. Stark-white bone peeped out of a path plowed by a bullet above his temple.

McDougall reappeared with a quivering pan of water. "Where's Finnegan?" she asked.

"Here." Finnegan moved to her side. "Do you want me to take over for you?"

"No," she said, trying to concentrate on the work at hand. Another rip of his undershirt and it fell away, exposing his chest. "This is my job."

Dipping the last piece of her new petticoat into the water, she wiped at the dried blood around the oozing shoulder wound.

"Cover him up with that quilt." She nodded toward the cover folded neatly on the foot of the bed.

"McDougall, why don't you see to the horses,"

Finnegan said as he pulled the quilt across Adam's chest. The young constable lost no time in hurrying away.

"How on earth did you make such a mess?" she whispered as the blood came away in bright red streaks. "How long have you been hurt?"

Finnegan laid a hand on her shoulder. "Lauren."

She paused and turned.

"I'll be more than glad to do this for you." His compassionate eyes were darkened with concern.

Lauren smiled. "I know what you're thinking. Adam didn't think I could do this, either, and if you want to know the truth, I'm not sure I can, but I have to try, Mike. He's my husband. This is part of the job. I serve, too, you know."

Finnegan smiled and patted her shoulder. "McDougall."

"Sir?" he answered from the doorway.

"Build us a fire and I'll cook you a good old Irish stew." Then, he passed through the hanging quilt, leaving them alone.

Lauren let out the breath she held, and her hands trembled uncontrollably. She dropped the cloth into the basin and clasped them together. Tiny blue lines etched across his closed eyelids, and gray bags shadowed his eyes. She pushed back a lock of blood-stiffened hair and stifled a sob.

"How long have you been like this?" she whispered to him. "How many days and nights?" A tear escaped down her face, and she wiped it quickly away. "There won't be any more crying," she told herself. "There will always be time later to cry." Then, drawing a deep breath, she picked up the cloth and finished cleaning around the wound.

With the removal of the dried blood, the bullet hole began to bleed anew, oozing out and over her fingers until the front of her dress was streaked. Gently, she probed the flesh. Once, Adam winced and moaned softly.

"Mike!"

Finnegan appeared at her side.

"See if you think there's a bullet in there."

She backed up, and Finnegan took her place. With knobby fingers, he felt the flesh, then raised Adam's shoulder and looked beneath. "No. It went clean through."

Lauren leaned over and saw the torn, ragged exit wound.

"Pour this in." Finnegan handed her a bottle of whiskey. Lauren tipped the bottle and let the amber liquid pour into the wound and out the other side, bringing fresh blood with it.

"We'll have to sew it up." Finnegan raised his eyes to Duncan who stood behind him.

"I'll get my needle and thread." Lauren brushed by McDougall hovering just outside the quilt wall. She opened her sewing box, selected needle and thread, and hurried back to Adam's side.

"Are you sure you don't want me to do that for you?" Finnegan had moved to the other side of the bed.

Lauren squinted one eye and poked the thread through the needle. Her fingers slowed. How easy it would be to let Mike finish the job. After all, William and Duncan looked dead on their feet and could probably use something to eat. She looked at Finnegan, then down to Adam's still face. He was her first concern. "No, I'll do it."

A chill ran over her, raising gooseflesh on her arms as she poked the needle through the skin. She had once sewn up one of her father's beagles when briars had ripped its skin on a hunt. Now, she tried to imagine Adam as that dog. "Talk to me, Mike."

"What about?" Finnegan asked.

"I don't care. Anything."

"Well, let's see. There was some gossip around the fort when we left. It seems that . . ."

Lauren ceased to hear the words, but Finnegan's voice, with its highs and lows for emphasis, lulled her, making some part of her mind follow his words while the rest was devoted to Adam. In and out the needle flashed. *Stitch, knot. Stitch, knot.* Careful to make the stitches even and secure, she closed the front wound neatly.

"Now, raise him up." Wiping bloody hands down the front of her smeared apron, she rethreaded the needle and closed her ears against Adam's deep groans as Duncan and Finnegan raised his shoulders off the bed. Straddling Finnegan's legs, she quickly secured every ragged edge of the exit wound and heaved a sigh of relief as the men lowered Adam back into the mattress.

"Now, quick. Wrap it up," Finnegan said, wiping a thin sheen of sweat off his own brow with the sleeve of his shirt.

Lauren wound clean strips of cloth across Adam's shoulder and beneath his arm, then tied the ends neatly together.

Finnegan probed the surrounding flesh with his fingers, then laid a hand on Adam's forehead. "Blood poison's already set in."

Lauren gazed down at Adam's face, so still in sleep. "What should we do?"

Finnegan tugged the quilt to cover Adam's arm. "Nothin' we can do, lass, but wait and see."

The *pop* and *snap* of the barrel stove was fit accompaniment to the snoring going on all around her. Lauren pulled a shawl tighter across her shoulders. Faint orange light turned the sparse room into a world suspended in time. Nothing seemed quite real except the raucous noise coming from the jail. Lauren gave her rocking chair another little shove, and it swayed back and forth on sighing floorboards. Only the gentle rise and fall of her favorite quilt told her that Adam teetered between life and death. The deadly infection held his life in its grasp, his dry, hot skin evidence of the struggle beneath.

Leaning her head back against the chair, Lauren closed her eyes. She should have told Adam about the baby before he left on patrol that day. She opened her eyes at Adam's soft moan. Would he live to see his child? Would he ever hold the life growing in her belly?

Adam threw an arm across his eyes and mumbled incoherently. Lauren leaned forward and felt his cheek.

"Would you like me to take the watch for a time?" Duncan's soft burr came to her from the darkness. He rose from his bed on the floor and stood, his white undershirt bold against the dark room.

"No. I'll stay."

Duncan moved closer, yanking the end of the quilt over Adam's exposed foot. "No sense wearing yourself out. The sun will be up soon."

She watched Duncan tuck the quilt securely around Adam's feet. Adam had mentioned the quiet Scotsman a time or two, always with admiration and respect. He was older than the other men, she gathered, and had assumed a fatherly role to many of the young constables. With a final tug at the quilt, he moved away, back toward his makeshift bed.

"I know." She crossed her arms and settled back in the chair. "I couldn't sleep anyway."

"He's strong. He'll fight his way out of this one." She heard Duncan rummage in his saddlebags, and he stepped back into her line of sight, a pipe and tobacco pouch in his hand. "Do you mind?" he asked, holding up the carved bowl of a brierwood pipe.

"No, of course not," she answered with a shake of

her head. Her father had smoked a pipe. She could close her eyes and still smell the soft, sweet scent that clung to him and his clothes.

Duncan filled the bowl and opened the stove door with a soft squeak. He poked a sliver of wood inside, then lit his pipe with the glowing end. Smoke encircled his head, and he stepped backward to sit gingerly on the end of Adam's bed.

"How long do you suppose he was out there?"

Duncan glanced backward at Adam. "Can't tell. A day or two, maybe."

Lauren began to rock, comforting herself against the fear and pain that welled up. "He was in pain and hungry." Her voice broke, and she clamped her lips together. She'd vowed to be strong, to prove herself a fit Mountie's wife. It wouldn't do to break now.

"You can't be thinkin' about things like that, lass. It'll prey on your mind. Adam's a fine lad and a good officer. He's found himself a place here, and he's doing what he loves." Duncan paused and took another pull on the pipe.

"I was shot myself sometime ago. I crawled inside a log out of the rain. Of course"—he paused to tamp down the tobacco—"in a couple of hours it occurred to me nobody could see me in there, either." Caught between his teeth, the pipe quivered as he rubbed his knee. "But he found me." He nodded toward Adam and drew in long on the pipe.

Lauren opened her mouth to comment, but a lump in her throat blocked the words.

"He looked all night, Griesbach told me. I never saw rain like that. Poured like somebody was dumping it out of a bucket. About daybreak, I heard somebody scuffling around outside. Then, I see a face at the end of the log. 'About ready to come out?' he asks, calm as you please."

Duncan took the pipe from his mouth and blew smoke rings over his head. "I crawled out, and he was wetter and dirtier than me. If I hadn't known him, I'd have sworn he was a whiskey trader. Three days of beard." He stroked his chin. "Coat torn and ragged. Picked me up like a sack of potatoes and threw me over the back of my horse." He clamped the pipe back between his teeth. "Damned uncomfortable ride home, as I remember."

Lauren looked down at Adam, imagining him leaning down, peering in the end of a log, the corners of his mouth twitching in amusement. Tears blurred the vision. Blinking rapidly, she swallowed a sob.

"He's more man than most," Duncan said with an odd catch in his voice. "He'll pull through. You'll see."

Silently, Lauren nodded, then she felt Duncan's hand clamp down on her shoulder and realized he had moved to her side.

"I've been in the Force fifteen years, and I've seen a lot of men come and go. Some of them came for the job and some for the adventure, but Adam, he was born to it. And you can rest assured he'd rather be laying there shot than livin' the life his da had planned for him."

Startled, Lauren looked up.

Duncan smiled and shrugged. "The days and nights get long on patrols, and past history comes up. But I can tell you this." He took the pipe out of his mouth and pointed the end toward Adam. "His da couldn't see past what he wanted the lad to be instead of seeing what he was. So, if you've got any doubts—"

"I don't," Lauren snapped, then smiled her apology. "I don't. I've always believed in him."

"I think he married the right woman for the job." He winked and strode away into the dark, disappearing into a cloud of his own sweet tobacco smoke.

* * *

Dawn played across the rough log walls with long pink fingers. Lauren nodded, her whole body aching with exhaustion. William and Duncan roused from their hard beds and left. Then, as the first light of dawn burst through the window, Adam moved and opened his eyes.

He stared at Lauren vacantly for a moment, then smiled weakly. "Where'd you find me?" he said drowsily.

"I didn't find you. Jake brought you home." Tears stung again as she imagined him cold, hurt, alone.

Adam scanned her face. "You look tired. How long have I been here?"

"We found you yesterday afternoon."

He groaned and moved his shoulder. "I don't remember much after the bullet knocked me off my horse."

"You must have gotten back on somehow."

Adam tried to sit up, but caught his breath suddenly and fell back against the pillow.

"Finnegan said you have blood poisoning." She laid her hand on his forehead. "The bullet went all the way through, but you still have a fever."

Concern flickered across his face, and his eyes found hers. "You must have been scared to death."

Lauren glanced away. "I managed."

The grip of his fingers was strong and warm as they closed around her hand. "I love you."

Lauren looked down. Blood-stiffened hairs covered the back of his hand, and creases in the calluses of his fingers were stained red. "And I love you."

She rose, and Adam reluctantly released her. She looked exhausted, gray shadows haunting her eyes. "I'll get you some broth," she said over her shoulder as she passed through the quilt curtain. He listened as she shuffled across the floor and rattled around the stove. Then he heard a sniff and knew she was crying. Staring up at the exposed beams overhead, he waited, helpless to comfort her, knowing she didn't want him to see.

When she came around the quilt again, there was no trace of tears except for the redness of her eyes.

"How long has it been since you ate?" she asked in a brave voice, sitting back down in the chair at his side.

"Oh, I don't know. A day or two." Actually, it was more like a few days, except for an occasional sip of water.

She lifted a spoonful of soup and raised it to his lips. Her eyes avoided his as he took the nourishment.

"That's good. What is it?"

"A little rabbit. A little squirrel."

"Did Finnegan get these?"

She lifted another spoonful. "No, I did."

Adam swallowed. "You did? How?"

Lauren smiled, tilting the corners of her eyes merrily. "With a snare."

Adam laughed, then grunted against the pain even the smallest movement brought. "Tell me about it."

"Oh, it's a long story. Maybe when you're better." As he opened his mouth to protest, she crammed in another spoonful.

Little by little, she fed him the entire bowl of thin soup. With each swallow, Adam watched her hands—delicately holding the bent and scarred spoon, deftly maneuvering the utensil to his mouth, careful not to spill the hot liquid. She smiled with each swallow he took, then carefully wiped his mouth with a bit of cloth. Despite the pain in his arm, he couldn't remember ever feeling better or more loved, not since childhood. How he wished he could be sure she felt as secure in their union, but he suspected she did not.

"Lauren." He caught her arm as she rose from the chair.

"Yes?" She paused, the bowl balanced in her hand. Questions blurred through his mind and carefully thought-out statements vanished. "I'm sorry you were alone for so long." The words sounded shallow and inadequate.

"It's all right. I managed." She shrugged and moved away with a gentle swish.

Adam turned his head and studied the wandering bear's-paw pattern on the quilt hanging at his side. Little sounds came from the other room: Lauren washing the bowl; Lauren restocking the stove; Lauren sinking into the straight-backed chair. More than anything that had come before or would come again, he loved her. But, he admitted with a sigh, love might not be enough to sustain them.

"It's glad I am to see you alive."

Adam jerked awake at the thick Irish dialect. Finnegan stood at the foot of the bed, grinning.

"If not for you, I might not be, friend," Adam grunted and pushed himself up onto the pillows.

"Ah. Jake woulda found his way home. Eventually."

"All the same, I'm glad you were here with Lauren."

Finnegan moved to the side of the bed and sat down. "I had me doubts when you brought your bride into our midst, but she's a fine lass, a strong woman. Bandaged and stitched you herself, she did. Wouldn't let me help a lick."

"Where is she?"

"I shooed her off up to Ansgar's. She was lookin' a might peaked, and I thought an afternoon away from you might just be the medicine."

"How did she take this, really?" Adam watched Mike's face, struggling to see through the mask his friend was so adept at creating when he didn't want his emotions read.

"Like any woman lookin' down at her man, a hole blown through him."

Adam flexed his shoulder and winced. "Angus is here, Mike, in all his glory. He's got an operation big enough to move out of the territory.

"Did you see him?"

Adam shook his head. "No. He was gone south with a wagonload."

"Who shot you?"

"I don't know. I was tying up one of his men, and suddenly I was tasting mud; then everything went black. When I woke up, I was out in the brush, alone. I had a Cree guide with me, but he disappeared, too."

"Do you think I need to go back to Fort Saskatchewan for more men?" Finnegan asked with a frown.

"No. I want to look around some more first."

Finnegan stared down at his hands.

"All right, Mike. Out with it."

Finnegan sighed. "It's none of me business, mind you."

"Say it."

"I don't think she's well."

"Lauren? Why?"

Finnegan shook his head. "She hasn't said a word, but she looks . . ." Faltering, he searched for the word.

Adam let his head drop back against the pillow. Surely, the weeks she'd spent alone had been hard on her. Old fears surged to the surface.

"I've been doing most of the cookin' for the lads and me outside, but she insists on lookin' after us."

Adam closed his eyes and imagined Lauren alone and afraid, as he had done a thousand times. "As soon as I can get out of this bed, I'll build her a proper kitchen so cooking won't be so difficult."

Finnegan turned and fixed him with an amber stare. "She needs some time to adjust, lad, and she'll be fine. I tell you, she's stronger than you think. It's just that womenfolk don't take to this sort of thing as quickly as us fellows." Finnegan rose and moved to the tiny window that overlooked the lake.

Adam laughed at Finnegan's evaluation, then winced at the pain the movement created. "How long do you think she'll be gone?"

Finnegan stared out at a single figure down at the lake's edge. "Not much longer, I'm thinkin'."

Fourteen

Lauren hugged herself against the suddenly brisk wind. Spring had painted the landscape with pastels, and the delicate, abundant colors made one light-headed. Stopping, she looked out over the lake's surface mirroring the azure sky above. What a beautiful place to bring up a child. She let her fingers trace down to her abdomen where life stirred. She'd tell Adam tonight, but for now, she'd keep the secret to herself a bit longer.

Glancing over her shoulder, she saw Finnegan leave the cabin, followed by Duncan and William. She had to get back. Adam would be needing her. With a final glance at the budding trees, she turned and headed across the moist, rich ground. Finnegan smiled and nodded as he passed her, his horse outfitted with equipment for hauling logs. He was building an addition to the house for the men's barracks.

"How are you feeling?" she asked Adam, removing the scarf from around her head and hanging it on a nail.

Adam sat upright in the bed, his chest bare except for the bandage wound around him. Even above the bandage, the flesh was still red and angry.

"I'm feeling like I want my wife." He grinned at her, his teeth white beneath his mustache.

Lauren moved to the bedside, her mind whirling. They would only have a short time alone together until the men returned. She had to tell him now, but how could she? What words should she use? Would she see fear, dread, in his eyes or joy?

Adam grabbed her hands and pulled her across his lap. Prickly mustache hairs tickled her nose as his lips pressed warm against hers.

She slid into that warm oblivion his kisses created, a safe place where nothing could touch either of them.

"I want you, Lauren," he whispered. "It's been so long."

His quavering words struck deep into her soul. "What about your arm?"

He smiled seductively. "My arm won't play much part in loving you." Her cheeks reddened at his frank words, yet her body responded instantly.

"What about Finnegan?" she protested hollowly as he fumbled with her buttons, one-handed. She pushed his hands away and slipped off her dress, leaving on her chemise.

"He'll be gone for most of the day. I made sure."

"Are you sure you're strong enough for this?" Lauren stopped him with both hands on his bare chest as he pulled her to his side and flipped the covers over them both.

He stared down at her. "I don't remember much after I was shot, but I do remember wanting to come home to you. I think maybe that's why I found my way to Jake and he found his way home." He pulled her closer. His chest rose and fell in gentle cadence, and his warmth crept through her, comforting and familiar.

"I'm glad you didn't listen to me and get back on that train," he said, his hand slipping down her body.

She stretched like a lazy cat as his hand covered one breast possessively. He kissed her hair, the tip of her nose. With an occasional grunt, he turned toward her and attempted to roll her underneath him. Suddenly, he stilled, and his face blanched. He sank into the mattress with a groan.

"I told you it was too soon. Are you all right?" Lauren scrambled to her knees and felt his forehead, sliding the backs of her knuckles along his cheek.

"Stop touching me, woman," Adam said, his words muffled by the pillow. Slowly, he rolled onto his back, cold sweat dotting his forehead.

Lauren yanked her clothes back on, then stretched across him to check the bandage. "Oh, Adam. You're bleeding again. You're so muleheaded." Angry and frightened that he might have undone some of his early healing, Lauren rolled out of the bed. "You're not only stubborn; you're obstinate." She smiled and looked down at him. "A fine example you'll set as a father."

Realization took a few seconds to dawn, then Adam's eyes found hers. In that moment, she felt that she saw into his soul. Slowly, he smiled and cupped her face in his palm.

"A baby?" he whispered. "When, how . . . ?"

"Around Christmas, I think. Maybe after. And for the how, well . . ."

He smiled broadly. "I think I can use my imagination." His gaze shifted from her face to her abdomen. Hands, trembling and hesitant, paused in the air for a moment like those of a reluctant child. Uncertain fingertips traced across her stomach until his wide palms spanned her width. He slid his hands around her legs and pulled her closer, laying his cheek against their sleeping child. His shoulders began to tremble, and hot tears soaked through the thin material of her chemise. Entangling her fingers in his hair, she held him as he cried, and beneath his cheek, she felt the first flutterings of life.

* * *

"Ouch. Damn." Adam plopped back onto the bed, his jacket clamped in his teeth and one boot on. His right arm lay confined in a sling across his chest.

"Are you trying to get dressed alone?" Lauren's voice quivered with humor from the other side of the quilt.

"Damn fine mess when a man can't even get his own clothes on," he muttered around the mouthful of fabric. He poked his left arm straight into the sleeve and shook it, hoping the jacket would slide down his arm enough for him to throw the other side across his right shoulder.

"I told you I'd help you in minute." Lauren pushed back the quilt and stepped into their bedroom.

"I thought I could at least get my clothes on by myself." Adam dropped his arm, now numb from being over his head. "Heaven knows, I haven't been able to do much else alone lately."

Lauren crossed her arms. "You are the most stubborn man I have ever known. It hasn't been that long. Only a week. Besides, I'm your wife."

Adam raised his eyes to meet hers. Apparently, pregnancy agreed with her. She had bloomed like a summer rose in a few short days, no longer the drawn, faded woman he had come home to. What went on inside the female body to make such changes happen so quickly? "How are you feeling today?"

"I'm fine." She stooped down and put his boot on. "A little nauseous this morning, but nothing bad."

They had not yet discussed the baby at length since Lauren's announcement. Days after, he had been feverish and fitful. Yesterday and today were the first days he'd felt like himself again.

"Lauren." He gripped her arm with his one good hand. She stopped lacing his boot and looked up. "I'm happy about the baby. I don't remember telling you that."

She smiled. "You did." Then she frowned. "No doubts?"

"None."

Her face brightened, and her eyes sparkled with mischief. "I only hope he's not as much trouble and as messy as his father."

Adam felt his face flush, and Lauren laughed.

"Adam McPhail, you are the most tenacious, prideful man I've ever known." Lauren stood and planted both fists on her hips. "Honestly, you'd have thought I was trying to tend to an old-maid schoolteacher. I have done this before, you know. I looked after Father."

"It's not the same." Adam's cheeks began to burn in embarrassment.

"How so?"

"Well . . . It's just not. I'm your husband."

"And what difference does that make?"

"I don't know. It just does. I'm supposed to be looking after you." Adam wrestled with the one arm in his jacket sleeve. If he could just get it on himself, somehow he'd just plain feel better.

"If I had been the one hurt, wouldn't you have cared for me?"

"Oh, of course I would. Ah. There." Adam lurched to his feet, reached across his chest, and yanked the coat over his shoulder.

"So, then, what's the difference?"

Lauren stood toe-to-toe with him, her head tipped back. Pink and moist, her lips were inviting him to kiss her. As much as he wanted to, wanted her, he knew his body wasn't going to cooperate. "I don't know. It just doesn't feel right having to be looked after. It makes me uncomfortable, makes me feel . . . useless, I guess, is the word I'm looking for."

Lauren's arms slid around his waist, and she pulled him against her. "I like looking after you. It makes you less . . . stoic. You always know what to do.

You're always confident, and I'm just not. Having you here at my mercy evens things a little."

Adam laughed and wrapped his arm around her shoulder. "If I have to be at anyone's mercy, I'd want it to be yours."

Lauren laughed and moved away. "Take care you don't hurt yourself or else you'll end up back in that bed for me to do with you what I want," she tossed back over her shoulder as she stepped into the next room.

Comfortable sounds came through the fabric separating them, and Adam closed his eyes and sighed. Thoughts of Lauren having this baby scared him to the very soles of his boots, but he couldn't let her see that. She had to believe he had everything under control and had come to terms with his fears.

"I hope you're not thinking of going on patrol today," she admonished, unseen from the kitchen.

"I thought I'd see how Finnegan was coming on the corral. Help me with this, will you?" He stepped into the living room and handed her his lanyard and gun belt.

"I don't see why you're even wearing this. You can't use your right arm."

"I feel naked without my gun. Besides"—he lowered his nose into her hair as she settled the cord around his neck and threaded it beneath his right arm—"it gives me a chance to do this." He swept her against him and kissed her hard.

The swell of her stomach pressed against him, and a surge of possessiveness jolted through him. She sighed softly as he held her close, and suddenly his need of her was painful.

"What if you were naked except for your gun?" she purred.

"That's enough." Reluctantly, he set her away. "You're torturing an injured man."

Lauren laughed and sashayed away to the stove. "When will you be back?"

Adam watched the sway of her hips as she darted about the house, straightening. "Just as soon as I can, believe me."

Lauren shot him a reproachful glance and turned back to her work.

Outside, June struck him with its full orchestra. Birds warbled in the trees overhead, bobbing up and down on branches barely large enough to hold them. Insects hummed down near the water's edge, and a warm wind wrapped itself around him. Breathing deeply, he winced as long-unstretched muscles expanded.

The *thump, thump* of a mallet drew him around the corner of the house and down toward the edge of the forest where Finnegan, William and Duncan took turns pounding posts into the unyielding ground. The partially finished skeleton of a corral twisted like a snake behind them.

"Adam." Duncan straightened, a hand to his lower back, then propped his forearm on the handle of the mallet. "How is the shoulder today?"

"Better." Adam propped one foot on the newest section of fence and rested his left forearm on the top rail. "Are you about ready to take a little trip into the bush?"

Duncan's brows gathered into a frown. "Surely you're not thinking of going on patrol?"

"While I was laid up in bed, Angus got just that much ahead of us."

"You know I'd have been willin'—"

Adam held up a hand to stop him. "I know you would have, Duncan, but this is my job."

"Still and all, you're no match for the likes of Angus now."

"I just want to take a look around."

"That's what you were doing when you got yourself

shot." Duncan wiped sweat away with the back of his hand and thumped the mallet head on the ground.

"I'll be more careful this time."

Duncan regarded him steadily for a minute. "When were you thinking of going?"

"First thing in the morning."

Duncan scraped his fingers across a bristly chin. "Lauren won't like it."

Adam sighed and looked at his feet. "I know she won't, but this is part of the job she's going to have to learn to accept."

"To a woman, accepting is one thing. Making a man's life miserable for his actions is another."

"She's a good Mountie's wife. She'll understand."

"You're going to do what?" Lauren planted her hands on her hips, a dishtowel slung across her shoulder, and faced him over a table covered with jars of beans.

Adam reddened and cast a glance toward Duncan, who was standing in the doorway, grinning around the stem of his pipe. "I've been away from my work long enough."

"Your arm's not even out of the sling." She poked at him with a long wooden spoon.

"We're just going out to have a look around, go onto the reserve, and see if anybody's seen anything of Angus."

She darted a glance at Duncan. "Are you going with him?"

"Yes, ma'am," he answered.

Chewing at the corner of her mouth, she squinted one eye closed. "Will you be careful?"

Adam's shade of red deepened. "Duncan. Could you give us a minute?" The tone of his voice said she'd gone too far.

The door closed softly on Duncan's chuckle, and they were alone.

"I wish you wouldn't question me in front of my men." He strode to the window, his shoulders straight and stiff, a sure sign he was angry.

Well, she didn't care. If he didn't want to look after himself, then she'd do it for him. "I was only concerned that you might be doing too much too soon."

"I know." The words came out as a sigh. He took off his hat and raked a hand through his hair. "I know you thought you were doing what was right for me, but I can't have my authority undermined."

"I won't undermine your authority," she mocked as she turned away to lift another jar out of a pan of boiling water on the stove. "You're doing that yourself, behaving so foolishly."

Adam watched her turn and place the jar on the table, but she didn't raise her eyes or meet his gaze. "I won't be late," he offered.

"Be careful." Still, she didn't meet his eyes.

Adam plopped his Stetson onto his head and headed for the door, grateful for the fresh air that greeted him. The right words had eluded him. He should have said something to reassure her. Duncan and the men waited for him by the horses, each staring down at their feet, looking ill at ease.

"We'll swing north as far as the bend in the river, here." Adam traced the route of the Saskatchewan River with a stick in the dirt. "Then turn due east for about, oh, ten miles." He stabbed the stick into the ground. "Angus is here."

"Do you think he brought in more men now that he knows you're on to him?" Finnegan asked.

"I wouldn't doubt it, now. I suspect that Johnson has come in from Saskatchewan to join him"—he dragged the stick across the ground again—"and that Frenchie has come up from the border." Adam dropped the stick and rose from his squatting position.

"We'll poke around and see what we can find out. When we take him, we'll need more men, but I can't send for them until I'm sure what we're dealing with."

Finnegan stood, holding his reins in his hand. "The lads and I will be glad to go." He nodded over his shoulder to where Lauren watched from the doorway.

"No."

"She's worried about ye, lad." Finnegan lowered his voice and stepped closer. "That's not a bad thing, and every one of us understands."

Adam glanced toward her again. "I know."

They mounted the horses and started out of the yard. "Be careful, men," he said. "Angus knows I'm here and that I'm coming after him sooner or later." They entered the forest, and he glanced back once more to where Lauren sat rocking on the porch before tree limbs slid into place to hide her. "He knows, and he'll be ready with everything he can muster," Adam muttered to himself.

Lauren watched them until they were tiny dots against the black spruce forest. Then, she rose from her chair on the porch. Her hand was on the door latch when someone spoke her name.

"Fox," she said, stunned to see the Cree woman standing in her yard. Fox stood quiet and solemn, knots in her hair, furs hanging from her shoulders. She wore a long, loose dress, making her look larger than before. Displacing the arrogant expression she had worn before was a furrow of concern. "What do you want?" Lauren thought of their last meeting.

Fox paused, obviously searching for words that did not come easily to her. "I have news," she said in broken English.

"What kind of news?"

"I have a dream." Fox paused again. "About you."

A chill ran up Lauren's spine. "Please come in," she said, and opened the door.

The shady inside was a welcome relief from the

midday heat and the mosquitoes that buzzed incessantly. Laying her floppy hat on the table, Lauren moved to the new kitchen table William and Duncan had completed while Adam was sick. "Would you like a cool drink?"

Fox didn't answer as she sank into one of the chairs. "I have a dream. A bad dream."

Lauren poured herself a cup of cold water, keeping her back to Fox while she tried to get her emotions under control. Fox unnerved her. She couldn't decide if it was her quiet way of appearing and disappearing so suddenly or the fact the woman seemed to know things that, by all that was logical, she should not know.

"Tell me about it," Lauren said, turning and moving to the table.

Fox's fingers worried the edge of her wrap. "I see storm, terrible storm. Wind, ice, deep snow. Very dark. It comes to sweep everything away." She took in the circumference of the room with a wave of her hand.

Lauren swallowed a lump of dread growing in her throat. She's crazy, she told herself. Don't listen to her.

"Storm take away your baby, too."

Lauren sat down into her chair with a flop, her hand immediately going to the gentle rounding beneath her dress.

"You are alone in this storm." Fox leaned forward, fixing Lauren with a stare. "All alone, with only your man. No woman."

Lauren took another sip of water, trying to gather her thoughts. Adam's reassuring voice crooned in her mind even though he was miles away. She closed her eyes and imagined his face before her. *I have to stay calm. It's not good for the baby.*

Lauren opened her eyes. "I'm not afraid here with Adam."

"Mountie husband know nothing about birth." She shook her head vigorously.

"Adam's delivered babies before," Lauren said, summoning her strongest voice while remembering the snatches of conversation about the stillbirth he delivered before she arrived. "Why did you come here to try and scare me?"

Fox frowned, wonderment on her face. "I not try to scare you, Mrs. McPhail. I come to warn you. I see things." Delicate fingers sketched in the air, forming a picture known only to Fox.

"Well, you're frightening me, and you must know that's not good for the child."

Fox's face mellowed, then appeared sorrowful as she stared at Lauren's stomach. "Little Mountie baby is not meant to be born. Another baby. Another winter."

"I think you should go." Lauren rose suddenly, tipping over the cup of water and soaking the front of her dress.

Fox stood slowly. "You and I will meet again . . . soon. Then I will owe you." Without another word, she pivoted regally and left the house in a flurry of furs, as silent as she had arrived. Trembling, Lauren moved to the bedroom to change her dress. After removing her blouse and skirt, she stood in only her chemise and pantalets before the cracked mirror Adam had hung on a nail. Smoothing the fabric, she turned sideways and studied her stomach. The swelling was only slight, almost indistinguishable beneath her clothes, yet standing here, she could see evidence of the life within her, and a fierce protectiveness washed over her. Cupping her abdomen with both hands, she whispered, "I won't let anything happen to you, little one. Nothing."

Fifteen

"What's wrong?" Adam frowned and studied Lauren's pale face looking up at him. He swung a leg over Jake's back and groaned. They had ridden all night, been gone longer than he anticipated, and the trip home had been hellish, knowing Lauren would be worried.

"Nothing." Lauren shook her head and tried to smile, but a sob caught in her voice.

"McDougall, take the horses to the corral." His eyes locked with Lauren's as he handed his reins over to the constable. "What happened?"

"Adam. The boys and I thought we'd bed down in Ansgar's barn for a spell." Mike spoke from the edge of the yard.

Adam met Mike's meaningful gaze with a slight nod.

"Lauren," Adam called after her as she whirled and hurried through the door.

She was standing in front of the washbasin, both hands planted on the tabletop. "Fox came to see me yesterday." She turned to face him, her hands clasped together. "I'm sorry. I didn't want to worry you with this."

Adam grasped her shoulders, alarm rising. "What is it?"

"Oh, this is silly." Lauren shook her head. "She said she had a dream, a dream about me and . . ." Her voice broke, and she bit her lip. "She dreamed the baby died."

Adam drew a silent breath of relief. He had imagined all kinds of horrors in the last few seconds. "You know the Cree think she's crazy. You can't believe anything she says."

"I thought that, too, but . . . I don't know. She seemed so . . . sure."

Adam stepped forward and drew her against his chest. "You shouldn't let a crazy woman's ravings upset you like this."

"I know. I'm just being silly." She drew back and wiped her cheeks with both palms. "Did you find Angus?"

Adam moved away, shedding his tunic. He threw it over a chair back and reached for the dipper hanging on the side of the bucket. "Not a sign. His camp was as clean as a whistle, not even an empty bottle."

"Maybe he's moved out of the territory." The hopefulness in her voice was unmistakable.

I doubt it, he wanted to say, but reconsidered, content to let her think some of the danger was gone. "Maybe so. What's for supper?" he asked, lifting a dipper filled with water to his lips, careful to hide the trembling of his hands. Despite Fox's reputation for being crazy, she was also right in her predictions more times than she was wrong, according to the men of her village.

For a moment, Lauren didn't answer or stir from her place by the table. "I thought maybe fresh beans. Some are ready in the garden." Even though the words were ordinary, the tone was distant, preoccupied. Adam let the dipper slide back down into the bucket.

"Lauren?" He moved to her side, and she lifted her eyes to his. "I'll take care of you." He pushed back

a lock of curly hair that had strayed onto her forehead.
"I said I would, didn't I?"

Lauren nodded.

"Well, there you have it." He moved away and sat
down in his chair pulled up to a small wooden desk
he had recently made. Papers shuffled; then the
scratch, scratch of his pen filled the silence between
them.

Reports. Always reports, she thought as she
snatched up a basket and let the door shut with a bang.
So, what if she was being silly? This one time in her
life she should be permitted to be a little silly.

Slimy mud oozed up around the soles of her shoes
as she stepped over the rows of vegetables. Above her
head the sky was brilliant blue, and dabs of white
clouds floated lazily by. The sharp scent of beans settled in around her as she stooped to pick them. Her
feeling of apprehension slipped away as the methodical motion of her hands soothed her. The day was
perfect, the weather warm and clear. Happiness filled
the holes left by her fears, and she giggled softly. What
a ninny Adam must think her. She glanced toward the
cabin window where his desk sat, and guilt pricked
her. She shouldn't have worried him with her fears.
He had enough on his mind.

Off in the forest a shot sounded, followed by a
whoop. Fresh rabbit stew for tonight, she thought, or
maybe elk or deer. One of the men apparently couldn't
sleep. Straightening, she pushed back her floppy hat
and shaded her eyes to peer toward the forest's edge.
She expected to see the flash of scarlet as the hunters
rode home; instead, a lone rider on a dark horse sat
motionless. She squinted. Who was he? How long had
he been there? Tiny hairs on the back of her neck
stood up. Again, she glanced toward the cabin. No
sign of Adam. Still the rider sat, hunched over, both
hands draped over his saddle horn. She couldn't make
out his face beneath a dark wide-brimmed hat.

Dropping her basket, she started toward the house, concentrating on remaining calm and appearing that way. She didn't dare call for Adam, else she'd alert the man. His eyes drilled into her as she moved across one row, then the next, the sticky mud grabbing at her feet.

Once, she glanced back at the man. He sat straight in the saddle, the reins gathered in his hands. Another step. Another. Then she touched firm ground. Gritting her teeth against her fear, she moved languidly toward the house, her sight fixed on the window over Adam's desk. Out of the corner of her eyes she saw the man punch his horse in the side and start to move toward her, angling across the backyard instead of going around the house toward the front. Rising panic threw her heart into a furious beat. She longed to hike up her skirts and run but knew he would be on her before she reached the porch.

"Ma'am," the stranger called in a raspy voice, only a few feet behind her now.

"Yes?" Lauren stopped and whirled around.

The man swayed in the saddle. "Could I have a word with the inspector?" Beneath the brim of the floppy hat, his face was pale and speckled with red sores. Lauren drew back from him.

"Wait here," she answered, and hurried up onto the porch. Adam was stretched across the bed, asleep. "Adam." She shook his shoulder.

"Wha-?" Groggily, he turned his head toward her.

"There's someone here to see you."

"Who is it?"

"I don't know, but something's wrong with him."

Adam rose quickly and peeped out the window. "Damn," he swore, and snatched his gun out of the holster. "Get into the bedroom and don't come out. Understand?"

"What's wrong?"

"Just stay there." Wearing only his undershirt and trousers, he moved catlike to the door in sockfeet.

Lauren sat down on the bed and dug her toes into the ends of her shoes to keep from following Adam. She heard a quiet exchange outside, then raised voices. She stood and moved to the curtain to peep out. Beyond the opposite window, she could see nothing except the garden. Eerie quietness settled in, and her curiosity got the better of her. Carefully, she stepped out into the room and listened; then she tiptoed to the window by the door. No one was in the yard, and there was no sign of Adam. She moved to the window over his desk. The spot where the man had spoken to her was empty. She listened and heard nothing. Easing open the front door a crack, she peeped out and saw Adam leaning over the front railing, his revolver dangling from his hand. A ring of sweat stained the back of his underwear shirt.

"Adam?"

"I thought I told you to stay put." He whirled on her, his finger on the trigger, an indescribable expression on his face.

She stumbled backward until the rough plank wall bit into the cloth of her dress. "Who was that?"

Adam lowered the gun slowly, unable to keep the trembling out of his hands. Then he turned away and stared out across the still waters of the lake.

"Adam? Who was that?"

Again, he paused without answer.

Lauren approached him, laid a hand on his shoulder, and felt his body tremble. "Adam?"

He turned toward her, and she caught her breath. Never in all the years she had known Adam McPhail had she seen such fear on his face. "Smallpox," he whispered.

"Dear God. Where?"

"On the reserve."

Lauren swallowed, remembering an epidemic when

she was a child. Papa had left her with Aunt Matilda
while he quarantined himself with his constables in
the barracks. Despite his efforts, she had contracted
it. Her only true memory of the time was Aunt Matilda's face above her, creased with worry, holding cold
towels to her naked body as she lay on a cool sheet.
But she had recovered, as had Papa, but not so with
many of his men.

"How bad?"

Adam ran a hand over his face. "Bad."

"Where'd the man go?"

Adam jerked a thumb toward the garden. "He's
dead."

Lauren peeped around the corner of the house. The
man lay spread-eagle on the ground.

"Did you shoot him?" she asked, panic rushing
through her.

"No, of course not." Adam holstered the gun. "He
was beyond help and knew it. He came here to get
help for his people. You go up to Eric and Gretchen's.
Stay there until I send for you."

"Where are you going?"

Adam moved toward the door. "Up to the reserve
to see if I can help." He paused with his hand on the
latch. "They're so many sick already; there's no one
to tend them."

"Let me go." Lauren stopped him with a hand on
his arm.

"Are you crazy?" he snapped. "In your condition?"

"I've had it."

"What?"

"I had it when I was a child." Lauren tightened her
grip on his arm. "How about you?"

His eye met hers, and he shook his head. Her heart
began to pound. "You can't go, Adam. Let me."

"No."

"Adam, please. I may be the only person here who's
had it."

"Are there guarantees you won't get it again?"

"Most people say . . ."

"You want to risk your child's life on what most people say?"

Lauren had no response. He was right, of course, but if he left, she might never see him again. He could contract the disease and die without time for anyone to get word to her. "What about your men?"

"They'll go with me." He let the door latch drop from his fingers, then turned to face her. "I'll be careful." His hands slid up her arms to her shoulders. "I promise." He pressed her against him for a moment, then let her go and stepped outside. The door closed, hollowly echoing in the empty room.

Acrid smoke tinted the dawn a heavy gray, shielding the sun and subduing its light. Lauren shook out a rag rug over the porch railing and glanced toward the woods where Adam had disappeared three days ago. Smoke rose in a lazy column in the distance, and she shook off a wave of revulsion, knowing that Adam burned diseased bodies to keep the epidemic from spreading. Stubbornly, she pushed away terrifying thoughts and gave the rug a last vicious shake.

She tossed the rug onto the floor and was adjusting it with her toe when a grunt came from the porch accompanied by a thud against the door. She waited, fear prickling at the base of her hair; then she crept across the floor and placed her ear against the door. Labored breathing wheezed in and out. She peeked out. A man stretched across the porch, his feet on the steps and his head against the wall.

"Dear God," she said, rushing out to turn him over. His hat fell off, and she snatched her hand away. The erupting pustules of smallpox dotted his face. A hand to his chest confirmed that his heart still beat and he was still alive, but his skin burned with fever. Ridicu-

lous laughter rose in her throat as she realized the
irony of her situation. The very thing Adam sought to
protect her from now lay on her very doorstep.

She rocked back on her heels and chewed the corner
of her mouth, trying to decide what to do. How on
earth was she going to get him inside? She glanced
in the direction of Eric's store, then remembered Eric
and Gretchen had gone to Edmonton this morning to
buy supplies and wouldn't be back for more than a
month.

She lifted one arm and gave it a pull. He slid a
little on the smooth porch boards, so she planted her
heels and pulled again. This time he moved more. Bit
by bit, she dragged him inside, then dropped his arm
when he was in the middle of the cabin floor. But
once there, she knew she could never get him into the
bed.

"You'll just have to stay on the floor," she said more
to herself than to him. Gently, she placed a pillow
under his head and tugged off the heavy fur coat flung
around his shoulders. He was a young man with light
brown hair and a ragged beard. Grime darkened the
creases of his face. Lauren studied him, trying to decide if she knew him.

"He's probably a trapper," she said to herself as she
sloshed water into the kettle from the bucket by the
door. Throwing in another stick of wood, she stoked
the fire, then slammed the door and wiped the soot
off her hands onto her apron.

Moving back to her patient, she knelt at his side
and tried to remove the filthy, slick clothes that covered him, but the material was too tangled. She got
Adam's knife from the table and began to cut away
the shirt. An eye-stinging stench rose from him, and
she put her hand over her mouth to stifle a gag. As
the fabric fell away, she saw that his body was covered
with ruptured and oozing sores, some already deep
scars.

The more she cut, the worse the smell. Lauren paused and covered her nose with her arm for a moment before continuing, swallowing against nausea.

Scrap by scrap she removed his shirt, revealing a broad, strong chest. Then, she split his filthy trousers up the front of the leg and across his abdomen. The pants fell away, and he was naked underneath. Averting her eyes, Lauren placed a square piece of torn linen over his private parts and turned her attention to bathing him.

His skin was searing to the touch, hot and dry. As Lauren sponged water over his body to both cool and cleanse, pox sores ruptured under her hand, and she prayed over and over that she wouldn't catch the disease, not here, alone.

When he was clean, Lauren covered him with a clean sheet, applied cold cloths to his head, and flopped into her rocking chair. The sun dipped into a scarlet sunset outside the window, and she thought of Adam, wondered if he was well. She sat transfixed by the ribboned sky until darkness crept in and she realized that the day had passed without her notice. She rose and lit the lamps, filling the cabin with golden light. Her head ached, and her throat was dry and parched. She warmed a little broth on the stove and drank some, then tried to pour some down the man's throat, but it bubbled across his lips, to soak into the pillow beneath his head.

Night came quickly on twilight's heels and with it grateful cooling of the day's heat. Night insects tuned up, and the breeze sighed gently over the lapping water, ruffling the curtains. Lauren couldn't remember feeling so alone. She nodded in the rocking chair and dreamed that Adam was there, that he was reaching out to hold her, his fingerstips touching hers. . . .

Lauren jerked awake. Some inner clock told her it was late, past midnight. The comforting night sounds had faded into the quiet expectancy of predawn. She rose from the chair, knelt down, and placed a hand on the man's forehead. His skin was still hot and dry. He mumbled and thrashed, calling out the name "Molly." She fetched more water from the pail, dipped the cloths again, and laid them against his fevered brow and across his bare chest to ease the fever. Who was this woman he called for? His wife? Mother? Some lover?

Satisfied she could do no more for now, Lauren stepped to the window and laid her forehead against the facing. A gaunt face looked back at her, reflected in the glass against the curtain of night. Without even the company of dawn, she felt alone, lost in the vastness outside her window. Where was Adam right now? Was he safely asleep in some lodge? Her fingers curled around the window casing, growing white from her grip. When would he come home? When?

Night slid into dawn and dawn into day. Cheerful birdsongs awoke Lauren. She rolled her head on her shoulders and rubbed at a stiff neck from sleeping sitting up in the rocking chair. She leaned down and placed a hand on the man's forehead and thought it felt a bit cooler. Flinging open the door, she took the bucket and stepped out into the morning's moistness. She breathed in the cool, fresh air, just realizing how stuffy the cabin was, even with the windows open.

On her way back from the lake, she glanced again at the tree line, hoping to see Adam and his patrol emerging, but there was only the dark green of the spruces. She stepped up on the porch and into the cabin.

The pallet on the floor was empty.

Wary, she set the bucket down by the door and glanced around the room. Moving to her bedroom, she snatched aside the quilt, but no one was there. She whirled. The jail was empty, too.

"Sorry I startled you." A husky voice came from behind her, and she jumped, her heart in her throat.

The man clung to the door, rags of clothes wrapped around his waist.

"You shouldn't be up," Lauren admonished through her fear. She stepped forward and took his arm.

"A man has to do some things for himself," he said, his voice shaky and weak.

Lauren helped him past the pallet on the floor to her bed and stripped away the covers. With a groan, he lay down, his head settling into the soft pillow.

"I ain't smelled clean sheets since I left home." He turned his head to the side and inhaled. "Where'd you find me?"

"You were on my porch, Mr . . . ?"

"Bolen. Richard Bolen." He ran a shaky hand across his face. "I musta made it here by myself, but I cain't remember a thing."

"Do you know you have smallpox, Mr. Bolen?"

"Yeah. Caught it, I guess, from that bunch of whiskey traders I run up with down in Edmonton." His eyes widened. "You ain't got no little'uns runnin' around here, do you?"

"No, no children." Lauren shook her head.

"Damn pox. We had a bout of it back home a few years ago. Molly and me lost a little one to it."

"Where are you from?" Lauren asked as she tucked the quilt around him, then took the rags he pulled from around his waist beneath the cover.

"Montana."

"You have family there?"

"Yes, ma'am." His eyes found hers. "A wife and two little girls."

"Whatever are you doing up here?" Lauren retrieved a pan of water from the other room while she spoke.

"Most everything's trapped out down there. I heard there were pelts aplenty up here." He squinted at her as she wiped his face with the damp cloth. "You're the Mountie's wife, ain't you?"

"I'm Mrs. Adam McPhail."

"A trapper down on the Saskatchewan told me there was a Mountie detachment." He glanced around the room. "I guess this is it."

"You'll have to talk to my husband about trapping up here, Mr. Bolen." Lauren dropped the cloth back into the basin. "As for you, do you feel like you could drink a little broth?"

Bolen nodded weakly.

"Doesn't your wife worry about you being so far from home?" Lauren asked as she poured some soup into a tin cup.

"Yes, ma'am, she does. Molly says all the time how she wishes I'd just settle down there at home and find something to do that wouldn't keep me away at night. She hates the nights alone." He wriggled up in the bed and took the offered cup.

"How long had you been sick?" Lauren asked, folding her arms across her chest and watching him take a tentative sip.

"Days, as best I can remember. I laid down there in a cabin with more holes than walls for days, hoping somebody'd come by, but nobody did. Then I remembered somebody saying there was a Mountie here, and here I am."

Lauren sat down in the chair across from him. Beneath the dirty skin and ragged hair he was a fairly attractive man. Her heart went out to the woman waiting for him, wondering if he was dead or alive, sick or well. Maybe if Adam became sick, some Cree woman would care for him, too.

"You're very ill. You should stay here for a few days." She took the cup when he held it out to her.

He shook his head. "I can't waste any more time. I gotta get further north if the fur's to be any good at all. Molly and the babies will be needing money by next spring."

Empathy for his wife brought quick, hot tears to

Lauren's eyes. She complained when Adam was gone a few days. This woman would have to wait months to find out if her husband was ever coming back.

"Going out there sick won't solve anything, Mr. Bolen, except make a widow out of your Molly." Lauren whirled, marched around the quilt to the table, and set the cup down with a clatter.

"You sure do remind me of her; my Molly, that is."

Lauren braced her hands on the table and stared out at the empty woods. If she didn't do anything else, she would see to it that this man left her house well and fed. She could do that much for Molly.

Adam straightened and flexed his back. Death was heavy in the air, and the stench of burning flesh filled his nose. Light was rare, and dust particles danced on the one shaft that poured in through a crack in the boards.

"Paskapisis? Can you hear me?" Adam leaned down into the pockmarked face, holding his breath against the wave of odor that rippled up to meet him. "Paskapisis?"

The old man opened his eyes and squinted against the dim light. "Inspector?"

"How do you feel?" Adam asked.

Paskapisis swallowed and ran a swollen tongue across cracked lips. "The fever has left me?"

"Yes. You're one of the lucky ones."

Paskapisis studied Adam's face. "Your wife will not think you so handsome when you return home." A twinkle of humor sparked in the old man's eyes.

Adam ran a filthy hand through his hair, wincing as tangles caught in his fingers. "No, I don't suspect she'll let me in the house like this."

"How many have died?" The twinkle left Paskapisis's eyes.

"Too many to count," Adam answered.

Paskapisis looked away, trying to hide the tears that appeared at the corners of his eyes. "How many are left?"

"A few people survived, mostly young men."

"The women?"

Adam shook his head, feeling the sorrow in his own heart. "One I know of lived; another might live if she survives tonight."

Paskapisis squeezed his eyes shut, and sobs racked his thin body. "What has brought this to us, Inspector? What have we done to anger the Father of All that he has brought us this terrible sickness?"

"Whiskey traders brought you this, Paskapisis, not God. The firewater has weakened your people." Adam opened the door to the hut, and Paskapisis threw his arm across his eyes against the bright light. "We have to get some air in here." But the air that poured in was anything but fresh; instead, it was thick with stench.

"I'm going outside for a while. Do you want anything before I go?"

Paskapisis shook his head. Adam ducked and left the shack. Blackened skeletons of houses poked up like dead fingers. A fine layer of ash coated the ground and turned the trees' green foliage gray. Gaunt dogs lurked around corners, growling and fighting over morsels of food cast off by long-dead masters. Adam ran a sleeve across his forehead and noticed his underwear was no longer white but a nondescript gray, like everything else as far as he could see.

"How is Paskapisis?" Duncan asked from behind him.

He put a hand on Adam's shoulder, and he winced. Days and nights crouched at bedsides, holding hands putrid with pus and sores, had taken its toll on him. He turned and saw the same fatigue in Duncan's eyes he felt down deep in his own bones. "I think he'll make it. What about Mike and William? Are they all right?"

"Neither got the pox. Both said they had something called inoculations back East."

"I read in a paper someplace doctors could do that now."

"It's a shame and a pity they couldn't come here." Duncan looked around them at the devastation.

"I have to get home to check on Lauren. Can you and the others finish here?"

"Sure. Go home to your wife."

Adam ducked back inside Paskapisis's house, then quickly left, throwing his scarlet tunic around his shoulders. How he and Duncan had missed contracting the disease, he'd never know. Somewhere, sometime, the two of them must have come in contact with small-pox long enough to become immune. Over the years, they'd passed through many villages rife with it and nursed many stray men they suspected carried the disease.

He headed Jake out of the village and rejoiced silently as he passed out of the last remnants of ash and fire and into the green forest of summer. Breathing deeply of the fresh air, he felt better immediately.

When he emerged from the forest and spotted the tendril of smoke rising from his home, a wave of thankfulness swept over him that threatened to buckle his knees had he been walking. He punched Jake into a trot and hurried across the open area to the porch, where he quickly swung down and tossed the reins over the post. No sound came from inside as he opened the door. The house was still and quiet, neatly cleaned and tidied, but Lauren was not there.

"She's probably gone up to Gretchen's," he muttered, and strode outside.

The wind buffeted him, tossing the grass recklessly in his path. Lauren stood down by the lake's edge, arms folded, her skirts whipping around her legs. She stared out over the water, watching a distant figure move slowly around the shore.

His arms slid around her easily, and she leaned back against him without turning.

"Are you all right?" she asked, pressing her head against his throat.

"I'm fine. Tired and dirty, though." He rested his chin on her head and breathed in the familiar scent of her.

She turned in his arms and searched his face. Staring down into her eyes, he knew he was home at last.

"Come home with me and I'll fix you a bath and some supper." They started out across the expanse of scrubby growth, her arm around his waist.

"Who was that?" he asked, tossing his head toward the lake.

"A trapper from Montana. I found him on the porch one morning."

Adam stopped and took her by the shoulders. "Was he sick?"

Solemnly, she nodded, her eyes locked with his.

Adam's heart skipped a beat, and he quickly searched her face for spots. "Pox?"

Again, Lauren nodded.

"You're not sick?"

She smiled, love shining from her face. "No, I'm not sick." Then, she smoothed his face, and he felt the cinders of ash slide away underneath her fingers. "I told you I'd be fine."

He clasped her to him, the strength of his emotions overcoming him.

"What's wrong?" she asked, her voice muffled against his dirty tunic.

"Nothing," he said, his voice slipping. "The suffering I've seen in the last few days. I was worried—" He cut his words off and Lauren felt his jaw tighten against her head.

"I told you I'd be fine." They stood together, the

soft wind sliding over them. "His name is Richard Bolen. He's a trapper from Montana, and he left his wife and two little girls behind, waiting for him. He came for help because he heard there was a Mountie detachment here." She pulled back and searched his face. "Wasn't that what you wanted? People to know if they needed help, you would be here?"

"You're twisting my words again," Adam said.

Lauren smiled slyly. "Come home with me." Her fingers intertwined with his, and she stepped away, pulling him after her.

Sixteen

"Curses be on ye. Are ye a blathering idiot, boy?" Finnegan jumped off his horse and stalked toward a chagrined Constable McDougall.

Lauren laughed from her vantage point in the rocking chair on the porch. The men were putting the last boards on the barracks that connected to the side of the house. September was almost over, and winter was already evident in the nippy mornings and cool nights. Soon summer, with its melodious insects and soft, wafting breeze would be gone, and winter would again hold them in its icy grasp.

"Can ye not see, lad, that when I say, 'Swing left,' I mean swing left and not right?" Finnegan snatched the guiding line out of the young man's hand and positioned the beam himself. He lowered it gently into Duncan's waiting hands, where it was hammered into place.

"Can I get you something?" Damp hands, covered with sawdust, slid around her shoulders.

She turned in the chair. Shirtless, Adam stood behind her, his suspenders hanging off bare shoulders and slapping the sides of his blue pants.

"You look tired." His hair was plastered back with sweat, and the yoke of his pants was soaked.

"I am, a little. I want to get this finished so we can put up the barn before the first snow."

"You don't think that will be soon, do you?" Even the mention of a storm brought Fox's words back to her.

Concern knitted his brows together briefly; then he said, "Could happen anytime now."

Lauren gazed out over the lake, now teeming with life, and marveled that in weeks all this comfort would be gone.

"Mrs. McPhail?" Young McDougall hung over the porch railing, sweat running down his face in rivulets. "Could I trouble you for a cup of water?"

"Of course, William." She started to rise, but Adam pushed down on her shoulders.

"Stay. I'll get it." He shuffled off into the house.

McDougall's face reddened. "I'm sorry. I could have gotten it myself, but I was worried about tracking up your floors." He raised a boot encrusted with mud.

"It's all right. Adam worries too much." Lauren rose, half rolling out of the chair around her increasing stomach. "I can't sit in this chair all day."

"You can if it means the baby will be healthy." Adam reemerged and sat a bucket of water down on the top step.

Again McDougall colored and dipped himself a cup. Lauren glanced back at Adam and frowned. Ever since she had told him of her pregnancy, he had become overprotective to the point of distraction. He even cut short his patrols to be home at night or else made sure one of the men was.

"Adam. Can I talk to you a minute?" She moved toward the door and saw Finnegan throw Adam a raised eyebrow before he followed her.

"You've got to stop fussing over me," Lauren scolded once they were inside the house. "You embarrassed poor William. He's been a great help to me this summer, and the least I could do is get him a cup of water."

"Just don't overdo it, that's all." Adam wiped sweat off his forehead with the back of his hand. "This weather is certainly strange. I've never seen it this hot in September. Usually by now we have snow."

"Well, I'm grateful for the extra warm weather." Lauren moved toward the kitchen and stared at the stove. "Do we want to light this tonight?"

"No." Adam stepped into the bedroom and emerged pulling his undershirt over his head. "I don't think we can stand any more heat in this house tonight. Except"—he slid his arms around her waist from behind and laid his cheek against her head—"heat that we make ourselves."

Lauren pushed him away playfully.

"I'll be right back." He swept his coat up off a chair back and banged through the front door.

She stepped to the window to watch him stride around the corner of the house when suddenly a pain cut through her midsection. Doubling over, Lauren gripped her stomach and groaned. Then, as quickly as it had come, it was gone. Straightening, she breathed deeply. "Was that you kicking, little one?" she said to the swelling that shoved out the front of her skirt. "I wonder if it's supposed to be that hard?" she muttered out loud. Standing in front of the window, she turned her thoughts inward, taking inventory of each breath, waiting for another pain, but none came. "I guess that was just your way of saying hello." She moved to a worn sheet of paper nailed to the wall. "September, October, November, December. Maybe you'll be here by Christmas. You can be your daddy's Christmas present. Then I won't have to finish that scarf I'm knitting."

"Oh, I don't know. I kind of fancied having a scarf about six feet long."

"Adam! You peeked."

Adam stepped inside, fastening the last button on his coat. "No, I reached under the bed for my boot, and it jumped out at me." He picked up his gun belt and fastened it around his waist. "I thought it was a snake until I saw the red-and-white stripes. Help me with this." He buckled his belt in front, then tossed it over his shoulder.

"If you aren't good, you won't get anything for Christmas." She gave the strap an extra hard yank, and Adam grunted.

Lightning quick, he turned and encased her in his arms. "All I want for Christmas is a healthy baby."

"And I'll see you get that present, husband." She tilted her head back to meet his gaze.

"Harrumph." Finnegan scraped and scratched at the door, making as much noise as possible. "Beggin' your pardon. The boys and I'll be goin'."

"Mike." Adam stepped out of her embrace and moved toward the open door. "Be careful. I think the weather's about to change."

The two men stood inches apart, and Lauren was struck by the odd nature of their friendship. Their very lives often depended on their trust in each other and nothing else. Ultimate trust.

"I will, lad." Mike winked, then turned and thumped away.

"You're not going with them?"

"No. I'm going over to the reserve. The smallpox epidemic seems to have tamed down the whiskey trade some. I think I'll have a little talk with Paskapisis. Plant a few doubts about Angus." Adam drew his Enfield revolver, checked the chamber, then holstered it.

Lauren squinted one eye shut. "You're not staying because of me, are you? I'm fine."

"No. I'm staying because I have work to do and as much as I like them, I want Mike and the men out of our house and in theirs as soon as possible." Adam filled the doorway, his shoulders nearly touching each side.

"Well, I think I'm going to take a walk down by the lake and enjoy the warmth as much as possible." Lauren picked her hat up off the nail by the door and plopped it onto her head.

"Be careful," Adam warned. "Stay in the clear and out of the brush so Eric can see you if anything happens."

Tell him about the pain. Lauren pushed the voice of caution away. Hadn't she been perfectly healthy? No problems? Even the nausea had lasted only a few weeks. Adam would only worry. Maybe later she'd go up to Gretchen's and mention the pain to her. Surely she would know about that.

Change was heavy in the air as she stepped down off the porch. She breathed deeply and missed the birdsongs of only a few weeks ago. Now the air was still, expectant, eerie. As she walked, the feeling of apprehension increased, bearing down on her, twisting the pleasant feeling from her. She found no joy in the softly lapping waves, no pleasure in the fluffy speeding clouds overhead. Finally, she turned back and headed home. But as she neared, the dread grew.

She swung open the door and stepped into the cool interior. Waiting for her eyes to adjust to the dim light, she removed her hat. She turned, and her breath caught. Sitting in the center of the table was a package tied up with a bit of ragged cloth. She glanced around quickly. Someone had been in their house.

She moved toward the bundle and lifted it. It was light, almost as if nothing were there. Sniffing it, she found no smell. The knot holding the edge of the cloth together came untied easily. Inside was a small packet of fine brown powder and a note in a handwriting she didn't recognize.

"Drink this and rid yourself of the sorrow to come. Fox."

Lauren let the package drop to the table, scattering the powder all over. Rubbing her hands down the front of her skirt, she backed away, the horror those words imparted dawning on her. Rid herself of Adam's child? The thought was unthinkable. Flattened against the wall, she felt the baby stir inside her.

Boots scraped on the porch. She jammed the bundle of cloth into her pocket and scattered the spilled contents onto the floor with a sweep of her hand.

"What's the matter?" Adam paused, holding his hat above a nail in the wall.

"Nothing," she lied, moving toward the stove and opening the door to the firebox. "I thought you were going to the reserve."

"I did," he said, suspicion in his voice. "What's wrong?"

"Nothing. I just didn't realize so much time had gone by." She couldn't turn around and face him now. He'd see the fear in her eyes, and she didn't want to worry him. She picked up a piece of wood and prepared to toss it into the firebox.

"Leave it," he whispered in her ear as he drew her back tight against him. His fingers crept down her arm to her hand and removed the stick of firewood. He dropped it to the floor, then spun her around to face him. "The men have gone hunting. Let's make good use of this time."

He lifted her into his arms, strode to the bedroom, and laid her on the soft mattress. He loosened his lanyard and gun belt and dropped them and his coat to the floor with a thud. In a few minutes, he was on the bed with her, his shirt hanging open down the front.

"Lauren," he breathed against her cheek while his fingers flipped open button after button on her blouse. He pulled the fabric back and slid a hand inside, cupping it around her breast.

"Adam—" Lauren caught her breath with another

pain. Fear quickened her heartbeat. Maybe she shouldn't have gone riding yesterday.

"What?" He paused in his caresses.

"Maybe we shouldn't. I mean . . . well, the men could be back anytime now and . . ."

"What's wrong?" Adam frowned and sat up.

"Nothing. It's probably nothing."

"Lauren." He slid to the edge of the bed and leaned over her, one arm on either side.

"I've been having some pains. Just little ones." She closed her eyes to shut out his face.

Quietly, he rose and padded to the window, the muscles rippling across his back, making the bullet scar dance on the surface of his skin. "Maybe I should ride for a surgeon."

"Oh, Adam, that's silly." Clasping her blouse together, Lauren rolled out of bed and went to stand at his side. "The women in my sewing circle told me you'd have some little pains. I said it's probably nothing, but I tought it might not be a good idea to—"

"No. It wouldn't be a good idea." He smoothed back her hair, tracing its loosened length with his fingers. "We have to get this baby into the world safely."

Lauren laid her cheek against the soft mat of fur on his chest and heard his heart beat, felt his warmth. As long as she could stay here, in his arms, she would be safe, she told herself. He sat down in the rocking chair and cradled her in his lap. They rocked together in silence, their thoughts intertwined.

Boots clumped on the porch boards, and a deep voice cleared its throat.

Adam planted a quick kiss on the top of her head, stood, and shrugged into his shirt. Lauren scurried back to the bedroom and quickly dressed.

"Lad, take the horses to the corral." Duncan handed the reins of his horse over to William as Adam opened the door. "We're not back too soon, are we?" he asked with a crooked smile.

Adam chuckled. "No. Oh, and thanks for the time."

Duncan glanced away and smiled sadly. For all the three years he'd known Duncan McLeod, he still knew little about him. Only that he'd left a wife and children back in Scotland. Rumor was she'd thrown him out of his house in favor of another man. He'd left his beloved Scotland and come to Canada. Beyond that, Duncan McLeod disclosed little about himself.

"Well, hunting was slim." He plunked down a grouse and two rabbits. "But we saw some deer tracks deeper in the woods. Might be worth a trip out this week."

"Yes." Adam leaned over the porch railing, propped on his forearms.

Duncan studied his face and frowned. "Something you want to get off your mind, lad?"

"Let's walk around back a bit." Adam snapped his suspenders onto his shoulders as they walked. "I think I should go for a surgeon for Lauren."

Duncan stopped. "She's not in trouble?"

"I don't know. She's in some pain." Adam shrugged his shoulders. "I don't know what to do."

Duncan looked over his head at quickly scudding clouds. "Weather's about to change. The woods were unusually quiet, and we saw almost no game. She needs you here more."

"If I left tonight and rode straight through, I could be back in two weeks."

"And kill yourself in the bargain. Do you think that's what she wants?"

"I can't just sit here and wait." Adam kicked at a piece of firewood, sending it skittering away.

"Lad, your place is with Lauren. If anybody's to go, let it be me."

"I can't ask you to do that."

"You don't have to ask."

Adam gripped Duncan's arm. "What would I have done without you all these years?"

"Pretty poorly, I imagine." Duncan's blue eyes danced and twinkled, then quickly sobered. "But there's something else you should know. The lads and I saw hoofprints all along the edge of those woods, and they weren't ours."

"What are you saying?"

"I think Angus is playing with you."

Adam raised his eyes to the edge of the forest. "You think Angus has been coming here?"

"Looks like the tracks of the same horse he rode here that day."

"What do you think he wants?"

"To worry you into making a mistake."

"You know he tried to buy me off that day. Offered me quite a sum of money to turn my head on his operation."

"And if you didn't?"

Adam glanced toward the house. "He said he'd strike when I expected it the least." He stared off at the distant tree line on the other side of the lake. "He's declared war on the Mounted Police."

Lauren fastened the last button on her blouse and stared out at the scurrying clouds. Birds disappeared from the trees at the lake's edge, and leaves tumbled along the ground, hurrying after balls of dust and spruce needles. This morning's warm temperatures were now oppressive, threatening, as if gathering strength for a change. Dark clouds snaked along the horizon, poising for the strike.

"I'd better get some wood up on the porch," Adam said, scraping clods of mud off his boots on the edge of the boards.

Lauren nodded as their eyes met, her unspoken fear known between them. A storm. Fox's prediction. "Where's Duncan and the constables?"

"Duncan's going over to Frog Lake, and Finnegan and William are out riding patrol."

"Why Frog Lake?" Lauren picked up her broom and brushed dried mud off the porch.

"Police business," he said curtly.

"What aren't you telling me, Adam McPhail?" Lauren leaned on her broom.

"That I want you all to myself." He laughed as he picked her up and set her out of his way.

"But Adam, they just got back from a hunt."

Adam released her, stepped away, and headed for the water bucket, his mind whirling for a good answer. He didn't want to worry her, and he would if he told her Constables McDougall and Finnegan were out scouting the area for Angus and that Duncan was riding hard for Frog Lake and a well-known midwife who administered to settlers there.

"They'll be back before it gets really bad, and if not, Duncan has been out in these before."

"Adam, this isn't like you. Why would you do this?"

He let the dipper drop back into the bucket with a splash. "Let it alone, Lauren."

Her silent pause was as intense as if she'd slapped him.

"I'm sorry," he said, turning. She stood behind him, her arms crossed over her chest.

"This has something to do with Angus, doesn't it?"

He studied her face and felt a slow smile creep across his face. She knew him better than he'd imagined. "Yes, now don't ask me any more questions."

"I won't," she answered, and turned away as the first snowflakes hit the windows with sharp *splats*. The tinkle of ice soon followed.

"I'll get that wood." Adam snatched his hat and coat off a nail by the door and ducked outside.

Ice pellets stung Lauren's hands as she slammed down the last window sash. In minutes, the front yard was a sheet of dancing ice, mixed occasionally with lazy snowflakes in ridiculous contrast.

"The weather's been saving up for this one." Adam stomped in through the front door, sleet skittering across the floor as he shook the ice off his Stetson.

Lauren took the branch of wood he offered and turned to put it into the stove. As she straightened, a dizzying pain cut across her midsection. She groaned and grabbed her middle.

"Lauren!" Adam sprang to her side.

"Oh, God. It hurts," she said between gasps. "It's never been this bad. Get me to the bed."

Adam scooped her up into his arms and eased her gently down into the mattress's softness. As he removed his arm from beneath her legs, his coat sleeves came away red with blood. Their eyes met, and his widened with fear.

"I'm going after Gretchen." He crossed the room in three steps, but when he opened the door, the wind rushed inside, blowing down the quilt curtain wall of their bedroom. Whereas hours before the last minutes of summer had died peacefully, lazily, now a solid sheet of white shut them off from the rest of the world.

"No, Adam."

He turned, the door still open in his hand.

"Don't leave me," Lauren pleaded from the bed, her pale face a speck amid the fan of golden hair framing it.

"I have to go for help."

"You'll never make it, and I need you here with me more."

Adam glanced toward the thickening snow, solid white outside the window. Part of him needed to stay at Lauren's side, yet another part shamefully longed to fetch Gretchen and wait in the next room for what was sure to be bad news.

"Adam, please." The imploring in her voice ran up his spine. Again, blinding images of the stillbirth flashed before him, and he closed the door. The cracking floorboards shouted at him, taunting him as he crossed to Lauren's bedside. Her fingers were cold and clammy as he picked her hand up off the quilt.

"I know what you're thinking." Fright widened Lauren's blue eyes as she held his gaze. "I don't blame you for this."

Adam clamped his teeth together, wishing he could turn back time to their first day in Edmonton when he should have sent her home. He looked down at the delicate hand with the tiny golden ring signifying their vows. Her fingers curled around his and squeezed. She was comforting him when the reverse should have been true.

"I'll stoke up the stove." He disentangled his hand from hers, rose, and rehung the quilt. Maybe things would be all right, he told himself as he hooked the edges of the quilt over the nails. Maybe the bleeding would stop, but a niggling voice deep down inside said no.

He counted the months as he threw in two pieces of wood and stirred up the orange coals. It was far too early for the baby to be born. Their child wouldn't live. Slowly, he closed the door.

Lauren groaned again. Pictures of the other birth, the other dead child, the other frantic mother, spun in his mind, dizzying him as he shucked out of his coat. Drafts snaking through the cabin chilled him beneath his linen shirt. He sloshed water in a basin from the bucket in the kitchen and set it atop the stove to warm.

When he returned to Lauren, she lay very still, her eyes closed. "Lauren?" Adam's heart lurched.

"I'm all right." She opened her eyes and smiled. "The baby's still moving, so maybe he's all right."

"I have to get you out of these clothes." He rolled up his sleeves and pulled back the quilt. Lauren lay in a puddle of her own blood. It had soaked through all her clothes, the bedclothes, and the mattress. If the flow didn't stop soon, she'd die. Again, he thought of going for Gretchen. Maybe she or Eric had something to help. He glanced over his shoulder to the window and saw that the snow had whited out everything. If he left and lost his way, Lauren would be here alone. Chills of premonition racking his body, he removed Lauren's skirt and blouse. He gazed down at the ruined undergarments and drew his knife from his belt.

"What are you doing?" Lauren asked, eyes wide.

She doesn't know. "You're bleeding. Your under-clothes are ruined."

"Don't cut them. I'll clean them later."

There may not be a later. "I'll buy you more." The blade sliced through the thin batiste with a tiny tearing sound.

"Adam." Her hand covered his, and he stared down at her fingers. "I love you."

Seventeen

Unexpected tears threatened. Adam clamped his jaw tight. "I love you, too. I better see to the water." He pulled the quilt back up over her and ducked quickly into the other room.

The stove cracked and groaned cheerfully, but the room seemed cold. Adam splashed cold water from the bucket over his face, fighting rising panic. He ran a hand over his face as he peered into the cracked mirror, wondering if the same fear and panic were evident on his face that had been on Pierre's.

"Adam. Ohhh, Adam."

He grabbed the basin of water and quickly returned to the bedroom. Bedsheets knotted in each hand, Lauren lay on her back, her body stiff. "It hurts so much," she ground out.

"Maybe this will help." Gently, Adam sponged away as much of the blood as possible, but it seemed the more he washed away, the more appeared. He wrung out the cloth, then dipped it into the hot water and spread it across her abdomen. "Does that feel better?"

Lauren's eyes were squinted in pain, but she nodded. He fished another sheet out from under the bed and slid it under Lauren. Quickly, it was soaked with blood. *Oh, God.* He sat down at her side in a chair and smoothed back her hair. Now, there was little else he could do but wait. Either she would die, or the baby would be born, or both.

Outside, gusts of wind shook and rattled the house, driving tinkling ice before it. Shingles clicked and clattered as they clung to the roof beneath the relentless wind. Where were Duncan and the men? Were they trying to make their way home? If he knew Duncan, he was most likely holed up somewhere in the forest, waiting out the storm, and he hoped William and Finnegan had done the same. Inside, there was silence except for the pinging of the stove and Lauren's occasional groan.

Daylight dwindled, and Adam got up to light a lamp. The wick threw a yellow pallor over everything, making Lauren's face look even more ghastly. By nightfall, she was unconscious, only the gentle rise and fall of her chest evidence she lived. With trembling fingers, he probed her swollen stomach for some sign of life, some evidence his child was alive. Beneath his touch, he felt a stirring, ever so slight, ever so faint.

Eyes closed, Lauren's face was blank and pale, crossed only by a grimace when the pains came. Withdrawing his pocket watch from his pants, Adam checked the time. Minutes passed. The remaining light faded until only he and the bed were circled in the remaining light, the rest of the cabin cloaked in darkness. He pulled down the quilt, feeling suddenly trapped in the tiny space. The stove glowed orange, throwing shadows on the floor.

Lauren stirred and frowned, and Adam checked his watch. Fifteen minutes apart. Pocketing the watch, he again probed her abdomen and felt a faint movement. Quick tears sprang to his eyes. Safe and warm in its nest, their child was about to be thrust into the world before it was ready. Chances of its survival were slim. Spreading his fingers, he massaged, committing to memory how his child felt, how it moved slowly, turning beneath his palm.

"It's tearing me in two!" Lauren screamed, pulling the sheets up around her face.

"I'm here, Lauren." He bent over her, but she never opened her eyes.

"It's coming!"

Adam threw aside the quilt covering her and bent her knees. How could someone lose so much blood and still be alive? he wondered as he tried to stem the flow. Her pale face reddened with effort, and he knew the birth was imminent. A tiny head appeared first; then a perfect but tiny body slid into the world. A boy. Tears clouded Adam's vision as he cut the cord and cradled the child in his two palms. So small. So thin. He wiped his son clean and held him upside down. Fluids drained from its mouth. He mewed like a tiny kitten, forever imprinting that sound on Adam's soul.

But Lauren had to be his first concern. He wrapped the baby in some of Lauren's underclothes and laid it in a basket by the stove. Then, he ripped up Lauren's petticoat and waited. The afterbirth arrived, and with it, the bleeding slowed. He wiped Lauren's face with a damp cloth and covered her. There was nothing more he could do. Her life was in God's hands.

Standing over her, he'd never felt so helpless and alone in his life—and so angry. Clenching his fists, he turned back to the stove and jerked open the door. Another piece of wood slammed against the back of the firebox. Why did he bring her out here? Why didn't he listen to the little voices that warned him of impending doom? He slammed the door shut. Why did he listen to his heart?

He picked the baby up out of the basket and sat down in Lauren's rocking chair. Pulling back the swaddling cloths, he peered into the tiny face, blue veins etching across translucent skin. A hand curled around the end of his finger, so small it barely fit. *I wonder what color his eyes will be?* Adam shook his head. Even through the thick bundle of cloth, he felt the baby's body heat ebb away. Despite the roaring fire in the stove, the drafty house was still cold.

Adam unbuttoned his shirt, unwrapped the baby, and placed the tiny body against his skin. Then he pulled his jacket across them both and slid the rocking chair closer to the fire. His head sank into the cushion Lauren had carefully cut and sewn to fit the chair. All their hopes and dreams for the future had come to this. He closed his eyes, listening to the storm. Inside his shirt, the baby mewed again and moved against him. The tiny heartbeat fluttered against his chest. He wanted to open his shirt, to caress the delicate skin, but he knew the baby needed heat, so he focused his thought, his senses, on the small life clutched against him.

His jaws ached from clenching them, but he knew if he gave way to the tears, they would tear him apart. Hours passed, and the fire in the stove grew low. Several times he reached over to check on Lauren. She now slept peacefully, the bleeding stopped, unaware her son was dying.

The storm's rage abated, leaving a steady snowfall. The baby moved, then drew a deep breath and sighed away his tiny life. Adam knew the moment his son was gone, yet they continued to rock, swaying back and forth, back and forth, as time and the night ebbed away.

Dawn arrived red and angry, the sun a bloodshot eye behind the layers of storm clouds. Adam jerked his thoughts back to the present as light crept through the cabin. *Lauren.* He started to stand, then remembered the baby pressed tightly against his chest. He threw off the coat and opened his shirt. The tiny bundle was cold except for the warmth absorbed from his own body. He opened the cloth and stared down at the lifeless face, eyes closed gently in sleep. A sob threatened to burst his chest, but he swallowed it, laid the baby back in his basket, and moved to Lauren's side. She lay still, and for a panicked moment, he couldn't see the covers rise and fall with her breathing. He laid a hand on her shoulder and felt the warmth of life.

"Adam?" she whispered, her face a shadow in the dark.

"I'm here." He sat beside her on the mattress.

"The baby?"

Adam's chest tightened until he could hardly breath. "He was so little—"

"A boy?"

"Yes."

"Is he dead?"

Adam ran a hand across his face. Sorrow settled on his shoulders. "We had a son. A tiny, perfect son, but he didn't—"

"God, no," Lauren sobbed. "I want to see him."

"I don't think—"

"I want to see him."

Adam rose and retrieved the tiny body from its basket. Lauren looked down as he nestled the tiny form beside her. She pulled back the swaddling cloths and touched the now-cold skin. "He's perfect," she murmured. "All his toes and fingers. I believe he has your mouth." She looked up, smiling.

"I should take him now."

"No." Lauren pulled the baby away, raw anger on her face, her eyes a little too bright. "I won't let you take him from me."

Adam ran a hand through his hair, true terror rising within him. He eased down onto the bed. "Lauren, he's gone. He was too little, born too soon. He only lived a few hours."

She stared at him, a blink the only evidence she'd

even heard his words. "I know. I just . . ." She handed him the bundle, then covered her face with her hands.

Comforting words could not fight their way out of his own despair. Adam turned away, and as he did, a primeval sound rose from Lauren, echoing against the thick log walls, quavering, then dying with a small sob. Shaking, Adam pressed his forehead against the cold glass of the window and gasped for a breath. Lauren was in a place he could not go. A wall of regret and despair stood between them. Yet Lauren still needed his attention.

Willing himself to do what must be done, he laid the tiny body in his basket and moved back through the curtain to Lauren. She lay still, her head turned to stare at the wall. He checked for bleeding and found it had stopped. Then he went through the motions of bathing her, dressing her, changing the bedclothes in a daze. Her eyes open and unseeing, she allowed him to tend her but made no move to acknowledge his efforts.

When finally he was finished, he felt drained, tired, old. He sat down on the edge of the bed and bathed his own face with a damp cloth.

"Lauren?"

Ashen, her face showed no emotion, no sign of life. He felt her forehead and found it hot. "Dear God," he whispered. A fever. As much blood as she'd lost, she didn't have the strength to fight off a fever, or the will.

He spoke her name again, and she opened her eyes. Outside, the snow drifted down in flakes so fat, they shut out the sunlight, casting a grayness over the cabin. The absence of the roaring wind fostered a loud silence that was deafening.

He opened his mouth to speak but stopped when tears sprang to her eyes and spilled over her lids. "Can we name him?" she whispered.

"Of course we can."

"Derek Butler McPhail, after Father."

"That's fine." Adam pushed a strand of hair off her forehead and noticed her fever was rising.

"I wish I could bury him at home."

Adam swallowed. "We can bury him here, where he was born."

Lauren turned her eyes away from him to stare out the window. "I wish I had died, too."

"Shh. Don't talk that way. We can have other babies." The words sounded callous and hard, but his mind could think of no easy way to voice his hopes. God's intent was clear. Tiny Derek Butler McPhail had not been intended to live in this world.

She swung her gaze back, hard and steely. "I don't want to have any more babies here. Gretchen lost three. I can't . . . won't go through this again."

"Just because Gretchen lost three doesn't mean we will."

"We will. We're cursed."

Adam frowned, noting her speech beginning to slur.

"When I die, I don't want to be buried in this awful place. Promise me you'll send me back to Regina." She gripped his forearm so hard it hurt.

"You're not going to die." Her words frightened him.

"Yes, I am. Please don't bury me here. Promise me, Adam."

The thought of living without Lauren was unthinkable. But she was so weak, so drained.

"If I die, I can see the baby," she said with a smile; then she frowned. "Do you think I'll go to heaven, Adam?"

"Don't talk like that, Lauren. You're not going to die." Adam ran a hand through his hair, fighting down fear.

"Do you think so?"

Frantically, he searched his mind for something to

reassure her, words she could hang on to that would give her hope. Then his gaze fell on his jacket discarded on the floor. The insignias of the Force gleamed on the collar. Swiftly, he rose and removed the pins. He held them in his hand a moment, remembering the day Griesbach had pinned them on him. Clamping his hand shut, he strode to the bed. He took Lauren's hand, opened her palm, and pressed the crowns against her skin. Then he closed her fingers over them.

"I give you these as evidence of my promise," he whispered.

Lauren stirred and cracked open her eyes.

"Fight to live and I'll take you out of here. I'll take you back home to Regina."

There was no sign she heard or understood him. He eased her hand to the bed, then tucked it beneath the covers.

Adam returned to the baby. He lifted the bundle out of the basket and opened the cover. He wanted to memorize every detail of his son's body—his wispy sprigs of light hair, his tiny hands and feet. For all appearances, he could have been peacefully asleep.

Tears came in great gulps that threatened to explode Adam's chest. Droplets fell on the baby's body, and for a moment, he desperately thought his tears might bring him back to life.

Morning passed into afternoon without Adam noticing. The swaying of the rocking chair transported him into another world, occupied only by himself and the tiny form he clutched. Shadows moved across the floor, and the sky lightened.

Someone pounded on the door. Adam tore his gaze away from the baby. Again, pounding. He rose and willed his feet to move across the floor. Snow spilled inside as he swung open the door. A snow-covered figure stared back at him from beneath ice-encrusted eyelashes.

"Duncan?"

"Sweet Mother of Jesus." Duncan shook snow off his Stetson and slapped it against his leg. "What a storm. I never made it to Frog Lake. On the north side of the lake, the snow's deeper than here—"

Adam tried to make his mind function, tried to remember why Duncan had gone and why he suddenly stopped speaking.

"What's happened?" Duncan frowned. "Where's Lauren?" His eyes swept the interior, then focused on Adam's arms. "Can I come in, lad?" he said gently. He moved forward, and Adam stepped back, letting him enter.

The fire in the stove was nearly out, the inside cold and clammy. "You need a little wood on the fire." Leaving wet footprints, Duncan walked to the stove and tossed in two more sticks. "There. That's better." He turned and rubbed his gloved hands together, feeling the morbidity of the room creep in on him. He locked eyes with Adam and knew. "What do you have there?" He indicated the bundle pressed against Adam's chest.

"My son."

A chill ran over Duncan. "Where's Lauren?"

Adam nodded toward the shrouded bedroom.

"Is she all right?" Horror began to creep into his blood.

"Yes—" Adam's voice broke, and he cleared his throat.

As the wood caught and the room grew lighter, Duncan saw Adam's face, gray and drawn, his eyes bloodshot, his blond hair tousled. Bloody handprints streaked the front of his shirt.

"Why don't you let me hold the wee one and you go and see to your wife?"

Adam hesitated a moment. Lauren. He had to see

about Lauren. He handed Duncan the baby, then moved toward the bed, each step an effort. But as he moved, the fog that had muddled his mind cleared. He had to fetch Gretchen. Lauren would need her now that the storm had stopped. Then he'd bury their child. Maybe on that knoll behind the house.

Lauren lay on her back, staring with unseeing eyes at the ceiling.

"Can I get you anything?" he asked.

The look she turned on him chilled his insides. "No."

"I'm going after Gretchen."

Lauren didn't answer. Instead, she swung her gaze back to the beams over her head. He felt as if she'd slapped him.

Adam turned, then met Duncan's tearful stare. "I'm sorry, lad."

Adam clamped his teeth together. "Wasn't meant to be, that's all."

"How is she?" He nodded toward the curtained room.

Adam ran a hand over the stubble on his chin. "I don't know."

"Adam. I want to see the baby again," Lauren called.

Duncan's eyes met Adam's. "I wouldn't advise it."

Adam took the baby from Duncan and placed it in Lauren's arms. Fresh tears washed away old tear tracks as she parted the wrappings. "A boy. He was a boy." Her voice broke, and her shoulders shook with sobs. "This is what Fox said would happen. We're cursed, Adam. Cursed."

"Shh." He sat down at her side and smoothed away knotted and tangled hair.

Irritably, Lauren brushed his hand away. "Don't touch me."

"She's upset, lad," Duncan whispered behind him. "Give her some time."

Lauren turned her face away and let her hands fall away from the baby, her fist still closed. Adam picked up his son and placed it back in the basket. "I'm going after Gretchen. Stay with her. Then I'll build a coffin."

Swirling the ragged buffalo coat around his shoulders, Adam disappeared out the door. Duncan moved to the window and watched him trudge through the thick snow toward Eric's house. He had chosen to walk instead of ride the horse still tied to the porch.

Duncan removed his dripping coat and jacket, then stripped off his boots and soaked socks. He placed the wet clothing by the fire and put the rest of his belongings beside the door. When he returned and peeked in, Lauren still lay staring at the ceiling.

Duncan poured water from the bucket into a pan, dipped in a soft cloth, then came to sit on the side of the bed. "You've a fever, lass." He wrung out the cloth and applied it to her forehead.

"Do you have any children, Duncan?" she suddenly asked.

"Yes. Two daughters."

"Where are they? Is your wife waiting for you back East?"

Duncan stared into her feverish eyes. She was slipping away, into that dark place where minds go when they cannot grasp the magnitude of what has befallen them. Duncan knew well that place.

"No, they are back home on the Isle of Skye."

Lauren frowned slightly, her eyelids drooping sleepily. "Are you going home to see them soon?"

"Maybe someday soon," he lied, patting her forearm. There was no place for Duncan McLeod at his wife's table. Another man sat in that chair, bounced his children on his knee, kissed away their scrapes and heartaches.

"I should have listened, Duncan. I should have. Adam was right. Fox was right. Even Gretchen was right. This is no place for a woman and children." She gathered the edges of the sheet in her hand. "Damn this infernal wilderness. Damn it all for taking away my baby."

"Now, Lauren—"

"Don't you dare spout duty and honor to me, Duncan McLeod." She raised up on her elbows. "I don't want to hear one word about the Mounted Police."

"You'll not hear that from me. Now lie down, Lauren, before you start the bleeding again. You won't want to do that, now, would you?"

"No," she said, her voice barely a weak mew.

"Could I get you some tea?"

"I don't want any damn tea!" she shouted. "I want to be done and through with this damned wilderness once and for all." With a feeble heave of her arm, the gold Inspector's insignias clattered against the opposite wall.

"Suffer the little children to come unto me." Biting arctic wind snatched the words out of Duncan's mouth almost before they left his lips. He dropped the handful of dirt and snow into the small hole, then raised his eyes to the tiny group surrounding him. Adam stood straight and stiff, inches away from Lauren, yet not touching her. Lauren stared past them all, eyes unseeing. Duncan shivered even beneath the ragged buffalo coat, but it was the cold from within that chilled him. Adam and Lauren's grief went so deep, they could not find a way to reach out and comfort each other. Words, harsh and bitter, flew between them far into the night.

Constable McDougall wiped tears from his eyes, then picked up a shovel.

"We better get you back to the house and out of this cold," Adam said to Lauren, touching her on the elbow.

"No. I want to stay and see it finished." She yanked her arm out of his grasp.

Adam's jaw tightened.

"I don't think it's wise, lass," Duncan said. "The boys and I can handle it."

"No!" She clenched her fists at her side. "I'm not a child. I'm perfectly capable of deciding what's good for me, and I want to see my baby buried."

Adam had lifted his hands to place them on her shoulder, but he paused and let them drop.

"Let's get the job done quickly, lads," Duncan murmured.

McDougall threw in the first shovel of frozen soil, then winced as the shovel bit into the partially frozen ground. They'd tended a fire on the spot all night to thaw the ground enough to dig the grave, and their hands were a mass of blisters.

Another shovelful echoed against the simple wooden box Adam had made. Little by little the hole filled up, and Lauren never took her eyes off the ground. Then, lastly, Finnegan stacked rocks over the grave to keep out predators.

Without a word, Lauren whirled and started back toward the house, her steps faltering and uneven. A week had passed since the birth. In that time, she and Adam had argued bitterly over whether or not she should leave her bed. Finally, Adam had given in and let her have her way. Now, watching them walk away, Duncan's stomach sank. Lauren tottered on her feet. Adam walked at her side, a steadying hand on her elbow. He persisted in his aid even when Lauren pulled away. It was as if their love had evaporated like snow beneath the warm breath of a Chinook.

"What do you reckon will happen now?" McDougall nodded, packing his gloves with snow to ease the burning.

"Only God knows. Let's get back in by the fire."

Finnegan took the shovels and trudged back toward the tiny cabin afloat on a sea of white.

Lauren hung her coat on a nail by the door and sat down in her rocker, her eyes focused on the floor, oblivious to the world. Adam had run out of words days ago, and efforts to take her in his arms only resulted in her shoving him away without explanation.

With a sigh, he hung his coat beside hers and stepped to her side. He got down on his knees and picked up her hand, holding it firmly in his despite her efforts to jerk it away.

"Lauren. We have to talk about this. Calmly and rationally."

"I don't want to talk to you at all." She raised her eyes, and he saw only pain and hatred in them. "I want to go home."

He reached out a hand to smooth her hair, but she pulled away from him, flashing him a look of pure venom.

"When spring comes, if you still feel that way, I'll take you home."

She stared straight ahead without acknowledging his offer. He knew she loved him; she lashed out at him to avoid lashing out at herself. Perhaps if he were gone for a time and she didn't have to face him every day, maybe then her pain would begin to heal.

"I'm going after Angus. I'll be gone for several weeks."

No answer.

"I'm leaving Duncan here to man the detachment and stay with you."

Still no answer.

Adam clasped tighter the limp hand held in his. "I love you, Lauren." Emotion tightened his throat as he brought her fingertips to his lips. "I always will, no matter how you feel."

Slowly, she drew her hand away.

When Duncan entered the door to the barracks, only silence came from Adam's quarters. A movement outside the window caught his eye. Both hands braced on the porch railing, Adam hung his head while the cold wind buffeted his open jacket.

"I'm going after Angus," he said as Finnegan stepped to his side.

"Do you think now's a good time?" Duncan fumbled in his pocket for the bag that held his pipe tobacco.

Adam straightened, his face gray, his eyes shadowed. "I have to go, Duncan. Angus's reach is lengthening every day I spend here at home. Besides, I bring no comfort to her." He nodded toward the closed door of their cabin. "The sight of me is only a reminder of what she lost and why. She's made that very plain."

"She's in a great deal of pain, lad. Give her time to heal." Duncan dug the bowl of his pipe into the bag.

"She says she never wants to see me again. She blames me for the baby's death; maybe rightly so." Adam shrugged his shoulders and stared off at the frozen lake. "I never should have brought her here. I knew it from the start."

"It's herself she's blaming. Blaming herself for loving you and for wanting to follow you here."

Adam shook his head as he did up his buttons. "I wish I could believe that, but I know it's not true."

The match flared briefly, then gasped for breath beneath the relentless wind. "When will you be back?" Duncan mumbled around the pipe stem clamped in his teeth.

"Weeks, probably." Adam's face softened, and he

placed a hand on Duncan's shoulder. "Gretchen said she'd stay with her some, but I'm about to ask something of you I wouldn't entrust to another living man."

Duncan stared into the boyish face, now aged by the elements. "Ya know I won't refuse, lad."

"I'm taking McDougall and Finnegan with me. I want you to take care of duties here, but most of all I want you to see after Lauren."

"You know you don't have to ask."

"But I am."

"Then you know the answer."

Adam smiled and stepped toward the end of the porch.

"Won't you think about this again before you go?" Duncan asked.

"You aren't deaf, Duncan. You've heard the things we've said to each other, things no man and woman should ever say. Maybe she will come to accept the loss if I'm not here."

"She needs you by her side."

"No, she doesn't need me." Adam slowly shook his head. "Maybe she never will again."

Eighteen

Lauren pressed her cheek tightly against the glass, reveling in the biting cold that numbed her skin. Outside, the air was filled with snowflakes falling softly, silently. Earlier she had sat on the porch and listened to the silence, to the slow, muffled plop of each flake, carefully taking note of where it fell.

I wonder if it's this silent in the grave?

If she walked to the end of the porch and craned her neck and squinted, she could just make out the tiny lonely cross, brown and drab against the mantle of white.

She glanced down at the paper in her hand. Smudged and smeared, Edmund's elegant hand still sprawled across the yellowed paper.

Please reconsider your decision to pursue your marriage.

How prophetic those words were now. *Please reconsider.* She should have.

If you should ever need me, you have only to telegraph.

Should she? She rubbed her thumb over the rough grain of the paper again, as she'd done a thousand times in the last weeks. Adam had ridden off with only a curt nod good-bye, and no one had heard from him in all that time. Terrible words echoed in her head, and regret tasted bitter in her mouth. A tear dropped onto the paper, further smearing Edmund's script. The loss of the baby wasn't Adam's fault. Gretchen had said it wasn't meant to be. Yet somehow she felt the need to rail at Adam, to curse his stubbornness and his devotion to this terrible wilderness. Only once had he lost his temper and returned her barbs stab for stab. After that, he had been strangely silent, even until the day he left.

You deserve better and I can give you that and more as my wife. I will start divorce proceedings for you, and I will come without hesitation.

Yours,
Edmund

Carefully, Lauren folded the paper and slid it into her pocket.

I will come without hesitation.

"I'm going to Eric's. Anything you want?" Duncan's muffled voice asked from behind the quilt separating the quarters.

"Come on in, Duncan." She pushed away from the window and wrapped the crocheted shawl tighter around her shoulders. Her cheek still stung from the cold. "Can I get you some coffee?"

"No." He pushed aside the fabric and entered, his coat already buttoned up around his neck. "I have a pot already warming on my stove."

"Can I go with you?"

Duncan frowned. "Are you sure you're up to the walk? It's cold."

"I have to get out of this house or I'm going to go crazy. Please?" She clasped her hands together. An afternoon away from the tedium of the cabin and the reminders of what had happened there seemed like heaven.

"All right." He stumbled backward from the force

of Lauren's hug. "But bundle up and wear that old buffalo robe. It'll keep your legs from freezing. Adam'll have my hide if he comes home and finds out I let you get sick again."

Lauren let her arms slide away from Duncan's neck. "He's not coming back, and I think you know it."

"He'll be back, lass. You shouldn't be thinking such things."

"You can say all you want, Duncan, but I don't believe he'll ever come back. Oh, he'll come back for his things and to take me to Edmonton. We just weren't meant to be. I know that now."

"Let me tell you something. Adam McPhail never walked out on anything in his life, and he's not about to start now." Duncan picked up the buffalo robe and spread it across her shoulders.

"Oh, no. What about his family in England and school at Stanbridge?"

"That was different."

Lauren shrugged. "It's all the same. When things became difficult, he ran to Canada. How do I know he hasn't gone back to England and left you stranded with me?"

"You're talking nonsense, and you know it." Duncan squinted his eyes. "Now hush that kind of talk before you start believing it yourself." He grasped her forearms and shook her slightly.

"I'm sorry." Lauren ran a hand over her forehead. Where had such thoughts come from, and why was she saying these things to Duncan? "I just need to get out of this house for a while."

"Well, get your walking shoes on before I have a stroke under all this fur."

The cold stabbed at Lauren's lungs as she stepped off the porch into snow nearly ankle deep. The sun flirted with fast-moving clouds, and an occasional snowflake drifted down to land on the dark wool of her gloves. The air was so fresh, scented with sultry spruce. Birds chirped and argued in the branches of a snow-laden black spruce, knocking the snow off in comic maneuvers.

"I appreciate your bringing me, Duncan."

Duncan walked silently at her side, his eyes on the ground. "Are you sure yer warm enough? I can go back and get the horses."

"No, it feels good to stretch my legs." As they moved across the yard, Lauren concentrated on not looking toward the graveyard, not checking the alignment of the wooden cross, as she did after every storm. Today she wouldn't look. Today she'd let things be as they would for a while. "Do you think there'll be anyone at Eric's?"

"I doubt it after this last storm. Winter's moving in fast, and most folks have either left or holed up for the season."

It was only the last week in November, and already snow had stacked against the door. What if Adam was gone all winter? What if he never returned?

"Maybe I'll buy myself something. I have a little money."

"That's a good idea. Something to treat yourself."

"Maybe something to make Christmas presents." Before the words died on her lips, tears started in her eyes. The baby was to be their Christmas present. A sob worked its way up from the depths of her, but she swallowed it back. Not today. She wouldn't cry today.

The porch of Eric's trading post was stacked with furs. A few men from the Cree reserve admired the pelts, fingering the luxurious hairs. Blankets streaked with sunset colors were wrapped around their shoulders. Steel traps tinkled in a sudden breeze. Their conversation ceased, and they turned as Duncan stepped up on the porch. They parted silently to let them pass, and Lauren felt their eyes on her back. Fox had been right. By now word had circulated, but she hadn't seen a glimpse of the mysterious woman.

"Ah, Lauren." Eric's warm hands encased hers as his soft Swedish accent surrounded her. "Gretchen is in the house. Why don't you go over?"

"I will. I wanted to look around first, if that's all right?"

"Sure it is," he drawled. "You look." He waved his arm toward the tables piled high with trade goods and supplies shipped in from the East. A shelf of books caught Lauren's eye. How long had it been since she'd read a book? She moved between the tables and selected a volume off the rough shelf. *"Romeo and Juliet,* a play by Mr. William Shakespeare," the spine read. Lauren slipped her finger between the pages and opened it. As she read the familiar words, the plight of the star-crossed lovers took on another meaning. Here was a tragedy of young love, yet, too, here was a mother's loss. Two mothers' losses. Lauren snapped the book closed and searched the shelf again. *Moby Dick.* This should be safe. Tucking the book under her arm, she was weaving her way back to the counter when a strange voice caught her attention.

"Pack it good, Ansgar. It'll be a long trip back to Regina." Regina. Home. Lauren paused behind a stack of blankets and closed her eyes. The streets would be covered with snow, and everyone would be out in their sleighs. Bells on horses' harnesses would jingle, and the *swoosh* of the runners would slice through the air. Later, groups would gather at each other's houses for tea and cakes.

"I'm going down to Edmonton and catch the train back before all the passes are closed."

Lauren peeked around the blankets. A tall man stood at the counter covered head to foot in rich tawny fur. His pack bulged and bunched, pots and pans tied to the sides.

"You're not going to the Yukon to make your fortune?" Eric's voice asked, accompanied by the sound of leather latigo cinching up the sack.

"Only fools are going into the Yukon this time of year. The last paper I read said more are dying than making it over the pass."

"You are wise to get out now. Wait and I will get your flour." Eric stepped around the counter and headed for the storage room in the back. Edmund's letter crinkled in Lauren's pocket, almost like a voice urging her on.

"I beg your pardon." Lauren stepped to his side, and the man looked startled. Duncan had sauntered to the back and was asking Eric if he could be of help. "Did I hear you say you were bound for Regina?"

"Why, yes." His kind eyes brightened when they swept over her.

"Could I get you to take a letter for me?"

He studied her for a moment. "I reckon so."

Lauren leaned over the counter and snatched out a piece of paper. "I haven't seen my sister in almost a year, and we were so close." Furiously, she wrote to Edmund, confessing her failure and asking for his help. "She lives on Williams Street, and her husband's name is Edmund Higginbotham." *Please, Edmund. Come for me. I made a horrible mistake.*

"He is a physician and a dear, and I'm sure he'll compensate you for your time in delivering this." She quickly folded the letter and dripped wax on it from a candle burning on the counter.

The man stared at the note for a moment, then smiled and slipped it inside his shirt. "I'll see that it's delivered."

"Oh, and don't say anything about this." Lauren lowered her voice and batted her eyelashes. "My husband over there"—she pointed at Duncan striding toward her—"has forbidden me to write to her because I get so sad. But I just have to talk to her. It's so isolated here."

"Yes, ma'am. I surely do understand." He leaned forward, engrossed in all that she said.

"You're a dear man." Lauren laid a hand on his arm for a moment before moving to the door. "Eric, I'm going over to see Gretchen."

"Yah," he grunted, a bag of flour hefted up on his wide shoulders.

Lauren stepped outside and shut the door. A rush of something passed over her. Relief? Revenge? She couldn't put a name to it. What had she just done? She stepped to the edge of the porch railing and stared out over the lake. It seemed like years ago they had come here. Two people just starting out. Now she felt like an old woman, ragged and tired. Edmund would probably never get the note, anyway.

She turned from the porch and stepped up to Gretchen's door. Rapping twice, she pushed the door open and was greeted by the familiar scent of cinnamon and apples.

"Something smells good." Lauren inhaled and laid her book and coat on the couch.

"It is the pie. Eric wants a pie even though I save the apples for Christmas." She waved the bottom of her apron in disgust. "How are you feeling?" She talked with her back turned, stirring a large kettle on the stove that bubbled and hissed.

"Better, I guess." Should she tell Gretchen she had just betrayed Adam?

Gretchen hustled up to her and gripped her face with both hefty hands. "Your color is back." She turned Lauren's face from side to side. "But how are you on inside?"

Lauren colored. Gretchen had stayed with her those first terrible days after Adam left. Cheerful as a sparrow, Gretchen had tried to cheer her up, but her presence reminded Lauren of how hard life could be here, how unforgiving. Finally, Lauren had told Gretchen she preferred to be alone, and graciously, Gretchen had left with understanding words.

Gretchen smiled widely. "Pretty soon you have another baby in there." Gretchen patted Lauren's stomach and laughed.

The swallowed sob from earlier tried again to escape, but Lauren pushed it away for a second time. She would get through one day without crying. She would. "I don't know. I don't know if I can take the chance again."

"You will. Come here." Gretchen caught her arm and pulled her over to a southern window. There, in a simple clay pot, bloomed a beautiful pink flower. "It is snow rose. I bring it from home in Sweden from my mother's garden. It has rough time in life. First the ship, closed up in box. Then, traveling here, it get spilled, lose dirt, but still it live." Gretchen gently touched one of the pink blossoms. "Once it get burned, cold try to kill it, but still it come back." She smiled as if it were all so plain. "Now it blooms beautiful."

Abruptly, Gretchen hurried back to the kitchen and lifted the black pot off a stove eye as the scent of scorching apples filled the air. "Pot always boils over," she grumbled, wiping at the stovetop with a towel.

"I don't think I can go through that pain again." Lauren moved around the room, touching the fine articles Gretchen had gathered around her. Were they what had helped her keep her sanity when her children died? Or was it sheer willpower?

"Who says another baby will die?" Gretchen asked. "Maybe not. Babies are natural thing. You have man and woman, then baby." Gretchen clasped her hands together and smiled. For the first time, Lauren detected something different, something almost joyful in her tone. She studied Gretchen's round, pudgy face. Why, she almost . . . glowed?

"Gretchen. You're not . . ."

She rubbed her stomach and nodded.

"Oh, Gretchen. No." Lauren hadn't meant the

words to be so sorrowful, but Gretchen only smiled, a flicker of disappointment in her eyes.

"Gretchen, I'm sorry." Lauren stepped forward. "I didn't mean it the way it sounded. This is wonderful news. I just didn't expect . . . I mean I didn't think you would . . ." Lauren let her hands drop, absorbed in her embarrassment.

"Time will pass; pain will ease. Will be same with you." Waving her spoon, Gretchen moved to the table and flopped a generous piece of dough on the floured surface. "You will see."

No, I won't see because I won't be here. Lauren sat on the couch, surprise taking the starch out of her legs. How could she stay here with no husband, a burden on poor Duncan, and watch Gretchen and Eric enjoy their new family? Guilt at her selfish thought pierced her, and tears fogged her vision. What kind of a self-centered monster had she become? "I'm so glad for you, Gretchen," she said over a rattling pot.

"Eric, he is glad. Strut around like rooster."

Adam strutted just like that when I told him. "I guess most men do." Her fingers entangled in the delicate fibers of a doily as she struggled to keep tears at bay. Self-pity banged at the inside of her rib cage, and she pushed away the ugly feelings.

"This will be summer baby. Born when the air is warm and weather is good. This time he live."

But I won't be here to see it. By June, I'll be in Regina. And Adam will be here.

"I make all new curtains and things for baby. Bad luck to keep others. You help me sew." Gretchen paused in her attack of the pie pastry and peered at Lauren over cheeks smeared with flour. She was the picture of domestic happiness. *Why, God, can't I have just a little of that? Haven't I earned it?*

"I have to be going. Duncan is waiting for me." Lauren rose and picked up the buffalo coat.

"Where is Inspector McPhail?"

"He's out on patrol somewhere." She shoved the matted fur away from her mouth as she settled the heavy coat on her shoulders.

"He will come back soon?"

Lauren paused, her teeth numb from clamping them against the silent sobs that came with more and more frequency. "I don't know."

Gretchen frowned. "You don't know? He will be gone for long time?"

"Yes. He will be gone for a long time." Lauren fiddled with the arm of the couch, wishing her brain weren't so numb, wishing she could think of something lighthearted to say to take her leave of Gretchen.

"You are welcome to stay here with Eric and me." Gretchen moved around the table, wiping her hands on a cloth.

Lauren forced a smile. "No, I wouldn't want to intrude. Besides, the cabin is home now."

"Yes. But you are welcome here."

"I know." Feeling as though her chest would burst, Lauren opened the door. "I'll come back soon." Then, gratefully, she stepped outside. Cold air helped still the sobs threatening to overcome her. She breathed deeply again and stepped off the porch into the snow.

"I'll deliver your letter," a voice called across the distance. Lauren shaded her eyes, then waved to the man trudging around the shore of the lake. Her future was set. If Edmund got the letter, her marriage was finished. The thought brought her crashing back to reality. *Oh, God. What have I done?*

"Wait!" she called, but the man didn't hear her. She took a step forward.

"Lauren?" Duncan's voice spoke over her shoulder.

"What?" Lauren jumped at his voice.

"Are you ready to go?"

"Yes. In fact, I'm getting cold." Wrapping the coat tighter around her, she set off in the direction of the cabin, doubts filling her mind. Duncan lingered behind. When Lauren turned, he was watching the man disappear around the lake's edge.

"Well, at least we know where they are now." Adam lowered the spyglass from his eye and squinted against the white glare. Below the rise where he, McDougall, and Finnegan crouched, a thin brown line of wagons and horses crawled along, struggling through the snow.

"I guess Angus delivers despite the weather." Adam ran his hand over the rough stubble on his cheeks. "He's headed for the border, and my guess is he'll have to freight it all the way." Adam stood and stowed the spyglass in his saddlebag. "This must be an important shipment if Angus himself is delivering it."

"Are we going to follow them all the way to the border?" McDougall asked, shifting in the saddle.

Adam turned toward the two men at his side. For weeks now they had followed him without complaining, even when he drove both them and himself beyond endurance. Not a word had they said, even though he was sure they knew the source of his motivation. "No. I think it's time we went home."

The two men exchanged glances of relief.

"We can get reinforcements from Fort Saskatchewan, now that we're sure of his trail, and clean him out."

"Think we'll be home by Christmas, Inspector?"

Adam mounted Jake, then shifted in the saddle, feeling every mile he had ridden in the last two months in his bones. "We should be if there's not another storm like the one last week." A sudden blizzard had torn across the prairie with a vengeance, obliterating landmarks and dumping two feet of snow on their cave shelter. For three days they had huddled together, waiting to die. Then a Chinook had melted the snow and granted them pardon. During that time, poised between life and death, Adam thought of nothing else save Lauren. The bitter words between them had faded. The baby's death had been no one's fault, but Lauren's pain was bottomless. She'd lashed out at him because he was an extension of her. She'd blamed him because she blamed herself. Now it was time to go home and set things right.

"We leave in the morning." Adam drew up his reins and turned his horse.

"Hold it right there, McPhail," a voice growled, accompanied by the unmistakable click of a revolver's hammer. A throaty chuckle vibrated behind him. "The woman has made you slow, McPhail. A year ago I couldn't have gotten within half a mile of you."

Angus released the gun hammer, and Adam heard it slip smoothly into a holster. He whirled and stared into Angus's grinning face.

"That's twice I've got the drop on you, Mountie. Twice." He held up two dirty, beefy fingers.

Adam searched for words, his brain suddenly devoid of comment. How could Angus have slipped up on all of them this way? He glanced up at the two chagrined constables. He couldn't have if they weren't all so dog tired. He had pushed them past their limit and endangered their lives.

"Now if I was of a mind to kill you, I would." Angus twisted the ends of his beard. "But I ain't. Not just yet, anyway." He sauntered around them, hands stuck into the band of his pants. "First I got a present for the inspector here." He reached a hand into his pocket and pulled out a woman's undergarment, delicate and fragile in Angus's grip. Adam immediately recognized the chemise as Lauren's.

"You bastard—" Adam leaped from his horse's back, but McDougall landed lightly at his side, a hand on his gun arm.

"Easy, Inspector. Let's hear what he has to say first," William whispered.

Angus hooked a thumb in each side of the garment and held it up. "Imagine the trouble I had getting this." He grinned broadly.

Adam willed his face blank, commanded his heart to stop thumping so loudly, and ordered his brain to think. "If you had taken that off my wife, Angus, you'd be showing some scars."

McDougall chuckled, and Angus's glance darted in his direction. Adam detected the first sign of uncertainty.

"She weren't in no condition to protest, as I remember."

From the corner of his eye, Adam saw Finnegan slowly draw his revolver. "Finnegan. No."

Finnegan glanced at Angus, then Adam, and holstered his gun.

Adam frowned. "What do you want?"

Angus smiled again. "It ain't what I want. It's what I don't want, and that's you on my tail. Interferes with business, you see." Angus dropped the chemise on the ground. "Yore lady's safe, leastwise she was when I saw her last, but I snuck these out of yore house without anybody knowing, and I can do the same again."

"So, you want me to let you alone while you cart whiskey out of my territory by the caseload."

"That's about the size of it."

"Or you'll what?"

"Or the next time I bring you these,"—Angus ground the fabric into the snow with the heel of his boot—"yore wife'll be in 'em."

Nineteen

"Where is my chemise?" Lauren muttered, staring at the clothesline. "I hung it out here last night." She stalked over to the rope strung between the house and a scrubby black spruce. Even the clothespins were gone. She scanned the snow, then squatted and examined hoofprints that had churned the snow into brown mush.

Apprehension raised the hair on the back of her neck. Slowly, she straightened and searched the edge of the woods, remembering the day Black Angus had come before. She began to back toward the house, watching the tree line, wondering if he sat on his horse somewhere in there, deep in the bare forest, watching, waiting.

When her fingers slid across the metal door handle, she grasped it and shoved the door open, then slammed it behind her. Relief poured out in a sigh.

"Duncan!" There was no answer from the barracks. "Duncan?"

Nothing.

Where could he have gone? He had been inside when she went out to the clothesline. Every crack and pop of the stove jolted her. Every window yawned wide, and she felt eyes on her from every side of the house. Her back against the wall, she slid around the room, keeping the side yard in her sight. Adam's extra rifle lay beneath the bed, where he had left it. Lauren reached the hanging quilt. If she went behind the quilt, she couldn't see, and yet if she didn't, she couldn't get the gun.

With a final glance outside, she dove inside and snatched up the gun. She fumbled with the buckskin case, and the rifle slid out and clattered on the bare wood floor.

"Are you all right?" Duncan stalked through the door without knocking, his suspenders swinging loose.

"N-no," Lauren stuttered. "Outside, at the clothesline. Somebody's been here." She pointed toward the back of the house.

"Since last night."

Duncan frowned. "Stay right there and put that gun down." He disappeared, then reappeared with his revolver in hand. "I'm going out to check," he said, snapping his suspenders back over his shoulders. "Now, don't shoot me." He peeped out the door, then slid through. Lauren slammed the door shut, threw the bolt, and moved to the window. Duncan was nowhere to be seen. She listened for the crunching of his boots but only heard the gentle sigh of wind caressing the corners of the house. Minutes ticked by like hours, and with each passing second, her nerves tightened.

Then the silence was broken. A sharp yelp and quick words filtered through the cabin's thick walls. Lauren crept to another window and peered outside. The snow was smooth and unbroken. Voices ebbed and flowed softly, and she couldn't recognize them. Gathering all her strength, she shoved through the front door, the rifle clutched in her hand.

Duncan stood in the yard looking up at a man on a dun horse. Two others flanked him.

"Adam," she said, weak with relief.

Adam turned from his conversation with Duncan. His eyes were bloodshot and dim, his face shadowed by a scraggly beard. His once immaculate jacket was now torn and stained.

She propped the gun up against the wall, wanting to rush into his arms, but there was no welcome in his eyes. Their last words were a faint memory, dimmed in her mind by the pain that had fogged her thoughts. All she could clearly remember was the pain in his eyes when he'd walked out the door.

"How have you been?" His words were flat, toneless, as though spoken to a casual acquaintance.

"I've been fine," she lied, trying to keep her voice as flat as his. He stared at her a moment more before returning to his conversation with Duncan. Lauren strained to hear but couldn't make out the words. She shifted her gaze to Jake, lathered and exhausted, great clouds of fog erupting from his nostrils. Apparently, Adam had ridden hard to get here. He dismounted and handed Jake's reins over to McDougall. His steps were tired and plodding as he waded through the snow. She thought he would come toward her, and a thousand things rushed into her mind, words she'd turned over and over for the last months. But he veered and strode toward the barracks's entrance instead.

All of the wilderness laughed at her. She heard it in the swishing tree limbs bowing under the voice of the wind; she heard it in the soft cluck of a bird hidden in spruce boughs. "You won't beat me. You won't," she said to the sky. "You won't take him away from me. Not again."

"She's been like this for weeks now." Duncan nodded out the window at Lauren, fog from her breath showing as she spoke out loud. "She's been talking to herself, acting jumpy and jittery. Then, this morning"—he let the burlap curtain drop closed—"she found tracks out under the clothesline."

"Tracks?" Adam asked, rubbing his hands together in front of the barrel stove in the barracks.

"Shod horse. Not more than a day old."

Adam unbuttoned his jacket and took if off. "Why the clothesline?"

"Now, that's an odd one." Duncan clamped the pipe stem between his teeth and stirred the bubbling pot of stew. "She said her chemise was missing," he said, his speech slurred by the pipe.

Adam felt the blood leave his face.

"That mean something to you?" Duncan asked.

Hands behind his back, Adam walked to the window and raised the curtain. Lauren had disappeared from the porch, and soft movements from the other side of the wall betrayed her presence in their cabin. Adam reached into his pocket and pulled out Lauren's chemise, dirty and ragged. "Angus brought this to me," he whispered.

Duncan's eyes widened. "He was here?"

"He or one of his men."

"Holy Mary and Jesus. And what were you doing talking to the likes of him instead of tying him hand and foot?"

"He had me at a disadvantage." Adam slipped the garment back into his pocket.

"And what did the scoundrel want?"

"About what you'd guess. He wants me to look the other way and he'll stay away from Lauren."

"Are you or I going to Fort Saskatchewan for reinforcements?"

Adam stared out over the lake, its shiny surface reflecting the sun in silvery rays. Suddenly he felt very tired and old. "Send William and Finnegan the day after tomorrow. I'll draft a letter. Now"—Adam dropped the curtain and picked up his coat—"it's time I went home."

Lauren opened the door to the stove, and a rush of heat poured out, fanning tiny hairs around her face.

The scent of hot cloth swirled up around her as she pulled out the pan of biscuits and set them on the table. Casting a glance over her shoulder to the door, she slammed the stove door shut and straightened. Adam had been home for more than an hour without coming inside. Guiltily, her thoughts strayed to the hurried note she had pressed into the stranger's hand. "It'll probably never get there. He'll lose it before he's halfway across the country," she muttered, smoothing back loose hairs.

"What'll never get there?" Adam filled the doorway, cold air rushing past him. He looked wonderful. Despite the scraggly beard. Despite the ragged clothes.

"Nothing. Just talking to myself." Lauren took a step forward, then stopped. What did she see in his eyes? Welcome? Forgiveness? Need?

Slowly, he stepped inside and closed the door. Then he removed his gloves and his battered Stetson, placing each carefully in its place. All the while, Lauren searched for something to say, something to ease this awful awkwardness between them. By the time he had his coat off, she had finally formulated a question.

"How was your trip?" She winced as the words left her mouth, aware that they eerily echoed another awkward meeting less than a year ago.

That fact didn't escape him. "I seem to remember you commenting those weren't fit words after a long absence." He smiled, and she noticed the lines of fatigue around his mouth and eyes, the same shadows that had been there when he left, only now deeper.

"I don't know what to say to you." Lauren threaded her fingers together and forced herself to meet his gaze, barreling headlong into the conversation she had dreaded for weeks.

"Nothing needs to be said." His tone was brisk and straightforward, yet coolly polite.

"I don't remember much of what I said, but I remember that I hurt you. I'm sorry." Lauren watched his face for a reaction, but his training served him well, and she could tell nothing.

Adam stepped forward. Her arms tingled, and she longed to press her cheek against the comforting rhythm of his heartbeat; then he brushed past her and hung his tunic on a nail. He moved back and stood in front of her. His shirt was torn and muddy. A spot of blood stained one shoulder. She wanted to ask him if he was injured, but the steeliness in his eyes stopped her.

"I'm sorry for the harsh words between us." His tone was even, emotionless.

"I am, too."

Tiredly, he yanked his shirt out of his pants waist and slipped his suspenders off his shoulders. "We were both raw, and lashing out at each other seemed the natural thing to do."

In berating Adam for the death of their child, she had brought to life his worst fears, fears he had warned her about time and again.

"I was wrong to blame you." Lauren stepped closer, wanting to embrace him, but something about him was different, warning her away. "It was nobody's fault except maybe that of this eternal wilderness."

He glanced down at his boots. Mud caked his hair and spattered his face. "Would you like for me to heat some water so you can bathe?"

With a groan, he sat down in a chair and pulled off one boot. "That would be nice." The other thumped to the floor.

Lauren turned to the bucket on the counter, but it was almost empty. She picked it up, and Adam's hand covered hers.

"I'll fill it," he said. Too soon his fingers slid away.

Methodically, he put his boots back on and trudged outside.

Lauren watched him, coatless in the snow, as he bent at the lake's edge and filled the bucket. His steps were uncertain and shaky as he made his way back.

He poured water into a pot on the stove, then sat down. Lauren picked up his jacket to brush, then noticed the missing insignias. She realized she hadn't seen them since that day. Had Adam picked them up? Or had they gotten lost, swept out with the dirt and mud.

Adam stood and removed his shirt and pants. Standing in the suit of dirty underwear, he looked defeated. "Would you call me when the water's hot?" His eyes met hers for a moment; then he disappeared behind the hanging quilt. She heard the mattress protest as he lay down on it. In moments, his breathing was even and regular.

She took a brush down off a nail by the door and stroked the scarlet serge, stifling a sneeze from the cloud of dust that rose from it. As she brushed, she noticed that the material beneath the missing insignias was brighter than the rest. How many years had he worn this same coat? she mused.

Her fingers played over worn spots in the fabric. Here was the hole she had mended after he was shot. There a tear while carrying her through that awful storm last spring. She turned the coat inside out and held it to her nose. Despite the dirt on the outside, the inside smelled like Adam, like wood smoke and spruce needles and something else that was uniquely his. She closed her eyes and summoned the memory of that scent when they had made love.

More images flooded back. She smoothed the satin lining against her cheek. How deep was the chasm between them now? Would she ever inhale that scent again while clasped next to his pounding heart?

She let the coat drop to her lap. He had promised to take her home come spring. Should she remind him of his words? Could she separate the man from the land?

The lid on the pot jangled, and she jumped to her feet.

"I'll get it." Adam's voice spoke behind her. He reached over her shoulder and picked up the pot by the handle with a bit of cloth and lifted it off the stove. Then he padded barefoot to the door, opened it, and dragged the tub inside. He dumped the bucket out, then scooped up a bucket of snow from by the front steps and added it to the steaming water.

"I'll just see to these rips." She turned away as he slid the underwear off his shoulders and stepped out of the garment. She was suddenly shy, embarrassed at the sight of her husband's naked body. She heard the water slosh as he eased into the tub, then silence. His head was back against the edge, and his eyes were closed. Wisps of steam rose around him. "This feels good," he said in a throaty, tired whisper.

Lauren moved quietly into the bedroom and rummaged under the bed for her sewing basket. She sat on the mattress's edge and examined the coat closer. Regret filled her at memories of other, playful times. Naked, he'd chased her around the cabin while she shrieked that Finnegan or the constables might come in at any time. But now he remained silent except for the occasional splash of water.

"Do you want your other pair of underwear?" she called through the quilt.

"I already have them."

"Oh." She sat down on the bed and threaded a needle with the last length of scarlet thread. She'd have to remember to see if Eric had any more. "Do you want something to eat?" The thread swished in and out of the material, neatly closing one rip, then two.

"I ate earlier today."

Lauren bit off the thread, then held up the jacket. Bedraggled and stained, it would have to do for now. Dropping her hands to her lap, she waited for him to say something else, but he remained silent. She peeked around the curtain. The water was still, and he slept. Tiptoeing despite squeaking boards, Lauren skirted the puddles of water on the floor and tended the fire in the stove. She approached the tub and dabbled a finger in the water. It was still warm, but growing cooler.

"Adam." She laid a hand on his shoulder.

He jumped, blinked, then focused blurry eyes on her. "What is it?"

"Your water's getting cold."

"Oh." He looked down, bewildered for a moment. "I'll get out."

Lauren reached for the towel at his side, but not before his hand closed around it.

"Sorry." Lauren withdrew her hand.

He stood, unabashed, and dried off while Lauren's eyes scanned his lean body. He was thinner, tougher than before. There were two new scars on his shoulder where she'd seen the blood on his shirt. She looked up. His eyes met hers for an instant, then looked away. With a soft groan, he leaned down and picked up the clean set of underwear he'd left home and stepped into them. Reminded of their first night together, she thought again of how soft the fabric would feel if she could just lay her head on his chest.

"I mended your coat." She held up the garment. "But I'm almost out of thread."

He picked up his towel and threw it over the back of a straight chair. "Soon you'll have all the thread you need."

Lauren raised her eyes at the unfamiliar tone in his voice. "What do you mean?"

He leaned against the wall and crossed his arms

over his chest. "As soon as I have Angus in custody, I'm leaving the Force."

Regret outweighed the joy his words produced. The serge coat weighed heavy in her lap. "Are you sure you want to do this?"

He pushed away from the wall and padded toward her on bare feet. His stern expression melted. Lauren tilted her head back as he stopped in front of her and looked down. "I made you a promise."

Part of Lauren wanted to let him out of his commitment, but another part of her wanted desperately to quit this place. "I won't hold you to it." The words left her lips like dry sand.

"But I will." He cupped her face in his hands and drew her lips close to his. "Nothing on this earth is more important to me than you. Before, there was something in me that just couldn't let go. Now I can."

He was trying to soothe her doubts, but she knew deep inside his feelings about his job and his country had not changed. He was doing this for her, giving his life for hers. "Couldn't you work in the Regina headquarters?"

"The Northwest Territories are expanding, Lauren. Men are needed out here. There would be no guarantees I could remain in Regina. I won't take that chance."

Lauren looked deep into his clear gray eyes, searching for honesty, for some clue that he truly wanted to do this, but his eyes were guarded, giving away none of their secrets.

Adam watched Lauren struggle with his admission, saw the joy ripple across her face, followed closely by confusion and doubt. Now, as she searched his face, he felt a surge of love for her that floated him above the harsh words that had kept them apart. He leaned closer and tasted her lips, savored her flavor. Long-pent-up desires flooded out with such force that a chill rushed over him. Her arms snaked seductively around his neck, and fingers entangled in his hair. She drew in deeply, then breathed out slowly, languidly, and her warm breath on his skin aroused him with such a rush that his head spun.

He carried her to the bed and sank into the mattress with her. As his weight came to rest on top of her, she popped open each of his buttons. Satin fingers smoothed over his shoulders and down his arms, pushing his shirt down to his waist.

Crack! Pop! A hail of gunshots broke the silence. Adam rolled off the bed, grabbing his gun out of the holster hanging on a chair. "Get down, Lauren!" Flattening himself against the floor, he crawled to the door and flung it open. Bullets splintered the wood by his head and pinned him down so that he couldn't see who was shooting. Then, as suddenly as they had began, the shots ceased. He crawled to the edge of the porch and peered around to see Finnegan, calmly standing in the yard, taking aim at a mounted figure crashing out of sight into the dense forest. McDougall and Duncan were getting up from behind the woodpile.

"What's going on?" Adam shouted.

"Some crony of Angus's paying us a visit." Finnegan holstered his still-smoking revolver.

Adam stood and walked out into the yard. "Anybody hurt?"

"Nope. McDougall there saw the bastard ride up as bold as brass and take aim at your cabin. The lad was in the hip tub, but he climbed out soon enough." Finnegan chuckled, and McDougall colored. "Fired the first shot as naked as the day he was born."

"You want we should go after them?" William asked.

Adam squinted at the forest's edge and shook his head. "No, they're long gone. If his plan is to draw us out, separate us, I won't play along. Let's get inside. There's no guarantee Angus is through with us."

"No, but I think he's driving home his point."

"His way of saying, 'Get out'?"

"Something like that."

"Well, I'm not going. Not before I get him, at least."

Finnegan halted his steps across the yard and turned to look at Adam. "What are you saying?"

"I've promised Lauren I'd leave the Force as soon as Angus is in custody."

Finnegan frowned. "Are you certain?"

Adam stared off at the lake, then swung his gaze around to the emerald forest of evergreens. "As much as the Force means to me, as much as this land means, she means more, and life here is too rough for her."

"What will you do with yourself?"

"I don't know. I'm sure I can find something to do in Regina."

"Keeping store, maybe. Can you see yourself behind a counter waiting on impatient women buying yard goods?"

Adam smiled. "No, can't say as I can see myself doing that, but still, a promise is a promise."

"And what does Lauren say about this?"

Adam stared at the cabin window where he knew Lauren stood, her heart in her throat. "She hasn't said."

Lauren watched the two men's lips, straining to see what they said. But beneath the bobbing mustaches, she couldn't make out a word. Twining her fingers together, she willed her hands to stop shaking. Again, in a fraction of a second, she thought she'd lost Adam. As she watched, he scanned the lake and the trees, knowing he looked for trouble but also knowing that the beauty did not escape him. He'd said he was resigning, but what kind of man would he be then? What would he do? He walked toward her with long strides, then stepped up on the porch and into the house.

"What was it?" Lauren asked as he returned his gun to its holster.

"Angus sending his best." Adam moved toward her and tickled her neck with his lips. "Where were we?"

Lauren stopped him with fingers on his lips. "We need to talk about this."

"About what?" He brushed her hand away and kissed her.

"About your leaving the Mounted Police."

Adam sighed and released her. "There's nothing to talk about."

"Adam." She caught his arm as he turned away. "You can't just walk in here and announce you're resigning."

He padded on bare feet to the window and stared outside, where snow was beginning to fall again. "I knew when I brought you here that life would be hard, downright impossible sometimes. I knew you weren't up to that, but I hoped you would adapt," he said over his shoulder. "But when we lost the baby, I knew you'd never forgive either me or the wilderness for the loss of our son. I can't ask you to endure any more."

Something inside Lauren screamed no, but she stifled it, clamping her teeth together to keep from saying the words. They were going home, home to Regina and the comforts of modern life, away from the sorrow and trouble of a life devoid of so much. Maybe he would adapt, a little voice said; maybe he'd find something to do he enjoyed. He'll never be anything but a Mountie, another voice chimed in. Lauren pushed the second voice away, smothering it with an imaginary hand.

"What will you do?"

"I don't know." He turned from the window. "I'll find something. Now, come here." His eyes darkened, and he reached for her. As he clasped her close, pressed her cheek against his chest, the steady *thump, thump* of his heart seemed to taunt her, to scold her for her unfaithful thoughts. He picked her up in his arms, and as he passed through the quilt curtain and closed it behind him, thoughts of her letter to Edmond faded like ink left too long in the sun.

Twenty

The yard was a sea of jangling harness and scarlet-clad men milling around in the mud. Weeks ago, Adam had send McDougall to Fort Saskatchewan for reinforcements, and yesterday they had arrived. Adam was going after Angus with everything he had. Folding her arms across her chest, Lauren watched him moving between the men, his face solemn and strained.

Despite the blending of their bodies, there'd been no blending of their souls. He was holding fast to his promise to take her home, and she couldn't let him sacrifice all that he was for her.

"Mount up!" Adam's voice rang out across the yard as he turned and strode toward the house. Saddle leather creaked in unison as the men swung up onto their horses' backs.

Adam guided her inside the cabin and shut the door behind them. While his men waited for him outside, Adam smiled down at her. "Keep safe."

"I will. You, too."

He laid his hands on her shoulders. "Know that I love you. Despite all that's happened, that hasn't changed."

A lump threatened to choke off her words. "I know."

"William's going to stay behind. Don't hesitate to call on him for anything you need."

"I will."

Time hung between them, throbbing with urgency. She closed her eyes. His kiss brushed against her lips. "Good-bye."

When she opened her eyes again, he was halfway out the door. The detachment turned to leave before he was in the saddle, and he mounted Jake on the move. As he cantered to the head of the group, he turned back and waved.

"Is there anything else that needs to be done, Mrs. McPhail?" William asked.

Lauren swallowed. "No. I'm fine."

"I got some harness to fix, so I'll be in the barracks if you need me." He strode away, and loneliness descended. She had turned to enter the house when she heard a distant voice call her name. She paused, thinking Adam had turned back. But this voice was coming from around the lake, in the opposite direction Adam had taken. Discounting it as the wind, she started inside, but it came again, a low shout, almost lost in the wind's voice.

She walked back out to the edge of the porch and shaded her eyes. Far around the lake was a tiny figure on horseback, leading another animal burdened with packages.

"Hello," the voice called again.

"Edmund?" Lauren muttered. "Edmund!"

"Lauren! Hello!"

"Oh, my God, it's Edmund." She'd stopped thinking about the letter and had convinced herself the trapper had probably lost it someplace. Those horrid days were only a faint memory now, and the reality of his presence was a shock. What would she tell him? How would she explain her urgent request?

She watched him grow larger and larger until she could make out his rumpled, but stylishly cut, clothes.

Had he come all this way on his own? Hurrying inside, she smoothed back her hair in the cracked mirror and adjusted the neck of her dress. In the mirror's reflection she saw Adam's extra coat hung straight and neat on the nail, his pants flung across the bed, the rumpled covers from last night, tiny, intimate reminders of their life together.

Guilt weighed her down until she could barely make her feet move across the floor. She picked up the room, spread up the bed, then sat down in a chair to gather her thoughts. The wind changed its voice from a howl to a whine that grated on her nerves as she waited to hear hoofbeats in the yard.

Minutes ticked by. Lauren fought the urge to go to the window and look out. She turned her explanation over in her mind. How on earth was she going to explain such an impulsive, selfish act?

A knock on the door jarred her out of her thoughts. With a deep breath, she walked to the door and opened it. Edmund stood on the porch, a buffalo coat pulled high around his neck, a floppy hat shading his face. Several days' growth of beard shadowed his cheeks.

"Lauren." He clasped her hand and kissed her gently on the cheek. "I got here as quickly as I could."

"Edmund. It's so good to see you. Come in." She stepped back to allow him to enter. He took off the hat and smoothed back ridges of russet hair.

"Rustic, but quaint house." He laid the headgear on the table and took off his coat. "A trapper in Edmonton sold me this smelly thing. He said I'd need it, and he was right."

"Did you come alone?" Lauren closed the door and stood with hands clasped in front of her.

"I had a guide for about half the way; then one night he just disappeared. I came the rest of the way on directions and a compass." He smiled softly at her,

and guilt stabbed her like a lance. "Has it been horrible for you?"

Lauren looked down, unable to meet his green eyes.
"Edmund, I have to explain." She spread her hands
in a gesture of helplessness. "Life here has not been
easy, and I'm afraid I may have misled you."

"Oh?" He raised his eyebrows. "I have the feeling
this is something I won't like, so why don't we have
a cup of tea first." He reached into his suit coat and
produced a tin of Earl Grey tea—her favorite.

While Lauren set water to boil, they chatted ami-
cably about home and common friends, carefully
avoiding the subject of the letter. Finally, they sat
across the table from each other, hands wrapped
around their teacups.

"So, I am sated with tea and warmth and ready to
hear your confession." Edmund leaned back and
smiled lazily.

Lauren felt her cheeks throb with heat. "I have
taken grievous advantage of our friendship."

"Well, that is what friendships are for."

"Not in this case. You see"—Lauren shifted in the
chair, wishing somehow she could make this easier—
"somehow, Adam and I lost each other for a time. I
was lonely and in despair, and well, there was a trapper going back East. I had been reading your letter,
and—"

"You thought even life with good old Edmund
would be better than this." His harsh words cut
through her.

"No, that's not at all what I thought. I was terribly
homesick, and well—"

"I'll let you off the hook, my dear." Edmund leaned
forward and wrapped his hands around hers. "I understand. In fact, I thought it might be something like
that. I would have come, anyway, if just to see that
you were faring well."

Lauren stared into his gentle eyes and wondered

why some young woman had not already claimed his heart. The answer was a dull throb in the back of her head. "I don't deserve your friendship."

Edmund's eyes softened, and he tightened his hold on her hands. "I once offered you more than friendship."

"I didn't realize you felt that way. Why didn't you say something before I left?"

Edmund sighed, released her, and rose to wander to the window. "You're right. I didn't make my intentions clear, but then I didn't think I had to put into words what we felt for one another." He rested an elbow on the windowsill and scraped a hand across his beard stubble. "I thought that our time together would speak for itself."

"You were my friend when I needed one the most, but—"

"But Adam is in your blood."

"Yes. I guess you could say that."

Edmund moved from the window and came to stand in front of her. "I look forward to again meeting Inspector McPhail, absent slayer of young women's hearts."

"He's not here. He's just left on patrol."

Edmund raised his eyebrows. "Leaving you here alone?"

"No. Constable McDougall stayed behind with me."

"How long will he be gone?"

"I don't know. Days, maybe. He has a large territory to patrol."

Abruptly, Edmund squatted in front of her. He entwined his fingers with hers and leaned close, the scent of his favorite cologne swirling around them. "Are you truly happy, Lauren? Is he all you expected, the love of your life? Say that you are completely happy and I will gladly go back to Regina."

Niggling doubts popped to the surface of her

thoughts, and she shifted her gaze beneath Edmund's stare.

"I did not come on the request of your letter alone."

Lauren glanced up.

"The Regina paper is filled with stories of the expanding Territories, wild stories of whiskey traders and unyielding hardships."

"I knew what I had bargained for."

"But you didn't know it would be this difficult, did you?"

Tears pricked the backs of her eyes as traitorous thoughts flooded into her mind.

"I talked with Commander Griesbach in Fort Saskatchewan, Lauren." His grip tightened. "I know about the baby."

Lauren met his eyes, deep pools of compassion. A sob wrenched itself from her.

"That is a difficult loss for any woman, but under these conditions, it must have been horrible."

Lauren put a hand to her face, struggling to control her slipping emotions. For a moment, she longed to lose herself in Edmund's comfortable embrace, to place her burdens on his ample shoulders, as she had done at her father's death.

"You cannot say that you are completely happy, can you?"

Her brave front was crumbling.

"Can you?"

"No." The word rushed out as the last of her defenses fell. "No, I can't."

Edmund put a hand behind her head and pulled it to his shoulder. Shuddering sobs racked her body as she let her misery pour out. How she wished she could have cried with Adam. How she wished they could have held one another and let the sorrow and the disappointment flow out. But Adam was not the type of man to give way to his emotions like that.

"Harrumph."

Lauren sprang away from Edmund and saw McDougall standing in the open door.

"Pardon me, Mrs. McPhail." Nervously, he twirled his Stetson in his hands. "I knocked, but you didn't hear." He cleared his throat. "I was going up to the post and wanted to know if you wanted anything."

Lauren wiped her burning cheeks with both palms. "No, William. I think not."

He glanced at Edmund, and the shadow of a frown crossed his face.

"Oh. Constable William McDougall, this is Dr. Edmund Higginbotham, an old friend from Regina."

William nodded curtly. "Should I give Mrs. Ansgar your greetings?"

Was there a note of disapproval in his voice, or was her guilty conscience imagining it? "Yes, tell Gretchen I will see her soon."

Williams flipped his hat onto his head and pivoted on his heel. The door closed softly, and she swung her gaze back to Edmund's face.

"Is that guilt I see in your eyes?" Edmund rose to his feet and dropped her folded hands, which he had held during the entire exchange. "May I assume that you felt something you should now feel guilty about?"

"The men are very loyal to Adam."

"I met your husband only once, but I do not remember his being such an icon of virtue. In fact, I remember his making you very unhappy on your wedding day."

"He did what he felt was right."

Edmund moved away, going again to the window and staring out at a sky lowering for another storm. "I won't interfere in your life, Lauren. That's not why I'm here. Obviously, you regret, in some measure, your decision to follow Adam into this wilderness. I am only here to give you an option. The decision is yours."

* * *

Lauren ran her fingers over the tatted edge of a doily on Gretchen's couch. Intricate picots and knots tangled around themselves in delicate patterns. How like life the piece was, where beautiful joining tangled around the fragile thread of living.

"Something is wrong?" Gretchen asked, her fingers flashing in and out of a sweater she was knitting.

"No." Lauren shook her head and brought herself back to the present.

"You come to talk, but you don't say a word."

The words crowded to the front of Lauren's mind. How she would love to confide in Gretchen. But something kept her from putting her confusion into words. If she spoke her doubts, they would become more real, more threatening.

"Mr. Higginbotham, he is in love with you, too."

Lauren jerked her head up. "What did you say?"

Gretchen laid down her work. "You come to talk to me about your visitor, no?"

"Yes, I did."

Gretchen frowned and rose from the chair. Lauren diverted her eyes from the bulge just beginning to show beneath Gretchen's apron and felt a quick pang. Lauren remained silent as Gretchen prepared two cups of tea, then placed one in her hand.

"You are in love with Mr. Higginbotham?"

Lauren took the cup of tea. "No. He and I were friends in Regina."

"But he is in love with you?"

"Yes." There, the word was out.

Gretchen sipped her tea. "He has asked you to leave Inspector McPhail."

Lauren's hands began to tremble, and she set the cup down. "Oh, Gretchen. I've done a terrible thing." She covered her face with her hands as tears clouded her vision. "After the baby died, I was so alone. Adam was gone on patrol. I sent for Edmund."

"Do you love him?"

Lauren stood and wandered to the window. "It seems he has always been there when I needed someone the most, and Adam hasn't. He came all the way across the country for me."

"Good friend can do all these things for you. Do you love him?" She set down the delicate china and followed Lauren to the window. "Does he make you hungry for him?"

The intensity of Gretchen's words surprised Lauren, and she looked at her friend in a new light. "No."

Gretchen gripped her arm. "That is what it takes to stay here, Lauren. You cannot be two people joined by words. You must be one." Gretchen pressed her palms together.

"I love Adam. But this . . . place is there between us, and it's so big, so powerful I can't fight it anymore."

"So you take the easy way out and go home with Edmund?"

Lauren turned and stared into Gretchen's gentle eyes, eyes wise with hard-won wisdom. "Maybe Adam would be better off without me here. I should have listened to him in the first place. He tried to tell me."

"Inspector McPhail said those words for you, not him. He come here sometimes and tell me about you, how he missed you."

"He did?"

"You marry a man of the Territories, you marry the Territories, too."

Lauren shook her head. "That's one too many."

Gretchen paused and squinted her eyes. "For as long as I know you, you admire my house."

Puzzled by the turn of conversation, Lauren frowned. "Yes, I have."

"You think I do all this because I like to sew?"

"Well, I always supposed so."

Gretchen shook her head. "No. All that you see here is substitute for Eric."

"What do you mean?"

"When he was young man, his father offer him a job with fishing business in Sweden. This would be good life. We could stay home where our family is. But no, Eric has heard of Canada, of wild wilderness. So we come, just he and I. I had to make same choice as you. Do I throw all away and follow Eric into wild place, or do I stay where I know is safe?"

"Obviously, you followed."

"Not without price." Gretchen smoothed a hand down her stomach. "I sacrifice three little ones, but I know I cannot live without Eric."

"Are you saying I have no choice, that you had no choice?"

Gretchen smiled and enclosed Lauren in her arms. "I am saying that your heart made choice without asking your mind long time ago."

"Mary and Joseph," Finnegan cursed softly. "How many men does it take to run a load of whiskey?"

"He knows we're coming." Adam grunted and rolled away from the rock prodding into his chest.

"I see six, no, seven lookouts." Finnegan glanced back at their small detachment, all lying on the ground just beneath the rise of the ridge. "We're going to have to have more men."

Adam shook his head. "This is a game to him. Every time I send for more men, he gets more men. No, this time we take him."

"They're young, Adam." He nodded back at the men. "They're just lads who've never been under fire."

"They're Mounties, aren't they?"

"That they are."

"If they took the same oath I did, then they know what they're in for."

Adam slithered down the hill and stuffed the spyglass back into his pocket. He stood and brushed away the first flakes of snow. "This isn't going to be as easy as I had hoped, men." He glanced at the ten young, expectant faces surrounding him. The oldest couldn't be more than twenty. Each one proudly wore new scarlet. He squatted and picked up a stick. Brushing aside the snow, he sketched Angus's lair. "We're going to have to take Angus by force. He has armed guards at every entrance." He dabbed at the location of the guards. "Duncan, you take three men and circle around to the south." The stick scratched through the earth. "Mike, take three and circle to the north. Stewart"—Adam glanced up at an older man he'd known since he enlisted—"pick your man. Go to the east and cut off Angus's retreat into those hills. Watch out for these rocks here." He drew squares in the earth. "He and several of his men can hide in here. I'll take the rest of you and go in." He dropped the stick, placed his palms on his legs, and pushed to his feet. "Any questions?"

The young men glanced at each other nervously. Adam understood their fear. All morning he had banished Lauren's face from his mind. If something happened to him, he could only hope McDougall would see to it that Lauren got back to Edmonton and on to home. He sucked in a chestful of biting air and gazed up at the lowering clouds.

"Mike, I'll give you thirty minutes. You should be in position by then."

"Right." Mike swung up into the saddle. Adam stepped to his side and laid a hand on his leg.

"If something should go wrong, I've left a letter in a box under my bed. Will you see Lauren gets it?"

Mike smiled. "You're not predicting dire circumstances, are you? 'Cause if you are, you're taking all the fun outta this."

Adam chuckled. "I'm no fortune-teller and I wouldn't want to spoil your fun."

The men scattered in three directions, leaving only Adam and two new men to go into the camp. Adam mounted Jake, turned up his collar, and settled in to wait. A snowflake drifted down, then two.

Time crawled by. Adam took out his watch and checked. A half hour had passed. Everyone should be in position.

"All right, men," he said, clicking his watch shut. "We're going in with weapons drawn." He punched Jake in the sides, and they charged over the slight rise that had hidden them from view.

The first guard stood in a thicket of brush and rocks, his rifle cradled in his arms. At the sound of thundering horses, he looked up just in time for a revolver to graze him across the skull. A cry went up from other guards, and the camp came alive. Half-dressed men scurried out of the white canvas tents, some with drawn weapons, some searching for theirs. Adam saw Mike charge into view on the opposite side. Then a roar like summer thunder rocked the ground. One of the new men riding behind Mike vaulted off the back of his horse and slammed into the ground. Adam yanked Jake to a quivering stop and frantically searched the confusion. Then he saw it. On the far edge of camp stood Angus, a lit cigar poised over the butt end of a small cannon.

The crack of gunfire split the afternoon silence. Lauren screamed as a bullet split off another piece of wood near her head, sending shards of wood into her cup of tea. Edmund grabbed her by the shoulders and shoved her underneath the table as a hail of bullets zinged past.

The cabin door flew open, and she watched Mounted Police-issue boots clump across the floor toward the bedroom. As she crawled out, Adam flung a still form off his shoulder and onto the bed.

"Adam." She started toward him, then stopped. His face was pale, and sweat dotted his brow. One sleeve of his tunic was almost torn off, and blood cut a wide swath down his side, now dripping onto the floor. She glanced toward the bed. A young constable's face was marred by the path of a bullet.

Adam stared at her blankly, then swayed on his feet.

Lauren shoved a chair underneath him and guided him down with a hand on his shoulder.

"See to him," he whispered before his eyes went blank and his head dropped back.

Windowpanes shattered, and glass tinkled to the floor. Bullets pummeled the sturdy walls, and the acrid scent of gunpowder filtered into the house.

Ducking, Lauren fetched a wet cloth and washed away the blood from the young man's face. She felt his neck for a pulse and found one, rapid but steady. Behind her, Edmund was ripping Adam's jacket off to expose a gaping wound in his side.

"Oh, dear God." Lauren put a hand over her mouth. "Edmund, you have to do something."

"This is very bad," he said, holding a cloth over Adam's side to stanch the flow of blood. "Very bad."

Lauren dropped to her knees at Adam's side and pushed blond hair away from his face. Beard stubble dotted his smooth skin, and the weight of the days past showed beneath his eyes.

"He's lost a lot of blood." Edmund dropped the saturated cloth and grabbed another. "Get my bag over there." He nodded at his black medical bag stored with his other belongings in a corner.

Lauren raised her eyes to meet Edmund's. "Will he live?"

Solemnly, Edmund shook his head. "I can't honestly say. Get that quilt down. Let's get him on the floor."

The world dropped out from under her feet. More gunfire pelted them, pinging off the walls, breaking windows, even shattering dishes in the kitchen. Then she recognized the distinctive bark of the Enfield revolvers. Hoofbeats thundered into the yard, and the gunfire ceased as suddenly as it had begun.

"Is Adam in here?" Duncan barked, charging through the door. "Sweet Mother of Jesus." He stared down at Adam, then shifted his gaze to Lauren.

"Would you see to him" she asked, pointing toward the bedroom.

Duncan stepped into the bedroom and pulled aside the curtain. "Poor lad. Did any of the other men come here?"

"No. What happened?"

Duncan's shoulders sagged, and fatigue showed in his face. "Angus was waitin' for us with a cannon."

"A cannon?" Lauren looked down at Adam's tortured side, where Edmund frantically cleaned away blood.

"Can't imagine how he got that thing in the Territory without somebody knowing." Duncan shook his head.

Boots scraped on the porch, and more Mounties came inside. They stood almost timidly, crowding into the doorway, shoulders sagging. Some had bandages tied around arms and legs, some around heads.

Steeling her mind against the picture of Adam surrounded by a pool of his own blood, Lauren methodically began to see to the men, knowing that would be Adam's main concern.

As Edmund began to cut away his clothes, Adam stirred. "Duncan?" he mumbled.

"Right here, lad."

Adam's lips barely moved as Duncan leaned closer, then nodded and said something too low for her to hear. She moved toward them, anxious to speak to Adam, but as Duncan turned to leave, Adam's head sagged limply to the side.

Twenty-one

Hours crept by, turning the morning into a gray afternoon. Lauren made pots of coffee and cleaned a variety of wounds, all the while forcing herself not to think about Adam. Young Matthew Turner, the wounded constable, regained consciousness, and they moved him into the barracks and Adam into his own bed. Edmund cleaned out the wound and sewed it up, then said the rest was up to God.

As evening stole in, Lauren again kept vigil in her rocking chair.

"What do you honestly think, Edmund?" she asked, watching her shadow rock to and fro against the wall.

Asleep at the table with his head resting on his forearms, Edmund stirred, then looked up drowsily.

"You've asked me that every hour, Lauren, and I've given you the same answer every time."

"I know." Lauren rocked a little harder. "I'm sorry."

Edmund ran a hand over his face and got up for a drink of water. "I'm sorry I snapped." He held out a tin cup to her.

Lauren hadn't realized how thirsty she was until the sweet water ran over her lips. The tin cup clinked as she set it on the floor; then she tugged the quilt up around Adam's neck and felt his forehead. It was warm and dry, indicating a fever just beginning.

"Go to bed." Edmund grabbed her hand and pulled her around to face him. "I've made up the cot in the jail." He shrugged. "It's better than the floor."

Lauren nodded, incapable of thinking much further than her next step. As she lay down, the faint scent of unwashed bodies rose up around her, but she was too tired to notice.

When she awoke, light flooded the cabin. Edmund was bending over Adam. He swung a tired, defeated gaze toward her. "I fear he is worse."

Lauren moved to Adam's side. Dark beard stubble stood out in stark relief against pale skin. She picked up his hand and rolled his slender fingers between hers. "You don't think he'll live, do you?" she asked Edmund.

His pause furnished the answer before he spoke. "In a physician's opinion . . . I think his chances are poor."

Tears clouded her vision, haloing the yellow light from a lamp on the table. She blinked and raised her eyes to the window. The snow had stopped, and the new day dawned bright and clear. To the west, the Rockies shoved their snowy, chiseled peaks into the bluest of skies. If Adam died, he'd die happy here knowing he was to become part of the land that he loved.

"I'm sorry I was so blunt." Edmund rubbed his hand across her shoulder. "I thought you should know the truth no matter how harsh."

"Thank you. The only truth I've found here has been harsh."

Behind her, Adam moaned, and she hurried to his side. He stared vacantly up at the ceiling, then shifted his gaze first to Lauren, then to Edmund.

"His fever is very high, Lauren. He may not recognize you."

Adam's eyes flickered back to Lauren. "How are the men?" he rasped through dry lips.

A sigh of relief rushed out. "Most of them are well. Matthew Turner was injured the most gravely, but we attended to him, and he is comfortable in his own bed with Finnegan in attendance."

"Angus?"

Lauren shook her head. "I don't know. There was so much confusion."

Adam sighed and let his eyes drift closed. Lauren's heart leaped into her throat, and she lightly placed two fingers at the base of his neck to feel the jumping pulse there.

"I'm not dead." He opened his eyes again. "I couldn't feel this bad and be dead."

Lauren leaned over him and touched her lips to his. When she drew away, he was already asleep.

"Come with me." Edmund touched her arm. "There's nothing more you can do here for now. I want you to sit down while I fix you something to eat."

"You've been up all night," Lauren protested as she sank into the hard chair.

"I'm used to it. In fact, stamina was my forte in medical school. I'm quite accomplished at surviving on catnaps." He swung open the stove door and tossed in another two sticks of wood.

What a dear man he is, Lauren thought, watching him stir around her primitive kitchen. Guilt settled onto her shoulders. He should have been pursuing one of the young women smitten with him instead of carrying a torch for her. How long had he loved her without her knowledge? Did she truly not know? *No,* answered her inner self. *You knew. You were so lonely and desperate for company that you refused to see what was before you.*

"Gretchen brought these eggs over yesterday," he was saying as he cracked one into the pan with one hand. He laughed. "She looked funny tromping across the yard in the snow, her apron full of eggs."

Lauren sipped the cup of coffee he set before her. "That's Gretchen. Once she makes up her mind to do something, nothing will stop her."

"Seems a good attitude for one committed to living up here."

"Sometimes determination is all one has."

The frying pan sizzled as he dropped in another egg. "And love."

Lauren raised her eyes, but he was intent on the yellow swirl in the pan.

"I have found that love will sustain one even in the hardest of times." He flipped the eggs. "I only wish that one day I might find that kind of love."

Lauren set down her cup. "Edmund—"

"No. We will not talk of that today. I'm sorry I brought it up." He flipped the perfect eggs out of the pan and onto a plate. Following with a generous piece of bread, he set the meal before her.

"You are too good to me, Edmund." Tears hammered at the back of her eyes, burning her nose.

A commotion outside made them both look up at the door as it swung open. Duncan stumbled in, dragging a large man by one arm and the collar of the dirty, ragged jacket.

"Beggin' yore pardon, Lauren. I'll have to put him in the jail."

Lauren pushed her chair back and stood. "Is it—?"

"In the flesh," Duncan grunted as he shoved the man inside the bars and slammed the door. "Adam told me where he left him tied to a tree." Duncan shook his head. "I don't know when the lad had the strength to take Angus. The smoke was so thick, I never saw."

The man scrambled up from all fours and turned.

"Ah. We meet again." He smiled slowly, his eyes smoldering.

Lauren took a step backward and bumped into Edmund.

"Is that the man who has caused all the trouble?" Edmund asked.

"Yes." Lauren met Angus's gaze squarely. "This is Black Angus."

"As soon as some of the lads heal, we'll be movin' him to Fort Saskatchewan." Duncan crossed his arms over his chest, wincing as he flexed his own wounded forearm. "I'd tie him up in the barracks, but I don't trust the rascal not to escape and all this would have been for nothin'."

"I got out of your jail before, Mountie." Angus sneered at Duncan.

"Not without some help you didn't," Duncan shot back.

Lauren whirled. "How did he get out?"

"Fox. She's his woman." Duncan slid a chair out and sat down.

"How—?"

"Crept in here at night and got the keys. Let him out, and they both got away without waking a soul."

A chill ran over Lauren. So two people had looked over them while they slept.

"Leave him here. I want Adam to see him when he wakes up. And I can guarantee Fox won't get in this time."

Angus looked taken aback for a moment. "If the Inspector wakes up." He grinned. "My cannon ripped a hole in him, did it not?"

"He will wake up, and he'll come to your trial."

For five days Adam lingered on the threshold of death. Fever tortured his body until Lauren thought his skin would surely peel away from the heat. He mumbled and tossed, lost in his own purgatory. By day Lauren watched over him, sponged his body with cold water, then relinquished her watch to Edmund or Finnegan by night. Curled on a pallet of quilts on the bedroom floor, Lauren lay awake long after she had retired, listening to his mumbling and swearing. What demons tortured his mind? What fears did he face alone in his fevered brain. He called his father's name and hers. Each time, Lauren rose and soothed his forehead, speaking softly and hoping that somehow he heard her.

"Lauren?"

Lauren scrambled up from her bed on the floor. Adam stared up at the ceiling, a frown of confusion furrowing his forehead.

Tears flowed down Lauren's cheeks as she caught his hand. "How do you feel?"

"Terrible. Where am I?"

"You're home. With me. Thank God Edmund was here."

Adam searched her face, his mind moving infuriatingly slow. How had he gotten home? Who had bandaged the hole in his side? If memory served, he should be dead. Then he seized on Lauren's last words. "Edmund?" Another face moved in behind her, and he blinked. Was he still hallucinating?

"Adam. It's good to see you awake."

Edmund. What was his name? Lauren's father's doctor. Higginbotham. That was it. The author of the letter hidden so well in Lauren's reticule.

"What are you doing here?" Adam asked. Had he come all this way to bring Lauren news from Regina?

"I suppose I should say you were lucky I was here. In fact, I will say that. You're going to recover nicely." Edmund placed his hands on Lauren's shoulder and urged her to move from the chair, then he sat down in her place and probed the bandaged area. "Some of the swelling has gone down."

Adam glanced up at Lauren. Her eyes were on Edmund's hands, the bed, the table, anywhere but on his eyes. What was going on?

"I think you're out of the woods, old man." Edmund tugged the quilt up and rose. "Do you think you could stand a cup of tea?"

"Yes, that would be fine."

Edmund stepped out of the room, leaving Adam and Lauren alone. She opened her mouth to speak, but her lips began to quiver, and she clamped her teeth shut. Adam took her fingers in his hand and caressed them. "I've put you through hell again, haven't I?"

She looked down, away from his face.

"Why is he here?" he asked.

"Because I asked him to come." Tears glistened on her lashes, and the door to the cabin softly closed.

"You're leaving with him, aren't you?"

She looked up.

"I found the letter months ago."

The tears spilled over her lids and plopped onto his hand. "I was alone and scared, heartsick. I sent him a letter by way of a trapper at Eric's. I never thought he'd really come."

"But now that he has, you're leaving."

"I don't think I can do this anymore."

"I promised we'd go home to Regina."

"You don't belong in Regina. You belong here."

He swallowed down a pain sharper than any Angus could have dealt out, the pain of hard truth. She was right. He didn't belong in Regina. She didn't belong here. They'd promised for better or worse, but nobody had said anything about insurmountable. He closed his eyes, focusing his attention on what he could hear and feel. The touch of her hand. The soft whoosh of her labored breathing. The hammering of his own heart. And as he recorded all these things in his memory, the silken bonds of their vows silently slipped away.

* * *

"You look so much better, my dear."

Lauren turned from watching May flowers bob in a warm breeze. "Thank you, Auntie."

"For a time I feared we would never be able to put the pink back in your cheeks."

The soft strains of Beethoven's "Anise" floated on the warm afternoon air.

"Come back and join the party. Edmund is waiting for you. The Worthington sisters have just arrived with their new beaus." Auntie leaned close, her corkscrew curls bobbing. "They're twins," she whispered, as if that endowed the young men with special powers.

Lauren turned back to the window of the sunroom. Party gossip held no fascination for her. The grass in Auntie's garden bent under a soft breeze, and swirled patterns appeared in the tender blades. The trees at Onion Lake would be in full leaf now. Tiny wrens would hop about the branches, courting and cooing. A spring breeze would dapple the surface of the lake.

She glanced down at her empty left hand. She'd left her wedding ring on the quilt that was stained with Adam's blood. She'd left so much behind in cold, harsh Alberta. A son. A husband. Her ring. Her heart.

"Lauren?" Auntie touched her sleeve, concern knitting together her white eyebrows. "Are you all right, dear?"

Lauren blinked away the tears. "Yes, of course. You say Edmund is waiting for me?"

Auntie narrowed her eyes. "Maybe you would prefer I make your excuses? Everyone would understand."

"No, I can't spend the rest of my days sniveling over the past." She straightened her blouse and peered at her reflection in the window. The trip from Alberta to Regina had been hard, and she'd cried most of the way. Poor Edmund had offered what comfort he could, struggling not to take sides even when she alternated between railing at Adam and railing at herself. He deserved to at least see her some of the time without tears running down her face.

"You need time to heal, Lauren. Perhaps this party was a bad idea. Perhaps you're not ready to entertain yet."

"Nonsense, Auntie. I've been home three months. No, it's time I put the past behind me and carry on. That's what a good Mountie wi—" She stopped, the words frozen in her throat. "Daughter does," she finished weakly.

"Suit yourself. You always did," Auntie muttered, and rustled away in her ivory taffeta gown. With a last glance out the window, Lauren moved toward her aunt's parlor, steeling herself to smile and nod and make pleasant conversation.

Edmund stood across the room, engrossed in conversation with the Worthington sisters and their twin lovers. He caught Lauren's eye and nodded only slightly when she reappeared. Immediately, Mrs. Morris claimed her and led her toward the garden, an arm hooked in hers. Apparently, Auntie had briefed all of Regina on what not to ask her, for the complete omission of any discussion about the last year yawned like a chasm.

"Dear, sweet Edmund is completely enamored of you, my dear. And he is such a good man."

"Edmund and I are just friends."

Mrs. Morris rolled her eyes. "He looks at no one else the way he looks at you."

Edmund was indeed her friend. Perhaps her best friend. But that's as far as it went. He knew things about her . . . and Adam . . . that he probably should not know, confessions sobbed out on a rocking train car somewhere in the middle of a desolate prairie landscape. She'd never live long enough to deserve all he'd done for her. And she'd never live long enough to stop loving Adam.

She'd made a terrible mistake leaving him. She'd broken his heart, injured his pride, shamed him in front of his men. There was no going back. She simply had to put the past behind her and move on. Toward an empty life. One filled with comforts and security. And no love.

"Who could that be?" Mrs. Morris asked, straining to peek above the blooming peonies that blocked the sight of the driveway. A carriage door slammed shut, and the conveyance pulled away, its wheels crunching past.

"Everyone that was invited is here."

"I'll go and see." Lauren hurried toward the house. If unexpected guests had arrived, it might be the perfect chance for her to slip away, upstairs, where she could be alone and nurse this growing despair that insisted on clinging to her.

She stepped through the French doors, but no new face greeted her. Conversations ebbed and flowed as before. Maybe it was a delivery for the party. She was about to turn away when she caught sight of Auntie standing in her foyer, twisting a lace handkerchief. She glanced nervously at the guests, obviously upset.

"Auntie, what's wrong?" Lauren asked, stepping across the polished wooden floors.

Auntie's eyes widened, and she glanced toward the small alcove designed to hold wraps and coats.

"Who's here?" Lauren asked, trepidation growing.

"Hello, Lauren." Adam stepped out of the alcove. He wore a new uniform. The scarlet-lined dark blue cloak of an officer swept the tops of his polished black boots. He twirled a new Stetson in his hands.

"Adam," she managed to say without a flood of tears. "What are you doing in Regina?" She didn't dare hope she was the reason.

He shrugged lightly. "Police business. New men. New supplies. Could we have a minute, Aunt Matilda?" he said in his soft baritone.

"Oh, dear." She fluttered and glanced toward the guests. Conversation had ceased, and heads turned.

"It's all right. We *are* still legally married," Adam said with a wry smile.

Auntie hurried away, her cheerful comments a little too cheerful and her enthusiasm spoken in a high, nervous voice.

"Could we take a walk in the garden?" he asked, lifting a shawl off a hook and placing it around her shoulders.

They went back out the front door to keep from plowing through the crowd of curious guests and entered the manicured garden by way of a small white gate. He deftly guided her deep within the garden, where unruly shrubs hid them from view of the house.

While they walked, he kept a hand on her elbow, a gentlemanly gesture that sent unladylike thoughts to her brain and the pit of her stomach.

"I've received the divorce papers. I'll sign them, of course." He pinned her with his dark gaze. "If that's what you still want."

Did she? Her cheeks flamed, and desire uncoiled within her. No papers and no ink would ever quell the passion she felt for the man standing there with the afternoon sun glinting off his hair. Not when she'd lain with him, done erotic things to his body, and received in kind from his skillful hands and mouth. Not when she'd conceived his child and buried his immortality in cold, dark soil. No carefully worded sentences would ever sever this bond between them. "Is it what *you* want?"

He quirked his mouth into a bitter smile. "I think you know my answer to that. I just want you to be happy, Lauren. And if Edmund makes you happy—"

"No. Edmund and I are just friends. Period." She smiled. "There's nothing more."

"Ah," he said with a nod of his head.

She wanted to fling her arms around him and drag him past the horrified faces of Auntie's guests upstairs to her bedroom. To fling him across her maidenly bedspread, peel away his scarlet uniform, and remember firsthand the things he did to make her blood race and her heart pound. To have him remind her why she had followed him into the wilderness.

"Well," he said, inching away, "I should be going. I'm sorry I interrupted your party. I'll have the papers delivered to you tomorrow." He touched his collar, and she realized the gold insignias were missing.

He took a step away.

"Where are your crowns?" She touched her throat. His gaze darkened, and her heart pounded against her ribs.

"In my pocket."

"Why aren't you wearing them?"

He smiled softly. "I gave them away once."

"I wondered what had happened to them. I'm so very sorry."

He looked down then, his jaw working convulsively. "I had hoped"—he stopped and raised his eyes to capture her gaze—"that one day you'd put them back on me." Shaking his head, he laughed softly. "I had a ridiculous notion that that would somehow make everything right again."

Lauren swallowed and moved toward him, drawn as surely as if he held an invisible tether attached to her heart. She stopped and looked up into his face, so close she could see the finely shaved beard stubble.

"I've been reassigned," he said softly.

"Here? To Regina?"

"No. To the Yukon. Duncan and Finnegan, too. We're to police the Gold Rush." He was going farther away. Likely, she'd never see him again. Tears welled up, and her vision blurred. Could she live the rest of her life without ever again seeing his face? Without knowing his touch? Without feeling his body quiver to completion within her and wonder if he'd planted a child there?

She held out her hand, palm up. His eyes softened, and he reached inside his coat and dropped the two gold crowns into her hand.

"Dawson City is a wild place," he said softly, the timber of his voice sliding up her spine. "There'll be claim jumpers and prostitutes and illegal whiskey."

She slipped her hand inside his collar, her legs quickly turning to jelly as her knuckles brushed his warm skin. "Will you make love to me?"

"As often as time allows," he whispered as one insignia snapped closed.

"And will you build us a cabin with a jail in the corner and no kitchen."

"Anything you want."

She snapped the other pin in place and straightened his collar, taking full advantage of the chance to touch his bare skin. "I want you."

He reached back into his coat and took out her wedding ring, held between two fingers. "I won't make you any promises this time except that you will always have my heart." He slipped the cool metal onto her finger, then put an arm behind her back, the hard brim of his Stetson pressing into her spine. His lips were soft and warm and tasted as she remembered. If she couldn't have him right now, right here amid the primroses, she'd explode.

"Does this place have a bedroom with a grass-stuffed mattress?" he whispered against her lips.

"No. Will a feather bed do?" she whispered back.

"Uh-huh. Gotta have the crackling of the grass. Remembering that sound has lost me many a night's sleep in the last few months." He kissed her again, abandoning the politeness of the first, hauling her closer, letting her know how much he wanted her. Somewhere in her pleasure-induced fog, Lauren heard his treasured Stetson hit the ground with a soft thud.

Epilogue

Pressure, unrelenting and powerful, gripped Lauren, twisting her in its grasp. She clutched handfuls of her bedsheets, tangling them in her fingers until she ripped loose the neat corners that held them around the mattress. Single-minded, she tried to concentrate on the face that hovered above her, but the pain chased away everything except itself.

"Squeeze my hand, lass," Duncan said, his fingers locked with hers.

And she did squeeze—until she thought she'd break his hand. But he endured without a wince until the pain subsided. At least for a while.

Adam had been gone for days on patrol. Riding out in the face of an approaching blizzard, torn between two responsibilities, he'd been reluctant to leave. But she'd pasted on a smile and commanded him to go and do his job. The job he loved. And she'd stayed home to do hers.

The pains had begun at dawn, tiny twinges that could have been anything. But by the time afternoon darkened into night, she'd known she was in labor. Not bothering to light a lamp, she'd gone to her bed and waited, watching the moon move across the sky. Duncan had found her near dawn, returning late from his own patrol. She'd heard the hooves of his horse and called out Adam's name. Duncan came inside, lit a lamp, and sat with her through the rest of the night, regaling her with stories and soft, comforting words.

"Where's Adam? When will he be back?"

"Easy, lass. He'll be on in a bit. He should be back from patrol anytime now."

As another pain crept through her, more urgent this time, she gripped Duncan's forearm. "Don't let my baby die, Duncan. Promise you won't."

Part of her knew she'd just asked the impossible, but another, larger part only wanted some kind of guarantee.

"Shh, lass." Duncan soothed with his voice and the cool cloth he applied to her forehead. "You'll be fine. You'll see. We have to deliver Adam a fine son in his absence. That's our job now, you and me."

She stared out the window as dawn shrank away and a fat, lazy snowflake drifted out of a menacing sky to plaster itself against the glass. Some cruel twist of fate had duplicated the day on which she'd last given birth and lost her son. Unnerved, she closed her eyes and concentrated on the tiny life within her struggling to get out. Surely this angry, gnawing beast that possessed her possessed her child, too. Surely the tiny baby felt the contractions and pressure that threatened to rip her apart.

She closed her eyes. Another pain began as an itch deep within and spread throughout her. The interior of her home dimmed, as did Duncan's worried face, disappearing into a white fog of pain. Vaguely, she heard the door open and smelled the fresh, sharp scent of snow. Muffled voices moved around her. The warmth of Duncan's hand disappeared, and she felt cold skin entwine with her fingers.

As the pain abated, she sighed and opened her eyes. Adam leaned over her, smears of mud streaking his cheek and flecking the front of his jacket. He smiled, that soft, sweet smile that had seduced and lured her into her present predicament. Ah, but she'd do it all over again, she thought, smiling back.

"Come, lad, and let me give you a cup of coffee. It'll do her no good to hear our teeth rattle together and for you to freeze her with your icy hands."

"I rode all night to get here," he said, not taking his eyes off her face, his fingers gradually warming in her grasp.

The pain began again, moving lower to wedge itself between her hipbones, a hard ball that demanded ease.

"I think the baby's coming," Lauren said.

Adam rose, shucked off his coat, and rolled up his sleeves. "This is it, darling. Soon you'll have a baby to hold."

"Do you want me to stay?" she heard Duncan ask.

"No. We'll be all right," Adam answered.

The door closed, and she felt Adam flip back her quilts and position her feet as before. So much was like before. So much.

"Adam?" she said, raising her head.

He turned to her from washing his hands and arms in a bowl. "The baby moved yesterday." She paused, searching for a delicate way to tell him, then opted for the simple truth. "At least he was alive then."

Pain claimed her then, arching her body upward, tensing every muscle and sinew. She lost all conscious thought, focusing only on Adam's voice.

"Push, Lauren," he said. "Push."

She obeyed with clenched teeth. Minutes seemed to stretch into hours. The pain was unrelenting, coming back to torment her again and again without respite or rest.

"I can see the head, Lauren. Push once more. Just once more."

Lauren scrambled for better position, held her breath, and strained until her muscles quivered. Her child slid from her body into Adam's waiting hands.

"I've got him. We have a son, Lauren, and he's fine. He's just fi—" The words stopped abruptly.

Adam stood at the end of the bed, streaks of blood across the front of his white shirt. Tiny legs and arms waved, struggled as he held the baby upside down and gently swatted its backside. A tiny mew and then a lusty cry filled the empty corners of their home. Adam sobbed and held the naked baby to his shoulder.

From somewhere in the shadows Duncan appeared with one of her embroidered baby blankets in his hands. "Here, lad," he said softly. "Let me have him and see to your wife."

Reluctantly, Adam relinquished their son and returned to take away the afterbirth. Lauren's eyes followed the tiny bundle, which Duncan cleaned, dried, and quickly placed in her arms. Then he disappeared again, leaving them alone together. The baby squinted up at her, blinking against the dim light.

"He's perfect," Adam said, pulling aside the blanket. "Perfect and healthy." He sat down in a chair, barely disguising a groan.

A hat line dented his hair, and flecks of mud and blood stained his face. Fatigue haunted the shadows of his eyes and the planes of his face. What a sight they both must be, Lauren thought as a laugh bubbled out of her. Nine months ago, she'd convinced herself that life in the Northwest Territories was too harsh, too primitive, too real. Now she couldn't imagine the value of a life spent serving teas and organizing picnics.

She chuckled softly and flicked a splat of mud from Adam's cheek. It was fitting, somehow, that their son had been conceived in Aunt Matilda's gazebo on the evening of their reunion, the miraculous result of a passionate and frantic joining amid coolly disapproving primroses.

Adam leaned forward and planted a gentle, lingering kiss on her lips. "Thank you," he whispered.

She captured the back of his head with her free hand as he started to draw away. "I want another one," she whispered. "And soon."

Adam chuckled softly against her lips as the odor of snow and horse and wool swirled around them. "I'm not sure I can afford another trip to Aunt Matilda's gazebo."

"You won't have to. I know where there's a meadow of columbine. And they're not nearly as prudish as primroses."

Look for the next MEN OF HONOR novel,
THE SEDUCTION

Coming from Zebra Ballad in March 2002

Something is dirty in Dawson City. At least by
Samantha Wilder's reasoning it is. With millions of
dollars in gold dust pouring out of the Yukon Territory
and only a handful of North West Mounted Policemen
representing the law, somebody has to be on the take.
But who? Finding that out is going to win her the
much desired title of investigative reporter, Samantha
figures.

Until she runs into Inspector Duncan McLeod.

With fifteen years in the force behind him, Duncan
McLeod has seen everything. Or at least he thinks so
until he has to defend himself against a bedraggled,
pushy old-maid reporter bent on his destruction. Will
Duncan's impeccable reputation stand up to Samantha's scrutiny? And when thousands of dollars in gold
dust disappear, will Samantha risk her dream to stand
by the man she has come to love?

COMING IN FEBRUARY 2002
FROM ZEBRA BALLAD ROMANCES

__OUTCAST: The Vikings__
  by Kathryn Hockett   0-8217-7257-0 $5.99US/$7.99CAN
Vengeful clansmen have taken Nordic warrior Torin prisoner. His only
hope lies in the beautiful, brazen Erica, who promises to aid his escape
provided he take her with him. He cannot anticipate the peril that lies
ahead—or the relentless desire that will lead them to a grand empire . . .
and glorious love.

__COMING UP ROSES: Meet Me at the Fair__
  by Alice Duncan   0-8217-7276-7 $5.99US/$7.99CAN
Rose Ellen Gilhooley can see that handsome newsman H.L. May is only
interested in one thing. Trouble is, the more he squires her around the
grand Columbian Exposition, the more Rose yearns for the same! But
when H.L. swears he's not the marrying kind, Rose thinks it's high time
she taught *him* a lesson—about listening to his heart . . .

__CASH: The Rock Creek Six__
  by Linda Devlin   0-8217-7269-4 $5.99US/$7.99CAN
Daniel Cash was a ladies' man with a smile as quick as his draw. Yet the
gunslinger harbored painful memories of the girl he'd left behind. Cash
believed Nadine Ellington was better off without the man he'd become,
but when she rode into town, Cash was tempted to consider another future . . . with her by his side.

__SWEET VIOLET: Daughters of Liberty__
  by Corinne Everett   0-8217-7146-9 $5.99US/$7.99CAN
Violet Pearson is determined to prove she can manage the Tidewater Nurs-
eries. And now, with the opening of a lavish new conservatory by Gabriel
Isling, the Duke of Belmont, she is sure to make the business bloom! She
had not, however, counted on her intense attraction to this charming gentleman whose seductive gaze reveals nothing of the dangerous secret that
has led him to America.

Call toll free **1-888-345-BOOK** to order by phone or use this
coupon to order by mail. *ALL BOOKS AVAILABLE FEBRUARY
01, 2002*

Name _____

Address _____

City _____ State _____ Zip _____

Please send me the books that I have checked above.

I am enclosing $_____
Plus postage and handling* $_____
Sales tax (in NY and TN) $_____
Total amount enclosed $_____

*Add $2.50 for the first book and $.50 for each additional book. Send
check or money order (no cash or CODs) to: **Kensington Publishing
Corp., Dept. C.O., 850 Third Avenue, New York, NY 10022**
Prices and numbers subject to change without notice. Valid only in the
U.S. All orders subject to availability. **NO ADVANCE ORDERS.**
Visit our website at www.kensingtonbooks.com.

Enjoy *Savage Destiny*
A Romantic Series from
Rosanne Bittner

___#1: **Sweet Prairie Passion**   **$5.99**US/**$6.99**CAN
    0-8217-5342-8

___#2: **Ride the Free Wind Passion**   **$5.99**US/**$6.99**CAN
    0-8217-5343-6

___#3: **River of Love**   **$5.99**US/**$6.99**CAN
    0-8217-5344-4

Call toll free **1-888-345-BOOK** to order by phone or use this
coupon to order by mail.

Name_____

Address _____

City_____ State _____ Zip _____

Please send me the books I have checked above.

I am enclosing $_____

Plus postage and handling* $_____

Sales tax (NY and TN residents) $_____

Total amount enclosed $_____

*Add $2.50 for the first book and $.50 for each additional book.

Send check or money order (no cash or CODs) to:

Kensington Publishing Corp., 850 Third Avenue, New York, NY 10022

Prices and Numbers subject to change without notice.

All orders subject to availability.

Check out our website at **www.kensingtonbooks.com**.

The Queen of
Romance

Cassie Edwards

__Desire's Blossom 0-8217-6405-5	$5.99US/$7.99CAN
__Exclusive Ecstasy 0-8217-6597-3	$5.99US/$7.99CAN
__Passion's Web 0-8217-5726-1	$5.99US/$7.50CAN
__Portrait of Desire 0-8217-5862-4	$5.99US/$7.50CAN
__Savage Obsession 0-8217-5554-4	$5.99US/$7.50CAN
__Silken Rapture 0-8217-5999-X	$5.99US/$7.50CAN
__Rapture's Rendezvous 0-8217-6115-3	$5.99US/$7.50CAN

Call toll free **1-888-345-BOOK** to order by phone or use this coupon to order by mail.

Name_____

Address_____

City_____ State _____ Zip _____

Please send me the books that I have checked above.

I am enclosing	$_____
Plus postage and handling*	$_____
Sales tax (in New York and Tennessee)	$_____
Total amount enclosed	$_____

*Add $2.50 for the first book and $.50 for each additional book. Send check or money order (no cash or CODs) to:

Kensington Publishing Corp., 850 Third Avenue, New York, NY 10022

Prices and numbers subject to change without notice.

All orders subject to availability.

Check out our website at **www.kensingtonbooks.com**.